*Octavia's War*

# Octavia's War

## BERYL KINGSTON

First published in Great Britain in 2009 by
Allison & Busby Limited
13 Charlotte Mews
London W1T 4EJ
*www.allisonandbusby.com*

The poem on pages 246-7, 'Song and Dance'
by RG Gregory, has been used with the
kind permission of RG Gregory.

A CIP catalogue record for this book is available from
the British Library.

10 9 8 7 6 5 4 3 2 1

13-ISBN 978-0-7490-0756-0

Typeset in 12.5/15.5 pt Adobe Garamond Pro by
Allison & Busby Ltd

The paper used for this Allison & Busby publication
has been produced from trees that have been legally sourced
from well-managed and credibly certified forests.

PEFC
PEFC/16-33-111
CATG-PEFC-052
www.pefc.org

Printed and bound in Great Britain by
MPG Books Ltd, Bodmin, Cornwall

BERYL KINGSTON has been a writer since she was seven, when she started producing poetry. According to her, it wasn't very good but she had a few more years to hone her skills before her first book was published in 1980.

Kingston was a schoolteacher until 1985, becoming a full-time writer when her debut novel became a bestseller. She lives in West Sussex, and has three children and five grandchildren. *Octavia's War* is her twenty-second publication.

*www.berylkingston.co.uk*

**Also available from**
**ALLISON & BUSBY**

*Gates of Paradise*
*Octavia*

# Acknowledgements

The author would like to acknowledge the generous help that she received from the following people:

Jan Mihell of the Lightbox and the Woking Historical Society; Dorothy Gray, Coleen Moore and Sheila Barrett of Mayfield School, who were all evacuated to Woking; Norman Plastow of the Wimbledon Historical Society, for information on the Wimbledon air raids; the administrators and staff of Nuffield Hospital, Woking; Karen Eastwood, head teacher of The Park School, Woking, and her staff; Rosemary Fost and Bronwen Travis, head of development at St Hilda's College, Oxford; and finally Elizabeth Garrett and her writer's retreat 'Cliff Cottage'.

# Chapter One

'Why is it so dark, Aunty Tavy?' Barbara said. At five years old she was a sturdy child and curious about everything, so a sudden darkness at six o'clock on a summer evening was something to be wondered at.

'There's a storm coming,' her aunt, Octavia, explained. 'Look at the sky. Do you see all those grey clouds over there? Well, they're storm clouds.'

The child persisted, standing by her aunt's elegant cane chair and squinting up at the sky. The clouds were so very grey as to be almost black and there was something about them that she didn't like at all. 'Why aren't they white?'

'Because they're full of rain,' Octavia said. 'They're like big black ponds up in the sky. Presently they'll make a rumbling noise that we call thunder – I expect you've heard that before, haven't you – and then they'll spill all the water out and we shall have a storm.'

Barbara's baby sister, Margaret, was standing beside the chair too. Now she edged a little closer to her aunt and held on to the sleeve of her cardigan, just in case. 'Shall us get wet?' she asked.

'We shall if we stay out here in the garden,' Octavia told her. 'But not if we get indoors quickly enough.'

'Shall us run?'

'Like greyhounds,' Octavia said, smiling at the child's earnest face.

'What's a greyhound?' Barbara wanted to know.

'Time for us to go,' their mother said, striding towards them across the lawn. 'I hope you're not being troublesome.'

Octavia smiled at her reassuringly, dear Edith, with that thick auburn hair and those clear blue eyes and that oddly endearing anxiety. 'They're being intelligent and curious,' she said, 'which is exactly as it should be. Ask Pa.'

Her father had been watching the exchange in his quiet way, enjoying the children's curiosity, thinking, as he always did on such occasions, that Octavia was so easy with children and wishing she could have married Tommy and had children of her own. It would have been so good to have had grandchildren. But there, you can't have everything in this life and she was a great lady, one of the leaders in the world of education and much admired.

'They're no trouble,' he said to Edith, 'but Tavy's right. I think we should be getting in. It's all very well for you little ones and your Aunt Tavy with her long legs. You *can* run like greyhounds if it starts to rain but I can't. I'm more of a tortoise.' He picked up his stick like the explanation it was and the movement dislodged the newspaper he'd been reading earlier and had set aside on the garden table. It fell on the grass, where it lay untidily, its pages fluttered by a sudden breeze. He watched as they turned, one after the other, until they gave a final flick and settled at the morning's chilling headline, *Storm clouds over Europe*. How apposite, he thought, but even as the words came into his mind, the first thunder rumbled overhead and the rain began to fall, spattering the paper with large damp spots.

Within seconds the garden was full of movement: Emmeline puffing towards them across the lawn, moving as fast as she could, given her weight, and unfurling an umbrella as she ran. 'Quick, Uncle,' she called to him. 'Let's get you indoors. I can't have you taking a chill.'

Edith grabbed a child in each hand and all three bolted like rabbits, Margaret squealing, 'Us'll get wet, Mummy. Us'll get wet.'

Octavia brought up the rear with the paper and the tea tray, skimming across the lawn with the tea cups rattling and thinking it was just as well the milk jug and the teapot were empty. They tumbled into the drawing room one after the other, dampened, laughing and breathless, and Emmeline took the tray from her cousin's hands and said she'd be back in a jiffy with some towels. By that time it was raining heavily and so dark that Octavia had to switch on the light as though it was already night time.

'That's the trouble with storms,' Emmeline said, busily towelling Margaret's short bob. 'They're on you before you can breathe. You'll have to stay here till the worst of it's over, Edie.'

'I can't do that, Mum,' Edith said. 'I've got to be back for Arthur's tea and we're late already.' Feeding her man was very important to Edith Ames and tonight's meal was even more important than usual because she had something difficult to tell him and she wanted him to have a good tea inside him before she did it. 'Don't worry. We've got our umbrellas.'

'Umbrellas!' Emmeline snorted, glaring at the window. 'Oh, for heaven's sake, Edie, they won't be any use. It's coming down like stair rods.' Both little girls turned their heads at once to see if rain really *was* like stair rods and were impressed to find that it was. 'Hold your head still, Maggie, there's a

13

good girl. You don't want to catch a cold.'

The instruction was as much a warning to her daughter as her grandchild. But Edith was firm. 'They won't catch a cold,' she said. 'They'll run like the wind, won't you, girls.'

'You'll all get drowned,' Emmeline warned, turning her attention to Barbara. 'That's what'll happen. Never mind running like the wind. Anyway, aren't you going to stay to see your brother? He'll be home any minute. You'll stay to see *him*, surely to goodness. Ten minutes. I mean, what's ten minutes?'

'Enough to make us late,' Edith said. 'It's no good you going on, Mum. I can't be late for Arthur's tea. Not even for our Johnnie. You know that.'

Octavia had cleaned her rain-spattered glasses and was drying her own frizzy hair in her vigorous way, listening to them with her usual concentration, turning her towel-hung head to watch their faces as the argument progressed. She was aware that Emmeline was being overprotective of these much-loved grandchildren of hers, that Edith was being too dogged in her determination and that neither would give way to the other. There's nothing for it, she thought, dabbing at her damp sleeves, I shall have to intervene. As head of the family it was her job to try to keep the peace and to suggest whatever compromises she could, just as she calmed tempers and suggested solutions as head of her school. 'How would it be if you went home in my car?' she said to Edith. 'Then you wouldn't be late and the girls wouldn't get wet.'

Emmeline relaxed at once, saying, 'Very sensible,' but her daughter looked worried.

'That's ever so good of you, Aunt,' Edith said, 'but what about your dinner party?'

'I shall be back in plenty of time for that,' Octavia said,

14

speaking with a confidence she certainly didn't feel, for preparations for the meal were well under way, the agency cook and the waitress were busy in the kitchen and in less than an hour her guests would arrive.

'But isn't it Major Meriton?' Edith persisted.

'Major Meriton is a very old friend,' Octavia told her. 'I'm sure he won't mind if I'm a bit late.' But that wasn't true either. Now that he was middle-aged and a senior official at the Foreign Office, Tommy Meriton had become a stickler for punctuality. It was sometimes quite hard to remember what a relaxed young man he'd been when they were both young. Relaxed and handsome and easy to be with. What a long time ago it all seemed!

'I'll keep him amused if you *are* late,' her father said. 'But I'd cut off quickly, if I were you. Time is getting on.'

'There you are, you see,' Octavia said to Edith, handing her damp towel to Emmeline. 'Everything's taken care of. I'll go and get the car out of the garage. Wait in the porch. I'll drive it to the door.'

It was a cheerful journey to Colliers Wood, even though it was so dark that she had to put the headlights on and the rain was torrential, hitting the roof as loud as sticks on a tin drum and sluicing the windscreen with constant streams of water. Propelled by her private urgency, Octavia drove faster than she should have done, persuading herself that there was no danger because there were very few cars about. When they reached the bottom of Wimbledon Hill there were puddles halfway across the road and she drove through them at speed too, so that the impact made a palpable thud and water rose from her wheels in a dramatic white arc. The girls were thrilled with it, calling out 'Wheeee!' at each new impact, and Edith said it was like being in a ship at sea, adding, 'Not that I've ever been at sea, but I can imagine it.'

'It was always such fun driving with you,' she said to Octavia as they passed the curved steps of Wimbledon Theatre, dramatic on their corner. 'Off to the theatre to see the pantomime and going home after Christmas at your place in Hampstead all squashed together in the back seat. We had some good times.'

They bumped across the tramlines, heading for the underground at South Wimbledon. The pavements were crowded with rain-drenched women carrying baskets and shopping bags, bent against the wind and struggling with tugging umbrellas. 'Soon be home,' Octavia said. 'And by the look of it, it's just as well. This is getting worse. Have you got your brollies?'

'We shan't need them,' Edith said. 'It's only a step.'

Which was true enough, for Wycliffe Road was short and narrow with the merest scrap of a front garden between the gates and the houses, so she could reach the door of her maisonette in two strides. It only took a few scrambling seconds for all three of them to run into the house.

Now, Octavia thought, waving to them, I can get back. With a bit of luck and some fast driving she could be home and changed before the Meritons arrived.

But her luck didn't hold that afternoon. The Silver Cloud was standing in the drive. On the one evening when she could have done with Tommy's predictable punctuality, he'd decided to come early. Sighing, she garaged her car and let herself into the house. Her guests were in the drawing room being entertained by her father. She could hear Tommy laughing in that throaty way of his and his wife saying something in her soft voice that made him laugh again. And as she hung up her keys on the hall stand, the agency waitress walked out of the kitchen carrying twelve glasses and a dish of peanuts on a tray. The evening had begun. Emmeline must have heard her car and given the signal for the aperitifs to be served. There wasn't time for her to change. Ah well, she thought, removing her cardigan and tucking it into the hall seat, there's nothing for it, this blouse will have to do. She tried to pat her hair into some sort of order, failed, straightened her glasses, and took a deep breath. Then she opened the drawing room door and walked in, prepared to be teased or scolded.

Fortunately, Elizabeth Meriton was the first person to turn towards her, elegant as always in an understated evening dress, in powder blue pleated silk, as Octavia was quick to notice; her short hair immaculately waved, her nails and lips painted the same bright colour, and Elizabeth was every inch the diplomat's wife, smiling warmly and saying exactly the right thing. 'Tavy, my dear. J-J tells us you've been on an errand of mercy. Why does that not surprise me? How good to see you.'

The two women kissed cheeks and then Tommy took Octavia's hands in his and kissed her too. There was no teasing or scolding, he was too pleased with himself for that. 'We've had *such* an afternoon,' he said and looked at her eagerly, waiting for her response. 'I can't wait to tell you.'

What's he been up to? Octavia wondered. It had to be something special. She took a Dubonnet from the proffered tray, thanked the waitress, sipped it, and looked a question at him. 'Well, tell me then,' she said.

'We've been buying Lizzie's uniform,' he said happily. 'She's all kitted out and ready for school and she looks superb, doesn't she, Elizabeth?'

'He's been like a dog with two tails all afternoon,' Elizabeth said, laughing at him. 'You'd think there'd never been another

17

eleven-year-old requiring a school uniform in the entire history of education.'

'Ah, but what an eleven-year-old, my dear, and what a school!' Tommy said, beaming at Octavia. 'These were no ordinary purchases.'

Which provoked a murmur of amused agreement, for there wasn't a soul in the room who didn't know it had always been his ambition to send his much-loved, only daughter to Octavia's school. His sons were settled at Dulwich, which was right and proper, but his daughter had to go to Roehampton Secondary School and be educated by the great Octavia Smith.

Watching his ardent face Octavia was remembering the evening when he'd first told her how important it was to him, here, just outside those french windows. 'There's a war coming,' he'd said, 'and open cities will be bombed.' How terrible those words had seemed to her then but it had been an accurate prophecy and she knew it now after what had been happening in Abyssinia. 'London schools will be evacuated,' he'd said. 'They are already planning it. I want her to be at your school with you. I want you to look after her.' She'd laughed at his eagerness, for Lizzie couldn't have been more than six or seven at the time, and teased him that he'd have to wait till 1936 until she could be enrolled at Roehampton Secondary School. And now it *was* 1936 and she *was* enrolled, and what was happening in Europe grew more alarming by the day.

The doorbell was ringing. More guests were arriving. She excused herself from the Meritons and walked across the room to greet them.

In her maisonette in Wycliffe Road, Edith had given her daughters their nightly mug of cocoa and put them to bed. Then she'd set the table and cooked Arthur's supper all nicely in time for his return. It was liver and bacon and fried onions, which was one of his favourites, and they'd both enjoyed it. Now, he was sitting in his armchair in the kitchen, smoking a cigarette with his legs stretched before him and the lower button of his waistcoat undone to make room for the meal, reading the *Evening Standard*, happy and satisfied, the difficulties of the day behind him.

'Good?' she asked him unnecessarily, as she put the dirty plates in the sink.

'Smashing,' he said, looking up from the paper. 'You done me proud.'

His praise pleased her, as it always did. 'I do me best.'

'You're a giddy marvel how you manage,' he said.

She filled the kettle and set it on the gas stove ready to boil some water for the washing-up, swept the tablecloth, folded it, and put it away in the dresser. Then she sat down at the table again.

'Thing is,' she said, 'I got something to tell you.'

'Oh yes,' he said, eyes still on the newspaper.

'Listen to me, Arthur.'

'I am,' he said, still reading.

'No, really listen. It's important.'

He set the paper aside. 'I'm all ears,' he said, smiling at her.

Now that the moment had come she didn't know how to begin. She looked round at her nice neat kitchen, at her nice dependable gas cooker that she kept so clean and her nice white sink and the pot full of wooden spoons and kitchen knives, at the pretty flowery wallpaper that Arthur had hung for them and the curtains she'd run up on her Singer and the rag rug she'd made for the hearth, at the mantelpiece clock that he'd given her that Christmas because it looked cheerful. And now she was going to lose it all and the clock was ticking reproach at her, in a leaden inevitable way, clunk, clunk, clunk. 'Thing is,' she said again. 'Thing is, I think I'm expecting. Well not think, actually. I know I am.'

He was so shocked he couldn't disguise it. 'Oh blimey, Edie!' he said. 'That's torn it.' Then he was rescued by disbelief. She couldn't be. He'd always been so careful. I mean, what's the good of being careful if it happens anyway? 'Perhaps you've got it wrong,' he hoped. 'I mean, people do. Women, I mean.'

Her distress tipped into anger. 'Women!' she shouted. 'It's got nothing to do with women. This is me. Edie. I don't get things wrong. If I say I'm expecting, I'm expecting and I ought to know.' Then her emotions tipped again, propelled by that awful repetition. She put her head in her hands and burst into tears. 'What are we going to do?' she wept. 'We can't have another baby, Arthur. We simply can't. We can only just manage as it is without another mouth to feed. We'll have to leave this house and just when we've got it so lovely. Oh, Arthur, I'm at my wit's end. What are we going to do?'

'Come an' sit on my lap, old thing,' he said, stretching out to hold her hand. He'd spoken out of turn, by hoping it was a mistake. Now he must make amends. Poor Edie.

She crept into his lap like a miserable child needing comfort, which was most unlike her. Normally she'd have kept him at arm's length for quite a long time after a mistake like that. Now she put her head on his shoulder and wept into his shirt.

He put his arms round her and held her close, stroking her back and thinking hard. There had to be an answer. There were always answers. Come on, Arthur Ames. Use your wits. Think. The baby was on the way. There was no doubt about that. So what was to be done? He'd have to earn more money.

That's what. He hadn't got the faintest idea how he would do it but it would have to be done.

Edie pulled a handkerchief out of her pocket and blew her nose. She was still awash with anxiety, drowning in it. 'What are we going to do?' she wept. 'What if you get laid off?'

'I'm a skilled mechanic,' he told her, with some pride. 'We don't get laid off. There ain't enough of us to go round.'

She wasn't convinced. 'You very nearly did that time, when the garage closed and everything. If you hadn't been took on by old man Murchison it would ha' been all up with us. We'd ha' been on the dole.'

'But we wasn't,' he said. 'It never come to it.'

'It'll come to it this time,' she said miserably. 'I don't see how we can avoid it.'

And he suddenly saw how. Like a light being switched on. 'I shall join the Territorials,' he said. 'They're advertising for car mechanics. I saw it in the paper only the other day. Good life. Out in the open air. Uniform provided and that'll save on clothes. Good grub and that'll save on food. Good pay, or so they said. Can't be worse than what I earn now anyway. Could be a lot more. That's the answer. I shall join the Territorials.'

'But that's the army,' Edie said. 'You'd be a soldier.'

'Only part time. You come home nights. Most nights anyway. You can go on with your trade. That sort a' thing.' He wasn't entirely sure of his facts because he'd only scanned the advertisement but he had to make it sound acceptable. 'Could be just the ticket.'

'But what if there's a war?'

'There won't be.'

'That's not what they say in the *Mirror*. They reckon there's a big war coming. They're always on about it.'

All perfectly true but he didn't want to be reminded of

21

it. Not now. He couldn't afford to be faint-hearted now or to think about what might – or might not – happen. He'd made his decision and he would stick with it. 'You don't want to take no notice of the *Mirror*,' he said cheerfully. 'That's all newspaper talk. They don't mean half of it.'

'I don't want you in a war,' Edie said. 'I don't hold with wars.'

'I could do with a cup of tea,' he said, changing the subject. 'What say you put the kettle on?'

At Octavia's dinner party the talk had turned to war too. They were twelve to table and four of the guests were old friends of her father's who belonged to the Fabian Society and consequently kept well abreast of the latest news.

'I used to think Winston Churchill was just a warmonger,' Frank Dimond was saying, 'but I'm not so certain now. The situation in Spain is absolutely appalling and as to what is happening to the Jews in Germany...'

'I still think the League of Nations should be taking action,' Octavia said. 'I know Hitler has taken Germany out of the League but that's no reason for the rest of us to ignore what he's doing. That's just playing his game.'

'But what action could we take?' Elizabeth Meriton asked. 'If he ignores the threat of sanctions, as he invariably does, what other weapon do we hold?'

'That,' Tommy said, dabbing his mouth with his table napkin, 'is the nub of the League's problem. Without an army to back up their demands there's nothing much they can do. Any international power needs an international army if it is to stand up to an international bully. It was a major oversight not to set one up right at the beginning.'

The storm had blown itself out and now it was a peaceful

summer evening. There was a blackbird singing in the garden and sunlight flowed through the windows in long visible columns, making the glasses shimmer and warming their earnest faces.

'I feel as if we're all drifting,' Emmeline said sadly. 'Nobody in their right mind wants another war and yet we're drifting towards one. That's what will happen, isn't it, Tommy? If the League can't do anything then we shall have to.'

'I wish I could say no,' Tommy said, 'but I fear you may be right. As far as we can see at the Foreign Office, since Hitler occupied the Rhineland he's had carte blanche to do what he likes and so has Mussolini. Gassing defenceless Abyssinians was against every code of warfare that's ever been written and yet he got away with it. It's a very serious situation.'

'What I can't understand is why the government will go on talking about appeasement,' Frank Dimond said. 'They must know it isn't going to work.'

'It's more diplomacy than hope,' Tommy said. 'They know how important it is for people to believe that peace is possible, and of course they don't want to spread alarm. It's a different matter behind the scenes. There are no official statements about it, naturally, but they're actually beginning to make preparations, pushing for more men to join the Territorials, manufacturing gas masks, stepping up on the production of arms. That sort of thing. Churchill's pressing for more, as you would expect, but at least it's a start. They've put in orders for the new fighter plane too, the one called the Spitfire. I expect you've heard of it.' Heads were shaken around the table. 'No? It was on show at Southampton. Me and a few chaps went down to see it. Fastest thing in the air, so they say, and I can well believe it. Rolls Royce engine. Twelve cylinders. Handsome little plane. Just the sort of thing we shall need if it comes to it.'

'How many have we got?' Octavia asked.

'Six,' he said, and when she grimaced, 'but there are more on order.'

Six, she thought, against an entire German Air Force. What good is six? If we're going to fight them we shall need hundreds and the young men to fly them. Then she noticed that Johnnie was listening just a little too ardently and that Emmeline was watching him and looking anxious, and she tried to think of another subject to distract them.

J-J was thinking the same thing. Now he leant into the conversation. 'What a topic for a fine summer evening!' he said, smiling at them. 'Have any of you been following the Berlin Olympics, I wonder?'

They had and took his lead at once, grateful to be thinking of something other than death and destruction. The wonderful performances of Jesse Owens in the hundred and two hundred metres were remembered and praised – 'He's the fastest man in the world, imagine that, and he's modest about it' – Hitler's rudeness in snubbing him was deplored – 'But what can you expect? He's a nasty vulgar little man' – the British success in the four hundred metres relay was enjoyed again. The dinner party relaxed and eased. Only Octavia sat a little apart, contributing to the general talk in a vague way but still thinking and worrying. There had to be some way to stop this war. She couldn't just sit there in her comfortable chair in her comfortable room and ignore it. It wasn't in her nature. Once or twice, Frank Dimond looked across the table and gave her a brief smile as if he knew what she was thinking, but she kept her thoughts to herself. She would talk to Pa after the guests were gone and see what he thought about it.

But as it happened, it was Frank Dimond who brought up the topic again, and he did it when most of the other guests had left and he and his wife were putting on their coats and saying goodbye to Octavia in the hall.

'A most enjoyable evening,' he said to Octavia. 'And very informative, if I may say so. I had no idea the government had so many preparations under way.'

'Nor had I,' Octavia told him and smiled. 'I think our Tommy was being rather indiscreet and thank God for that. I've never been in favour of official secrets.'

'In that case,' he said smiling at her, 'may I ask you a question?'

'Of course,' she said, wondering what it would be.

'I belong to an organisation that might interest you,' he said. 'Or perhaps I should say a committee, for that's all we are at the moment. But committee or organisation, our aims are the same. We are doing what we can to get as many Jews out of Germany as possible. We're afraid Hitler might close the borders, so time is of the essence. Would you be interested in helping us?'

'Of course,' she said again. 'If I can.' It was just the sort of thing she ought to be involved in. 'You must tell me more.'

'I will ask our Mrs Hutchinson to contact you,' Frank said, and turned as J-J and Emmeline walked into the hall to say goodbye too. 'A splendid evening, J-J.'

'I'm glad you enjoyed it,' J-J said, shaking his hand. 'It was good to have your company.'

'A lovely dinner, Emmeline,' Mrs Dimond said. 'Splendid food, lovely wine, good company, what more could anyone want?'

They left smiling and Octavia smiled too, although rather absent-mindedly. She was wondering when Mrs Hutchinson would get in touch and what she would say when she did.

Her phone call came two weeks later. And it caused a row.

# Chapter Two

Octavia had spent the morning in her school. The start of the autumn term was only nine days away and she wanted to be sure that everything was ready for it, that the new stock had been delivered, that the repairs to the science rooms were completed, that everything was clean and in order. She and Maggie Henry, the school secretary, had inspected every room, noting everything that wasn't entirely to her satisfaction and she'd returned to Parkside Avenue, with Maggie's notes in her attaché case, ready to deal with anything outstanding. That afternoon she sat in the garden, smoked a few necessary cigarettes and wrote a lot of necessary letters, while her father talked to Emmeline and enjoyed the afternoon tea she'd provided for them. The sound of the phone suddenly trilling inside the house was decidedly unwelcome. It had to be answered, of course, the new term being so close, because there was no knowing who it might be, but it was a nuisance.

'Yes,' she said shortly into the receiver.

The voice that answered sounded unsure of itself. 'Miss Smith?' it asked.

'Speaking.'

'Ah,' the voice said and gave a nervous cough. 'Um, my name is Stella Hutchinson. Mr Dimond asked me to contact you. Is this an inconvenient time?'

Frank's committee, Octavia thought. Of course. She'd been so busy she'd forgotten all about it. She moderated her tone at once. 'No, no,' she said. 'I've just rushed in from the garden that's all. I'm a bit breathless. How I can help you?'

'Well...' Mrs Hutchinson said, 'how much do you know about our organisation?'

'Only what Frank told me,' Octavia admitted, 'which wasn't a great deal. I know you're trying to get as many Jews out of Germany as you can, which seems admirable to me – and necessary given what's going on there.'

'You know about the concentration camps then.'

'I've heard rumours. Yes.'

'From the newspapers?'

'Yes. I have no other source of information.'

There was a pause, then the gentle voice went on, 'The situation is much worse than anything you'll read in the newspapers. Worse than you could possibly imagine. From what our refugees have been telling us, it looks as though the camp guards are deliberately starving the inmates to death.'

The voice was cool, quiet, almost emotionless but that made the impact of the words even more terrible. 'That's appalling,' Octavia said, and instantly began to think of some action she could take. Some action she *must* take. It was imperative. A letter to *The Times* perhaps. A petition. 'Something must be done,' she said. 'How can I help you?'

'Our most pressing need at the moment,' Mrs Hutchinson said, 'apart from raising funds, is to find people in London who could offer our new arrivals temporary accommodation until we can move them on to something more permanent. Would that be possible?'

'Yes,' Octavia said at once. 'Of course. We've got a spare room they could have.'

The voice changed, became businesslike. 'How many does it sleep?'

'There's a double bed and a small single but we could squeeze another single in if there were four of them.'

'When could it be ready?'

'When would you want it?'

'Would next Tuesday be possible?'

'Of course,' Octavia said. There was no doubt in her mind. 'You will need my address.'

She strolled back into the sunlit garden feeling undeniably pleased with herself. From the ease and affluence of her life here with Pa, she was going to do something positive, to help people who needed help, to make a difference. It was right and proper and she was buoyed up with the satisfaction of it.

'There you are, Pa,' she said when she reached his chair. 'I'm going to do something useful with my life.'

'Which of course you've never done up to now,' her father laughed. 'What particular good work is it this time?'

She sat down beside him and gave him a smile. 'Taking some of the wind out of Hitler's obnoxious sails,' she said. 'You remember what Mr Dimond was saying at the dinner party, about the committee – the people who are trying to evacuate the Jews from Germany – well, he put me on to the secretary and she's just rung and asked me if I will take some of her refugees in, and I've said yes.'

'How many?' Emmeline said, and her voice was ominous.

Octavia was too caught up in happy altruism to notice. 'Two, three, four, it depends,' she said.

'And how long would we have to have them?'

'Two or three days,' Octavia said. 'Until they've found

28

somewhere permanent for them to go to. Not long.'

'So when are all these people coming?' Emmeline asked, and this time the tone of her voice was unmistakable.

'Well, actually, it's next Tuesday,' Octavia admitted, and now she was worried because her cousin looked cross. 'But that shouldn't be a problem, should it? I mean we've got the room and the beds. It will only be a matter of making them up.'

Emmeline shuddered. 'Only!' she cried. 'Only! Oh, Tavy, for heaven's sake! You double the number of people in the house and you tell me it'll only be a matter of making up a few beds. Have you any idea how much work this will make? They'll need feeding and looking after and sheets washing – you think what it'll be like if the children wet the bed and ten to one they will – and dirty clothes every five minutes and dirty nappies I shouldn't wonder, and double the shopping every day – and I have quite enough shopping to do without that – and clearing up after them and I don't know what all. I can't do it, Tavy. It's too much.'

Octavia tried to reassure her, 'We'll help you, Em…' but her words were waved away as if they were flies.

'Oh, don't talk such *rubbish*, Tavy. You won't help me. You won't be here. You'll be at school all day and Johnnie'll be at work and you can't ask Uncle to make beds and fetch and carry – not at his age. And don't say you'll help when you're at home. That's no earthly good at all. The work's all been done by the time you get back.'

'There's Mrs Benson,' Octavia pointed out.

But that only provoked a snort. 'Mrs Benson,' Emmeline said sternly, 'only comes in twice a week for two hours. She's a help, I'll grant you that, but four hours will be a drop in the ocean if we're going to have the place crawling with foreigners.

Oh no, I shall bear the brunt of it. That's who it'll be. Me. On my own. And I've got enough on my plate without taking on a lot of refugees. Why can't they stay where they are?' She was hot with distress, her cheeks flushed and her untidy grey hair escaping from its pins.

'Because they'll get sent to a concentration camp if they do,' Octavia said. 'Come on, Em, we can't have that.'

Emmeline was truculent. 'I don't see why not.' She was very near tears and she knew she was being unreasonable but, really, this was all too much. 'And there's Arthur joining the Territorials, as if this isn't bad enough. I don't know what's to become of us. The world's gone mad. Stark, staring, raving mad.' And she stood up quickly before they could see her cry and half-walked, half-ran off towards the house.

Octavia was on her feet at once, feeling guilty and ready to run after her. She couldn't have Em upset, not her dear Em whom she loved so much and had lived with for so long, not when she worked so hard and looked after them so well. And she was right, of course she was right, she *would* do the bulk of the work. I must do something about it, she thought.

Her father caught her by the arm. 'Leave her,' he advised. 'Give her time.'

'But she's upset and it's my fault,' Octavia said. 'It's no good making that face, Pa. It *is* my fault. I shouldn't have sprung it on her. It was thoughtless. I should have asked her about it before I said yes.'

'Then you must think now before you say anything more,' her father said. 'We must both think.'

Octavia was thinking already and thinking aloud. 'I can't back out of this now, Pa. It's too important. And I've given my word. But she's right about me not being able to help her. I can't leave the school and stay at home. Not at the start of term. There's too much to do and it wouldn't be fair on the staff to leave them. And with the best will in the world, you can't help her either. So there's really only one answer, isn't there. We must *hire* some help. I think we could run to it. No. I'll rephrase that. We must run to it. There isn't any option. I can't have Em upset. What sort of wages should we offer?'

'Sensible ones,' her father said, reading her mind.

'Four pounds a week.'

'Be reasonable, Tavy. That's far too much. You'd be inundated with applications.'

That had to be admitted. 'Well, three pounds ten then.'

'I would say twenty-five shillings,' J-J advised. 'However, given your views on exploitation, perhaps thirty.'

So the wage was agreed, with the proviso that if they found the right person it could always be increased, and Octavia went indoors to her study to write the advertisement. Then she walked across to the kitchen to make it up with her cousin.

It took a considerable time and much hugging for Emmeline was profoundly upset and needed to tell her cousin all over again that she simply couldn't do so much work. 'Not with the best will in the world.'

'But if we can get a good girl,' Octavia urged, 'that will make all the difference, won't it.'

Eventually after demurring for a long time, Emmeline agreed that it would and, as the matter seemed to be settled, she dried her eyes and put on her straw hat and the two of them went off arm in arm to post Octavia's letters.

'It's so peaceful here,' she said as they walked beneath the burgeoning lime trees in the avenue. 'You don't think there's really going to be a war, do you?'

The anxiety on her face reminded Octavia of something

she'd said in the garden. 'What's all this about Arthur joining the Territorials?' she asked.

'And that's another thing,' Emmeline said. 'I can't think what's got into him. Edie told me this morning. "Joined the Territorials," she said. And I said, "Whatever for?" and she just shrugged. You know how she does. I don't like it, Tavy. I mean, that's the army to all intents and purposes. If there *is* a war he'll be in the thick of it and we don't want that. We had quite enough of that with our poor Cyril.'

'He hasn't been laid off, has he?' Octavia asked. It seemed the most likely explanation.

'Oh no,' Emmeline said. 'Nothing like that. I asked her. But there's something going on. She had that look, you know the one, all sort of stiff faced and not telling you anything, like she had when he was laid off that time. I tell you, Tavy, I don't like it one bit.'

They'd reached the letter-box on the corner. Octavia slipped her letters into the slot while Emmeline watched. Now whatever was going to happen next would depend on what sort of answer they got and both of them were privately praying that it would be a good one.

What they actually got in the next two days were three bundles of letters each tied together with an elastic band.

'Good heavens above,' Octavia said. 'I know there's a lot of unemployment but I never realised there'd be this many people looking for work in Wimbledon. It'll take for ever just to read them and sort them through. And we'll have to see them on Monday by the latest, Em. It doesn't give us much time.'

'We'll do it between us,' Emmeline told her. 'Three piles: definitely possible, quite good, and no good at all.'

By the end of the evening they'd sorted the letters into

possibles and impossibles and reduced the possible pile to the six women they most liked the sound of. Then there was nothing more to be done except answer the letters and wait until their six candidates arrived.

They were a varied bunch and they'd come from all over the British Isles: South Wales, Tyneside, Slough, West Ham, Glasgow. 'No work, you see, Miss Smith,' they explained. 'Not where we live.' But they were all very eager to please, so eager, in fact, that Octavia was touched to the depths of her socialist soul and wanted to employ them all. However, one was all she needed and that one soon emerged from the group.

Her name was Janet Sanderson and she was pale and skinny and looked as though hard work would make her collapse, but there was something endearing about her. With her stick-thin legs and her chirrupy perkiness and that bright red jumper, she reminded Octavia of the robin who sang to her every day in the garden. She said she came from Tyneside and lived with her cousin in Putney.

'She works on the telephoane, miss,' she told Octavia. 'They wouldn' tek me on account a' me accent.'

'Are you used to housework?' Octavia asked her.

'I ought ter be,' the girl said, rather ruefully. 'I done enough of it.'

'It's a big house,' Octavia warned her. 'There would be a lot of work.'

'Couldn't be worse than the doale, miss,' Janet said, and grinned at her.

I like her, Octavia thought. She's got the right spirit. I think she'd suit us very well.

That was Emmeline's opinion of her too, although for a different reason. She was much too sensible to entertain any romantic notions about robins and red jerseys, her concerns were entirely practical. 'I think she'd be more likely to do as she was told,' she said to Octavia as they walked round the garden while their six applicants waited in the study, 'being young. Some of the others would have their own ways of doing things and I'd prefer to have things done my way.'

So the decision was made to Janet's very obvious delight.

'We would want you to start at half past eight tomorrow morning,' Octavia said. 'Would that be agreeable?'

'Yes, ma'am. It would.'

'Don't be late,' Emmeline warned. 'We've got a lot to get through tomorrow.'

'I'll be there on the dot, ma'am,' the girl promised.

And so she was, appearing at the kitchen door as the clock struck the half-hour and donning her apron ready for work as soon as she was inside the kitchen. 'Where would you like me to start, Mrs Thompson?' she said. It was the perfect opening.

'I've got a list here,' Emmeline told her, pointing to her little notice board. 'We'll start with the breakfast things. Use the trolley.'

So the trolley was used and the table was cleared and brushed free of crumbs – 'Use this little brush and pan, do you see? I keep that specially for crumbs' – and the dirty dishes were washed and put neatly away and the list was followed obediently and cheerfully for the rest of the morning. But just as they were preparing the lunch, the doorbell rang and change arrived with a shuffle of small feet and terrible smell.

'If you please, Mrs Thompson,' Janet said, returning to the kitchen when she'd answered the door. 'You've got company.'

'Tell Miss Smith,' Emmeline said, not looking up from the pudding she was mixing. 'She deals with company.'

'I have, ma'am,' Janet said, 'onny she said I wor to tell you, like.'

'Oh, for heaven's sake!' Emmeline said, putting down her spoon. 'They're not here already, surely to goodness, wretched people. And just when we're getting on so well. It's too bad.' And she went off to attend to them, scowling all the way.

There was no doubt how wretched they were. She could see that as soon as she stepped inside the study. They stood together in a small huddled group, four dark-haired children, in foreign-looking clothes: three little girls wearing cotton frocks, dark coats and berets, and a little boy in a cloth cap several sizes too large for him, who was clinging to his sister's hand and shivering.

Their escort was a handsome woman in a tweed suit who was talking to Octavia. She turned as Emmeline came in and introduced herself as Stella Hutchinson. 'These are the Cohens,' she said and explained unnecessarily, 'I'm afraid they've been rather seasick.'

Emmeline looked at their stained clothes and sniffed. 'So I see,' she said. 'Do they have a change of clothing?'

'They've got a case,' Mrs Hutchinson said. 'But I haven't had time to see what they've brought in it. They're rather bewildered, poor little things, so I thought the best thing to do would be to get them here to you as soon as I could.'

'They'll need a good wash,' Emmeline said, 'clean clothes or not. We can't have them standing around smelling like that. It's not pleasant. Do they speak English?'

'I'm afraid not.'

'But you speak German presumably.'

'I do.'

'Then tell them my name is Mrs Thompson and that I'm going to give them a bath and they're to do as they're told and then they shall have dinner afterwards. They look as if they could do with some nourishment.'

Mrs Hutchinson spoke to the children in German and at some length while Emmeline rang for Janet, fidgeted with impatience and wrinkled her nose against the smell of vomit. Eventually the children seemed to have understood for they were all nodding and at that Emmeline took the little boy by the hand and walked towards the door.

'Come along,' she said, and brisked them all out of the room and upstairs to the bathroom, with Janet following in attendance. 'Two at a time, I think,' she said, 'and we'll wash their hair while we're about it.'

When Octavia came upstairs half an hour later to see how they were getting on, she found the two eldest children sitting on the bathroom floor swathed in towels while Emmeline and Janet had the two younger ones on their laps and were rubbing their hair dry.

'They haven't got much in the way of clothes,' Emmeline said. 'I shall have to go out presently and buy them some knickers. Poor little ducks. We'll have our dinner first though,' she said to the child on her lap, 'eh? I expect you could do with it.'

*Poor little ducks*, Octavia thought, smiling at the words and the affection with which they'd been spoken. It was what Emmeline had called her own children when they were babies. Dear little ducks. Despite her worries, this was going to be all right. Em might get cross and complain, but when it came down to it her heart was in the right place. 'I'll leave you to it then,' she said.

Emmeline was disappointed when her new little ducks ate so little at dinner time but she was ready to excuse them. 'We can't wonder at it,' she said to Octavia. 'Not after being so seasick. I shall make some little light cakes for their tea and see if that will tempt them.'

'So it will be all right for me to go to school tomorrow?' Octavia said, grinning at her.

'I don't see why not,' Emmeline said. 'We've got everything under control, haven't we, Janet? Now I'm off to get those knickers and I think I might buy them some warm cardigans too. Their coats are very lightweight.'

The start of a new autumn term was always a joy to Octavia. It was so good to be back in school, to see her old colleagues again and hear what they'd all been getting up to during the summer holiday, and taking her first assembly invariably filled her with a sense of ineffable well-being. It was so good to be sitting in her familiar chair on the platform with the staff sitting behind her, the new prefects ranged at the back of the hall in their red sashes and their black gowns, and all the little first-formers, wide-eyed and bandbox neat in their new uniforms on the front benches. My school, she thought proudly, as she always did. My fine, strong, intelligent, lively school.

But the talk in the staff room at their first break was more serious than she'd ever known it, for Helen Staples, who taught English, and Phillida Bertram, their Art teacher, had spent the entire holiday in Germany. They'd gone to Munich to see the latest paintings in the 'House of Art' but they'd come back talking about the terrible things they'd seen and heard in the city streets.

'There are troops everywhere,' Helen said. 'We saw a parade in Berlin, didn't we Philly, and there were hundreds of them all marching along like robots with guns on their shoulders and the most dreadful helmets you ever saw, bellowing some awful song. They scared the life out of me.'

'All very ugly,' Phillida agreed. 'Oh, they're smart enough.

Their uniforms are very fine, a sort of grey-green, and everything's polished and clean but it's the impression they give. They don't look human. You feel they'd be absolutely ruthless if it came to obeying orders. They'd do as they were told without a thought, no matter what it was. I find that alarming.'

'And what were the paintings like?' Octavia asked.

'Horrible,' Phillida said. 'Either pornographic, or – well, what shall I call them, Helen?'

'Militaristic,' Helen said. 'Handsome young men in grey-green uniforms, all looking healthy and well-fed, off to war waving flags, looking noble. And invincible, of course. About as far away from the reality of war as the artists can get and all of a piece with those bellowing men in the streets. Propaganda, of course.'

'It makes you wonder what's going on behind the scenes,' Morag Gordon said, putting down her coffee cup. 'You hear such rumours.'

So Octavia told them about her refugees. 'If the next family I get can speak English,' she said, 'we might find things out.'

The four children left her two days later wearing their new cardigans and with a shopping bag full of fruit and sandwiches for the next stage of their journey. Four days after that they were replaced by a young woman called Gerda, who had a babe in arms and a toddler and was worried about her husband who'd been left behind. 'Very bad,' she said. But as Octavia quickly discovered, that and 'Thank you' was all the English she knew.

'I shall have to learn German,' Octavia said to her father. 'That's all there is to it. Not being able to communicate is very trying.'

Gerda stayed for four days and when Mrs Hutchinson came

38

to collect her, she said goodbye to Octavia and Emmeline with tears in her eyes. 'You good,' she said passionately. 'You rescue good.'

'It's the least we can do,' Octavia told her. 'The least any of us can do and we're glad to do it.'

'They're grateful for so little,' she said to her family over dinner that night. 'It makes me wonder just what horrors they've had to endure. I wish they could tell us. I'd like to know what's really happening out there. Morag's right. I'm sure we don't know the half of it.'

But it wasn't until the Mannheim family came to stay with her that she heard what was going on.

They were an obviously middle-class family from Berlin, mother, father and two little girls of seven and eight called Miriam and Rachel, and they came to stay in the middle of November, bringing money and jewellery stitched into their clothes so that they could pay their way. They said they'd had terrible trouble trying to get out of Germany, 'you would never believe how difficult it is', and now they were planning to take ship to America, where Mr Mannheim hoped he would be able to get a job. They were well dressed and courteous and they all spoke English, in the father's case extremely well. He'd been a journalist, he told them on his first evening at Parkside Avenue, 'but of course, that is no longer permitted.'

'Why is that?' J-J asked. 'Are people afraid to employ you?'

'No, sir,' Mr Mannheim said. 'It is because it is against the law. Jews are not allowed to teach, or farm, or work in films or the radio, or be journalists, by order of the Führer.'

Professor Smith was shocked. 'Has it come to that?' he said.

'Actually, that is the least of our worries,' Mrs Mannheim told him. 'We might perhaps tell you a little more about it, but later in the evening.' And she flashed a warning glance in the direction of her two daughters.

'Yes, quite,' the professor said. 'We mustn't forget the pudding. Emmeline has something rather special for us tonight.'

Later that evening when Johnnie was out with his friends and Miriam and Rachel were safely upstairs and well out of earshot, the Mannheims told their hosts what life was like in Hitler's Germany.

'For a start,' Mr Mannheim said, 'you must understand that nobody is allowed to oppose this man. Not that many would dare to now. It is altogether too dangerous. Since May, he has established a new court which he calls "the people's court", but which of course is no such thing. It consists of two judges chosen by Herr Hitler and five high-ranking Nazis, also chosen by Herr Hitler, naturally, and its function is to try cases of treason against the state, or in other words, disagreeing with Herr Hitler. It sits in camera and there is no appeal against its judgement.'

It sounded corrupt in the extreme. 'What sort of punishments can it impose?' Octavia wanted to know.

'Death,' Mr Mannheim said, 'or banishment to a concentration camp, which could well be tantamount to death.'

'Even his own followers are not safe,' Mrs Mannheim said. 'You have heard of the Night of the Long Knives, doubtless.'

There had been something about it in the papers. 'The night they shot Ernst Roehm,' J-J said.

'He and hundreds of others,' Mr Mannheim told him. 'It was what they call a purge. And these men were all members of the SA, don't forget, the Storm Troopers association, his closest allies.'

'Dear God!' Octavia said. 'It sounds like a nightmare.'

'It is a nightmare,' Mr Mannheim said. 'Nobody is safe, and the Jews least of all.' Then he stopped and turned to look at his wife and there was pain on his face.

'I would not wish to pry,' J-J said, 'for we know how difficult this must be for you, but we know so little that anything you can tell us would help us to understand, and I do feel we should try to understand. It seems to me that it is only by ordinary people telling one another what is happening that the truth will emerge.'

'What we are facing,' Mrs Mannheim said, 'and face every day on every street, is hatred. Hitler hates the Jews. I don't know why, except that it must be something very deep-seated, something in his psyche. But for whatever reason, he hates the Jews. There is no doubt about that at all, he makes no secret of it, and he and his henchman, Dr Goebbels, have taught the Germans to hate us too. None of us are safe. We can be spat at, or sworn at, or punched and kicked for no other reason than because we are Jews and happen to be in the way of someone who wants to vent their anger on us. I have not dared to let my daughters out in the street for a very long time. It is very ugly.'

'But why?' Octavia said, struggling to understand. 'What is the matter with them?'

'I think,' Mrs Mannheim said, 'it is because they need someone to hate, and we are there. They are angry. They have no jobs. They have been poor and unemployed for years. They do not count for anything. They have no self-esteem. Then they are told that we are a threat to them and so they lash out. We have become scapegoats.'

41

Emmeline had been listening quietly. Now she joined in with a pertinent question. 'You said it was difficult to get out of Germany,' she said. 'That's right, isn't it? Well, now that doesn't make sense. At least it doesn't to me. If they hate you so much, I would have thought they'd have been encouraging you to leave.'

'Yes,' Mrs Mannheim said, 'you would think so, wouldn't you? That would be the reasonable thing to do. But this is not a reasonable situation. This is a situation where prejudices and needs come into play. I think they need to have us there so that they can punish us.'

That was an extraordinary idea. 'Really?'

'I wish it were not so,' Mr Mannheim said, 'but yes, really. I have watched their faces when they are kicking someone or painting the Star of David on a shop window or shouting their hatred at us as they pass and I have to say, they enjoy it. They are swollen with the pleasure of it. They look twice the size. It gives them a sense of power.'

'That,' Octavia said, remembering Holloway gaol, 'is hideous.' But she could believe it.

'Yes.'

'It's not something I've ever seen,' Emmeline told them, 'so it's hard for me to understand.'

'It is for most people,' Mrs Mannheim said.

'And yet you understand it and talk about it calmly. I would be raging.'

'It is my profession,' Mrs Mannheim explained. 'I am – was – a psychiatrist.'

The idea kept Octavia awake for most of the night. Unlike Emmeline she *had* seen hatred in action. She'd seen it in Westminster when mounted police baton-charged a suffragette march and in Holloway gaol when she herself was held down and forcibly fed, so she knew how brutal and unreasonable it was. If the Germans were being encouraged to hate, they would be perfect cannon fodder. A belligerent army is just the place for men full of hatred. After all, if you're allowed to hate one race, you can be persuaded to hate another. Jews today, French and British tomorrow. Unless the League of Nations can stop this man, she thought, there will be a war. I don't see how we can avoid it.

The Mannheims stayed at Parkside Avenue for nearly six weeks and they were excellent company, teaching Johnnie to play chess and talking politics to J-J and Octavia late into the night. But eventually Mr Mannheim came back from one of his sorties to the shipping offices to say that he had tickets for New York at last, 'sailing on Thursday from Southampton.'

'We shall miss you,' Octavia said, as she saw them off at the gate. 'You must write and tell us how you are getting on.'

The promise was given, the goodbyes were said. 'One day,' Mr Mannheim told her, 'we will meet in Berlin.'

'I hope so,' Octavia said, but she was thinking what a hard road they would all have to travel before that day could arrive.

# Chapter Three

'You *must* tell her, Edie,' Dora said. 'You can't go on wearing that great cardigan all the time and hoping no one'll notice. You're really showing now. It's not fair. Think how she'll feel if she finds out from someone else. Her own daughter not telling her. And Christmas coming and everything.'

'It's my baby, Dora,' Edith said sullenly. 'I'll tell her when I'm ready. Just not now.'

'I don't see why not,' Dora said, drinking her tea. 'I would if it was me.'

'But it's not you, is it?' her sister said. 'It's me, and it's my baby.'

Dora put down her tea cup, took a drag at her cigarette and looked at her sister levelly. 'I'm beginning to think you don't want the poor little thing,' she said.

'Well, I do,' Edith told her stubbornly. And it was true. She hadn't wanted it a bit, not at the start, but now that it was kicking she felt really sorry for it and was ashamed to have been so unkind. It must be the worst possible thing for a baby to come into the world and for its own mother to say she doesn't want it. She was drawn with pity at the very idea.

'Have bittick?' Margaret said, looking at the biscuit tin. 'Please, Mummy.'

'One piece,' Edith allowed, adding sternly, 'I don't want you spoiling your dinner.' Now and then, as a great treat, she bought half a pound of broken biscuits and the girls loved them.

'And me,' Barbara said. 'Please, Mummy.'

'Since you've asked nicely,' Edith said and watched while they made their choice. 'Then I shall have to get on.' There was a pile of ironing waiting on the ironing board and dinner to cook. 'I *will* tell her Dottie. Only in my own time. I can't rush it.'

'Well, I've said my say,' Dora sighed. 'I can't do more than that.'

'It would be easier if the house wasn't full of foreigners all the time,' Edith said, putting the biggest iron on the trivet. 'It's not something you can tell your mother with a lot of foreigners all over the place.'

'Take her out for a walk,' Dora suggested.

'Oh, come on, Dottie,' Edith protested, 'when does she have time to go out? She's always working. Mind you don't go near the iron, Margaret.'

Emmeline had taken to her new job as hostess and carer easily and with enthusiasm. The Mannheims had taught her enough German to be able to welcome her guests, and to enquire if they needed another blanket or if they would like a second helping or another cup of coffee, and from then on and with Janet to help her, she'd been coping if not entirely happily then at least with the satisfaction of knowing she was doing something well worth while. Coffee had been a problem to start with because she really wasn't very good at making it, but it was a problem solved when Mrs Mannheim offered to do it for her and actually found a delicatessen where they sold freshly ground coffee which made a lot of difference. From then on she simply handed the job over to someone else, surprised to see that even quite small children could manage it.

'What you're used to, I suppose,' she said to Octavia. 'It wouldn't do for me but it takes all sorts. What are we going to do about Christmas?'

'We shall invite them to join us,' Octavia said. 'We'll give one another presents and we'll buy a few little gifts for them and we'll treat it as a holiday. They have a religious ceremony at Christmas time too. It's called Chanukah. I've been looking it up. Perhaps we could combine them.'

But as it turned out, there were no refugees to join them that Christmas. Mrs Hutchinson rang Octavia in the middle of December to tell her they were having great difficulty in getting anybody out at all. 'It could be better in the New Year. We must hope so. I will keep you informed.'

So it was a simple family holiday after all and a cheerful one. They spent most of their Christmas dinner happily castigating King Edward, although, as Emmeline said, 'I suppose we can't call him that now.'

'He's a fool whatever we're going to call him,' Dora said trenchantly, as she helped herself to more bread sauce. 'Fancy giving up the throne of England for that ugly woman. She's got a face like a flat iron.'

'She's no beauty, I'll grant you that,' J-J said, encouraging her. 'But we can't all be beautiful. She must have other charms.'

'I can't see what,' Dora said. 'She's got no figure to speak of, she's American, she's plastered in make-up, she's had two husbands. I mean, two husbands! What does that say about her?'

'I think she's a gold digger,' Edith said. 'She wanted to be Queen and wear ermine and jewels and drive about in the

46

state coach. Good riddance to her, that's what I say.'

'I wonder what the new king will be like,' Johnnie said, spearing a Brussels sprout. 'They say he's a timid sort of bloke. Got a stutter apparently. Can't get his words out.'

'The Queen's all right, though,' Dora said, 'as far as you can tell. At least she's pretty.'

'And they've got two pretty little girls,' Octavia said. 'Like you, Edie.'

The pause that followed her remark went on just a little too long, so she looked up from her plate to reinforce her compliment with a smile – and then realised that Emmeline was giving her daughter the oddest look, that Dora was flashing an eye-warning to her, and that Edith was blushing. What have I said? she thought. It's almost as if I've put my foot in it.

'Not quite like you though, eh, Edie?' Emmeline said, heavily. 'If I'm any judge, you've gone one better.'

'I *was* going to tell you, Ma,' Edith said, looking shame-faced. 'Only there were always so many people round. I mean, I never got you on my own. I mean, it's not something you can say in front of a load of foreigners.'

'When is it going to be?' Emmeline said. 'If we're allowed to know.'

'When's what going to be?' Johnnie asked. The conversation seemed to have taken a turn he couldn't follow. He looked round the table at them all, his eyes questioning.

'We're expecting,' Arthur told him, rescuing Edie. 'Beginning of April.'

'Good-oh!' Johnnie said, and returned to his meal.

His nonchalance made them all laugh and the tension broke into a chorus of congratulation led by J-J. 'What good news, Edith, my dear!'

47

'Yes, it is, isn't it,' Dora said, this time giving her mother a warning glance. 'We're all really happy for you, Edie. Aren't we, Ma?'

And John Erskine echoed her, 'Good news, Edie. Really good news.'

Margaret had begun to suspect that something was going on. 'What is, Mummy?' she said. 'What's good news?'

'Nothing that you need to know about,' Edith told her firmly. 'I hope you're going to eat that all up like a good girl.'

The child scowled and appealed to her father. 'What's good news, Daddy?'

'That we've got two pretty little girls,' he said. 'Like the new Queen.'

That was a better answer. 'Has she got two pretty little girls?'

'Yes, she has,' her father said, 'but they're not as pretty as mine.'

It was such a splendidly affectionate and diplomatic answer that there were smiles all round the table, even from Emmeline, who was still feeling annoyed that she hadn't been told before, and took care to have the last disapproving word. 'I hope it doesn't choose to arrive on All Fool's Day, that's all,' she said.

But the baby, who turned out to be another girl, to her father's secret disappointment, was a creature of great good sense. Not only did she stay where she was until the foolish day was past, she arrived quickly and with very little fuss in the middle of the morning on Sunday the 5th of April, so that her sisters could tiptoe into the bedroom and see her as soon as she was born and her father could walk to the corner of the road and phone her grandmother with the good news.

Emmeline put on her hat at once and took the tram to Colliers Wood. And fell in love at first sight. 'Such a little

48

duck,' she said to Edith, sitting beside the bed and slipping her finger into the warm, curled fist of her new granddaughter. 'Just look at those dear little dimpled hands. Couldn't you just eat her? What are you going to call her?'

'Joan,' Edith said. 'I think she looks like a Joan, don't you?'

'I think she looks like a little duck,' Emmeline said, as the baby clutched her finger. It was the most loving and natural approval.

Later that day, when Emmeline had come happily back to Parkside Avenue glowing with delight at her new grandchild and full of plans for the clothes she would make for it – 'I shall get the wool first thing tomorrow morning. She'll need a nice new matinee jacket. Edie's kept her baby clothes very nicely but there's no warmth in hand-me-downs' – Octavia and her father sat by the fire in the study and told one another how relieved they were that everything had gone so well.

'To be truthful, I thought she might take against it,' Octavia admitted. 'She was so touchy at Christmas.'

'We live in troubled times,' J-J said. 'I think it is making us all touchy.'

That was true enough, Octavia thought. Far too many people were quick to take offence these days and usually with very little cause. 'It's all this talk of war,' she said. 'We live under a shadow.'

'I'm afraid we do, my dear,' J-J said, and sighed. 'We know what we're in for this time, that's the trouble. We know what's coming and we can't do anything to prevent it.'

'If the League of Nations had taken action against Mussolini when he invaded Ethiopia, we wouldn't be in such a mess now,' Octavia said. She was seriously disappointed in that organisation. 'They asked for help, specifically asked for it, and all they got was a lot of useless talk in Geneva and no

49

action at all. We should have sent in an army to drive him out.'

'Exactly so, my dear,' J-J agreed, 'but we didn't have an army. Tommy is right. An international organisation needs an international army. Moral force is useless against a dictator, I'm sorry to say.'

Octavia was sombre. 'How long do you think we've got, Pa?'

'There's no way of knowing,' her father admitted. 'It depends on Herr Hitler and what he does next.'

What he did next, on a peaceful April day while Edith and her two little girls were walking their old pram and their new baby up the long slope of Wimbledon Hill to visit their grandmother, was to order the German Air Force to bomb a small market town in northern Spain. A small market town called Guernica. He chose his moment brutally because it was a Monday so the market square was crowded with men, women and children.

The attack was described in shocked and shocking detail in all the English newspapers the following morning. On their first bombing run, the planes dropped high explosives, on their second they set the shattered streets alight with incendiary bombs, and then, as if they hadn't done enough damage, they flew low over the wreckage and machine-gunned the fleeing inhabitants. Eye witnesses spoke of the shock and terror of it, of injured people sitting by the roadside too dazed to speak. *Soldiers were collecting charred bodies,* one man wrote. *They were sobbing like children. The smell of burning human flesh was nauseating. Houses were collapsing into the inferno. It was impossible to go down many of the streets because they were walls of flame.*

J-J was always the first person to read the paper in the morning, usually as he sat at the breakfast table while Em and Tavy were busy making the tea and cooking the breakfast. Then he would pass the paper on as soon as Johnnie had come yawning downstairs and they were all settled. But that morning he was so upset by what he read that he was very near tears and couldn't trust himself to speak. He held the paper up so that they could all see the headlines and passed it to his daughter without a word. She read it quickly, frowning and troubled, and when she'd passed it on to Emmeline, she got up, lit a comforting cigarette and switched on the wireless.

'It's almost time for the news,' she said. 'They might know more.' But she kept the volume turned right down so that her father wouldn't be disturbed by the preceding programme. Light music is all very well, but it can be irritating when you're distressed.

Presently, the well modulated voice of the newsreader spoke into the quiet of the room, as Emmeline wept and her son smoked and read the newspaper grimly. The horrific details of the air raid were given calmly and without emotion in the time-honoured tradition of the BBC. Yesterday morning there had been an air raid on the Basque border town of Guernica. It had been carried out by squadrons of German planes, Heinkel 1-11's and Junkers 52's, with fighter support. The town was almost completely destroyed. There were many casualties. 'This morning survivors are evacuating the town.'

'I don't understand it,' Emmeline wept. 'These are ordinary young men, that's all, ordinary young men like our Johnnie, and they do a thing like this. It's hideous. Dreadful. Don't they have mothers and sisters? I mean what's the matter with them? Why are they killing Spaniards? There's no sense in it.'

Octavia was remembering what Mrs Mannheim had told

51

them. 'They've been taught to hate,' she said. 'That's what's the matter with them. They're not like Johnnie. They've been turned into fighting machines. They obey orders.'

'Then they could attack anybody,' Emmeline said.

'Yes,' Octavia told her sadly. 'That's what they're for.'

'They could attack us.'

'Yes.'

There was a long fraught silence. Outside in the garden the new grass was freshly green, the ancient apple trees grew tender with pink and white blossom, daffodils fluttered as disarmingly as butterflies in all the borders, the blackbird was singing his passionate yearning song. Spring was waking their world with the promise of new precious life and they sat in their comfortable kitchen, at their familiar table, facing the possibility of death and destruction. This house could be blown to pieces, Octavia thought, this warm, comfortable, peaceful house, where we've lived so happily and easily all these years. She could already see it as a pile of rubble.

'What on earth would we do?' Emmeline said.

'The children are going to be evacuated,' Octavia said, thinking aloud. 'They've had plans drawn up for years, according to Tommy. He told me about it ages ago. Very well then, once I know where we're going, I shall rent a house big enough for all of us and evacuate you too.'

'And leave this house?' Emmeline said.

Octavia's answer was brusque with the distress she was hiding. 'If it's likely to be bombed, yes, of course.'

'It would be a load off my mind if I knew you were out of it,' Johnnie said.

'Oh dear,' Emmeline said. 'You're all talking as if it's bound to come.'

'It is bound to come, Ma,' Johnnie said, brown eyes serious.

'In fact...' Then he paused and gave thought to what he was going to say. He knew it would hurt her but it would have to be said sooner or later and this seemed as good a moment as any. 'The fact is...I was going to tell you this in a day or two anyway. The fact is, I've joined the RAF.'

The silence that followed his announcement was complete and intense, all three of his relations watching him with total attention. Then Emmeline began to howl. 'Oh, my dear, good God! Don't even say such a thing, Johnnie. You can't do it. You simply can't. What were you thinking of? You'll get killed.' She picked up the paper and waved it at him. 'You see what they've done. They kill people.' She was weeping in earnest now, the tears streaming down her cheeks. 'Tell him, Tavy. He can't do it. Oh, I can't bear it. Not with the baby and Arthur in the army and everything. Didn't we have enough last time? Tell him, Uncle. Oh, please somebody, tell him.'

Johnnie got up, walked round the table, sat beside her in Octavia's empty chair and tried to hold her hands, but she shook him away, weeping terribly. 'Don't touch me!'

He was very upset but he tried to be reasonable. 'The bombers will come, Ma,' he said. 'There's no doubt about that now. You must see that. They will come and we've got to be ready for them. I knew it would upset you but I had to do it. I couldn't just sit by and leave it to other people.'

'I don't see why not,' Emmeline wept. 'Why does it have to be you?'

'I'm going to learn to fly one of the new fighters,' he told her patiently. 'Look, I shall be called up eventually, Ma, we all will. You do know that, don't you. You must. It's been in all the papers. We'll all get called up. We shan't have any choice about it. So I thought if I've got to go anyway I might as well go now under my own terms. This way I can get to do the job

I really want, instead of being drafted into something I might not like. It's all right, really it is. I shan't take risks.'

'Oh, oh, oh,' Emmeline wept. 'I don't want you to go at all. You're my only son. Can't you see that? The only one I've got left. I don't want you to go at all.'

He looked across the room at Octavia. 'Aunt?' he appealed.

'I don't want you to go either,' she said. There was no criticism in her voice, only admiration. 'None of us do, if we're honest, but I can see that you must. I think you've done a very courageous thing. And so does your mother. It's just a shock to her at the moment, isn't it, Em?'

But Emmeline was drowned in tears and couldn't answer.

'It's the only thing I could do,' he told Octavia. 'I can hardly go on designing buildings when they're going to be blown up. That would be nonsensical. Still, I'd better go and do it now or I shall be late and that won't please Mr Carmichael.'

Emmeline managed to stop crying long enough to kiss him goodbye, but when he was gone, she sat in her chair and cried most bitterly. 'It's just like the last time all over again,' she wept. 'Why can't those stupid fools in Geneva do something to stop it? They must have seen it coming. That was supposed to be the war to end all wars. They kept on and on about it. The war to end all wars. And now look where we are. First Squirrel, and then my poor little boys, and now my Johnnie. And baby coming along so well too. And Arthur in the Territorials, and God knows what will happen to him either. I don't think I can bear it.'

'The trouble is nobody's asking us whether we can bear it or not,' Octavia said. 'They're just assuming we will.'

Emmeline raised a tear-streaked face to her cousin. 'I don't think I can, Tavy.'

'Whatever happens,' Octavia promised, 'we will bear it together. All of us. And now I *must* go to school or I shall be late and there's a lot to do. We'll put our minds to all this as soon as I get home. Ah now, here's Janet come.' What a relief to have that sensible girl to look after Pa and her poor Em. 'More tea I think, Janet. We've just heard the news about Guernica.'

'I'll have it on the table in two shakes of a lamb's tail,' Janet promised, putting on her apron. 'Doan't you worry, Miss Smith.'

The advice was unnecessary, for Miss Smith was not a woman to worry. She was a woman who took action. If there was a problem she would deal with it. By the time she got back to the house that afternoon, she knew what had to be done and set about doing it at once.

First she wrote a careful letter to *The Times*. She described the attack on Guernica as cruel, callous and totally unjustified, and pointed out that the Spanish people were no threat to Germany, and that to allow a military power to bomb an open city and kill and maim its inhabitants was completely intolerable. 'Something must be done to deter Herr Hitler,' she said. 'The man is a bully and needs to be stopped.'

Then, since she was fairly sure that her letter and others like it would be ignored – how could it be otherwise when the League had no military power with which to respond? – she turned her attention to matters which were within her competence. She picked up the phone and asked for Tommy's number.

It was a relief to hear his sensible voice. 'Tavy, my dear. What an unexpected pleasure.'

'It might not be quite such a pleasure when you hear what I want,' she warned him.

'I presume this is about Guernica.'

'Yes,' she said, 'it is, although not directly. I need some information.'

'Fire away,' he said. 'If I can give it to you, you shall have it.'

Straight in, blunt and to the point. 'Where is my school going to be evacuated to?'

There was a pause while he gathered his thoughts. 'That may take a bit of finding out,' he told her. 'It's all very hush-hush at the moment.'

'But they've made plans for it, haven't they?'

'And they want to keep them secret. It wouldn't do for the Germans to get wind of them. We wouldn't want them dive-bombing the trains.'

'No,' Octavia said, shuddering at the thought. 'We would not. But I don't need to know the details. It's nothing like that. Just where we would be going. A hint would be enough. I'd keep it to myself.'

'I'll see what I can do,' he promised. 'You'll have to be patient though. I can't rush it. How's the family?'

'Johnnie's joined the RAF. He wants to fly a Spitfire. Em's in a terrible state.'

'That's two of them then. Mark joined up last week.'

Octavia could feel her heart sinking. 'I thought he was going to Oxford.'

'So did we. But apparently not. He says it's something he's got to do and Oxford will have to wait. Foolhardy, of course, but admirable.'

'Like father like son,' she said. 'I can remember what you said when you joined up.'

He laughed. 'It's more than I can.'

'You said it was the done thing. It was expected of a chap.'

She could remember his voice saying it.

'*Plus ça change, plus c'est la même chose*,' he said.

'Heaven help us all,' she said and meant it.

Her letter was published in *The Times* the next morning and so were several others from some rather eminent people. But, just as she feared, nothing came of it. The League of Nations deplored the attack but went no further, the British Government discussed it but decided that nothing could be done, the newspapers continued to print letters about it for a day or two and then dropped it and after that, to her annoyance, everything went quiet and the horror seemed to be forgotten. The people of Guernica buried their dead, General Franco, encouraged by the unchecked power of his German ally, redoubled his attacks on the government army in northern Spain, convinced that his rebellion would soon be successful and that he would be the next European dictator, and the British press turned its transient attention to the coming coronation.

'And what good that will do to anyone,' Octavia said, 'I really can't imagine. All this silly flummery. We should be concentrating on the things that matter.'

'It won't stop our young men joining the Forces,' Emmeline said bitterly. 'And that's all I care about.'

Johnnie got his expected letter two weeks later and passed it to his mother at the breakfast table. She took it better than Octavia had feared and only wept in private where none of them could see. Tommy and Elizabeth came to dinner with the news that Mark had already gone, and the two mothers commiserated with one another when they were all walking in the garden afterwards. Octavia was glad they had one another for comfort and company, and besides, it gave her the chance to ask Tommy if he'd found out what she wanted to know.

'I have tried,' he said. 'But nothing yet, I'm afraid. I can't push it or they'd smell a rat.'

'I only need to know the name of the town,' Octavia told him. 'That's all. Uprooting a Dalton school is going to take a lot of organisation. We need more space than most schools and better timetabling. We need to start planning it now.'

He smiled at her urgency. 'Yes,' he said. 'I know. I've seen Lizzie's timetable. Couldn't understand a word of it. Don't worry, old thing. I'll persevere. You'll get your name in the end.'

But it was very unsatisfactory and her face showed it.

The summer progressed as though the world was still normal. The much vaunted coronation was held – despite her poor opinion of it – in May and exactly as planned only with a different king and queen, both archaically grand in state crowns and velvet cloaks. The two little princesses wore cloaks and crowns too, to Margaret's intense interest, and although rain was threatening all day, it held off until after the ceremony which the papers said was 'a good omen'.

'Good omen my eye!' Emmeline said when she read the newspaper accounts at breakfast the next morning. 'Still, at least it's over and done with. I was getting heartily sick of it. All that fuss. Now I suppose his silly brother will marry that awful woman of his.'

'I don't think it matters what he does now,' Octavia said, buttering her toast, 'providing he keeps quiet.'

'No,' Emmeline agreed, 'you're probably right. Personally, I shall take the children to Eastbourne, as soon as Johnnie goes. They could use a holiday and Arthur's going to be away with the Territorials, so Edie says. You and Uncle can manage

58

without me for a week or so, can't you? You've got young Janet.'

In fact she was away for a month and, during that time, Tommy and Elizabeth came to dinner again, Johnnie wrote to report that flying was an absolute joy and, down in Sussex, Barbara and David celebrated their sixth birthdays and wore paper hats and had a special party at the boarding house.

According to Edith and Dora, who sent their aunt a daily postcard, all four children were enjoying the seaside very much and were being very good. 'It might be the last holiday we get,' Dora wrote, 'so we're making the most of it.'

It might be the last holiday I get to organise this evacuation, Octavia thought, and I can't even start. Oh, come on, Tommy. Buck your ideas up!

But September came and the new term began and she was still waiting. And to make matters worse, Hitler seemed to be starting up again. At the end of the month, the papers were full of pictures of him at his annual Nuremburg rally, posturing and shouting on a stage backed by an enormous swastika, and all of them reported his boast that the Third Reich would last for a thousand years. Then, as if he hadn't made his point abundantly clear, he appeared again, in the Olympic Field of May, dramatically spot-lit, with the hideous Mussolini pouting like a toad beside him and an audience estimated to be almost a million strong. Both men talked about their countries need for an empire. 'Without colonies,' Hitler said, 'Germany's space is too small to guarantee that our people can be fed safely and continuously.' Germany needed *Lebensraum* and he was determined to give it to them. 'The attitude of other Powers to our demands is simply incomprehensible.'

Octavia wrote a postcard to Tommy that evening. 'This

war is rushing down upon us at a rate of knots,' she said. 'I need that information.'

Four days later he rang her at school. 'Tavy,' he said, 'I believe you were thinking of taking a holiday in one of our country towns.'

'Yes,' she said.

'I could recommend a trip to Woking.'

# Chapter Four

Octavia drove to Woking on the very next Saturday. It was a warm October morning and, once she'd cleared Kingston and was out in the country, the roads were bordered by shorn fields wreathed in smoke-blue mist and trees and hedgerows in a blaze of autumnal colour. It quite lifted her spirits to see them. Whatever this town was going to be like, she would do everything she could to make it a comfortable refuge for her girls.

It turned out to be a small, rather sleepy place. It had a sizeable railway station (which is where we shall arrive) facing an imposing Victorian hotel called the Albion – (I'll get something to eat there later on) – a small narrow High Street and a longer street called Chertsey Road which ran at a sharp angle from the square in front of the station and was full of shoppers. She parked the car in front of the hotel and set off to explore. Small shops, and lots of them. She noticed a MacFisheries, Boots the Chemist, Woolworths, Timothy Whites, Burtons, several good butchers (that'll please Em), bakers, grocery stores, even a bookshop, library and stationers run by one WA Elton, where she stopped to buy a map of the town. It struck her as she walked along the pavement that this was a gentle sort of place and that the people she was passing lived at an even quieter pace than the one she was used to in Wimbledon. Groups of women stood on the pavement passing the time of day with their neighbours, errand boys cycled and whistled along the middle of the road, women pushed prams with their toddlers trailing behind them and there was hardly any traffic at all. She watched two cars driving by at a sedate pace and there was a horse and cart waiting patiently outside the fishmonger's, but, except for a gang of small scruffy boys who were obviously on their way to the Saturday pictures, nobody was in a rush. Yes, she thought, we could enjoy life here.

But where was the school? That was the important thing. I'll go back to that hotel, she decided, and have a pot of tea and take a good look at my map.

She was impressed by the Albion Hotel, which was spacious and comfortable, with Turkey carpets on the floor and armchairs to sit in while you drank your tea and a waitress in neat black and white to serve you. The map wasn't anywhere near so helpful, for although various schools were marked on it, there was nothing to indicate what sort of schools they were. The waitress said she didn't know, explaining, 'I've only been here three weeks, ma'am,' but suggested asking the barman. That worthy wiped the counter dry, gave it a final polish with his sleeve and then spread the map out to take a good look at it.

'What sort of school were you after, ma'am? If I may make so bold.'

'A grammar school.'

'That would be a private school, I daresay?'

It amused her to think that he saw her as a prospective parent. 'No,' she said. 'It's a county school I'm looking for.' They'd hardly be likely to expect a small private school to share its premises with a large London county school.

'Well, we've got two of those,' he said. 'A boys' and a girls'. Which would it be, ma'am?'

'The girls' one.'

'That's in Park Road,' he said, tracing the road on the map with a finger so broad that it totally obscured it. 'It's a fair old walk.'

She smiled at his concern. 'I've got a car.'

'Ah, well then,' he said. 'Park Road, that's what you want. Over the other side of the station. You can't miss it.'

What she missed wasn't the road, but the school. She'd driven from one end of the road to the other, following it uphill and round several bends, admiring the new detached houses with their neat front gardens and their large windows and their carriage drives, noticing what a lot of fine trees there were, passing a long holly hedge and thinking that there must be a particularly big house behind that, but she'd seen no school. He *had* said Park Road, hadn't he? So it must be here somewhere. Sighing, she turned the car and drove slowly back the way she had come, looking carefully to the right and left. Then she saw what was behind the long holly hedge and realised her mistake. She'd been looking for a school building, thinking vaguely that it would probably be something like her own at Roehampton. What she'd found was a line of huts. There were five of them and they stood in considerable grounds, but they were just huts!

Oh dear, she thought, staring at their inadequacy. There'll never be room for all my lot in five huts, even if we have the whole place to ourselves, never mind if we have to share it. And she parked the car and went to take a closer look. She was peering in at the window of a science lab, feeling relieved that at least they had one of those, when someone walked up beside her. It was a man in his shirt sleeves, carrying a mop and a bucket. 'Can I help you?' he said.

He thinks I'm trespassing, she thought, and assumed her headmistress's voice at once. 'Ah, good morning,' she said. 'Are you the school keeper?'

He was and looked at his bucket to prove it.

'Then you're just the person I want to see,' she told him briskly. 'You would know how many pupils there are in this school.'

'Three hundred and ten,' he said promptly, 'as of this September.'

Two forms a year, she thought, calculating swiftly. It *is* small.

'Were you thinking of sending a girl here?' he said. 'If I may make so bold as to ask.'

'Yes,' she said and added, 'actually I was thinking of sending more than one,' wondering what on earth he'd say if she told him it would be somewhere between four and five hundred.

'Oh well, in that case ma'am, perhaps you'd be better to come in again on Monday and see the headmistress.'

He's easing me off the premises, Octavia thought. 'I shan't be here on Monday, I'm afraid,' she explained. 'I'm only here for the day, getting my bearings so to speak. I shall be moving to Woking some time in the future.'

The explanation satisfied him but he watched her until she was back in her car. She approved of his vigilance. He's a good school keeper, she thought. He takes his duties seriously. Fancy mistaking me for a parent! I must look more motherly than I thought. But there was no time to consider her appearance, motherly or not. Now she had to find an estate agent and see what properties were available for rent.

By the time she finally drove home late in the afternoon,

she was tired and hungry but well pleased with herself. She had the details of seven large houses in her handbag, and there were pictures of all of them in her camera, three that would suit her family and four that were big enough to be turned into schools. If the school they were evacuated to was too small, the LCC would have to be persuaded to rent a house for them as well. Or two if need be. Now, her next task was to tell the staff. This war was coming and it was her job to see that they were all prepared for it.

Emmeline had spent a happy afternoon with her grandchildren. She hadn't had any refugees since the middle of September, so it really looked as if Mrs Henderson was right and Hitler had closed the borders. She felt sorry for the poor things who hadn't managed to get out but she'd been glad of the chance to get her house back into some sort of order just the same. She and Janet and Mrs Benson had given the place a late spring-clean and now everything was spotless, which was just how she liked it, and that afternoon it had been so warm they'd had tea in the garden, which had been another treat. She and the three older children had played croquet on the lawn while Edie was indoors feeding the baby, and they'd all enjoyed it very much. It had been so normal, as if there wasn't a war coming, and Arthur wasn't in the Territorials and Johnnie wasn't in the RAF. So when Tavy came home with details of the sort of houses they would have to stay in if they were evacuated she was none too pleased.

'Yes,' she said crossly, flicking a glance at them. 'I'll look at them later when I haven't got a dinner to cook.'

'Would you like a hand with it?' Octavia offered.

'No thank you,' her cousin said, stiffly. 'I can manage.' And retreated to the kitchen as though it was a fortress.

'Oh dear,' Octavia said to her father.

'She can't face it, Tavy,' he sighed.

Octavia sighed too and sat down in her chair rather heavily. 'It's been a day for disappointments,' she said and told him about the hutted school.

He listened with his usual quiet attention but without the concern he'd been feeling for poor Emmeline. The one thing he could be sure of with Octavia was that, however hard the difficulties she might have to face, she would press on until she found an answer to them. It was a great source of pride to him. 'So what will you do?' he asked.

She put her bundle of specifications on the coffee table between them. 'Get the LCC to rent one of these,' she said.

He smiled at her. 'Of course,' he said and leant forward to pick them up and look at them.


By the time she held her next staff meeting, Octavia had her plans in order. She plunged straight into them as soon as the more mundane matters had been dealt with.

'Since the bombing of Guernica,' she said, 'I don't think there's much doubt that we are heading for a war with Germany. I wish I could say otherwise but I'm afraid I can't. Mr Chamberlain may speak of appeasement but behind the scenes the fact is we are preparing for war. Plans are already drawn up to evacuate the children from London, as I daresay several of you know.' Many of her colleagues nodded at that, for they were following events as closely as she was. 'Very well then. You won't be surprised to know that I spent Saturday in the town that our school will be evacuated to. I can't tell you where it is because it's all very hush-hush, as they say, but as soon as I'm officially notified you will know too. For the moment, all I can tell you is that it's a small, quiet town not really all that far from London and the school whose premises we shall be expected to share is extremely small. So we have some detailed planning to do. We shall all need to know exactly which books in our subject libraries are essential and which could be temporarily left behind, we shall need to have syllabuses for the next year written and run off and stored because we could find printing them difficult – at least for the first term or so – and we shall need to choose our prefects with particular care. They will have a considerable burden to carry.'

The staff were nodding at that too, for the house officers and prefects ran the school house system and that could be a cohesive force if the girls were going to be dispersed in strange homes all over a strange town. But their newest entrant, a quiet and rather diffident young woman called Mavis Brown, who taught History and Geography, was worried. She looked up at her headmistress, mutely requesting permission to speak.

'Mavis?' Octavia encouraged.

'I realise I probably shouldn't say this, being the newest – um – the most recently appointed...' Mavis said, blushing, 'but what I'm wondering is, are we going to continue with syllabuses? I mean it's going to be very difficult, isn't it? Maybe we should try something a bit easier. I mean with a war coming and evacuation and everything.' She was finding the famous Dalton system very hard going, much worse than she'd expected and, from what Miss Smith had just said, it looked as if being evacuated was going to make it ten times harder.

Octavia was rather taken aback. She knew there were bound to be reservations and worries and that some of the staff would find it hard to produce a year's worth of syllabuses because they were used to working a term at a time but she hadn't expected the system to be questioned. 'What do the rest of you think?' she asked, looking round at her team. She could have answered Mavis herself but it would come better from her colleagues.

Morag Gordon spoke first, after adjusting her long cardigan and pushing her glasses up her nose while she got her thoughts into order. 'This is all perfectly true, Mavis,' she said. 'Preparing syllabuses of all the work we propose to do for every pupil in every subject for a full year, maximum and minimum, will take a bit of doing, but syllabuses are the key to the system we run here. If we are going to go on expecting our pupils to take responsibility for all the work they do, we must provide them with syllabuses. They must know exactly what the work is to be well in advance of the lessons that will, if we've planned them well enough, trigger the interest that will set their research going. That is the essence of the system.'

'We can't let Herr Hitler bully us into changing our system,' Phillida said. 'It's bad enough the way he bullies the Jews. We saw that when we were in Berlin, didn't we, Helen?'

'Yes, we did,' Helen Staples said firmly, 'and it was absolutely appalling. We need to stand up to the man. I don't think we should change a thing.'

'Even if it means a lot more work?' Octavia asked, smiling, because she was so sure of the answer.

Helen and Phillida replied with one voice. 'Yes. Of course.'

'We shall need young women who can think for themselves more than ever if we're going to war,' Mabel Ollerington said. 'There is a regrettable tendency for governments to tell us what to think when we're combatants. I can remember that from the Great War. It is understandable but nevertheless regrettable. We must nourish the critical faculty in every way open to us.'

'I don't write syllabuses,' Joan Marshall said, which was true because she taught Games and PE, 'but I'm with the system every inch of the way. I don't think we should change a thing.'

And no more we will, Octavia thought. Not if I have anything to do with it. But she spoke calmly. 'Is that the general opinion?'

It was and even Mavis agreed with it when she saw how strongly it was being supported.

'Of course it would help us if we knew how long we've got,' Alice Genevra said.

'It could be months,' Morag told her. 'It could be years. It all depends on that wretched man and what he does next.'

That wretched man kept rather quiet that winter, except for giving a speech in which he claimed that there was no room for independence in the rearing of children and that in future, every German child would grow up knowing only Nazi values.

'Odious little man,' Octavia said to her father.

'He is afraid of anyone who can think for himself,' J-J said. 'That is the mark of a dictator. Everybody has to agree with him or run the risk of being sent to a concentration camp.'

'Exactly so,' Octavia said. 'He's an odious little man.'

But Christmas was coming and baby Joan was crawling about and Johnnie had written home to say he'd wangled some Christmas leave, so she put the coming war out of her mind for the holiday. After that the spring term was so busy she barely had time to think of anything beyond the needs of the day.

First of all, they had to have a gas mask drill, which the girls made a great joke of. Then, they were given instructions as to what they would have to do when evacuation was 'imminent' and told that further and more detailed instructions would follow 'in the event'. And then when the staff were scrambling to write the last of their syllabuses, news came through that the German army had invaded Austria, apparently 'by invitation' of the new Austrian leader, Seyss-Inquart, who had pushed his predecessor aside only the previous day.

'Now we're for it!' Joan Marshall said, flexing her muscles, as if she were about to oppose the invasion single-handed. 'They won't let him get away with this.'

But nothing was done and three days later triumphant German troops escorted their Führer through Vienna in a precision of jackboots, tanks and field guns, to what was described as tumultuous applause. There was newsreel footage of young girls in national dress throwing flowers into Hitler's car and shots of young people waving and cheering. Austria was now part of the new German empire and all of it done without a shot being fired.

Within a week the German newspapers were bragging that Austria was being given 'a spring cleaning'. Jewish judges had all been dismissed before they could protest and Jews were now banned from all the professions. It was soon plainly obvious that another vicious pogrom had begun. The plebiscite that followed in April was a foregone conclusion. Ninety-nine per cent of the Austrian population, no less, voted in favour of Hitler's annexation of their territory.

'Of course they have,' Octavia said, giving her copy of *The Times* an angry shake. 'Who would vote against him? They wouldn't dare. Mr Chamberlain must take action now. He can't go on appeasing the man for ever.'

Mr Chamberlain's policy of appeasement was discussed

with more and more heat at every dinner party she and her father gave during the following winter. Tommy, playing the statesman, did his best to point out that their Prime Minister was doing everything he could to avoid another war and argued that his actions were understandable if not exactly admirable. Emmeline took his side every time, saying none of them wanted to see another bloodbath like they had last time. Frank Dimond, on the other hand, had no doubt at all that a war would come sooner or later, and said that the sooner it came the better.

'Jews are being rounded up all over Austria,' he told them passionately. 'Rounded up and sent to concentration camps. Are we to sit by and let it happen? We must take action. Or be branded moral cowards.'

'Better a moral coward than dead,' Emmeline told him fiercely. 'We lost enough young men in the Great War. A whole generation blown to pieces. Are we to go through all that again?'

'We must hope not,' Elizabeth Meriton said gently. 'If there is a peaceful and honourable way for these difficulties to be resolved, I'm sure Mr Chamberlain will find it.' And she changed the subject in her usual deft way. 'Have any of you been to the new cinema in Victoria? I'm told it's very splendid.'

Meantime, Octavia thought, we go on waiting and worrying and none of us getting anywhere. It's dreadful to have to face it, especially for poor Em, but Frank is right. This war will come, sooner or later, no matter what we think about it.

As it did.

# Chapter Five

Being Miss Smith's secretary at the famous Roehampton School was a position of considerable responsibility. Maggie Henry, who'd held it for more than fifteen years, was totally devoted to it and never stopped bragging to her friends about her Miss Smith – she always spoke of Octavia as her Miss Smith – who was the most wonderful woman alive and an absolute inspiration, although she did occasionally add that there *were* times when she thought her heroine worked too hard. Take this last week as an example.

It was all very well saying it couldn't be helped because they were all waiting for this dratted war to be declared. She knew that. Everybody knew it and they had known it ever since Hitler started arresting Polish shipworkers in Danzig for some unaccountable reason and arguing about some place called the Polish corridor, that no one had ever heard of. Provocation, that's all it was, although why he should want to provoke a war with Poland over a small port and a little bit of land was beyond her comprehension. But there you are, he did, and he'd done it. And now there were German storm troopers swarming into Poland and Mr Chamberlain had sent him an ultimatum about it, which everybody knew he'd ignore, and they were all waiting for the war to start and her school was waiting to be evacuated, and life was altogether extremely difficult.

Not that it needed to be. The authorities could have made a better fist of this evacuation if they'd put their minds to it. She could have organised it with one hand tied behind her back. It had been a week of bedlam in the school. Absolute total bedlam, with her Miss Smith on the go from early morning to late at night, her brown button boots going tweak, tweak, tweak along the corridors and papers sticking out of the pockets of that old tweed suit, and her fuzzy hair so wild it looked as though she hadn't combed it for weeks, and the staff packing up their books – there were tea-chests in every room – and the phone continually ringing. It's a wonder we're not all exhausted. And now they had the girls sitting about in their winter uniforms for the second day running – and it was so hot, poor things, they must be baking – with their gas masks and their luggage all mounded up round them – and a nice old muddle that was – waiting for the signal to leave. And there were people all over the place checking lists. There was no end to all the lists. Lists of books, lists of the helpers who were going to accompany them and make sure that everybody got onto the train – that nice Mrs Meriton was one of them – lists in the registers of all the girls who'd signed to be evacuated so that they didn't leave anyone behind. As if Miss Smith would allow that! Even the house officers had lists and were checking that the girls in their group were wearing their name tags and had all got their gas masks and their stamped postcards so that they could write home to their parents at the end of the day. And that dratted phone, brr, brr, brr all the time. Could they speak to Miss Smith?

There it was again.

'Roehampton Secondary School,' she said politely. 'How can I help you?'

'I'm calling from County Hall,' a man's voice said. 'I have a message for the headmistress.'

This is it, Maggie thought, but she stayed calm and polite although her heart was racing. 'If you will hold the line, please,' she said. 'I will get her for you.'

It took a little while even though she walked through the throng as quickly as she could, with the girls pulling their luggage out of her way and standing aside to let her pass. She found her heroine in the music room talking to Miss Jones. 'Excuse me, Miss Smith,' she said. 'You've got a call.'

Octavia was alerted by Maggie's expression. '*The* call?' she asked.

'I think so.'

'Very good,' Octavia said. And she walked off at such a pace that Maggie couldn't keep up with her.

Two minutes later she was standing on the platform blowing her whistle. The crowded hall was instantly attentive.

'Girls,' she said. 'I have just heard from County Hall that it is time for us to walk down to the station.' There was an instant buzz of excitement and apprehension and some of the first-formers looked up at her anxiously. Poor little things, she thought, smiling at them. It will be very hard for them to leave their homes and their friends and come away with us when they're so new to the school. They hardly know us at all. She held up her hand to still them all into attention. 'There is no rush,' she said. 'The train will be waiting for us. We will leave in our house groups through the foyer, exactly as we did in our rehearsal yesterday, and Miss Henry will be at the door to check with each house officer in turn that everyone in her group is present. Miss Fennimore has our school number and

74

will lead the way. If you will raise your pole, Miss Fennimore, so that we can all see the number. Thank you. If you can't see Miss Fennimore, you will certainly see our number.'

Miss Fennimore raised the pole even higher and turned it from side to side so that they could all see it. There was a ripple of laughter. That was better.

'However, before we set off,' Octavia said, changing the tenor of her voice, 'I have something to say to you all and I hope you will take it to heart. Read, mark, learn and inwardly digest as our Miss Gordon would say.' Another ripple of laughter and Miss Gordon waved at them, turning her grey head from side to side so that she could look at them all, smiling. 'What I have to say to you is this. Nobody can predict what lies ahead of us. Wars are unpredictable by their very nature. There will be good times but there may also be bad ones. The staff and I will do everything we can to ensure that the life and spirit of this school continue as they have always done but there are bound to be changes. I don't need to tell you that if you welcome change and are not afraid of it, it is easier to cope with. You are strong, resilient young women and all of you are capable of standing on your own feet and thinking things out for yourselves. That is the gift that the Dalton System has given you. You are also generous and compassionate. If there are people in need of help and comfort I know you will give it. But don't be afraid to ask for help if you need it yourself. Don't keep your own grief and difficulties hidden. We are all in this new adventure together and we will all help each other.

'Now I want to say a special word to our first-formers. Coming to a large school for the first time after being in a much smaller one is always daunting and you have come to this school for the first time in very unusual circumstances. You have a different journey ahead of you from anything that any of our previous first-formers have ever undertaken, so you are special. If you need help, no matter where you are or what it is, talk to your house officer. She is the one who has been elected to look after you. And if you can't find her, which might happen – who can tell? – and if you can't find a member of staff, then look for any other girl who is wearing our uniform and a house officer's badge. You know what that looks like, don't you? Good. Find a house officer and she will help you.

'And now, as this is the first day of a new term and a new school year, we will sing the first verse of our usual opening hymn, "Lord behold us with Thy blessing, Once again assembled here." We don't need hymn books, do we? No, I thought not. When you're ready, Miss Jones.'

There was a moment while they all stood up as well as they could among their bags and baggage and then the hymn was sung lustily by everybody in the hall except for the first-formers and the helpers.

'And now,' Octavia said. 'If our helpers would join their groups please, you can start moving out as soon as your group is ready. Good luck to all of us!'

Lizzie Meriton took her headmistress's words to heart, as she always did, and started looking after her own first-formers straight away. There were two of them, a tall girl called Sarah who had the longest plaits she'd ever seen and a little girl called Iris who had green eyes and very dark hair. They were both very quiet so they were probably nervous.

'As soon as Mary gets back with her mum, we can go,' she said to her group. 'You two can walk with me and hold my hands, and then I shall know I won't lose you.' Her belongings were all in a knapsack, which had been Pa's idea so as to leave her hands free. Dear Pa. He was always so sensible. It had been Ma who'd fussed. She'd had to talk to her quite sternly about it.

'I don't mind you coming as a helper,' she'd said, 'just so long as you don't expect to help me. I'm the one who has to do the helping now. Miss Smith said so.' She'd touched the little blue shield that was her badge of office and that Miss Bertram had pinned on her blouse in front of the whole house. She was very proud of being a house officer. It marked her out as someone important, someone the other girls knew they could depend on. When the votes had been counted and Miss Bertram had told them the result, she'd felt so proud to be chosen that her chest was almost bursting. And when the house meeting was over and Miss Bertram had spoken to all the house officers privately, she'd said something that made her feel prouder than ever.

'You will probably be the most important house officers this school has ever had,' she'd told them. 'There's a war coming – I don't have to tell you that, do I – and we shall be in the thick of it because this school will be evacuated into the country. It will be your job to look after all the girls in the house. It will be a great responsibility and a great privilege. I know I can depend on you.'

And now, here they were, packed into the school hall with their luggage all round them, and there was Mary O'Connor with her mother beside her and the group was all present and correct and they could go.

'This is it!' she said, taking her two first-formers by the hand. 'Follow me.'

It was extremely hot out there in the sun and walking made it worse. The pavements were hard under their feet, their winter uniform was stifling and their luggage grew heavier and heavier and their gas masks more and more of a nuisance with every step they took. Lizzie held on tight to her first-formers' hands and jollied them along as well as she could, telling them they would soon be there, even though she knew they had at least half a mile to walk. Their long navy blue column marched on ahead of them and straggled behind them as far as she could see. She couldn't help thinking what a very big school they were and began to wonder whether there'd be room for them all on the train.

'I'm baking,' Iris complained.

'Soon be there,' Lizzie said again, and this time she meant it. 'We're nearly at the end of Augustus Road now – do you see? – and then we'll turn the corner into Wimbledon Park and you'll see the station.'

What they saw were two more columns of laden children toiling along in the sunshine. One was a line of boys in full school uniform, caps and all, the other was a junior school with lots of little'uns, wearing enormous labels and holding on to one another's hands. Heavens above! Lizzie thought, stunned to see so many children. They'll never get all this lot on one train. Still, that's their problem. All I've got to do is make sure my group keep together and that we all get into the same compartment. 'Don't get lost,' she said to them. 'This could be quite a crush.'

'Look!' Iris said. 'There's a sweet shop. Can we stop and get a drink, Lizzie? It says soft drinks. On the placard.'

'No, you most certainly can not,' Lizzie said in her sternest voice.

'It wouldn't take a minute,' Iris persisted. 'We're nearly there.'

Lizzie was adamant. 'I'm not having you getting lost,' she

said. 'Just keep on holding my hand. You can have a drink later on. There's Miss Henry, look, just by the entrance, waiting to check us in.'

'How did she manage that?' Mary wanted to know. 'She must have run all the way.'

'She came in Smithie's car,' Lizzie said, spotting it beside the pavement on the other side of the road.

'Heavens!' Mary said. 'They *are* organised.'

'Here we go,' Lizzie said, shepherding her group towards the entrance. 'Keep together all of you.'

Her warning was timely because Southfields Station was crowded with children and their luggage. Miss Gordon was standing on the platform with the school number raised high and Miss Smith beside her, and there were teachers everywhere urging them to spread out so that they would all be in position and ready for the train when it came, but there was no sign of a train. The minutes passed and more and more children poured onto the platform. Lizzie took off her knapsack and put it down at her feet and the rest of her group followed suit. Iris said she was hot. They waited. And waited. A quarter of an hour went by according to the station clock. And they waited. And waited. When the train finally approached – much, much too slowly – they were so relieved they gave it a cheer. Then there were several minutes of jostling confusion as they picked up their luggage and struggled into the nearest carriages while their helpers ran up and down the platform trying to make sure their groups were all on board, but at last Lizzie and her charges were all together in one compartment and could take off their impossible hats and coats and put them in the luggage rack.

'Sit tight for a minute while I open the windows,' she said, pulling on the leather strap to let the nearest window down.

'Once we get going we shall get a breeze and then we'll all feel a whole lot better.'

But once the train began to move, her first-formers felt a whole lot worse and Iris began to cry. She didn't say anything, she simply sat squashed between Mary and Sarah while the tears rolled down her cheeks and dripped off the end of her nose. Lizzie couldn't think what to say to comfort her. *It'll be all right* would be banal, especially when none of them knew whether it *would* be all right, and *'cheer up'* would be worse. But while she was trying to think of something suitable, Mrs O'Connor took action. She moved across the carriage, told Sarah to shove up, sat down between them and put her arms round them both.

'You'll see her again in a day or two,' she promised. 'You've got your postcard, haven't you? Well then. You just send that off the minute you know where you're going to be staying and I bet your mum'll be down to see you on the next train.'

'Will she?' Iris said, still weeping.

''Course she will,' Mrs O'Connor reassured. 'Like a shot. You got a hanky, have you? Good. Dry your little eyes and have a good blow of your nose. That's the ticket.' She looked round at all the serious faces in the carriage, disentangled her right arm from Sarah and pulled a paper bag out of her handbag. 'Would any of you like a humbug?'

The little sweets cheered them all. That's what I should have thought of, Lizzie told herself. I'll know next time. There's an art in being responsible for people and part of it's working out what you're going to need before you need it.

It was an art her headmistress had been exercising at full stretch over the last few crowded days. At that moment she was driving her little black Ford down Melrose Avenue, heading

80

for Wimbledon and the next stage of the journey, with Maggie Henry in the passenger seat beside her and young Janet in the back seat with her shopping basket and Maggie's typewriter.

'That went quite smoothly, all things considered,' she said to Maggie as she drove past Wimbledon Park Station and another long crocodile of trudging schoolchildren. 'At least we didn't leave anyone behind. And the staff know where we're going. You did give them all their letters, didn't you, Maggie?' She'd sat up late as soon as she knew the evacuation was imminent and written a personal letter to all her staff telling them where they were going and giving them the address and phone number of the house she'd rented in Woking so that they would know where to find her. *I hope we will all be able to meet there at ten o'clock tomorrow morning*, she'd written, and had added. *Good luck to us all.*

'Of course,' Maggie said. She'd handed them out as they walked through the foyer. 'Everything's under control.'

Octavia smiled at that. It was so typical of Maggie Henry. The sky could fall and she would still be well organised.

They were approaching Wimbledon station. 'We shall have to look lively,' she said, 'or the train will be here ahead of us.'

It came in as she and Maggie were walking onto the platform. She'd only just had time to find a porter and was asking him which platform they needed for their next train, when it steamed in, hissing and creaking. 'Stay where you are,' she said as her pupils emerged from every open door. She walked along the platform telling them group by group. 'You don't need to change platforms. Stay where you are.'

It was another long wait but they accepted it patiently, standing together, still in their groups with their luggage at their feet. When their train moved out Octavia could see that every platform on the station was full of waiting children.

81

There must be millions of us, she thought, all on the move. It's a major undertaking. She watched as other trains pulled in, were loaded and left, and more children arrived.

'I don't think much of this for organisation,' Maggie grumbled. 'I hope they haven't forgotten us. It's nearly midday.'

'Then we're at war,' Octavia said, remembering. 'Mr Chamberlain was going to make a statement at eleven o'clock this morning.'

'Damned Hitler,' Maggie said. 'He ought to be shot. All this fuss. Ah, here it comes. And about time too.'

This time it was easier to get all their charges on board, although there were tears when the helpers said goodbye and every window was a white flutter of waving hands and handkerchiefs as the train drew out. Even Lizzie was swimmy-eyed because her mother had walked the length of the platform to say goodbye to her.

'Look after yourself, my darling,' she said, reaching up to the window to hold her daughter's hand, 'and don't forget your postcard.'

'As if I would,' Lizzie said, trying to be flippant. But it didn't work and the train was moving. Oh God! The train was moving.

'I'll see you soon,' Elizabeth promised, walking along beside it. 'Take care of yourself.' Oh my dear, darling girl. I do love you so much. Take care of yourself.

'Now for Woking,' Octavia said to Maggie Henry. 'Gird your loins, Miss Henry. It's going to be a long day.'

'I've had 'em girded since I got up,' Maggie said and was glad when Octavia laughed.

\* \* \*

The station at Woking was a sizeable place and well used to crowds but they'd never had to accommodate quite so many people as they did on those three hot days in September. On that particular morning evacuees had been streaming out of the open doors into the station approach since nine o'clock, so the buses that had been hired to carry them to various halls and gathering places had been hard at work for nearly four hours before Roehampton Secondary School arrived. By that time the drivers were more than ready for their lunch break and in no mood to wait until various school friends could find one another. The girls were simply bundled into the nearest waiting vehicle as they emerged from the station and were driven away as soon as the bus was full and the statutory number of teachers was aboard. In the muddled rush of their arrival, Lizzie and Mary O'Connor were separated from their group before they had a chance to check where they all were.

Lizzie was most upset. 'How can I look after them if they whip them away from us like this?' she said to Mary. 'It's ridiculous splitting us up. Where's Miss Fennimore?'

But there was no sign of that lady and no sign of Miss Smith either, and the next bus was drawing up beside the station entrance. 'All aboard the Skylark!' the conductor called. 'Mind the step.'

There was nothing for it but to do as they were told, although Lizzie grumbled about it all the way to wherever they were going. 'How are my first-formers going to get along with no one to look after them?' she said. 'This is a shambles.'

She was even more aggrieved when they arrived at their destination because it turned out to be a golf club in the middle of nowhere, and although there was a lady in the green uniform of the WVS waiting on the step to welcome them, there was no sign of her group.

'That's right,' the lady said, as they stepped gingerly out of the bus. 'Come right in, dears. I expect you'd like a drink after your journey. This way.'

'Are you bringing us all here?' Lizzie asked

'Us?' the lady asked.

'Roehampton Secondary School.'

'Oh, I shouldn't think so, dear,' the lady told her. 'You're a big school, aren't you. We're using dispersal centres all over the place. Don't worry. We'll look after you, wherever you are. Go in and have your drink. You must be ready for it.'

The club house was crowded with children, some standing in a queue, some sitting at trestle tables, and most of them from a junior school and looking decidedly scruffy after their journey. She couldn't see anybody from her group at all, although after a while she caught sight of Miss Bertram standing by one of the tables and went across at once to see if she could tell her anything.

'Not much, I'm afraid,' Miss Bertram confessed. 'Apparently you're going to be fed and watered and the nurse is going to take a look at you, and then they're going to take you to your billets – as they call them.'

'Nurse?' Mary said. 'What nurse?'

Lizzie had seen her, sitting at a table at one end of one of the queues, small-tooth comb in hand. 'It's a Nitty Nora,' she said in disgust. 'That's all we need. What sort of children do they think we are?'

'Well, I don't know about you,' Mary said, pulling a paper bag out of her case, 'but I'm going to have my lunch. I'm starving.'

'Very sensible,' Miss Bertram said. 'I'll tell the others. Your friend Poppy's over there, Lizzie.'

Oh, what a relief to find one of her friends. 'Poppy!' she

called. 'Have you still got your group?'

Only half of them apparently, but among them was one of Mary's friends so there was a double reunion.

'Stick together,' Poppy said. 'They're taking us to our billets in a minute.'

'Have you seen the Nitty Nora?' Mary asked

'Yes, I have and she tugs! I say, you haven't got any spare sandwiches, have you? I had a pie and it got squashed and I'm absolutely starving.'

Lizzie opened her packet of sandwiches and held it out to her friend. She did it casually and without thinking about it, the way she'd done so many times in the school hall – but then suddenly and with a palpable tug at her innards, she remembered her mother wrapping it up for her. She could see her standing in the kitchen folding the greaseproof paper, saying, *'There you are, sweetheart, that should keep you going,'* and she yearned to see her again, to be with her in their nice, wide, clean kitchen instead of being cooped up in this foul club house waiting to be seen by some ghastly Nitty Nora. I didn't even kiss her goodbye, she thought, and she had to blink to stop herself crying. 'I hate being evacuated,' she said.

When Octavia arrived at the station with her two helpers, the dispersal was well under way. She saw at once that the drivers were in a rush and that her comfortably organised groups were being split up and parted from one another, but there was nothing she could do about it, annoying though it was. They obviously had their system, even if it wasn't a very good one, and if she tried to change things she would only be getting in the way. She stopped to talk to the girls who were climbing aboard the first of the two buses in the square, so at least she knew where they were going and could follow them there, and while she was wishing them luck, she saw Miss Fennimore still standing guard with her pole.

'Can't help you much, I'm afraid,' Miss Fennimore said. 'It's all being done so quickly. They're going to a golf club somewhere, that I do know, and a village hall, but apart from that I'm afraid I don't know where they are. I've told the staff to keep a note of the girls' new addresses, if they can manage to do it.'

'Don't worry,' Octavia said. 'This is a start and you've all got my phone number so you know where I am if you need me. I'll see you all at ten o'clock tomorrow morning.' Then she set off, determined to find as many of her girls as she could and knowing that it might be a job.

'I'll take you to the house first, Janet,' she said, as she drove away.

'Yes please, mum,' Janet said, 'if you doan' mind. I got a list a' things I got to do there as long as me arm. Mrs Thompson give it to me this mornin'. An' the supper to get, which'll be a little ham salad if that's agreeable, bein' it's so hot, like, an' I doan't know when you're likely to be hoame.' She patted her basket. 'I got me things.'

It felt most peculiar to Octavia to be turning in at the drive of an unfamiliar empty house. When she'd decided to rent it she'd thought it was quite a pleasant place, built in the Edwardian style with a wide bow window to light the drawing room on the ground floor and a good-sized kitchen and four bedrooms, one with its own dressing room. There were also two extra rooms in the attic both completely empty, so they would have plenty of space. But now, as she put the key into the lock and smelt the dank, unwelcoming odour of dust and emptiness, she felt homesick and irritable, recognising in that instant that she didn't want to be there, that she dreaded this war that none of them had wanted, that she needed the familiar smell and order of her own home. She shook the thoughts from her head at once. This was no time to get maudlin. There was work to be done, a challenge to face, children to be cared for.

'Let's have the windows open,' she said to Janet, walking into the dining room. 'This place needs an airing. And then we'll get the luggage in.'

So windows were opened all over the house and they carried in the cases and boxes between them and left them in the hall for Janet to sort.

'What a difference a bit of fresh air *does* make,' Octavia said. 'Now we must get on with our treasure hunt, Maggie, and see how many of our pupils we can find.'

They drove about the town for the next four hours, visiting the dispersal centres they knew about, discovering others, praising the girls who were still there for being sensible and waiting so patiently, and questioning every WVS worker they found to try to discover who would have a full list of all the billets their pupils had been sent to. Eventually, when they were finally given a name and told that the lady in question would be outside the station at half past eight the next morning, Octavia decided that enough was enough.

'Let's go home and have supper,' she said to Maggie. 'I don't know about you but I'm starving. Then, I really must phone my cousin and let her know we've arrived and find out how her grandchildren have got on. They could have gone today too. And then we must see about getting you a place to stay.'

'I've got one,' Maggie told her with some pride. And when Octavia looked surprised, 'I did it when we first arrived, while you were talking to the girls. It's just round the corner. I told the lady I was your secretary and I had to be near the Ridgeway and she said that was the nearest.'

'Well, if that's the case, we'll get straight back for our supper,' Octavia said. And she drove them to Horsell and her house in the road called Ridgeway, pleased that she already knew her way there. This time as she turned in at the drive and saw the open windows and Janet busy in the dining room setting the table, the place felt more like home. It was a warm peaceful summer evening, and somewhere in a nearby garden a chaffinch was singing. 'What a day it's been!' she said.

# Chapter Six

'It's a gorgeous day,' Lizzie Meriton said, leaning out of the bedroom window. 'Come and have a look, Poppy. You can see for miles.'

Poppy groaned and turned over in her unfamiliar bed. 'It's all very well for you,' she complained, 'you were asleep all night.'

'Comes of having a clear conscience,' Lizzie told her. It wasn't true. She'd been awake off and on all night too, worrying because she hadn't kissed her mother goodbye, but you have to keep the side up. 'There's a common over there. I can see the trees. Tell you what, when we've had our breakfast, let's go and explore.'

'I'm exhausted,' Poppy said, struggling to sit up. 'Oh God! You're dressed.'

'Clean, clothed and in my right mind,' Lizzie agreed. She was surprising herself by how much better she felt now that it was morning. Smithie was right. It was all a matter of accepting things.

'You've even brushed your hair,' Poppy complained, admiring Lizzie's long blonde mane. It really wasn't fair for anyone to look that pretty first thing in the morning. She was so slim and she had such lovely long legs and such white teeth, and such beautiful grey eyes and long black eyelashes and everything. She hadn't even got spots.

'It's what I do,' Lizzie said carelessly. 'Fifty strokes both sides, every morning.'

Poppy's hair was thin and mouse-brown, and had to be put in curlers every night and combed and arranged in the morning so that it didn't look too bad, which took a very long time. She lumped from the bed and went to look for her dressing gown. It was in her bag somewhere. She remembered packing it. 'I wonder what's for breakfast,' she said.

'Bacon.'

'How do you know?'

'I can smell it cooking.'

She's such a brick, Poppy thought, tugging the dressing gown out of her bag – along with two pairs of knickers and the sleeve of her spare blouse. She takes everything in her stride, even this. I'm glad we're together. And she took out the first curler and began to start her day.

Emmeline was shaking a Beecham's powder into a glass of water, watching as the mixture fizzed and bubbled. 'There you are, Uncle,' she said, handing it to J-J, 'drink that down while it's fizzy. We can't have you with a cold.'

'I'm not at death's door, Emmeline,' J-J protested, sitting up in bed with his white hair sleep-tousled and his glasses on the end of his nose. 'It's only a cough.'

'Um,' Emmeline said, dubiously, 'well, there's no need to put up with it, whatever it is. What do you fancy for breakfast?'

'Porridge would be nice.'

'Porridge it shall be,' Emmeline promised and turned her head towards the bedroom door, listening. 'There's the phone ringing. I shall have to go and attend to it. You'll be all right, won't you?'

He smiled at her concern. 'Perfectly,' he said.

Emmeline went puffing down the stairs as fast as she could. The call would be from one or other of her daughters and she was eager for news of her grandchildren, who'd all been evacuated the previous day too.

It was Dora, sounding very calm and collected. 'Yes,' she said. 'He arrived safely. I had a card from him this morning.'

'Dear little man,' Emmeline said. 'What does he say?'

Dora read the card. 'He's in a village called Bracknell, wherever that is – and he's staying with a nice lady called Mrs – what is it? – Weather – that can't be right – and he's with Martin and Bob Cavendish. So you don't need to worry about him.'

Emmeline went on worrying. It was all very well for Dora to say what a big boy he was and how grown up he was getting, but he *was* only eight when all was said and done, poor little mite, and eight's no age to be sent off to the country without your mother. 'Did he say anything else?'

'No. It was only a postcard. I have got another bit of news for you though. I'm going to join the ARP. They want people to drive their ambulances. It was in the paper this morning.'

'But you've got a job,' Emmeline protested. She worked for an estate agent just down the road from her flat.

'This is extra,' Dora said firmly. 'When there are air raids. It won't stop me working. Anyway, I don't reckon there'll be much work for me to do now. I mean who's going to buy a property in Balham? It might be bombed. Nobody'll move to London with a war on. They're all moving out.'

'Don't talk like that,' Emmeline said. It made her flesh creep. Bad enough to have to think they might be bombed, without actually saying it.

'That's the way we've got to talk now, Ma,' Dora said. 'It's no good pretending. We're in it now. We've got to face things.

Anyway, must rush. The pips are going. I'll phone you tonight and let you know how I get on.'

Emmeline put the telephone back on its hook, feeling stricken. Her world was being turned upside down for the second time in her life and she couldn't bear it. Her nice comfortable order was wrecked and now look where they all were. Poor little David all on his own out in the country somewhere, her dear Dotty Dora driving an ambulance – and just think how dangerous that's going to be if they start bombing – no Tavy to talk to, and her dear, dear Johnnie flying his Spitfire with all those dreadful bombers in the air. Sighing, she stomped off to the kitchen to cook the porridge.

It was just thickening nicely when the phone rang again. She took it off the gas and set it aside so that it didn't burn and went off to see who it was this time.

It was Edie and she sounded upset and unsure of herself.

'Mum? Is that you?'

'Yes,' Emmeline said. 'Where are you?'

'I'm in the phone box at the end of the road.'

'What road?'

'My road. Where I live.'

'Didn't you go then? Have they put it off?'

'Oh no. Nothing like that. The girls went. They're in Guildford. I got a postcard this morning. I stayed here with Joanie.'

'I thought you were all going together.'

'Yes – well – we were,' Edie said, and then there was a long pause before she went on. 'Arthur's being sent to France, he got the letter yesterday, and I couldn't very well go off and leave him with that going on, could I? Not knowing where we were or having an address to write to or anything. Anyway, I've stayed. Me and baby'll go down later, when he's gone. I couldn't do anything else could I?'

Emmeline supposed not, since that was what Edie wanted her to say, but her chest ached with pity for those two children out in the country somewhere without their mother.

'I'll have to go,' Edith said. 'Lots to do.' And hung up.

Emmeline went back to the porridge, which had thickened in her absence and needed re-warming. Then she made a pot of tea and toiled upstairs to tell Uncle his breakfast was ready and to give him the news about her grandchildren. She was upset to find that he was lying down and looked rather flushed.

'I don't feel quite the thing,' he confessed. 'I might just stay here for a bit longer. Would you mind?'

She reassured him at once. Poor old Uncle. He was overtired. 'No, of course not. There's no necessity for you to get up yet awhile. You just have a little rest and I'll make you up a nice little tray and bring it up for you. I shan't be long.'

She took special pains over the tray, setting it with the best tray cloth and the prettiest china, and as a finishing touch she went out into the garden and cut the last of the roses so that he could have a little vase of flowers to cheer him too. It was quite a shock when she went back upstairs to find that he'd grown worse in the short time she'd been working on it. He was lying on his back with his eyes shut and looked really poorly. She put the tray down on the dressing table and went to sit beside him.

'Would you like me to get the doctor?' she asked when he opened his eyes.

He had to make an effort to answer her. 'I shall be better presently.'

'I'll phone him,' she said. And did.

\* \* \*

93

Dr Mullinger was an old man and a thorough one. He didn't arrive until late in the morning but he examined his patient most carefully, took his pulse and temperature, looked down his throat, sounded his lungs and asked him how old he was.

The question caused some distress because J-J had forgotten and was reduced to saying 'Um – um' and coughing while he struggled to remember.

'Eighty-six,' Emmeline said, patting her uncle's hand to reassure him.

Now it was Doctor Mullinger's turn to say 'Um', which he did thoughtfully as he put his stethoscope back in his little black bag and snapped it shut. 'I'm afraid your uncle is suffering from bronchitis,' he said to Emmeline. 'Keep him in bed and warm. Don't worry about feeding him. He's not up to food at the moment. Just give him plenty of fluids. That's most important. That, and keeping him warm. I'll call in again tomorrow.'

Emmeline thanked him as she escorted him downstairs and saw him out, but her mind was spinning. What a thing to happen. Now of all times, with everything at sixes and sevens and everybody all over the place. Well, there'll be no rushing off to Woking now, what with Edie and Joan still here and Uncle ill. I shall have to phone Tavy and let her know. Mustn't alarm her though. She's got enough on her plate without that. And she picked up the receiver.

Octavia was in the middle of what Elizabeth Fennimore called the first staff meeting of the evacuation and the news she'd had for her colleagues wasn't good. She and Maggie had been hard at work since six o'clock, and now there was a huge map of their new area hanging from the picture rail on the drawing room wall, with every street neatly labelled and coloured pins marking the houses where their pupils could be found, and a pile of typed lists on the coffee table detailing all their addresses. Her staff were sitting in a variety of chairs all round the room, smoking and drinking coffee and listening to her outline of what they had to expect in the next few days.

'As soon as we know exactly where they all are,' she said, 'we'll have named flags attached to those pins. And in the meantime if you could sign the list that's going the rounds so that I know where you are too... With phone numbers if you're lucky enough to have one. Then Maggie will get that circulated to you too.'

It made them all feel better to be organised. But the news of the school they were to share was nowhere near so good.

'I've seen Miss Jones, the headmistress, this morning,' Octavia told them, 'and been shown over the school, which as I told you yesterday – the day before – I've rather lost track – is not a school building, but a line of huts. She and her staff are very kind and I'm sure they'll make us welcome, but the premises are just not big enough to contain us, especially if we're to have an area for private study, and especially as we're only going to be allowed the use of the place on Tuesdays, Thursdays and Saturdays. The two schools have got to share it, Box and Cox style. There is some space for storing text books but class libraries will be a problem. And even if we doubled up some classes we still wouldn't all fit in. I've written to our Chairman of Governors to tell him we need at least two large buildings as supplementary accommodation and I've sent him details of seven that might be suitable.'

That provoked laughter. It was so typical of their Smithie. She smiled in answer to it and went on. 'However, that is only one of our problems. According to Miss Jones, nobody is going to be allowed to use her building at all until the local

95

authority has built air raid shelters in the grounds. So we've all got to wait. I don't suppose the girls will mind an extension to their summer holiday, especially as it's good weather, but it will make it difficult for all of us if we're delayed too long.'

'We ought to try to meet the examination girls and at least give them their syllabuses,' Elizabeth said. 'It's a short term and it'll be even shorter if they take a long time over these shelters.'

'We could hold some classes here for the time being,' Octavia said. 'There are two empty rooms in the attic and the dining room, of course.' The phone shrilled into her thoughts. 'Excuse me a minute,' she said, as she picked up the receiver. 'Octavia Smith.'

'Ah!' Emmeline's voice said. 'Yes.' And then paused.

The odd hesitancy was an alert. 'Is there something the matter?' Octavia asked.

'Um – not really – I mean it's nothing to worry about. Nothing important. Not really. It's just…Uncle's got bronchitis.'

'Have you had the doctor to him?'

'He's just this minute left.'

'And?'

'Nothing more than I've told you, really. He's got bronchitis and to give him lots of water and let him rest and he's going to call in again tomorrow. Only I thought you ought to know.'

'Would you like Janet to come back and help you?'

'No, no. I'm fine. He's no trouble. I mean, it's not much more than a chesty cough really. We shall manage.'

'I shall come back and see him tomorrow afternoon,' Octavia decided. She could visit Mr Chivers too and talk about those extra premises. Kill two birds with one stone. Or three, if she brought back some more books. 'Give him

96

my love, and don't worry too much.'

'I'm not worrying,' Emmeline said. 'I mean he's no trouble. I just thought you ought to know.' And she put the phone down and went worrying off to the kitchen. If only the house wasn't so empty. It was horrid having to cope with everything all on her own. And Arthur going to France, and Johnnie waiting for the bombers, and those three poor little children out in the depths of the country all on their own.

Lizzie and Poppy had discovered a canal. Their landlady had made sandwiches for them and given them an apple each which they'd packed in Poppy's shoe-bag, they'd made sure they had sufficient pocket money for drinks and since then they'd been happily exploring the territory. They'd found the common almost at once because it was at the end of their road, and when they'd walked right across it they'd turned south along a track called Well Lane and there was the canal.

Lizzie was thrilled with it. It was so green and peaceful and countrified. 'It's like walking through a green tunnel,' she said as they reached a spot where the trees curved towards each other across the water.

'There's a swan,' Poppy said. 'It won't attack us, will it?'

''Course not,' Lizzie said, although the big bird was hissing at them even before they were anywhere near it. 'Just walk past.'

'Maybe we should walk back,' Poppy said.

'Come on,' Lizzie said, striding along the towpath. 'There's a barge up there. Look.'

It was a big barge and it was being pulled towards them by a large mud-spattered horse which was plodding as though it had all the time in the world. As it came nearer they could see that the boat was painted scarlet and gold, which made it

97

look very bold among all that greenery, and that there were two scruffy-looking men, sitting on very small camp chairs on what little deck there was, smoking pipes. As the two girls drew level, they waved and the older one called out, 'You got a lovely day for it!'

'Yes,' Lizzie agreed, 'we have.'

'You 'vacuees, are yer?'

'Yes,' Poppy said. 'We got here yesterday.'

'Fancy! Well you got a good day for it.'

'I'll bet it's fun to live on a boat,' Poppy said, when they'd walked on and were out of earshot. 'Sitting out there in the sun with nothing to do.'

'It's another world,' Lizzie said. 'Like *Wind in the Willows*. Look at all those reeds. I can just see Mole and Ratty rowing along down there. It's all browns and greens and blue sky and ducks and swans. Oh look, there's a damsel fly. Over there on the reeds, long blue body, very pretty. Do you see it?'

Poppy was impressed. 'How do you know what it is?'

'We have them on our pond at home,' Lizzie said. 'There's another one. And two more over there. Aren't they pretty? Like little slices of sky. I tell you what, Poppy, I think being evacuated is going to be fun.'

Poppy was getting hungry. 'Is it time for dinner?'

'If we want it to be,' Lizzie said. 'We don't have to wait for mealtimes. We can do what we like.'

They found a grassy spot to sit on and unpacked their sandwiches. They were a bit soggy but they made good eating and the apples were lovely, very crisp and tasty.

'I'll bet they came out of her garden,' Poppy said. 'I'll bet she picked them this morning. I wonder what sort of apples they are.'

That was a bit too prosaic for Lizzie's present mood. 'This,' she said, gazing round at the scenery, 'is the most romantic place I've ever been in. It's like something out of the pictures. You know? The part where the hero meets the heroine and they fall in love and there are violins playing. It's just the place for a love scene. I tell you what, Poppy, I'm going to meet the man of my dreams by this canal. I can feel it in my bones. He'll come walking along this towpath and he'll see me walking towards him and it'll be love at first sight.'

Poppy threw her apple core into the water. 'How can you possibly know?' she said.

'I told you, I can feel it in my bones. It's a premonition. He'll be walking along, all tall, dark and handsome, not thinking of anything in particular, and then he'll see me and our eyes will meet and that'll be it.'

'You're potty,' Poppy said. 'Do you think we ought to go and find some of the others?'

'There's no romance in your soul,' Lizzie sighed. 'How can you even be thinking about looking for the others when we're in a place like this?'

Poppy persisted. 'But don't you think we should? I mean, we *are* supposed to be looking after them.'

'Oh, all right then,' Lizzie sighed. 'Let's see if we can find Woolworths. I bet that's where they'll be, and there's bound to be a Woolworths.'

There was and sure enough it was crowded with girls in navy blue uniform. It didn't take Lizzie long to find Iris and Sarah who were mooching about by the lipstick counter.

'Hello, you two,' she said. 'Everything all right?'

'Not bad,' Iris said. 'They eat some jolly funny food down here, though. We had the weirdest stuff for breakfast, didn't we, Sarah?'

'Baked up crumbs,' Sarah said. 'What did she say it was,

Iris? Grape something or other? Didn't look much like grapes to me. Have you seen Miss Bertram?'

'No. Have you?'

'She was in here a minute ago,' Sarah said. 'She says we're still on holiday. Isn't that wizard? She said there's a letter in the post for us telling us all about it, and they're going to write again and tell us when we've got to go to school and where it is and everything. We've been looking round, haven't we, Iris?'

An extended holiday was good news but there were practical matters to be attended to. 'Where's your billet?' Lizzie asked. 'I need to know where you are.'

It was rather a disappointment to find that the letter that was waiting for her and Poppy when they finally went back to their own billet had a different message. The gist of it was the same as the message Miss Bertram had given the little'uns – the holiday was to be extended until air raid shelters had been built at the school they would be sharing – but in their case, as they were examination candidates, lessons would begin at Ridgeway in two days' time at nine o'clock, when they would meet their teachers and be given their syllabuses.

'What a sell!' Poppy said.

'She's right,' Lizzie said, defending her heroine's decision. 'We've got a lot of work to get through. We'll just have to make the most of tomorrow.'

Tommy and Elizabeth were discussing the next day too, sitting in the comfort of their elegant parlour as they drank their after-dinner coffee. It was the smallest of their four reception rooms but they liked it better than any of the others, partly because it was set apart from the rest of the house, but mostly because they were the only ones who ever used it. The windows gave out to the green of the garden, it was decorated in pale blue, cream and biscuit brown, which were their favourite colours, with blue and cream swagged curtains to frame the view and heaps of pale blue tasselled cushions on every seat. They had their own easy chairs by the fireside, their favourite books were on the shelves above the chaise longue, and their favourite pictures adorned the walls. It was, in short, a calm and private territory in a house which was too often crowded with other and important people. And, naturally, it was the place where they had their most private conversations.

'I shall take the afternoon off tomorrow,' Tommy said, 'and we'll go down and see her. I've spoken to Toby about it and he's quite agreeable.'

'We mustn't rush her,' Elizabeth warned him. 'I'm not saying I don't want to see her. You know I do. But she wants to be independent. She was really quite stern about it. Maybe we ought to write back and ask her if it's all right.'

'No, no,' her father said. 'That's just our Lizzie being Lizzie. She was always independent. It'll be different when we arrive. We'll take her out to tea somewhere special and spoil her a bit. It'll be a nice surprise.'

# *Chapter Seven*

The two cars passed one another on the Weybridge to Woking road. Octavia recognised the Silver Cloud as it approached, but it took Tommy several seconds to realise that the black Ford he'd just passed was being driven by Tavy, and then he felt irritable. What did she think she was doing? She should have been in Woking looking after her girls, not driving to London. Then he saw that she'd pulled up, so he stopped too and, as there was no other traffic in the road, reversed until the two cars were boot to boot. Then he got out to find out what she thought she was playing at.

'Is the war over then?' he said, as he reached her open window.

'Pa's got bronchitis,' she told him shortly. 'Emmeline phoned me yesterday. I'm going back to see him.'

The news changed his irritation to concern. If poor old J-J was ill, that was different. He altered his tone at once, standing there in the strong sunlight, elegant in his grey suit, aware that she was anxious and doing her best to conceal it. 'I am sorry.'

She changed the subject, talk of her father being a little too hard to handle, when she hadn't seen him and didn't know how bad he was. 'Presumably you're going down to see Lizzie.'

'Spur of the moment sort of thing,' he explained. 'Little surprise. Thought we'd meet her at the school gate and take her out to tea.'

'Ah!' Octavia said and, explained why that wouldn't be possible.

He was irritable again. 'Oh well, I suppose we'll have to go to her billet then,' he said, 'and hope she's there.'

'If she's not, try Woolworths,' Octavia advised. 'That seems to be our unofficial annexe.'

His eyebrows raised in disbelief. 'Woolworths?'

'It's where they meet one another,' Octavia explained, 'so Miss Bertram says. The first-formers love it. It's familiar, you see, a sort of home from home.'

'Well, thanks for the tip,' he said. 'We mustn't keep you. Give our regards to your father.'

'Well?' Elizabeth asked, when he eased his long legs back into the car.

'J-J's got bronchitis.'

'Poor man,' Elizabeth said. 'We must hope it doesn't turn to anything worse.'


It felt most peculiar to Octavia to be driving alongside Wimbledon Common again. After the crowds of children she'd left behind in the streets of Woking, the wide expanses of the common looked empty, and Parkside Avenue was so quiet it could have been a Sunday.

Emmeline busied out into the hall the minute she heard the key in the lock. She'd been waiting in the kitchen for nearly an hour, fiddling with the tea cups, and with the kettle on and off the boil and the clock ticking the minutes away. Now she ran to her cousin in relief.

'How is he?' Octavia asked when they'd kissed.

'Bit worse, I'm afraid,' Emmeline admitted. 'The doctor came again this morning. He seemed to think it might be turning to pneumonia. He's asleep at the moment, poor old love. I went up to him a minute ago and he was quite peaceful. Let's have some tea, shall we, and then we'll go up and see him.'

The tea was very welcome after her drive and it gave Emmeline a chance to tell her everything that had been going on. 'I've been at my wit's end,' she said as she poured the first cup, 'what with Uncle ill and Edie not going with the girls, and those poor children all by themselves in the country.'

'They're probably having the time of their lives,' Octavia told her. 'My lot are. There are lots of people looking after them and they can't go to school yet because the building isn't ready for them, so they're roaming the countryside like gypsies.'

'That's as may be,' Emmeline said. 'But they're older. They can cope with it better. My poor little David's only eight. Would you like some fruit cake?'

'Oh, Emmeline, nothing changes,' Octavia said, smiling at her. 'Tea and fruit cake in the kitchen. When did you make it?'

'As soon as I knew you were coming,' Emmeline said. 'It gave me something to keep myself occupied.'

Octavia understood that perfectly. It was a pattern that had withstood every change, an easy, comforting pattern. Tea and fruit cake.

But change was waiting for them when they went upstairs and it was the change that both of them had been secretly dreading.

The bedroom was quiet except for the intermittent buzzing of a fat bluebottle that was pinging against the window. Everything was neat and tidy. There was a carafe of water on the bedside table with her father's spectacles folded beside it, the carpet was swept clean and the counterpane was so straight there was barely a crease in it. But there was a faint and oddly familiar smell in the room, a sour, troubling smell that reminded Octavia of something she found herself straining to remember. Her father lay on his back with his mouth open and his eyes shut so tightly they seemed to have sunk into their sockets. He was so still it seemed a pity to wake him but she walked to the bedside nevertheless and sat down in his little bedside chair.

'Pa,' she said gently, and leant forward to take the quiet hand on the counterpane. 'It's Tavy.' But the hand was limp and there was no response. He didn't even stir. And leaning forward she realised that his face was empty, vacated, not Pa at all, and then she remembered exactly what the smell was. It was the horrible sour odour that had filled her mother's room when *she* lay dying. She put her hand at her father's throat and felt for a pulse, knowing she wouldn't find one. 'He's gone, Em,' she said. 'I've got here too late.'

'He can't have,' Emmeline said, her face crumpling with distress. 'He was all right just a minute ago. I mean, I was up here and he was sleeping like a baby. I mean, he was all right.' Then she began to cry.

The two women wept together for a very long time, holding on to one another in an extreme of grief, until the clock in the hall struck six and they came to their senses a little and knew that there were things that had to be done. There were people to notify. The doctor must be called.

'You stay here and look after him,' Emmeline said. 'I'll do it.'

'No,' Octavia said. 'I'll do it. He doesn't need looking after now.'

Dr Mullinger came within half an hour and certified that Professor Smith was indeed dead. 'It was pneumonia, you see,' he explained to Octavia. 'It can be very quick sometimes. And merciful, I'm glad to say. He wouldn't have suffered.'

It was a consolation, but only a faint one.

'I must phone Janet and tell her,' Octavia said, when the doctor had signed the death certificate and suggested the name of an undertaker and left them. 'She's expecting me back for supper.'

'You go back,' Emmeline said valiantly. 'I can manage. I've done it enough times, God knows, over the years.'

'It's very dear of you, Em,' Octavia said. 'But I wouldn't dream of leaving you alone. The idea! No, we'll manage this together, and when everything's settled and the funeral's arranged, you can come back to Woking with me and let me look after you for a change.'

'Haven't you got to get back?' Emmeline worried. 'I mean, haven't you got things to do?'

'The staff will cope,' Octavia said, and it was a great pride to her to be able to say so. 'I'll send them a message to say I'll be back as soon as I can.'

'Oh dear, oh dear, oh dear,' Emmeline said.


Tommy Meriton had spent the entire afternoon searching for his daughter – without success – and he was feeling very irritable indeed.

'This is ridiculous,' he said to Elizabeth, as they drove down Chertsey Road for the third slow time. 'This place is heaving with little girls. Look at them. They're all over the place. We *must* find her.'

'We should have sent her a card to let her know we were coming,' Elizabeth said. This was so typical of Tommy. As a diplomat he was exceptional, and everything he did was thought through and planned to the last and smallest detail, but when it came to this precious daughter of his he lost all sense of proportion and was as thoughtlessly impulsive as a child. 'I did tell you.'

Tommy didn't want to hear it. 'Now, look at that,' he said scowling at a group of girls who had wandered into the road. 'Damn nearly under my wheels. This is ridiculous.'

'So you keep saying,' his wife said.

'And it's so damned hot. What's the good of us bringing her summer clothes if we can't find her?'

'You could have given them to her landlady.'

He snorted. 'What earthly good would that have done? The woman's a fool.'

'Just because she couldn't tell you where your daughter was doesn't give you the right to impugn her intelligence,' Elizabeth said, teasing him. 'I thought she was rather nice. Shy, of course, but very pleasant.'

'Oh, come on, child,' Tommy said to a small girl hesitating on the kerb, 'if you're going to cross the road then do it. Don't dither.'

He was waving his hand to urge her to cross when another larger schoolgirl suddenly appeared, took hold of her hand and led her into the road. And it was Lizzie. Just when he wasn't actually looking for her, it was Lizzie.

'My dear child,' he said, beaming at her. 'We've been looking for you everywhere. I'd almost given up hope of finding you. I was just saying so. Hop in and we'll go and have tea. How about a teashop in Guildford? How would that be?'

'Can Poppy come too?'

'The more the merrier,' Tommy said. He was in the most affable mood.

107

So the two girls climbed into the back seat and they all drove off to Guildford where they had a sumptuous tea, with buttered scones and cream cakes *and* éclairs.

'Would you like some more?' Tommy asked happily when their plates were empty. 'You've only got to say the word.' Oh, it was so good to see her again and looking so well and so pretty.

'Better not,' Lizzie said, 'or we shall never eat our supper.'

It was Elizabeth's chance to ask how they were getting on. 'I gather your landlady is looking after you.'

'She's nice,' Lizzie said. 'The food's a bit dull, between you and me, but she's doing her best. I mean she wasn't expecting two huge great girls like us.'

'I wouldn't call you huge great girls,' Tommy protested.

'Nor did she,' Lizzie said quickly, and explained. 'It's just we were a bit of a shock to her. She was expecting two nursery school kids. Her face was a study when we arrived, wasn't it, Poppy?'

'It was priceless,' Poppy confirmed. 'We laughed for ages.'

'And what about your schooling,' Tommy asked.

'Starts tomorrow,' Lizzie told him. 'In Smithie's house.'

'I'm glad to hear it,' her father said. But privately he was wondering whether 'Smithie' would be there.

Octavia and Emmeline sat up half the night talking and grieving, remembering all the good things J-J had done in his long life, from his long teaching career and his involvement with the Fabians to the patient and loving way he'd accepted his new life in Wimbledon when what he'd really wanted to do was to go on living in Hampstead. They told one another over and over again how much they would miss his good sense, how glad they were that he'd died without suffering and finally they agreed that it was a mercy that he didn't have to endure another war.

'We had quite enough of it the first time round,' Emmeline said, as the hall clock struck three. 'And a fat lot of good it's done us.'

'Shall you come back with me tomorrow?' Octavia asked.

Emmeline thought not. 'I'll stay here till after the funeral,' she said. 'I ought to know where Arthur's going to be sent by then. I wouldn't like to leave my poor Edie with all that hanging over her. When he's gone wherever he's going and she's taken Joanie off to Guildford I shall feel better about things.'

So Octavia left her early the next morning and drove back to Woking alone with her thoughts, in a pearly dawn. The roads were almost completely empty which was just as well for her brain was fuzzy and she was driving badly. It simply wasn't possible that Pa was dead. It was unnatural, unacceptable, like losing the roof of the house. Oh dear, dear Pa, she thought, it's going to be very hard without you.

But there was no time for tears. They might be streaming down her cheeks at that moment but she would have to dry her eyes when she reached Woking. There was a school to run and houses to be rented and adapted to provide the extra classrooms she needed, and the fourth-formers had to be started on their examination courses. And a war to be endured, whether she wanted to endure it or not.

In fact the war didn't seem to be beginning. A week went by and nothing much happened except for a couple of stern government directives. All windows were to be blacked out and headlights on all vehicles were to be covered with cardboard so that only two small bars of light were left to light the way.

That was followed by a warning from the new Ministry of Food that butter and bacon would be rationed by the middle of December.

'Just so long as they don't put us on short commons before Uncle's funeral,' Emmeline said. 'I'd like to give him a good send-off.'

The funeral was a very big affair, attended by so many of his ex-pupils that Emmeline said she couldn't count them and Tommy told her it was a sure sign of the value of the man. Three weeks later, Arthur was sent to France along with 158,000 others and a quarter of a million young men over twenty were called up, among them Dora's quiet John. Emmeline took a train to Woking and Edith went to Guildford with her baby and got lodgings for herself and all three of her children in a local farm. She wrote to her mother to report that everything was much better for them now they were all together. And Roehampton Secondary School finally moved into the huts and the girls were educated there on Tuesday, Thursday and Saturday mornings.

But still nothing much was happening in Europe. After over-running Czechoslovakia and Poland, Hitler was keeping uncharacteristically quiet and there were no new German invasions for the Allied forces to withstand. By the end of October the newspapers were calling it the phoney war.

Preparations for it went ahead notwithstanding. Everybody was given a National Identity Card and a ration book, and every street had an air raid warden whose job was to enforce a total blackout and who was considered an unnecessary busybody in consequence. The darkness led to a very marked increase in road accidents and falls, and after a while every other kerbstone was painted white and letter-boxes and pavement trees were given a bold white ring in the hope that this would reduce the number of collisions in the total darkness of a moonless night. And the wait went on.

It wasn't long before Octavia's pupils were asking their form mistresses if they could go home and see their parents at the weekend.

'I don't see any reason why not,' Octavia said, when the matter was brought up at one of her weekly staff meetings. 'Providing they don't travel in the blackout and providing staff don't mind them missing Saturday lessons. They're sensible girls and it's not a long journey.'

'What are we to tell them about the Christmas holiday?' Miss Bertram wanted to know. 'Some of them are asking about that too.'

'We'll make a decision nearer the time,' Octavia said. 'It's six weeks yet and we don't know what might happen in six weeks. The war might start. London might be bombed. I don't think we should commit ourselves to anything yet.'

What happened was that it started to snow.

Lizzie Meriton woke early that morning and for a few seconds she couldn't think why. Then she glanced at the window and realised that the light was odd and that the sky was completely white. No, to be accurate – and Miss Bertram said you should always be accurate when it came to colour – it wasn't exactly white because white was denser and this sky wasn't dense at all. It looked delicate with a faint touch of very pale yellow and an odd sort of sheen to it, as if there was a light shining on it from a mirror somewhere. But there couldn't be, could there? And lying there all warm and snug under the blankets, she suddenly thought of HG Wells's novel *The War of the Worlds*, the one they'd read in the third form, and remembered with a shiver of horror that the space ship had arrived right here in Woking. What if a space ship had landed during the night? But it couldn't have, could it? There were no such things as space ships and she was a sensible girl. Wasn't she? Yes, of course she was. She had to be. She was on her own now. She got up, put on her slippers and her dressing gown and went to the window to see exactly what was happening.

The world was completely white. The reflecting mirror was snow. 'Come and have a look at this,' she said to Poppy.

'What fun!' Poppy said. 'Is it a school day?'

Edith didn't think it was any sort of fun at all. She bundled her two little girls into the warmest clothing she could find and sent them off to school looking as fat as snowmen. They came home at the end of the day soaking wet and glowing because one of the local boys had let them have a turn on his toboggan.

'You should've seen us, Mum,' Maggie said. 'You come down the hill at a hundred miles an hour. Geoff said.'

'Well, don't go breaking your legs, that's all,' Edith told her. 'It's bad enough being here without broken legs.' She was finding life in a farmhouse extremely difficult, and sharing a kitchen with her landlady was a nightmare. 'Look at the state of your gloves.'

'That was the snowballs,' Barbara said happily. 'I like being off school when it's snowing. D'you think we'll be off tomorrow? Geoff said they close down when it snows because of the boilers.'

'I hope the snow goes on for ever and ever,' Maggie said, handing her sodden gloves to her mother.

'Heaven help us all,' Edith said.

The next day the snowfall was so heavy and prolonged that

the school *did* close down, to the girls' delight. They went tobogganing again and built a snowman that Maggie said was 'big as a house'.

'It looks as if it's set in for the winter,' Edith wrote to her mother. 'And my poor Arthur in France.'

'Look on the bright side,' Emmeline wrote back. 'At least there's no fighting.'

Which was true, for apart from occasional reports of running battles between the Russian Red Army and the Norwegians in the much deeper snows of Norway, the war continued to be more phoney than real.

Lizzie and her friends were thrilled with the cold weather. The canal had frozen solid and now they had an ice rink and could go skating whenever they wanted, and as Poppy said, 'This is the life! I hope it goes on for ever and ever.' And sure enough the cold weather continued. After a week or two, Woking WVS arranged to take over the gym in the boys' grammar school on Sunday afternoons so that visiting parents would have somewhere warm where they could meet their children and have a cup of tea. It was much needed for by that time the snow wasn't quite so pretty. The pavements had been cleared so many times that there were perpetual mounds of frozen slush at the pavement edge, much pitted by discarded cigarette ends and streaked yellow by the local dogs, and rather too many people were hobbling with chilblains and complaining that they didn't know how much more of this awful weather they could stand.

'Fat lot of good talking like that,' Emmeline said. 'The weather's like the war. We've just got to get on with it.'

'Christmas is coming, Em,' Octavia said. 'Look forward to that.' Her school was fizzing with preparations for it. The sixth form were rehearsing their customary Christmas play – and that always cheered everybody up – Miss Bertram and her art classes were making paper chains and Christmas decorations and cards, and nearly all the girls were going back to London to spend the holiday with their families. They might be evacuated but the school traditions hadn't changed. Despite everything, Christmas would be celebrated in its usual joyous style.

'Just so long as we don't have to cope with rationing, that's all,' Emmeline said. 'I'd like to ask the girls to join us – that's all right, isn't it, Tavy? – and I can't do that if they won't let me buy any meat.'

She was cheered when she managed to order a goose and a sirloin of beef from the local butchers, even though he warned her to make the most of it because it could be the last. And her life improved even further when Edith wrote to say that she and the girls would love to come and to ask if they could stay for the holiday, and Dora wrote that she and David would be all on their own because John couldn't get back, so they would love to come too.

'We shall have a house full,' Emmeline said.

'Just as well we've got all those bedrooms,' Octavia said.

'We can use Janet's too, of course,' Emmeline said, happily making plans. 'She's going back to Gateshead for Christmas. She asked me this morning if it would be all right.'

So the beds were made up, a cake was baked and iced and a pudding was steamed, presents were bought and wrapped, and a Christmas tree hung with baubles was set in the window so that they could be piled beneath it in the traditional way, and finally the dining room and the drawing room were draped about with paper chains so that, although Octavia's map still dominated the main wall, by dint of framing it with tinsel it was reduced to just another decoration.

'Now,' Emmeline said, surveying the room with great satisfaction, 'we're ready.'

Edith and her three little girls arrived surprisingly early on the first morning of the school holiday. They'd caught a bus to Guildford and come on by train from there. When they rang at the bell, Octavia and Emmeline were still in their dressing gowns drinking tea by the fire.

'We've been on a toboggan,' Barbara told them, as she was ushered into the hall. 'It went a hundred and twenty miles an hour.'

'Fancy,' Emmeline said. 'Let's have you out of that coat and then you can come and sit by the fire. I expect you'd like some tea, wouldn't you? Or a cup of cocoa. What do you think, Edie?'

'I don't mind what we have,' Edie said, hanging up her coat and hat, 'just so long as it isn't old Mother Hemmings cag-mag. I've had that woman up to here. You'd never believe how bossy she is.'

Emmeline grimaced. 'Oh dear.'

'You know how Joanie likes her little bottle to settle her at night,' Edith said, peeling the baby out of her woolly coat. 'We've had ructions about that from the first night. She's on and on at me the whole time. How I'm spoiling her and I'll deform her mouth and how I should make her grow up. It's more than flesh and blood can stand.'

'Well, you're here now,' Emmeline said, 'and she can have as many bottles as she likes, pretty dear. We've got a little cot for her in your room. And two little camp beds for Barbara and Maggie.'

'Which will be a darn sight more comfortable than what

they've been sleeping in at old Mother Hemmings,' Edie said. 'I tell you, Ma, if I have to stand much more of that woman, I shall put on my hat and coat and walk out.'

'I hope you won't go doing anything silly,' Emmeline warned. 'You don't want to end up back in London.'

Edie looked mutinous so Octavia moved to intervene. 'Come and sit by the fire and get warm,' she said, taking Maggie's hand, 'while your Gran makes that cocoa.'

It was a wise suggestion for the fire soothed them. And so did helping Gran prepare the lunch. By the time they'd had their first meal together, sitting round the table in a well-warmed dining room, Edith seemed to have forgotten her grievances.

She remembered them again when her sister arrived on Christmas Eve, but there was so much going on by then that there wasn't time to dwell on the behaviour of old Mother Hemmings. The cousins hadn't seen one another since they were evacuated and they all had tales to tell.

'We went on a toboggan,' Maggie said, 'and it went a hundred miles an hour. Geoff said.'

'That's nothing,' David told her. 'Me and Martin went skating. On a pond. An' if the ice had cracked we'd have fallen in and been drowned dead.'

'Just as well it didn't then,' Octavia said.

'But it might've,' David said. 'And we'd have been drowned dead.'

'Anyway,' Barbara said, determined not to be outdone, 'it wasn't a hundred miles an hour. It was a hundred and fifty. An' if we'd fallen off we'd have broken all our legs.'

'Who'd like a mince pie?' Octavia asked.

'Oh, it *is* good to be back together again,' Dora said.

\* \* \*

Despite the cold and the war, they had a happy family Christmas and ate well and sat around the fire afterwards to play all the old family games and tell one another all the old family stories. And although the adults were privately wondering where they would all be in a year's time, Edie kept quiet about old Mother Hemmings and nobody mentioned the future at all. What was to come would come and they would have to endure it as well as they could. For the moment, it was enough that they were enjoying themselves together.

# Chapter Eight

The war began in earnest on the 8th of April, to Emmeline's consternation. 'If this isn't bad timing, you tell me what is,' she said to Octavia, pushing that morning's *Daily Herald* across the kitchen table towards her. 'That wretched man's invaded Denmark. Just look at it. And just when Edie's gone back to London.'

Octavia put down her tea cup and glanced at the headlines. She was due to meet the Chairman of Governors at half past eight to inspect the house they'd finally decided to rent for the school and she was running late. There wasn't time to read the paper. Not that it mattered. The news was what everyone was expecting. It was alarming and unwelcome but it wasn't a surprise.

'Wouldn't you just know it,' Emmeline mourned. 'Just when my Edie's taken those poor little children back to London. I knew it was stupid. I did warn her.'

'I know,' Octavia said, putting on her hat. She was torn by her cousin's anguished expression but she couldn't stay and let her talk. She couldn't even say a few commiserating words or they'd be stuck in the kitchen for hours.

'I told her over and over again.'

'I know.'

'They never listen.'

'I'll be back as soon as I can this afternoon,' Octavia said, 'and then we'll see what we can do. I daren't stop now, Em. I'm late already.'

Emmeline sighed heavily. 'This damned war,' she said. 'I did so hope it wouldn't start.'

There wasn't the faintest chance of that, Octavia thought, as she took her bicycle out of the garage. Never has been. Not once we allowed Hitler to invade Czechoslovakia and Poland. We should have stood up to him then, instead of kowtowing to him all the time. It's a bit late now. And she went pedalling off towards Horsell Rise and the steep incline of Kettlewell Hill. I hope to God our Mr Chivers has found us something suitable, she thought, as she pushed uphill. We're going to need a good roomy house more than ever now. If they bomb London it'll have to be school and home rolled into one.

Mr Chivers, the Chairman of Governors, was a quiet, unassuming man in his early fifties, not much more than five foot six in height, with a round pale face, round pale eyes, rather sparse grey hair which he kept tidy with Brylcreem and a tendency to stoutness that gave him a rather barrel-like appearance, especially from a distance. He was waiting by the gate of a large house on the corner of Grange Road, gazing out over Horsell Common, and from the patience of his stance it looked as though he'd been waiting a long time.

'I'm so sorry I'm late, Ralph,' Octavia said as she cycled towards him.

'Not to worry, dear lady,' Mr Chivers said. 'You're here now. This is Downview. Shall we proceed?'

They proceeded into the front garden and stood looking up at the house. It's a sizeable place, Octavia thought, Victorian of course and built to last. The three windows on the first floor were flanked by white shutters, which was a pretty touch, and there was a Venetian window in the slight bay between them which probably marked the turn of the stairs. Downstairs there was a wide bay window to the left and a line of lesser windows to the right and beyond them an extension that was almost as wide as the original house and looked as though it had been added later.

'Is the front door at the side?' she asked.

It was and although it had an elegant porch it stood rather incongruously between two very tall brick chimneys, both of which were embellished with a coat of arms and one of which was marked by the date of its construction – 1888.

'It's the same age as I am,' Octavia told her old friend.

'A good omen, perhaps,' he said, producing a key from his pocket. 'Shall we go in?'

There was something about the eccentricity of the place that appealed to Octavia's sense of adventure. She propped her bicycle against the nearest chimney and Mr Chivers opened the door and they went in, he standing courteously aside to let her enter first.

A grand tiled hall, as she expected, with a grand oak staircase, expensively easy tread, nicely rounded newel posts, the Venetian window at the turn. A space designed to impress the visitor. Leading out of it a series of sizeable rooms, all of them big enough to withstand a class and to house the subject libraries they needed. The drawing room was splendid, capacious enough to serve as a school hall cum dining room cum study area. What a relief that would be for her beleaguered fifths and sixths.

'How big is the kitchen?' she asked, and followed as he led the way. Very big indeed with a separate scullery where the washing-up would be done and lots of storage space for all the china and cutlery they would need. 'We could have our school dinners here and get back to eating at house tables,' she said. 'The present arrangement isn't satisfactory at all. The seniors have been asking what can be done about it for weeks.'

Mr Chivers was beaming, his bland face lit by the pleasure of having found such a suitable place. 'And you still haven't seen upstairs,' he said.

They inspected the house from the capacious cellars to the third floor attics, which were long and narrow with windows in the eaves or, rather oddly, at floor level, but might serve as dormitories with a little rearrangement. There were a lot of girls who weren't happy in their billets and changes took time to arrange. I must give it thought, Octavia decided, as Mr Chivers unlocked the french windows in the drawing room. Then she walked out into the garden.

It was as big as a city park and had been laid out in a similar way, with wide herbaceous borders and a long avenue of yew trees which ran across the lawn from the house to a kitchen garden, where there was a tangle of raspberry canes and a neglected strawberry patch. Round the side of the house, there was actually a tennis court. Octavia stood in the pale sunlight and rubbed her hands with the satisfaction of it all. She could see her girls in this house already, eating their dinner in that fine big room, strolling between the yew trees arm in arm the way they did, playing tennis in the summer and netball in the winter.

'I gather you approve,' Mr Chivers said.

'I do indeed,' Octavia told him. 'This place could make all the difference.'

Mr Chivers beamed like sunshine. 'There is more to come, dear lady,' he said. 'This is just the half of what I have to show you. If you care to leave your bicycle here I will take you to the second half in my car. It isn't far.'

The second half was another house and it was almost as big as the first one. It was called Barricane House and looked like something out of a Gothic novel, its three high bays covered in ivy from the ground to the gables and a general air of unloved gloominess about it that was rather off-putting. But the rooms were an excellent size. There were eleven of them on the two floors and nine of them were quite big enough for classrooms, the bathroom could be converted into a row of toilets and washbasins, the kitchen would make a cookery room, and the drawing room had the right light for an art room. In fact it didn't take much imagination to see that if it was cleaned, painted and furnished, this house would make a very good Lower School and give the juniors a base where they could meet one another every day.

'Yes,' Octavia said, 'I don't know how you've managed it but you've provided us with almost exactly what we needed. With these two buildings and the occasional use of the science labs in the Woking school and the swimming pool in the town during the summer, we shall do very well.'

This time his beam was melon-shaped. 'I am glad to be of service,' he said.

That afternoon Octavia held an impromptu staff meeting at Ridgeway to tell her colleagues the good news and show them the plans of the two houses. They were delighted to hear that they were going to have adequate space for their teaching at last and they all asked the same question. 'When will they be ready?'

'As soon as Mr Chivers can get the conversions done,' Octavia told them. 'Possibly a few weeks, possibly a month or so. But we will certainly be in occupation by September.'

Mavis Brown was looking uncertain, as she so often did these days, her wide forehead wrinkled and her blue eyes troubled. 'The war could be over by then,' she said. 'I mean, if Hitler gets what he wants he'll stop, surely. I mean, he's always said he doesn't want to fight us.'

'Saying's one thing,' Morag told her, 'doing's quite another. We can't second guess *what* that man will do. I don't think anybody can.'

'I can't see why he wants Denmark,' Phillida Bertram said. 'I mean it's not as if they've got anything special.'

'It's a stepping stone to Norway and the port of Norvik where they ship the Swedish iron ore.' Octavia told her. 'That's what he wants. Iron for his guns.'

'And after that, if I'm any judge, he'll want Belgium and Holland,' Elizabeth Fennimore said, 'and then France and all her wine and wheat. He's building an empire, Mavis, and he'll fight anyone who gets in the way.'

Time to intervene, Octavia thought. Mavis was looking terrified and there was nothing to be served by frightening the girl out of her wits. 'However,' she said, 'for the moment our task is to plan how we're going to make the best use of our two new buildings. We must draw up a timetable and work out which would be the best site for our individual subject rooms. It's going to take a lot of work, especially for you, Joan. You'll be teaching on four different sites.'

Joan Marshall grinned, like the stalwart she was. Nothing ever seemed to throw her. 'Well, thanks a lot,' she said.

'I could help you if you'd like,' Mavis offered. 'I mean I could take some swimming lessons and netball. If you'd like. If Miss Smith… If I haven't got any History or Geography lessons then, of course.'

'We will bear that in mind,' Octavia said, 'won't we, Joan?'

\* \* \*

During the next four days the staff set about planning the new timetable, while the news from Europe grew more and more worrying. The Danes capitulated to the German army after a mere twenty-four hours, which was a shock to everybody, and the very next day Hitler gave the order to invade Norway. The landing took place at Norvik, before dawn and in a snowstorm, and despite the difficulties, two thousand troops all specially trained in mountain warfare were got ashore. The next day, British warships sailed into the fjord and attacked the German fleet and three days later, while the Germans were still recovering, British troops landed in Norvik and the German troops took to the hills. To the watchers in Great Britain, the second German war was now inescapably under way.

'At least it's not happening here,' Emmeline said, when she and Janet and Octavia sat down to dinner that night. 'That's not much consolation to the Norwegians I know, but they do seem to be holding their own.'

'Have you heard from Edie?' Octavia asked, helping herself to vegetables.

'She rang this morning, not that it did any good. She's so pig-headed, Tavy. I told her she ought to come back here where it's safe. But no. She wouldn't hear of it. She says she's going to stay where she is, if you ever heard of anything so silly. She says they're better off in their own home.'

'Which from her point of view is probably true at the moment,' Octavia said. 'She hated sharing a kitchen, you know. That was the problem.'

'And what will she do if they start bombing?' Emmeline said. 'She'll have to be evacuated all over again and she'll have to share another kitchen then. There's no sense in her.'

\* \* \*

In fact there was more sense in Edith Ames than her mother suspected. She and her remaining next-door neighbours had been discussing the best thing to do if the bombing started and she'd made up her mind that she would move all the junk out of the cupboard under Mrs Holdsworthy's stairs and make a shelter there. It would be a bit of a squeeze but it would be better than nothing. The air-aid warden had been round and taken a look at it and he thought it was the best thing. Mrs Holdsworthy said she was going to use the underground at South Wimbledon.

'Safest place,' she told Edie. 'Right underground. I mean, stands to reason. My Geoff says if they start their bombing I got ter go straight down the station and see what's what.'

They were surprising themselves by how matter-of-fact they were being, especially as they had no idea what was going to happen next, or when it would happen. Things were moving quickly now that Hitler had started his attacks. They hardly had time to take in one invasion before there was another one. But at least the Norwegians hadn't thrown in the towel like the Danes. They seemed to be putting up quite a fight.

'And that's something,' Ethel said. 'Though, course, they got our lads there with 'em an' that's bound to make a difference.'

Edie knew all about that. She'd been watching the papers anxiously in case Arthur got sent there and was very glad when she had a letter from him saying he was still 'kicking his heels' in France. You stay there, my lad, she thought, as she put the letter back into its envelope. I don't want you getting yourself killed.

All through that April while the builders worked on Octavia's two school houses and Emmeline fretted over her grandchildren, and Edith kept a careful eye on the news, the struggle in Norway continued. There were days when Octavia found herself sympathising with Mavis Brown and wondering why they were spending all that money and effort on converting these two houses when the Germans might invade. But it was being done notwithstanding and it was being done speedily.

'With luck,' she told her staff at the end of April, 'we shall be moving into Downview at the beginning of May.'

'Do we have a date?' Morag asked.

'According to Mr Chivers, Friday the 10th of May,' Octavia told them. 'It's a sensible choice. It will give us the weekend to settle in and then we can start teaching there on Monday. We'll let the juniors have a day off and ask the seniors to help us, as I'm sure they will. We can transfer the subject libraries from Woking school on Saturday, as that's one of our days. I'll order a couple of vans and if the weather holds we can have a picnic in the garden. It should be quite a red-letter day.'

Although she didn't know it then, it wasn't just a red-letter day for the school but an historic one too. It was the day Hitler poured his storm troopers into Holland and Belgium. Not that any of them knew it while they were transferring their books and taking possession of their spotless classrooms. It was a perfect summer's day and such a joy to be in a building that was theirs and theirs alone, that they simply gave themselves over to the pleasures of occupation. They had a picnic lunch out on the lawn, and afterwards the girls returned to the classrooms with the teachers they were helping and set up the desks and chairs. Then, because it was still light, they were allowed to explore the building.

Lizzie and Poppy were thrilled with it, especially when they found that there were dormitories in the attics.

'Who's going to stay here?' Poppy wondered.

'Me for a start,' Lizzie said. 'I've always wanted to go to a boarding school only Pa wouldn't have it. Oh I say! Look in here, Poppy. They've got a little window seat. I tell you what, I'd love to live in this room. We could sit in the seat and play cards or read or anything we liked. It would be our own world. Let's ask, shall we?'

'Who?' Polly asked

'I've no idea,' Lizzie admitted, sitting in the window. 'We'll find out on Monday.'

But by Monday the world had changed and when Smithie took her first crowded assembly in their freshly painted hall, her mood was sombre.

'The next few weeks will be difficult for all of us,' she said, 'and particularly for those who have fathers or other relatives in any of the armed services. We must help one another in any way we can. Miss Brown will put maps of Belgium and Holland and Norway on the wall in this hall and we will keep you all up to date on everything that is happening. If there is anything that is worrying you, speak to your house officer or your form mistress, or to me. Don't worry on alone.

'Now, we will say special prayers for the civilians and servicemen who are caught up in this new invasion. Then we will sing 'Lord behold us with your blessing' because whatever is happening in Europe, we are making a new beginning in this house and that is what we sing when we are making a new beginning.'

'It's bad, isn't it, Lizzie?' Poppy said, as they filed out of the hall.

'Looks like it,' Lizzie admitted. 'Not to worry though. I'll phone Pa and see what he says.'

It was the most disappointing call she'd ever made. For a

start he wouldn't tell her anything about the war, although she asked him three times, and then he said he was afraid he wouldn't be able to get down to see her on Sunday and that upset her, because he hadn't come the previous Sunday either.

'Sorry about that, little one,' he said, 'but there's a lot of work to do. We'll come down and see you as soon as we can. I promise.'

'This war is getting in the way of my life,' Lizzie complained to her friend. 'If my own father won't tell me what's going on I despair!'

'At least you can phone him up and talk to him,' Poppy said. 'Which is more than I can. My dad's in France somewhere and he only ever writes to Mum. You should count yourself lucky.'

Lizzie was chastened. Having a father in France was no joke. Hadn't they been saying prayers for the people in France and Holland and Belgium that very morning? 'I'm sorry about that, Poppy,' she said. 'I was being selfish. I wasn't thinking. It's just I want to *know*.'

'You can always read the newspapers,' Poppy said.

'They don't tell you the half of it,' Lizzie sighed. 'You can read everything they've got to say in ten minutes.' Which was true enough, for newspapers were restricted to four pages now so as to economise with newsprint and, as they usually put in a few pictures, it didn't leave much room for text. 'I'm sick of trying to glean things.'

'What else can we do?' Poppy asked.

'If we lived at Downview,' Lizzie said, 'we could get a wireless and listen to that.'

But for the moment picking up snippets was the only method of gathering information that they had and the snippets were decidedly unsatisfactory. The first one Lizzie found made her really cross.

'Look at that,' she said to Poppy, pointing at the offending article. 'The Germans say they've invaded Holland and Belgium *to protect their neutrality.* Did you ever hear such wicked nonsense? They're such liars! I'll send my army into your country and make you all do as I say and then you'll all be neutral. Neutral, my Aunt Fanny! They won't dare to speak. That's what'll happen. Especially if they're Jewish, and there are lots of Jews in Amsterdam. Pa told me.'

The news next day was better. There had been a twenty-four-hour debate in the House of Commons and at the end of it, Mr Chamberlain had lost the vote and resigned. 'Good job too!' Lizzie said. Now Mr Churchill was going to take over.

'Will he be better?' Poppy asked. 'I mean, will he know what to do?' Politics was really baffling sometimes.

'Let's hope so,' Lizzie said. 'At least he's a fighter. He fought in the Great War. Pa told me. And he's been on and on for ages about rearming.'

That first week in Downview was like something out of a previous life. It was so good to be there with all their friends around them, eating dinner in house groups again, talking to their first-formers, having lessons in their own classrooms and studying in a hall, instead of trying to write essays in their cramped bedroom or wandering round the town looking for somewhere quiet where they could read in peace. That in itself was a daily pleasure. And yet the papers were full of battles and surrenders and retreats.

By the weekend they were reporting that the Dutch had asked for an armistice and that Queen Wilhelmina had left The Hague and taken ship to London with her family and the Dutch gold reserves. And nine days later the Belgian army surrendered and the German army invaded France.

The maps in their new school hall were informative but very alarming, with arrows marking the points at which the Germans had invaded and charting the speed of their advance. Every day brought changes and every change was for the worse. As her father still wasn't telling her anything, Lizzie made it her business to check the maps every morning, concentrating hard, her face anxious, with Poppy standing quietly beside her looking equally worried. From the way the arrows were extending, it looked as though the British Expeditionary Force were retreating towards the English Channel and the Germans were encircling them.

'It looks awful, Lizzie,' Poppy said. 'I mean, it's worse than it was yesterday. Why aren't they heading for a port? I mean, that's where they should be going and then we could send troop ships and get them home. If they end up on a beach somewhere, they'll all be captured, won't they?'

'The nearest ports are Calais and Ostend,' Lizzie told her. 'If we lose them, they *will* be on the beaches.'

'And what will happen to them then?'

'God knows!' Lizzie said.

# Chapter Nine

Those last days of May were acutely painful to Octavia Smith. It was an agony to think that the British army was being defeated, worse to know that they were going to be caught in the noose the Germans were so obviously pulling tighter and tighter around them, worst of all to have to face the fact that most of them were going to be captured. She was full of passionate energy, which was how she always reacted in a crisis, wanting to do something to change things or at least to make them better, and knowing only too well that it was beyond her power to do anything at all. She missed the good sense of her father and the comfort of her own house; she ached for all her pupils who had fathers in France; she grieved for poor Edie who hadn't heard a word from Arthur since the fighting began and was now so tense with anxiety that she squabbled with poor Emmeline every time she phoned; and she was torn to anguish by the beauty of the apple blossom.

When she'd first moved into the house in Ridgeway, the trees had been heavy with fruit, and when Emmeline had finally joined her, they and Janet had set to work to harvest the crop. She'd thought what fine trees they were and how lovely they would look in the spring. Now she stood in the garden in the clear light of a May morning and wept because the delicate pink and white blossoms were so fragile and young and vulnerable and soon to fall. 'Dear God,' she prayed, 'save our soldiers. They're fighting a war that is none of their making and they don't deserve to die in a trap.'

Knowing that nothing could be done to save them dragged her down in the long days of waiting. She kept up her spirits at school for the sake of the girls and the staff but by evening she was drawn with fatigue, and when the phone rang, she answered it dully, merely repeating her number.

'Tavy, my dear,' Tommy's voice said. 'I've got some news for you. Keep it under your hat until it breaks because it's all hush-hush at the moment.'

There was so much excitement in his voice her heart leapt. 'Of course,' she said. 'That goes without saying. What is it?'

'There's a plan afoot for getting the army off the beaches,' he told her. 'Totally foolhardy but it just might come off. They're mobilising all the little boats they can find, mostly in the south-east, but they're searching further afield as I speak: pleasure boats, fishing boats, anything that can sail across the Channel and pick up a few men. Troop ships can't get ashore, you see, not on an open beach, but *they* could, and even if they only manage to take off a few, that's better than none at all. There should be quite a flotilla, if it all goes according to plan.'

It was imaginative, daring, a last hope, but a very bold one. It lifted her spirits simply to hear about it. 'Thank God!' she said. 'When are they going?'

'Tomorrow.'

Alvar Liddell, the BBC newsreader, broke the news the next afternoon, in his usual calm and measured way. 'A fleet of small ships especially mobilised for the purpose has been evacuating troops from the beaches at Dunkirk throughout the day. Several thousand men are already on their way back across the Channel and the evacuation is planned to continue. The men are reported to be in good spirits.'

The next morning, *The Times* was more forthcoming. 'British troops,' it said, 'are fighting a desperate rearguard action on the French coast around Dunkirk as German troops finally move in and surround them. The first men of the B.E.F. to be picked off the beaches arrived home yesterday. They told how they had been bombed and machine-gunned as they waded out to the ships. One private described how he had walked over thirty miles to the beaches with a bullet in his foot, another reported that the British artillery had put up a mile long barrage on one sector in an effort to stop the German advance. The Germans had advanced right into it and must have taken tremendous casualties. Despite everything, seven thousand men have been rescued in the first day alone and the evacuation is continuing.'

'Well it's not much,' Emmeline said, 'but it's a start.' The phone was ringing into her thoughts, alerting her to the possibility of more news. She eased herself to her feet. 'That could be Edie,' she said.

It was Dora, and she was in a state of high excitement. 'Isn't it wonderful, Ma,' she said. 'My John's been posted to Dover. I had a letter this morning. He says it's the best thing he's ever seen. Ever so big and hardly planned at all. They just gave the skippers fuel and charts and let them get on with it. Imagine that! It's his job to refuel them as they come in. They've been coming in and out all day long, he said, and there are still new ones arriving. Isn't it just the most wonderful thing?'

'Have you heard from Edie?' Emmeline asked.

'I went to see her yesterday. They're all right. No news of Arthur yet but, like I said to her, you wouldn't expect it, not

133

yet awhile. I mean there's a lot of men to rescue.'

'Ring me as soon as you know anything,' Emmeline said.

''Course,' Dora said. 'Chin up!'

The first troop train pulled in at Woking station later that morning, full of exhausted soldiers on their way to London. News of its arrival spread through the town like the ringing of bells. People went down to the station at once, some with urns to make tea, some with packets of postcards so that the men could write home, some simply to stand in the Broadway and cheer. Poppy and Lizzie went down with the rest, for as Poppy said, 'I might see my dad. You never know.' In fact there were so many people there it was hard to see who they all were, but the two girls handed out postcards and gathered up the completed ones and felt they were being useful. They were shocked by how dirty and exhausted the soldiers were and much impressed by how brave they'd been and, although they were late back for their next study period, nobody rebuked them. 'You've been on war work,' Miss Gordon said.

By the time the third train arrived, everybody was organised. The WVS were there to hand out tea, sandwiches and cigarettes, there were hundreds of postcards stacked in cardboard boxes, ready and stamped, and several senior girls, including Lizzie, Poppy and Mary, had been commandeered to act as interpreters for the French troops. It was, as the three girls told one another at the end of the day, a humbling experience.

The days passed, more trains arrived at their station, somebody calculated that they were handing out four hundred postcards every day, and as people all over England held their breath, the numbers taken off the beaches continued to rise. The newspapers and the BBC bulletins kept a daily tally –

ten thousand, a hundred thousand, a quarter of a million, and hopes and hearts rose with the figures. But there was still no news of Arthur, and Emmeline was irritable with anxiety, especially when the weather was bad.

'If we're going to get our boys off those damned beaches,' she said, 'we need sunshine and a calm sea, not all this wind. They're such little boats, Tavy, they're not built to withstand storms.'

'They're not built to withstand dive bombers, either,' Octavia pointed out, 'but they're doing an amazing job just the same.' What was happening on that French beach was beginning to look like a miracle. The total number of men who had been rescued was reported to be over three hundred thousand, and laden trains were still passing through Woking station where most of her senior girls were waiting to help them and interpret for them. It surprised her that the German army seemed to be holding off. The Luftwaffe went on strafing the beaches and bombing the ships, despite the most valiant efforts by the RAF, but the Panzer divisions had come to a halt. And thank God for that, whatever the reason.

'A few more days,' she said, 'that's all we need.'

By now messages were beginning to filter through to the many waiting relatives. Poppy's father had been taken back to England on the third day and had sent postcards to his wife and daughter as soon as he landed. Poppy wept with relief when hers arrived. She simply couldn't help it. After seeing all those weary, blood-stained soldiers in the trains and knowing what horrors they must have gone through, it was miraculous to think that he'd got home safely.

'He isn't injured or *anything*,' she said to Lizzie.

Lizzie hugged her and said she was so, so glad but secretly, and like the realist she was, she was beginning to wonder what would happen next. Once the British Expeditionary Force have pulled out, she thought, there'll be nothing to stop the Germans conquering the whole of France, the way they've conquered Holland and Belgium. And then what will happen? They could invade us too and we wouldn't be able to stop them.

'I'm glad I'm not in the fifth form,' she said, 'taking their exams with all this going on. At least we can skip lessons if we like and go down to the station to help, but they're stuck.'

In fact, the last day of the great sea rescue was June the 4th, which was the second day of the General School Certificate examinations. By the end of the day a total of 338,226 men had been taken off the beaches. There were more still waiting to be rescued but by evening the operation had to stop because the German troops had captured the town.

'What will happen to the men they've left behind?' Poppy wondered.

'They'll be taken prisoner,' Lizzie told her, still reading her newspaper. 'It says here there's a casualty station for the wounded still on the beach. The doctors drew lots to see which of them would stay behind and man it. Now, I call that really brave.'

'So do I,' Poppy said. 'When you think what it must be like. Oh, I'm so glad my dad's home and out of it.'

For a few days, the euphoria of the rescue carried them all along. Then Emmeline had two phone calls that brought her down to earth with a jolt. The first was from Johnnie, although he was talking in such an odd way that it took her a little while to realise who it was.

'Is that you, Mater?' his voice said.

The name made her cringe. He never called her Mater.

Ever. It was always Ma, never Mater. There was something the matter. She knew it at once and her stomach tensed with the dread of what was to come. 'Johnnie?' she said. 'Is that you?'

'Me as ever is,' he said, but his voice was too light, too casual, almost as if he was playing a part. 'Thought you'd like to know I've been in action.'

She suddenly found it hard to breathe. 'Action?' she said.

'Flown my first sorties, old thing,' he said, as casually as if he were talking about a trip in a balloon. 'Over Dunkirk. Shot down my first Stuka. Absolutely wizard.'

She didn't know whether to praise or commiserate. 'Oh Johnnie!'

'Knew you'd be pleased. Bunty bought it, though. That was a poor show.'

Bought what? she wondered, but didn't like to ask.

'Blighter came out the clouds. He didn't stand a chance.'

'Oh, Johnnie!' she said again. The conversation was making her feel quite ill. He was telling her about somebody being killed, not somebody buying something. How could he be talking like this, in this silly flippant way? It was hideous.

'That's war for you,' he said. 'Still, we're putting on a damned good show. I'll say that for us. Are you getting on all right?'

She told him she was. How could she say anything else? She could hardly tell him about her problems when he'd been talking about his friend being killed.

'Good-oh!' he said. 'Must dash.' And hung up.

'It was horrible,' she said to Octavia that evening. 'Like talking to a stranger.'

'I think this is something that happens when the fighting starts,' Octavia said, trying to comfort her. 'They learn a new way of talking to cover what they're feeling. Think how Algie wrote to us from the trenches. *I am in the pink. I am ticketty-boo. Please send more jam.'*

'You could be right,' Emmeline said, 'but I wish my Johnnie wouldn't do it.'

'I don't think he's got any option,' Octavia told her. 'It's probably the way they all talk. A sort of emotional camouflage. It must be pretty terrifying, if you think about it, fighting in the air, knowing they'll be shot down and killed if they make one false move. It's no good making that face, Em. None of us wants to think about it but it's a fact, whether we do or not. You can't blame them for finding ways to play their feelings down. I think it's admirable. And brave.'

But Emmeline's expression made it clear that she didn't want to think about it at all. 'I hate war,' she said. 'Changing my Johnnie. As if I haven't got enough to do with all this worry over Arthur.'

'Edie hasn't phoned then?'

'No, poor girl. And she's worried sick.'

'She'll hear soon,' Octavia comforted. 'It's bound to take time, given the number of men involved.'

In fact, she rang the very next morning, just as Octavia was leaving for work, and she was hysterical.

'He's been taken prisoner,' she wept. 'I've just had the letter. Some awful place I can't even pronounce, and God knows where it is or how he is and it's all my fault.'

'Oh, come on, Edie, be sensible,' Emmeline said, trying to reason with her. 'You can't help the war.' And she mouthed the news to Octavia who was standing beside her. 'He's been taken prisoner.'

Edie was wailing. 'You don't know the half of it, Ma. I knew this would happen. I've known it all along. I should have stopped him before he started. Only we just sort of… I mean, we were…' Her voice was so thick with tears and distress it was quite hard to understand her. 'Oh, my poor Arthur. It's all my fault, Ma. It is. All my silly fault. I should never have agreed to it. Only we were in such a pickle. I mean…' She blew her nose and wept and snuffled, while her mother struggled to think of something to say to comfort her. Then the explanation came out with a rush of tumbling words. 'If I hadn't fallen with our Joan he'd never have gone into the army in the first place. I knew it was a mistake, I've known it all along, but we didn't have any option, not if we were to stay in the flat and not with a baby coming, and now he's in a prisoner a' war camp and I shan't see him for years and years and it's all my fault. All my own stupid, stupid fault. I can't bear it.'

Emmeline tried to be practical. 'Is he hurt?' she asked.

But that brought another outburst. 'How should I know?' Edie cried. 'They don't tell you anything. Only where he is. They send you these horrible letters and they don't tell you anything. Just a prisoner a' war camp. I shan't see him again for years and years. I know it, and it's all my fault. Oh Ma, I can't bear it.'

Emmeline could hear a child crying in the background. One of the girls, of course. Poor little thing. 'I'll come back,' she decided. 'Go and give your girls a cuddle and try not to worry. I'll be there on the next train. Maybe it's not as bad as you think.'

'How can you say such a thing? It is! It is!'

'Put the letter on the mantelpiece,' Emmeline said, in her firmest voice, 'and we'll look at it together. Two heads are better than one.'

'I'll drop you off at the station,' Octavia offered, as her cousin reached for her hat and coat. 'We'll just let Janet know what we're about.'

'I'll take what's left of the fruit cake, if that's all right,' Emmeline said. 'I'll bet she hasn't thought to give those children their breakfast.'

Edith was standing by the window in the front bedroom when her mother arrived. She'd been prowling the flat ever since she put the phone down, fidgeting and worrying, picking things up and putting them down, unable to settle to anything. The sight of her mother's comfortable, comforting figure taking the last few waddling steps up her pathway triggered another outburst of passionate weeping. But then Emmeline was through the door and in the flat and she had her arms round her daughter and was patting her back and stroking her hair out of her eyes the way she'd done when she'd been upset as a child, and everything eased. They walked into the kitchen arm in arm. The three little girls were sitting round the kitchen table, subdued and anxious.

'Let's get that kettle on, shall we?' Emmeline said, smiling at them. 'I don't know about you three but I could go for a cup of tea. I'm parched. Now,' pulling the cake tin out of her bag, 'I brought a little bit of fruit cake because I thought you might like it. Could you fancy a slice?'

The kettle steamed and whistled, the cake was put on one of Edie's best plates in the middle of the table and generous slices cut for both adults and all three children. Joan's bib was found and tied around her neck, as she was told what a good little girl she was. And as the familiar patterns were reasserted, the day shifted and became normal.

They were drinking their tea and eating every last crumb of cake and Emmeline was carefully reading Edie's official letter when there was a ring at the door.

'Don't worry, Mum,' Barbara said, licking the last of the

crumbs from her fingers. 'I'll go.'

It was Dora, looking determined. 'Now what's all this?' she said to Edie. 'I couldn't make head nor tail of what you were on about on the phone. Is he injured?'

Emmeline handed her the letter. 'No, nothing like that,' she said. 'Your sister was a bit upset. That's all. Bit of a shock.'

Dora read the letter quickly. 'Ah!' she said. 'Yes. Well. I can see why you were upset, expecting him home and everything. But look on the bright side. At least he's out of danger. It must be horrible to think of him being locked up. I'm sure it is. I'll grant you that. And I don't suppose it'll be much fun for him. But at least you won't have to worry about him being injured or killed or anything. You'll get a letter from him soon, you see if I'm not right, and he'll tell you he's not hurt and he's all right and you're to keep your chin up.'

Edie was calm enough now to accept that all this was probably true. He would write. Of course he would. And even if he had been injured, they'd look after him, surely. They might be Germans but they weren't barbarians.

''Course not,' Dora said, in her pragmatic way. 'He'll be fine, you'll see.' She folded the letter, handed it back to her sister and turned to easier and more immediate matters. 'Is there any tea in that pot?' she said. 'I see you've scoffed all the cake.'

Emmeline stayed in Colliers Wood until Arthur's letter arrived. It was as sensible as Dora had predicted. He'd been taken prisoner with *the rest of chaps...being as we was surrounded,* and now they were all in the same hut, *or I could say the same boat.* He'd had what he called *a slight wound* but was better now and he signed off, *Keep your chin up. We shall soon be home.*

141

Edie cried when she'd read it but she wasn't as upset as Emmeline had feared she might be, so the worst of the shock seemed to have passed. There was no more hysteria, no more talk of everything being her fault, Maggie and Barbara were going to school as usual, the house was clean and tidy, they listened to ITMA in the evening and laughed at all the jokes.

'I think I shall get back this afternoon,' Emmeline said. 'You're all right now, aren't you?'

Edie was busy ironing. 'Yes,' she said. 'Better than I was anyway. I'm sorry I made such a fuss. It makes a difference getting letters, knowing he's safe.'

Which is more than you are, Emmeline thought, and she wondered whether she ought to say something about taking the children back to the country in case the Germans started bombing London. But on second thoughts she decided against it. The war seemed to have gone quiet again. The Navy was still rescuing troops from various beaches in parts of France that weren't occupied by the Germans but apart from that nothing much was happening. I'll speak to her later, she thought, when the time comes.

It came two days later with the news that the Germans had occupied Paris and that, led by their newly appointed Prime Minister, Petain, the French government had asked for an armistice.

'So that's it,' Octavia said at dinner that night. 'We're on our own.'

'God help us,' Emmeline sighed. 'What will happen to us now?'

'Doan't you worry, mum,' Janet said, jutting her chin. 'We woan't give in to them, no matter what.'

* * *

142

That was Mr Churchill's opinion too, as he told the House of Commons on the 18th of July. Britain stood alone but she would fight on, for years if necessary. 'Let us brace ourselves to our duty,' he said, 'and so bear ourselves that, if the British Commonwealth and Empire lasts a thousand years, men will still say, "This was their finest hour".'

# Chapter Ten

'Do you think they're really going to invade us, Lizzie?' Mary O'Connor asked, her plump face wrinkled with anxiety. 'My mum does. She says they'll be here any day. Bound to be, she reckons. I mean, they're only just over the Channel, aren't they. It's not far. She's laying in stocks of food, tins and that, just in case.'

'So's my mum,' Poppy Turner said, stopping to shake a stone from her sandal. 'She says there's nothing to stop them.'

The three girls were walking along the tow path, heading back to Downview. It was a bright, sun-warmed, peaceful day, the summer term was nearly over and they had the afternoon and the canal to themselves. Two swans sailed their easy magnificence along the olive water, a flock of finches flew like green darts from a nearby tree and swung in a graceful arc towards the bushes, a sandy-coloured mongrel trotted happily towards them wagging his tail and looking hopeful. It didn't seem possible that they could be invaded.

Mary repeated her question, hanging on to Lizzie's arm. 'D'you think they'll invade us, Lizzie?'

I must stop this, Lizzie thought. She's getting in a state. 'Not according to Pa,' she said. She wasn't really sure she believed what he'd told her but she passed it on anyway. 'He says there are three things in Hitler's way, two he can fight but he won't beat, and one he can't do anything about.'

'Like what?' Mary said. 'I can't see anything to stop him at all.'

'Three things,' Lizzie said firmly, and she counted them off on her fingers. 'First, there's the army we took off the beaches, and that's a lot of men and they're all experienced – well you know that, you saw them – then there's the RAF, and they've got the best planes in the air and the best pilots. I've got two brothers in the RAF now. You ask them. They'll tell you. And the third is the English Channel. Napoleon couldn't beat the English Channel and neither could the Spanish Armada, although Drake did have something to do with it too, I'll allow that, Poppy. You don't have to make that face. Anyway, whatever the reasons, they couldn't invade us and they got beaten and that was what mattered. And when it comes down to it, Hitler won't be able to either.' When she'd started her explanation she'd had little faith in it, now she was convinced of its probability,

'But you can't be sure, can you?' Mary said. 'I mean, anything could happen really, couldn't it?'

'Yes,' Lizzie allowed, 'it could, but I don't think it will, and neither does Pa and neither do my brothers. Anyway, there's no point crossing bridges till you come to them. We could drive ourselves silly doing that.' And she changed the subject. 'Now then, what are we going to do about getting a room in Downview?'

Poppy followed her lead. 'Do you think we can?' she said. 'I mean, it's for the little'uns really, isn't it?'

'Quite right,' Lizzie said, 'but they're going to need a few seniors to look after them, especially in September. You can't have hordes of first-formers charging about all over the place not knowing how to behave. They'll have to have someone to show them how to go on. That's obvious. So why not us? We'd be ideal. We could live in the room with the window seat.'

'You and that window seat,' Poppy said.

'Well, why not?' Lizzie said. 'I think we ought to go and see old Smithie and offer our services.'

'What, now?' Poppy asked.

'Why not?' Lizzie said. 'No time like the present.'

'You're so artful, Lizzie,' Poppy said. 'This is why we're going to Downview, isn't it? You've had this planned all along.'

Mary was looking worried. 'Didn't we ought to wait till she asks us?' she said.

'No, we didn't,' Lizzie said, trenchantly, if not particularly grammatically. 'If we wait to be asked someone else will get in before us and I'm not having that. Come on.'

Octavia had been in her office at Downview all afternoon, as Lizzie knew because she'd asked Miss Gordon. She and Maggie Henry had just finished making up the class lists for next year's first form, when the three girls arrived at her door. She was intrigued to receive their delegation but, true to her established custom, she didn't show it. She was well used to visits from her pupils now and took them all seriously no matter what they might be about. 'Let's go into the garden,' she said. 'It's lovely out there today.' And she led them past the quiet study in the hall and out of the french windows.

They walked towards the kitchen gardens in the strong sunshine. 'So how can I help you?' she said.

'Well…' Lizzie said. 'We were wondering if you needed any house officers to help look after the first-formers. The ones you've got living here, I mean. Miss Gordon says there are quite a lot of them.'

146

'Are you not happy in your billets?' Octavia asked.

How perceptive she is, Lizzie thought admiringly. Straight to the point. 'No, no,' she said. 'It's nothing like that. I mean they're very good to us.' Then she caught sight of the wry expression on Poppy's face and added, 'I think they'd have preferred a couple of rather younger children. They'd been told to expect two from a nursery school, so we were a bit of a shock, weren't we, Poppy?'

'You could say that,' Poppy agreed.

'But you've settled in well?' Octavia said.

'So far,' Lizzie said. 'But...' and she let the word hang, while she thought out what she ought to say next. If Smithie could be persuaded that they weren't happy where they were, she might be more likely to offer them a room. On the other hand they couldn't really complain because there was nothing to complain about. 'The thing is,' she said at last, 'I'm not sure they like having evacuees who are old enough to be out at work.'

'Have they said so?'

'Not in as many words,' Lizzie admitted. 'But they talk about how they were out at work when they were our age, and how things have changed, and I get the feeling they don't really approve.' And she gave her headmistress her most innocent smile, the one that always melted her father, opening her grey eyes wide.

'Um,' Octavia said. 'So if I take your point, what you are saying is that you would like to move while relationships are still good, is that it? And what about you, Mary? Are you happy where you are?'

Mary's answer was a surprise. 'Not really,' she said.

'Why is that?'

'I have to do a lot of housework,' Mary told her. 'I don't

mind. I mean someone's got to do it. But Mum says it's more than I should, and it does get in the way of my homework.' It would be much nicer not to have to do it and this was just the right moment to try to get out of it. Besides, it would be safer to live in a house with Smithie if the Germans were going to invade them.

'How much housework do you have to do?' Octavia probed. Several of her girls were being overworked in their billets, as she'd already discovered.

'Well, I make all the beds and do the washing-up – and I wash the kitchen floor of a Friday and then there's the ironing. There's a lot of ironing.'

'Um,' Octavia said again, looking from one to the other. Lizzie was so like her father – those grey eyes were exactly the same and she'd got his style. She'd been impressively diplomatic, you might even say cunning! She smiled at her briefly, knowing she would give her what she was asking for. Not immediately, of course. It wouldn't be sensible or helpful to allow her to think that she could get anything she wanted simply by asking for it. 'I will talk this over with Miss Gordon,' she said, 'and let you know what we decide.'

Lizzie wasn't fooled by her politic reply. 'It's in the bag,' she said to her friends when Smithie was out of earshot.

'How can you possibly know?' Poppy said.

'You watch,' Lizzie said, tossing her blonde hair, 'and see if I'm not right.'

Octavia walked back to her office, with her hands in the pockets of her long cardigan, deep in thought. Her interview with Lizzie and the others had brought a problem into inescapable focus. The three girls were being self-serving, the way girls often were, she knew that, but there was altruism in their request too. They had a valid point when they said the first-formers would need looking after. And it wasn't just the first-formers. If the Germans bomb us, she thought, and I'm sure they will, there will be a lot of girls in distress and they'll need a haven of some kind where they can be cared for and comforted. Downview was the obvious place but if it was to be used in a different way it would need different staffing. There would have to be more cooks for a start and someone permanently in charge of it, like a matron in a boarding school.

She opened her study door and there was Maggie Henry, hard at work typing up the lists. But of course. Dependable Maggie Henry, who'd been with the school from the beginning and knew the girls so well and had such a way with them. I will hold a meeting, just with the staff, she decided, and test their opinion.


'Capital idea,' Morag Gordon said. 'I've been thinking along the same lines myself. The girls need a base and a matron there full time to look after them. Our Maggie would be just the ticket. If we appoint her now she can be settled in by September.'

Several of the others spoke in favour of it too. 'I think we need to be quick,' Alice Genevra said. 'It doesn't look as though we've got much time now. I mean, I don't want to sound defeatist but we've got to be sensible, haven't we? I think we ought to get it up and running as quickly as possible, given what's ahead of us.'

'I hear some of next years' fifth-formers are moving in too,' Joan Marshall said. 'Young Lizzie Meriton, isn't that right, Morag? And Mary O'Connor? She's a duffer at games, of course, but she'll be lovely with the little'uns.'

'But who will be your secretary?' Phillida Bertram asked. 'I mean, if Maggie agrees to be a matron she won't be able to help you very much, will she. I'm not saying she wouldn't be good at it. I'm sure she would. But she's always been our school secretary, hasn't she? We're always saying we couldn't get on without her.'

Octavia had thought of that already and had found a possible solution. 'I don't want to lose her as my secretary either,' she said. 'She's much too valuable. But if she likes the idea of being our matron and agrees to it, we could hire an office junior, and Maggie could train her to take over all the routine tasks and then I could limit Maggie's part of the job as school secretary to the decision-making and planning, which is the bit she enjoys and where her experience is most needed. It would mean a lot of work but she's never been shy of hard work.'

'Capital,' Miss Gordon said again.

Maggie Henry was sitting on the wooden seat in the garden with her elfin face raised to the sun, her blue eyes closed, enjoying the warmth. She opened her eyes as Octavia approached her and smiled. She's so slim, Octavia thought, looking at Maggie's narrow wrists and the childish figure under her neat white blouse. There's hardly anything of her. And she noticed that there were white hairs in her secretary's short brown bob and more wrinkles round her eyes than she used to have. Or was she imagining things? Maybe we shouldn't be putting more burdens on her. But she sat beside her and told her what she had in mind, notwithstanding.

Maggie's reaction was so strong, they melted her doubts at once. 'I'd love to do it,' she said. 'If you think I could. I've been thinking about it a lot since the first-formers moved in. They've really been a bit lost you know, poor little things. It's a lot for them to cope with, away from their mothers and everything. They do need looking after. And it would be lovely to have a place of my own. I mean, my landlady's lovely but it's not the same as your own place. The only thing is, who would be your new school secretary? I wouldn't want to let you down.'

Octavia explained her solution.

'Perhaps we could try Bella Wilkins,' Maggie said. 'She wants a job in an office now she's left school, and she can't go back to London because her parents are in Scotland. She was telling me only yesterday.'

'A very good idea,' Octavia said. 'She would suit us very well.'

So it was decided and Miss Henry was appointed matron of Downview and Bella became the office junior and agreed to take over Maggie's lodgings when she moved, and Mr Chivers was asked for his assistance in the rather costly matter of transforming all the rooms in the attic and on the first floor into dormitories, which he gave willingly, saying he would do whatever he could – and Lizzie and her two friends moved into the room with the window seat.

Tommy and Elizabeth were having breakfast when their daughter's letter arrived, and Tommy was rather surprised by it. 'Changing her billet?' he said when Elizabeth had told him the gist of it. 'What on earth for? I thought she was happy where she was.'

'She says she's going to live in the school house and help with the juniors,' Elizabeth said, reading on.

That made sense to her doting father. 'Ah, I see,' he said. 'It's a special assignment. If that's the case, quite right too.

She'll make a fine job of it. Does she say anything else?'

'She wants to know if she can come home for the summer holidays,' Elizabeth said, passing him the letter.

Tommy frowned. 'Out of the question,' he said. 'She must know that.'

'And when we're going down to see her.'

'When I get back from Washington, and yes, I know, we can't tell her that. Tell her as soon as we can. When I'm not so busy. God, look at the time. I shall have to go or I shall miss my flight.'

'I'll get the car while you finish your coffee,' Elizabeth said. 'There's no rush.' As always she had everything under perfect control, his bag packed and loaded in the boot, petrol in the tank, passport, tickets and official documents in his attaché case. 'I'll tell her we'll see her in a fortnight. How would that be?'

'She won't like it but it will have to do. Did you pack any aspirins?'

Elizabeth smiled at him. 'Naturally,' she said.

In the second week in August when the school holiday was well under way and Bella Wilkins had been appointed as the office junior and Maggie Henry was happily moving into her new quarters on the first floor at Downview with half a dozen second-formers to help her, Lizzie Meriton was sitting in her coveted window seat on the third floor, complaining that her father never came down to see her and saying that it wouldn't hurt him to stir his stumps just once in a while. In fact, even as she grumbled, Tommy Meriton was using his very considerable diplomatic skill to try to persuade the American administration that they should ally themselves with Great Britain or, at the very least, support the British war effort. It

152

was a delicate and difficult task and it was made worse by the news that was coming through from England. The German Luftwaffe had just carried out their first, expected raids on airfields and radar bases in the south-east of England and there was little doubt that Hitler's invasion plan was now under way.

Both Tommy's sons were in action that day and so was Flying Officer Johnnie Thompson. The fighting was swift, brutal and exhilarating, and he returned to base exhausted, but cock-a-hoop at his successes, reporting two kills and being thumped on the back by his fellow pilots and told what a good show it was.

'Better phone the aged P and tell her I'm still in the land of the living,' he grinned, putting on the right show. It was taking him quite an effort because what he really wanted to do was to lie down and sleep for a week.

Emmeline had heard the news on the wireless that evening and had been worrying about him ever since, so she was highly relieved to hear his voice, even if he was still talking in his incomprehensible language. Still, once she'd gathered that he wasn't hurt, nothing else really mattered. She listened to his laconic account of his two kills, winced at how much he had changed and, when there was a pause in the conversation, ventured to ask when he was coming on leave.

'Leave?' he said, his voice incredulous. 'There won't be any leave while this is going on, Ma. There's a war on.'

Her heart contracted with misery but the pips were sounding and it was too late to ask him anything else. He was already saying goodbye. 'Chin-chin, old thing. Keep your pecker up!'

'And how can I do that,' she said to Octavia, 'when he could be shot down at any minute? I hate this war. It makes me dread to hear the news.'

But dreading it or not, she listened to every bulletin and was drawn with anxiety at the news of yet another raid on the following day. 'I hope they're not going to keep this up,' she said. 'We shall all be worn to a frazzle.'

'That's the object of the exercise,' Octavia told her grimly.

The next day it was raining heavily and the German attack was called off. 'Thank God, for that,' Emmeline said. 'Give our boys a bit of peace. At least we've got the weather on our side. Long may it rain, that's what I say.'

But on the 15th of August it was a beautiful summer's day with clear blue skies and perfect visibility and the Luftwaffe flew across the Channel in force. Five hundred and twenty German bombers crossed the Channel that day, aiming to bomb British airfields and the radar installations that were strategically placed along the south coast. The perfect sky was criss-crossed by the long white lines and graceful parabolas of chalky vapour trails, as Spitfires and Hurricanes battled to fight off the attack. By the end of the day, as the BBC was happy to announce, seventy-six German planes had been shot down at a cost of thirty four British fighters. And the bombing had come to London.

It was Edie who broke the news to her mother. She rang from the phone box on the corner of her street and her voice was breathless with the drama of what she had to say. 'They've bombed Croydon airport, Ma,' she said. 'I can see the smoke from here. Great back cloud, sort of hanging in the air. We heard them go over. Funny thing was they didn't sound the sirens until afterwards. Still never mind, we're all still here.'

'Oh Edie,' Emmeline said. 'Don't you think you ought to come back to Guildford?'

'And face old Mother Hemmings?' Edie said. 'No fear. I

had enough of her to last a lifetime. No, no. We're fine. I've made a shelter under the stairs with a mattress and pillows and everything. We'll be snug as a bug in a rug.'

'You haven't got any stairs.'

'Well, no,' Edie admitted, 'not stairs as such but I've got a cupboard under where Mrs Holdsworthy's stairs are. Mr Topham says it'll be fine. Not to worry, Ma. We'll be safe as houses.'

'Houses aren't safe at all,' Emmeline said tetchily. 'They get blown up.'

'Not our house.'

Emmeline decided not to remonstrate. There didn't seem to be any point. Not when Edie had so obviously made up her mind. 'Anyway, who's this Mr Topham?' she said.

'Our Air Raid Warden,' Edie told her, 'and if he says it's all right, it is. Trust me.'

'She's being perfectly damn ridiculous,' Emmeline said to Octavia when she'd hung the receiver on its hook. 'She'll worry the life out of me, Tavy, staying there. I mean, if they've bombed Croydon airport, what will they bomb next? It could be Colliers Wood. She hasn't thought of that.'

'That's where Tommy flies from,' Octavia remembered. 'Croydon Airport. I hope he'll be all right. The last time I spoke to Elizabeth she said he was due back tomorrow.'

'They'll have it cleared for his sort of plane,' Emmeline said. 'Bound to.'


But she was wrong. The airport was still out of action the following morning and Tommy's flight was diverted to Biggin Hill. He and his team stayed there for over an hour enquiring what had happened in Croydon and the news he brought back to Elizabeth was, as he admitted, 'pretty bad'. Three hangers had been hit in the raid and so had the terminal building

155

which had been very badly damaged because it was being used as an ammunition store. Sixty-two people had been killed and nearly two hundred injured, either on the airfield or in the town. 'We're in for a rough ride,' he said.

Elizabeth looked at his weary face and knew that his trip to Washington hadn't gone well but she didn't ask him about it. He would tell her in his own good time. Which he eventually did, when he'd eaten poorly and slept fitfully and woken late and disgruntled.

'Total waste of time and effort,' he said as he drank his breakfast coffee. 'We couldn't shift them an inch. Isolationists to a bloody man. I think Roosevelt would back us if he didn't have an election coming up but the rest of the team were intransigent. They're not going to join us this time round and we needn't think it. None too keen to help us in any other way either. We got them to agree to some trade deals, armaments and food stuffs mostly, but we've got to meet the costs of shipment. Apart from that it was a complete failure.'

'I am sorry,' Elizabeth said.

He put down his cup and smiled at her wearily. 'Let's go down and see our Lizzie,' he said.

'Today?'

'Why not?' he said. 'Give her a surprise. The Foreign Office can do without me for once. I've earned a day off.'

He is low, poor man, Elizabeth thought, and she leant across the table to pat his hand.

'Have you heard from the boys?' he asked.

'They ring every day.'

'They're good lads,' Tommy said. 'Whatever else, we've done a good job with our children.'

That 'whatever else' was telling. He's depressed, Elizabeth thought. I wish he didn't set himself such impossibly high standards. That's what comes of having a father who always wanted his own way. As she knew only too well for her own father had been similarly heavy.

The good lads were in constant action during that summer, for the German attacks on the British airfields were determined and incessant. The Luftwaffe took very heavy casualties – by the end of August they'd lost over six hundred planes – but they knew that Hitler's invasion of England couldn't take place without the defeat of Fighter Command, and as they'd been instructed to see that the defeat was complete and total before winter weather made it impossible for the German troops to cross the Channel, they kept on coming. The task that Fighter Command had set themselves was even harder, for they were fighting for survival. They, too, took heavy losses – two hundred and fifty-nine fighters were shot down during that August – and they were in an even more difficult position than their adversaries, for although the factories were working night and day to replace the lost aircraft, and new pilots were being trained at an impossible rate to replace the men who'd been killed or too badly injured to fly, by the end of the month there were so few pilots remaining that the survivors had to fly more sorties than anyone thought humanly possible, taking to the air again and again as soon as they'd refuelled. By the 31st of August they were in a parlous condition.

'Not good, old man,' Flight Lieutenant Mark Meriton admitted when he phoned his father. 'We shan't be able to keep this up much longer.'

'How long?' Tommy asked.

'If we go on losing planes at this rate,' his son said, 'a week.'

* * *

157

A week later, and totally unexpectedly, Hitler changed tack. If he couldn't defeat the RAF and Goering seemed to think that was now the case, he would reduce London to rubble and break the morale of the British that way.

On the 7th of September he sent four hundred bombers with full fighter escorts to attack the East End of London in broad daylight. The fires they lit with their incendiaries were still burning that night when another two hundred bombers returned to continue the pounding. It was the worst day of the war, so bad that the government issued an invasion alert. But it was a last minute reprieve for Fighter Command.

# Chapter Eleven

'Coo-ee, young Edie!' Mrs Holdsworthy called. 'You ain't 'alf took a long time with that shopping.' She'd been keeping watch at the window ever since Mr Topham told her the good news, and as soon as she saw Edie and Joan coming along the street she pulled up the sash-cord and leant out, both hands on the window sill and her face beaming. 'They've opened up the Tube for us, duck. What did I tell you?'

Edie was tired that morning. She'd had a bad night, what with the raid and everything and her shopping basket was dragging her arm down and Joanie was grizzling enough to try the patience of a saint, but she looked up at her neighbour and smiled at the good news. 'Thank God for that,' she said. 'High time they saw sense. Perhaps that'll stop my mum being on at me. When can we use it?'

'Tonight, so Mr Topham says. I'm gettin' me things together.'

Edie gave her daughter's hand a shake. 'Stop that row, Joanie,' she said. 'We're home now. You don't have to go on. I can't hear your aunty talk.' And when the child sniffed and stopped she looked up to question her neighbour again. 'What can we take?'

'He didn't say,' Mrs Holdsworthy told her. 'Just it was going to be kept open for us. Bedding I reckon, don't you. An' me flask. We shall need that. Cup a' tea.'

It'll be cold sleeping on the platform, Edie thought, as she put her key in the lock. I wonder if I've still got those old sleeping bags me and Arthur used to have. They'd be just the thing. Couple a' pillows.

There'd been an air raid every night for the last three weeks and she was heartily sick of them, hating the sound of those awful bombers overhead and the thud, thud, thud of the ack-ack, hating the fear that griped her stomach every time the sirens went and the fear she saw on her children's faces when the noise got too bad, hating everything about it. 'There you are, Joanie,' she said, as she took off her daughter's coat and hung it on the hook in the hall, 'we're not going to hear any more nasty raids ever again. We're going somewhere safe, right away from them.'

'And Barbara and our Maggie,' Joan said.

''Course. We wouldn't leave them behind, now, would we? Come on we're going to find some sleeping bags.'

'What's a sleepin' bag?' Joan wanted to know, but her mother was already standing on a chair in her bedroom, searching through the bedding on the top shelf of the wardrobe.

Just as Edie had feared, it was cold on the platform and the concrete floor was extremely hard to lie on, but she didn't care. For the first time since this awful Blitz began she felt safe, cocooned in the familiar sulphur-smelling darkness of the underground, surrounded by her sleeping children – and what a relief to see them fast asleep for once – with neighbours nearby to talk to and, most important of all, completely cut off from the horror of what was happening in the sky above the battered streets.

'Best thing they ever done,' she said to Mrs Holdsworthy, sipping her welcome mug of tea, 'opening up like this. They should ha' done it weeks ago. I shall bring a couple a' blankets down tomorrow. Pad these bags out a bit. Wait till I tell my Arthur. He's been worrying himself silly since this started. Now I can tell him he's not to worry no more. Best thing they ever done.'

Emmeline was relieved to hear her daughter's news too, although she still thought she ought to come back to Guildford and be really safe. There were occasional raids during the day and she could easily get caught in one of them – after all she couldn't stay in the underground day and night – and although the newspapers didn't say much about casualties, she knew very well that ever so many people were being killed and injured.

Octavia knew that better than most, for she and Maggie were coping with the terrible grief of girls who had lost their mothers or fathers or older brothers. There had been six of them since the start of the Blitz and each one seemed to be harder to comfort than the last. The most recent had been little Iris, who'd come to Lizzie's attic room before morning school began the previous day, weeping so terribly she could hardly speak and saying between gasping sobs that she wanted to go home.

By this time Lizzie could guess what had happened and knew exactly what to do. She found a handkerchief and dried Iris's eyes, then she put her arms round her and held her until she'd recovered enough to tell her what was the matter, the words gulped out between sobs. 'It's Mum. My – aunty – wrote to me. She's been – bombed.'

So it's bad, Lizzie thought, but she didn't press to be told any more. She simply took Iris's hand and led her down the back stairs to Maggie Henry's office. 'We'll go and see Matron,' she said. 'She'll know what to do. She's ever so good.'

Maggie Henry opened the door as soon as Lizzie knocked. She'd dealt with so much grief over the past few weeks her senses went into full alert at every knock. 'Tea,' she said to Lizzie as she led the little girl to the sofa. 'Three cups. When did you hear, Iris?'

'Yesterday afternoon. My aunty wrote to me.'

So she's been grieving all night on her own, poor little thing, Maggie thought. 'And it was bad, wasn't it?' she said.

'Oh, Miss Henry,' Iris cried. 'She's dead.'

'You cry, darling,' Maggie said, cuddling her. 'Cry all you want. It's a terrible thing. The worst.' And as Iris wept against her shoulder she began to rearrange the child's day. 'Take a look at the timetable,' she said to Lizzie, 'and see who's teaching her first lesson.'

The tea was made and drunk, the timetable was consulted, and Lizzie went off to find Iris's teacher and let her know what had happened, leaving Miss Henry to look after everything else. As she left the room Iris turned her poor little blotched face towards her and thanked her. It was all she could do not to burst into tears before she could get out of the room. She wept all the way to the classroom, torn with a dreadful aching pity. Poor Iris. What has she ever done to deserve this? It isn't fair!

The autumn term continued and so did the bombing. Bad news soon became a part of the school's life.

'We shall need an extra special Christmas this year to lift our spirits,' Octavia said, when the staff gathered at her house at the end of October for their regular weekly meeting. 'Perhaps we ought to start considering it. I hope the sixth form are doing their play.'

'It's already written so they tell me,' Morag Gordon reported. 'It's going to be *Snow White in Woking*.'

That provoked smiles all round the room.

'Thank God for the sixth form,' Octavia said.

'Are we going ahead with the music festival?' Jenny Jones asked. She'd had a festival planned since the end of the summer term, soloists, choirs, even the venue. The local Boys Grammar School was going to let them use their hall. 'I mean, do we think it's – um – suitable?'

'I don't know about the rest of you but I think it isn't just suitable, it's a necessity,' Octavia said. 'We need as many good things as we can cram into our lives.'

There was a murmur of agreement.

'Only the thing is,' Jenny said, 'the thing is, Iris was going to be one of our soloists, you see, and I wondered... I mean, I don't want to put pressure on her or anything now she's... I don't really know what to do for the best.'

'Let her make the choice,' Morag advised, flicking ash from her cigarette. 'If she feels she's up to it, it could be the best thing for her.'

'I think we ought to have a school party at Downview,' Helen Staples said. 'It would be a squash but I don't think they'd mind. Could be fun.'

'An excellent idea,' Octavia said and teased, 'Are you volunteering to arrange it?'

'I wouldn't mind,' Helen said. 'With a bit of help.'

Help was instantly forthcoming – from Alice Genevra, who offered to be Phillida's assistant and make the decorations, and Sarah Fletcher, who said she'd do the catering, and Elizabeth Fennimore, who said she would cost it and order all the things they needed 'within reason, of course'.

Not for the first time, Octavia thought what a good team

163

they were. They take everything in their stride, she thought, and they never complain, no matter what this war flings at them. 'Thank you very much, all of you,' she said to them, 'I don't know how this school would manage without you.' And she grinned at them and quoted one of their favourite hymns. '"He who would valiant be, 'gainst all disaster." Only, of course, it should be she in your case. Don't you think so Jenny?'

'It's us to a T,' Jenny said, blushing but pleased to be given such praise. That was what was so nice about old Smithie. She knew how to thank you.

Darkness descended on them earlier every day, the dormitories were cold, far too many girls had chilblains and head colds and Matron Maggie was kept busy with Wintergreen ointment and Vick. The first fogs of November swathed the town in a miserable dampness. The rations were reduced. And the Blitz went on, night after night. It was, as Tommy Meriton had predicted, a rough time.

Despite all the difficulties of the job she was doing, Dora Erskine was really quite pleased with herself. When the Blitz began and she first started edging her ambulance through the darkened streets, she was afraid she would hit a wall or a pillar box or run someone over, but she was surprised by how quickly she grew accustomed to the lack of light, even on nights when there was no moon and it seemed pitch black. It was partly because she knew how important it was to reach her casualties as quickly as she could and partly because she knew the roads so well, having walked through them by day. As the nights passed, she saw some terrible injuries but there was even a good side to that. It wasn't that she'd grown hardened to seeing people in pain and bleeding, it was because the familiarity of it made her philosophical. 'I've seen it all now,' she would say wearily at the end of her shift, and she would think, I've seen it and I haven't panicked. Before very long she became a steadying presence in the stink and darkness, someone who was totally dependable and always calm, the way she'd been taught to be.

'It's all right,' she would say, in her firm voice. 'We're here. We've got you. You're all right.' And she would light a cigarette and put it between her casualty's dust-caked lips and smile encouragement at them, even if their injuries were making her ache with pity. It was dreadful when the body lifted from the wreckage turned out to be a child or, even worse, was dead, but she even got used to that after a time.

'Bloody war!' she would say. 'I hope they put that bloody Goering up against a wall when all this is over and blow his bloody brains out. Bloody monster.' She'd never sworn so much in her life.

'Our Dora's a giddy marvel,' they said at the ARP post, and she took it as the compliment it was.

But it wasn't a job she could do night after night without a break and she was glad when she got time off, especially when she could persuade Edie and the kids to come to Balham and visit her.

'I don't see much of you what with one thing and another,' she wrote to Edie at the end of a particularly bad week. 'How about coming over this Saturday?'

It was such a good afternoon and the sisters enjoyed every chattering minute of it, remembering old times, drinking endless cups of tea, eating Dora's special scones, playing Pit by the fire the way they'd done when they were children. Outside their blacked-out windows, the November dusk cast its sooty pall over the High Street and people walked home as fast as they could with their coat collars turned up and their hands in their pockets for warmth, but inside the flat they were too cosy and happy together to notice how late it was getting. When the clock struck six, it made Edie jump.

'Oh, my good God,' she said. 'Look at the time, Dora. We shall have to be getting back or the sirens'll go. Come on you three. Chop, chop. Get your hats and coats. We're late.'

'Why don't you go on the Tube?' Dora said. 'That'd be quicker.'

But Edie decided they'd go on the tram the way they always did. 'We're used to it, Dotty. It's the way we go.'

It was a mistake, for the air raid sirens began to howl as they were passing Tooting Broadway and by the time they reached Colliers Wood it was completely dark and the raid had begun. As they stood on the platform of the tram, waiting to get off, they could hear the laboured drone of the German bombers overhead and ack-ack firing somewhere close by, fer-dum, fer-dum, fer-dum.

'I don't think we'll go back home tonight,' Edie decided. 'We'll stay on the tram and go straight to the Tube.'

'What about our pillows?' Barbara objected. 'What'll we sleep on if we haven't got our pillows?'

'You can use me,' Edie said, 'I don't mind.'

'What, all of us?' Maggie said. 'You'll be squashed.'

'I can be squashed for one night,' Edie told her. 'Don't make that face. Better to have no pillow than a lump of shrapnel sticking in your head. Come on. We're here.'

They climbed down from the tram and ran across the dark road as quickly as they could, dodging the traffic. All three children were panting when they reached the Tube station but none of them minded. They were safe. That was what mattered.

Nothing could hurt them once they were underground.

The platform was already crowded and noisy, as mothers tried to settle their children for the night and people gossiped with their neighbours. Mrs Holdsworthy was sitting with her back against the wall putting in her hair curlers. 'You're late,' she said. 'I thought you wasn't coming. There's tea in the flask if you want some. Where've you been?'

'We've come without our pillows,' Barbara told her.

''Ave yer, duck?' Mrs Holdsworthy said. 'Well, never mind. You can have a lend a' mine if you like. You'll 'ave ter keep your 'ead still or I shall spike you with me curlers.'

'You wouldn't,' Barbara said, much impressed. 'Would you?'

'Oh, I'm a devil with me curlers.'

'I'll make a pillow of my coat,' Edie said, and did. 'Now let's have you settled.'

'We don't have to go to sleep yet,' Maggie said. 'We've only just got here. It's not time.'

'It's past time,' Edie said firmly, 'as well you know, so yes ,you do.' It was chilly without her coat and she was beginning to wonder whether she ought to have risked it and gone home for the things they needed. The girls were warm enough all bundled up in their coats and scarves but it would be hard sleeping on the platform without the sleeping bags and blankets to protect them.

It was a long difficult night. Edie turned and fidgeted and couldn't get comfortable no matter what position she tried and the children were as restless as she was. All three of them woke one after the other and had to be escorted into the tunnel so that they could have a wee and then took ages to settle again. Their immediate neighbour was snoring and so deeply asleep that even when Edie gave her a good hard poke she

167

didn't stir, and there seemed to be people coming and going all night long. It's because we're not sleeping, Edie thought. They probably do this every night only we sleep through it and don't notice it.

She was really glad when the first train came through and people began to stir and make ready for the day. 'Come on you lot,' she said to her three girls. Now that the night was over, they were fast asleep rolled together in her coat and they looked really comfortable. It seemed a pity to wake them but they couldn't stay there now that the trains were running. 'Six o'clock. Wake up. Let's get home and have a nice wash. You look like gypsies.'

'I'll follow you down,' Mrs Holdsworthy said. 'Must do me hair. See you later gels.'

It had been a bad raid. Edie could tell that the minute she stepped out into the morning darkness. The air was full of the smell of bombed houses, that horrible combination of brick dust and gas and shit that she knew so well and found so appalling. And there was shrapnel all over the place and shards of broken glass glinting on the pavement.

'Mind where you're putting your feet,' she warned. 'There's a lot of glass. Hold onto my hand, Joanie, there's a good girl. I don't want you running off. And you two hold on tight to one another.'

'That's Mr Perkins' paper shop,' Maggie said, and stopped to take a closer look. Only half the shop was still standing and there was a great pile of rubble where the rest of it ought to have been and lots of men digging and a very strong smell of gas. 'Look, Mum, Mr Perkins been bombed.'

'Yes,' Edie said shortly. 'Come on. They won't want us in the way if they've got all this to clear up. I thought you wanted to get home.'

They trailed along beside her looking back at the wreckage, wide-eyed and serious. She gave their hands a tug to get them to walk more quickly because she didn't want them to see someone being dug out. That wouldn't do at all. 'Cup of tea,' she said, 'and then a nice wash.' And she turned the corner into Wycliffe Road.

Even in the poor light of a bombed dawn, she could see that there was rubble all over the road. Oh my God, she thought, it must be one of the neighbours. As they got closer to it, she saw that it was actually a long trail of broken bricks that led to a great jagged pile of bricks and planks and rubble. It looked as if it had just spilt out onto the pavement and it had obviously come from somewhere very near her house. Very, very near. Almost… Then she was stopped by a moment of disbelief and horror, too shocked to move on. Oh dear God, it was right where their house was. No, she corrected herself, not where their house was, where their house had been. She stood quite still holding her two youngest children firmly by the hand, stunned and staring. There was nothing left if it. Not a single brick. It was just a great gaping hole. Their home, where they were going to have a nice cup of tea and a nice wash. Oh my dear, good God! What am I going to do?

The girls were stunned too. They didn't cry and they didn't move and they didn't speak. They just stood where they were, holding her hand and staring. She knew she ought to say something to comfort them, poor little things, but her mind was stuck and she couldn't think of anything. This was my home, she thought. My lovely home. And there's nothing left of it.

She was aware that there was somebody standing beside her and looked round to see Mr Topham. At first she thought he looked like a ghost in that dreadful darkness but then she realised that he was covered in dust, his dark suit smeared all down the front, and his shoes so white it looked as though he'd been walking through flour. Even his moustache was dusty, poor man, and he looked so drawn that for a moment she barely recognised him.

'Yes,' he said. 'Direct hit, I'm afraid. We've had a right night of it. What a blessing you was in the Tube. Was Mrs Holdsworthy with you?'

'Yes,' she said, looking back at the hole that had been her home. Where had everything gone? It couldn't just have disappeared, all the sheets and the pillow cases and the cooker and her nice clock and everything. Then she saw that half of Arthur's chair was sticking out of the pile, covered in dust, and that two of her best cups were lying next to the legs all chipped and filthy. Bloody Hitler, she thought, doing this to me.

'I'll just make my report,' Mr Topham said, 'and let them know you're OK. Be back in a jiffy.'

Barbara was pulling at her mother's sleeve and whispering urgently. 'Mummy, Mummy. What are we going to do?'

She gave herself a shake and took a decision. 'We're going to catch a train and go to your Aunt Tavy's,' she said.

Octavia and Emmeline had overslept that morning and were sitting by the kitchen fire swathed in their dressing gowns gathering their thoughts before they began the day. It was Sunday so there was no rush.

'The nice thing about Sunday,' Emmeline said, 'is having time for an extra cup of tea with your feet on the fender.' And then, just as she settled her cup into its saucer, the doorbell rang.

'I'll go,' Octavia said. 'It's bound to be for me.' Janet was upstairs cleaning the bathroom and there was no point in calling her down just to answer the door. 'I'll get it, Janet,' she called from the hall.

The surprise of seeing Edie and her children on the doorstep quickly turned to shock when she realised what a dishevelled state they were in, their hair unbrushed, their faces filthy dirty, with no luggage.

'We've been bombed out, Aunt,' Edie said. Her voice was totally without emotion, as though she was speaking in a dream. 'It's all gone.'

Octavia was mentally checking them over, looking for signs of blood or injury and relieved not to find any. 'Never mind,' she said, comforting at once and by instinct. 'You're here now.' And she took the nearest child by the arm and led her into the house, calling over her shoulder for Emmeline. 'Em! It's Edie.'

Emmeline came out of the kitchen in a rush, took one look and ran towards them. 'Oh my dear, good God!' she said. 'What's happened to you? Are you all right?'

'They've been bombed out,' Octavia told her calmly, 'but they're all right. They haven't been hurt. Have you? No, I thought not. And I'll bet you haven't had any breakfast either.'

'We came straight here,' Edie said, still stony-faced.

'Quite right,' Octavia said, and turned to the girls. 'Let's get you into the kitchen and see what you could fancy,' she said. 'And then we must get you into a bath, mustn't we, Em?'

To her considerable relief, Em took her cue and led the children into the kitchen. 'Nice pot of tea,' she said. 'And then I'll rustle up some nice boiled eggs and soldiers. How would that be? Would you like a boiled egg, Joanie?'

And at that Edie began to cry, her whole body shaken by tearing sobs, on and on and on. Emmeline let go of Barbara's

171

hand and turned her full attention to her daughter. She put her arms round her, kissed her and held her, murmuring to her as though she was a child. 'Never mind my little lovely. I've got you. You're all right now. Never you mind. We'll look after you.'

Octavia left them to it. There were other things that had to be attended to and she was already thinking about them. People who'd been bombed out got special ration cards and allowances to help them with the things they needed, like food and clothes. They couldn't live in the same clothes for long so the sooner she saw about that the better. Now who would know? The WVS probably. What was the name of that nice woman who helped us when we first arrived? We must have a record of it somewhere. Maggie would have it. And she took the phone off the hook.

Maggie was having a bit of a lie-in too that morning. It had been a difficult week. But she got up at once when the phone rang and walked quickly across the room to answer it.

'You don't happen to have the name and address of that nice WVS woman, do you?' Octavia said. 'The one who gave us the list of all the billets when we first got down'

'I can't remember it off hand,' Maggie said, 'but I know where it is. Hold on a tick and I'll get it for you.'

Thank God for our Maggie, Octavia thought. Now what else has got to be done? She reached for a pencil and began to make notes on the telephone pad. Clothes. Make list. Where to buy? Primary schools. London or local? Beds and bedding. Chertsey Road? What a good job we've got those two rooms in the attic. Inform ARP at Colliers Wood. Register ration books. Library tickets.

* * *

After the shock of their arrival, Edie and the girls settled in extremely quickly. By the time the children had all been put in a warm bath and made presentable, Janet had given the attic rooms a quick brush and polish and made up the double bed for them. 'Now you have a nice little rest,' Emmeline said, tucking them under the clean sheets, 'and when you wake up you shall have dinner with us and then you've all feel much better.' Privately, she was worrying about how little food she'd got in the cupboard and thinking what a nuisance it was that it was Sunday and she couldn't go shopping, but it was a minor worry, she would soon work something out. The great thing was that they hadn't been hurt.

'Sleep tight, my ducks,' she said as she left the room. 'You're with me now.'

# Chapter Twelve

Lizzie Meriton was looking forward to Christmas that year. She knew she couldn't go back to London and spend it with her family. The bombing had put paid to that. But her brothers were coming down to see her, they'd promised faithfully, and so had her mother and Pa, and there was the sixth-form play to look forward to and the music festival and the Downview party. It was going to be a good time, Smithie said so. And if Smithie said so, you could depend on it.

The weather was foul, damp and cold and miserably dark, but inside their two school buildings the walls were sun-bright with paper chains and lanterns and there were boldly coloured pictures all along the corridors, thanks to Miss Bertram and her art classes, and they sang their favourite carols at every assembly. It was normal, like it had been in Roehampton, when there weren't bombs and people getting killed and injured, or dog-fights and people getting shot down and having to worry about your brothers, when it was peaceful and you could get on with your life in your own home and sleep in your own bed and see your Pa every day. What a long time ago Roehampton seemed! A lifetime. But Christmas was coming and it was going to be lovely. Smithie said so.

Edie was looking forward to the holiday too, which quite

surprised her, because when her house had been bombed she'd thought she would never be able to enjoy anything ever again. But there you are, she told herself, you get over things somehow or other and Aunt Tavy's making such an effort with this Christmas it would be unkind not to enjoy it. They were going to have a family party and Dora was going to try and get down and had promised that, if she did, she would bring David with her, and John too if he could get home, and Johnnie had written to Ma to say that he would do 'his darndest' to join them 'and he couldn't say better than that'. Of course, she kept thinking of poor Arthur, all on his own in that horrible prison camp, but she and the girls had sent him the best parcel they could put together, with a pair of hand-knitted socks to keep him warm and the writing paper and envelopes he'd asked for and even a bar of Nestle's chocolate she'd bought with her sweet ration, and she'd written him a long letter telling him how much she loved him and wanted to see him again, and the girls had painted special Christmas cards for him. Even Joanie had made a card of sorts scribbled all over with her coloured crayons and with her name written inside, with a bit of help from Maggie. And now everyone in the house was getting ready for Christmas Day.

Janet seemed to be everywhere all the time and always hard at work, making up camp beds and giving all the rooms a thorough good clean, answering the phone and the door, up and about long before everyone else, making the breakfast. She said she wanted to get everything good and ready before she went to Gateshead. Ma was in her element with all the family coming. She'd made a huge Christmas pudding. The house had smelt of it for days. There was a cake too, not iced of course because the sugar ration wouldn't run to that and in any case you weren't allowed to ice cakes, but a nice cake just the same. Aunt Tavy had made a wreath of holly and hung it over the door knocker; and the house was decorated with paper chains; and there were carols on the wireless; and the Christmas cards were beginning to arrive, even though it was only the 10th of December. We're eager for it, she thought, because it's the season of peace and goodwill. But thinking the words upset her because there was no peace, the bombing was still going on and Arthur was still a prisoner of war, and not much goodwill either. The papers kept saying that Hitler's U-boats were sinking our merchant ships every single day and hinting that the rations were going to be reduced again when the holiday was over. But for the moment it was Christmas and candles were lit behind the blackout. And the war couldn't go on forever. It had to end sooner or later.

Octavia felt she was carrying a heavy burden that season. It was important for everything to go well and for her family and her pupils to have the best possible time of it, but the closer it came the more she foresaw the possibility of failure, particularly at home. The rations were so tight now and there was so little extra food in the local shops that there were days when she wondered whether she ought to go to London and see if she could get a few extras on the black market. It was against her socialist principles but something had to be done.

In the end it was Tommy Meriton who solved her problem for her. He and Elizabeth arrived to visit Lizzie one dank afternoon at the end of December, asking for permission to take her to Guildford for tea, and when the school day was over and his daughter had been safely returned to Downview, he turned up on Octavia's doorstep carrying a hamper. It was obviously very heavy and he and Elizabeth were grinning widely.

'There you are, my dear,' he said to Tavy, when he'd carried it into the house. 'To add to the feast.'

It was a mouthwatering collection of Christmas food, an enormous turkey – how on earth did he get that? – a ham, tinned peaches, tinned pears, a box of marrons glacés, sugared almonds in a transparent paper cone tied with a trailing ribbon, shortbread biscuits in a tartan tin, three bottles of wine, a vintage port and a huge box of chocolates.

'Good God!' she said. 'However did you manage to get all this?'

'Trips to America, old thing,' he explained. 'I gather you like it?'

'I'm overwhelmed,' she said and it was true. 'Thank you so much.'

'Happy Christmas,' he said and kissed her.


So it was a luxurious Christmas after all and Emmeline's children and grandchildren all managed to get to Woking to enjoy it. The two Johns couldn't join them until Boxing Day but they were given such a rapturous welcome that it soon felt as if they'd been there all the time, and there was plenty of cold ham and turkey to feed them on and Emmeline was so happy she couldn't stop smiling.

'I don't know when I've had such a good Christmas,' she said when the meal was over and they were clearing the dishes.

'And there's still the evening to come,' Octavia said. She'd got a surprise for them and she couldn't wait to reveal it.

That afternoon as they digested their meal, they played Pit by the drawing room fire and pushed the chairs into a circle so that they could play charades and decided they really didn't want to listen to the news. 'It's bound to be bad,' Emmeline said. 'And we've had enough bad news. Who's for a cup of tea?'

Tea and a slice of her cake and then a pause, while she made up the fire.

'Don't put the chairs back round the fire,' Octavia said. 'Push them up against the wall.'

'Why?' the children asked. 'Why, Aunty Tavy?'

'Because we're going to dance,' Octavia told them.

'In here?' Dora said. 'But there's no piano. What'll we dance to?'

'There's a gramophone,' she told them, standing beside its unobtrusive cabinet. 'Look!' And she lifted the lid to show them the turntable and opened the fancy double doors to reveal a stash of records, all standing together neat and upright in their brown paper sleeves. 'What do you fancy? There's Roger de Coverley and The Dashing White Sergeant, or a quickstep or a waltz, or you could have a polka. Your choice.'

Barbara chose a polka, even though she didn't know what it was, and the record was pulled from its sleeve and put on the turntable, while they all stood round to hear what it would be like. 'Come on,' Tavy said, holding out her arms to the nearest child. 'One, two, three, hop. One, two, three, hop. See?'

Soon they were all squealing and hopping together, Dora and John, David and Barbara, Edie and Joan, Maggie and her Uncle Johnnie. The room was hot and grew hotter as they spun and giggled. And when the record stopped and Joanie said, 'Do it again!' they laughed and clapped and said, 'Yes, do!' until Tavy put it on again.

'Change partners,' she ordered. 'Johnnie to dance with his mother.'

'I can't dance,' Emmeline protested. 'You know that. I'm too fat.'

'Rot!' Johnnie said. 'You're just a good armful.' And he seized her round the waist and spun her away, still protesting but hopping with the rest of them. It was, as she said, when the dancing was finally done and the children were taken off to bed, 'the best Christmas I've ever had.'

But Octavia was wondering how people were getting on in London and whether there'd been a raid. It would be too dreadful to be bombed out on Christmas Day.

There were no raids reported in the papers next morning which pleased her even though she knew that the lack of news could have been because the editor had censored it. But there were more raids planned, nobody had any doubt about that, and the Blitz certainly wasn't over. On the 29th of December when there was a low tide on the Thames and a full moon – which Londoners were learning to call a bombers' moon – there was a massive and terrifyingly destructive raid on the City. Goering knew what he was about, for the first bombs to be dropped were thousands of incendiaries, so many, that when the AFS arrived to deal with them, the water in the hydrants ran dry. On every other occasion when this had happened, they'd taken the water they needed from the river, but on that night the tide was so low it couldn't be done and without water to fight them the fires raged out of control. St Paul's was ringed by a roaring inferno and the flames were so high and so fierce they could be seen in the suburbs. It was a terrible night. And Elizabeth Meriton was in the middle of it.

Tommy had been none too pleased when she'd told him she was going to a night club. 'Tonight?' he'd said.

'I did tell you, my dear,' she said, brushing her hair. 'It's Annabella's fiftieth birthday.'

'I'd rather you didn't.'

'I've promised her.'

'Put it off,' he said. 'It's my last night at home.' He was off to the States again the next morning, as she knew very well.

'I can't do that,' she said. 'You know I can't. I'll see you when you get back.'

'But that'll be weeks.'

'Eight days,' she corrected, smiling at him.

'You're a hard-hearted woman,' he said, pretending to complain. 'I was going to take you out to dinner, make a fuss of you, soft lights, champagne, sweet music and all that sort of thing. Now I suppose I've got to stay here all on my own and finish off the goose.'

'Afraid so,' she said, putting on her lipstick.

'What time will you get back?'

'Not till the early hours I shouldn't think. You know what Annabella's like.'

She looked quite delectably pretty sitting at her dressing table with her hair brushed and shining, her lips reddened and the pearl necklace he'd given her glowing against her throat. As he watched her, she leant forward towards the mirror so that he saw three images of her, with her left and right profile flanking the full beauty of her face and he was filled with the oddest yearning, almost as if he was seeing her for the last time. 'Please don't go,' he said.

She stood up, slipped out of her negligee and stepped into her dress, arranging it carefully. It was her red silk, the one he'd always liked the most. 'Zip me up, my darling,' she said, turning her back on him. He obeyed her, as he always did, and she turned to the mirror to check that everything was as it should be, saying, 'How do I look?' the way she always did.

'Beautiful,' he told her.

She took his face between her hands and kissed him, very gently so as not to smudge her lipstick. 'Darling Tommy,' she said. 'I shall be back before you know it.'

It was lonely in the house without her, so he went to his club, where he had a lively night with several old friends. They spent most of it in the cellars because the sirens went almost as soon as they'd arrived but that was no hardship because most cellars were pretty comfortably furnished by then, and there were cards to play and plenty to drink.

Just after midnight, Tubby Ponsonby arrived to tell them that all hell was breaking loose in the City and he and Tommy went upstairs to the third floor lounge to have a look. The long room was completely empty and the blackout tightly drawn so they had some difficulty edging their way past too many easy chairs in the smoky darkness, but eventually, after some cussing, they reached the window, opened the curtains and looked out into the night. Pall Mall was so clearly lit they could see every stone in the building opposite shining whitely in the moonlight. Above their heads, the black sky was patterned with the long white beams of the searchlights, swinging and searching. There was no doubt that there was a big raid going on. They could smell the smoke of the fires even behind their unopened window and hear the throb of the bombers, and when they craned their necks they could see a terrifying forest of flames, rising and writhing as thick as tree trunks amid sudden showers of red sparks.

'I wouldn't like to be in the fire service tonight,' Tubby said. 'And that's a fact.'

'I wouldn't like to be in the fire service any night,' Tommy told him, watching the flames. 'They're bloody heroes.' But he was thinking of Elizabeth and feeling relieved that the

181

Germans were attacking the City instead of going for the West End. She'll probably see all this too, he thought, if she can drag herself away from her friends, but she won't be at risk. It pleased him to think that they would be sitting at their breakfast table in an hour or so talking it all over. How callous you get in wartime, he thought. There are men out there risking their lives, people getting killed and injured, and all I'm thinking about is whether my wife is safe.

The night went noisily on. They played cards, drank whisky, dozed. At half past two Tommy decided he'd had enough of club life and ought to go home. 'Good idea, old fruit,' Tubby said. 'I shall follow you.' But he was too squiffy to stand up so he stayed where he was.

It was bright moonlight out in Pall Mall and Tommy's Silver Cloud was the colour of its name. As he drove off along the empty street, the sky was stained an ominous misty red by the fires and he could hear an ambulance ringing somewhere nearby. It'll be good to be home, he thought. I wonder whether Elizabeth is back.

She wasn't, which was a disappointment. But never mind, she'd be back soon. He switched on the bedside light and lay down on their bed to wait for her. And the next thing he knew his alarm clock was yammering and it was half past seven. It took him a few seconds to gather his thoughts. Then he realised that her side of the bed hadn't been slept in and went off to look for her in the spare room. She wasn't there either. So where had she got to?

He put on his dressing gown and went downstairs to find his housekeeper, Mrs Dunnaway. She was in the kitchen, capped and aproned and waiting to cook his breakfast. 'No, sir,' she said, 'Mrs Meriton hasn't come down yet.'

'I don't think Mrs Meriton has come home from her

party,' he said. 'I should think they all went on to breakfast somewhere.'

Mrs Dunnaway smiled benignly as if it was perfectly all right and the smile irritated him. Elizabeth had no business staying out all night, especially when he was going to the States. It wasn't kind.

He ate what breakfast he could, showered, dressed, checked that he had his flight ticket and his passport, and there was still no sign of her. I'll phone Arabella, he decided. But that was a waste of time because Arabella wasn't at home either and neither was her husband. Now there were only a few minutes left before he had to leave for the airport. He sat down at her dressing table and wrote her a note. 'Dearest Elizabeth, Who's a dirty stop-out? Ring me when you get back, my darling. Leaving now. 8.33 a.m.' Then he drove to Croydon, feeling aggrieved.

It was Octavia who took the phone-call. It was a man's voice, asking if he could speak to the headmistress. 'Speaking,' she said. 'How can I help you?'

'Ah!' the voice said. 'I'm trying to contact one of your parents. Percy Carswell. Air Raid Warden.'

'We've no one of that name, I'm afraid.'

'No, no,' the voice said apologetically. 'That's me. I'm Percy Carswell. No, The person I'm trying to contact is someone by the name of Meriton. Major Meriton. His housekeeper said he was one of your parents. Daughter called Lizzie, I believe.'

Octavia's heart gave a painful lurch. 'That's right,' she said. 'Is something the matter?'

'It's a matter of identification,' Mr Carswell said carefully. 'We had an incident in the West End last night and we were rather hoping that Major Meriton could help us. Could your pupil tell us where he is? His housekeeper said he'd gone to America, but she couldn't say where we could find him.'

'Washington,' Octavia told him. 'British Embassy. I've got the phone number if you'll hold the line for a moment.' And she searched through Maggie's careful files, her heart shuddering with alarm. If it was an incident in the West End it was either one of the boys or Elizabeth. 'Here it is,' she said, picking up the receiver again. And she gave him the number.

'Thank you,' he said. 'It's very kind of you.'

'Before you go,' she said, speaking quickly before he could hang up. 'Would you mind telling me something more about your casualty. I assume it was a fatality.'

'I'm afraid so,' he said, with weary sadness. 'But we're not allowed to divulge any details except to next of kin.'

'That's quite understood,' Octavia said, 'but I need some information if I'm to be ready to help my pupil when the identification is made. Is this a young man, in air force uniform perhaps, or a woman?'

'The latter,' Mr Carswell told her. 'Which is why we want to contact her husband.'

Oh dear God! Octavia thought. My poor Tommy and my poor little Lizzie. She didn't know which of them she felt most sorry for.

'Well, thank you again,' Mr Carswell said, and this time he did hang up.

For the rest of the day Octavia struggled to decide what she ought to do. As she cycled between her two school buildings, with her basket full of books and papers, her scarf flying behind her and her button boots slipping on the damp pedals, she turned the choices over. Should she tell her now, very gently of course, it would have to be done very, very gently,

184

or should she just throw out a hint of some kind to warn her? Or should she say nothing until she knew for certain who the person was? After all, it might not be Elizabeth. It could be someone else. In the end she decided to say nothing but to wait until she heard from Tommy.

When she got home from school that afternoon, Janet and Edie were full of news about the raid on the City.

'One a' the woarst raids they've ever knoan, so they say.' Janet told her. 'There's a photo here of St Paul's and you can hardly see if for smoake.'

'It's a wonder it wasn't burnt to the ground,' Edie said. 'They say there's nothing left of the City.'

Emmeline walked into the kitchen just as they were pushing the evening paper across the table for Octavia to see, and she knew at once, from the anguish on her cousin's face, that there was something seriously wrong. 'What is it, Tavy?' she asked.

'It's Tommy's Elizabeth,' Octavia said shortly. 'It looks as though she was killed in the raid last night. I had a warden on the phone asking for Tommy's address in Washington.'

They were all shocked and Janet and Edie were silenced. 'Oh my dear,' Emmeline said, her face full of concern. 'Does Lizzie know?'

'Not yet,' Octavia said, struggling to stay calm. 'They've got to identify the body before they can…' And then the words got choked in her throat and she had to sit down at the kitchen table and breathe quietly to bring herself under control.

'Of course,' Emmeline said. 'That's the way it is.' And she changed the subject. 'How did you get on with your nice Chairman? Is he going to be able to get the money for your extra beds?'

So they struggled through the bad moment and Edie hid the paper away. But it was bad, bad, bad and none of them could deny it or change it.

Tommy and his team were doing rather well on this latest trip. The reports that Alistair Cooke was broadcasting from London were beginning to change minds and, of course, Roosevelt had been comfortably re-elected and could back them rather more easily. Tommy was enjoying a cigar and feeling quite pleased with himself when he was called from the conference table to take 'a call from London'.

'Meriton here,' he said.

'Major Meriton,' the voice said. 'I'm sorry to trouble you, sir, but may I ask when you will be returning to London?'

'Who is this?'

Mr Carswell identified himself and spoke rather vaguely about a casualty 'whom you might be able to identify, sir. Your daughter's headmistress gave me your telephone number.'

Oh God, Tommy thought, he's told my poor Lizzie. He was suddenly uncontrollably angry. 'You had no business talking to my daughter.'

'No, no, sir,' Mr Carswell soothed. 'Nothing has been said to your daughter. You have my word on that. It was you I wanted to contact, seeing as…' And his voice drifted off.

Tommy's feelings plummeted from anger to an unnatural coldness. 'It's my wife, isn't it?'

'We're afraid it might be.'

'I'll be back as soon as I can get a flight,' Tommy said. 'Whom do I contact? You'd better give me a name and address.'

* * *

186

The morgue was ice chill and peculiarly dark after the bright light of his flight and every sound echoed, footsteps reverberating along the corridor, the door opening with an unnecessary thud, papers rattling, somebody coughing like an explosion, and even though the voices that spoke to him were muted they resonated with what felt like menace.

And of course it was Elizabeth, lying under a small white sheet – what were they covering up? – her hair matted with great clots of blood and her beautiful face so gashed and stained it was almost impossible to recognise her. In fact he might not have done, had they not drawn that awful sheet back to reveal one long white perfect hand for his inspection. He stood looking down at it obediently and was cut to the heart to see that there wasn't a mark on it and that she was still wearing her engagement ring. He controlled himself with a superhuman effort. 'Yes,' he said. 'This is my wife.'

# Chapter Thirteen

Lizzie and Mary and Poppy were in their dormitory discussing their academic futures. The three of them were sitting in the window seat in their dressing gowns, which strictly speaking they shouldn't have been doing, because it wasn't long before breakfast and they ought to have been down in the hall, dressed and ready. But as Mary said, 'There's no lessons and if you can't take a few minutes off to plan your life in the holidays, when can you?'

'The thing is,' Lizzie said, 'Miss Gordon will keep telling me I should be making my mind up about what subjects I want to study at Higher Schools, and I haven't got the faintest idea. I mean, how are you supposed to know what your favourite subjects are when you haven't taken them? I like French but I might hate it if I fail it. And the same with Maths.'

Mary said it wasn't such a problem for her. 'There's only two subjects I'm any good at,' she said, 'and that's English and Art, so I suppose that's what I shall choose, providing I get Matric.'

'What do you want to do when you leave school?' Poppy asked her.

'I'd like to be a nurse,' Mary admitted, 'but you have to have Biology for that and I don't suppose I'll pass that.'

'Yes you will,' Lizzie told her firmly, 'if you want to. You just have to put your mind to it.'

'What about you, Lizzie?' Poppy said. 'Do you know what you want to be?'

Lizzie gave it thought. 'Something adventurous,' she said. 'I don't want to teach or anything like that. Or work in an office. I'd be bored stiff in an office. I mean, imagine typing letters all day. And I don't want to be a nurse. I might like to be a doctor if it didn't involve too much blood. But not if there was a war on.'

'What about getting married and having children?' Mary asked. 'I've always thought it would be nice to work for a little while but I wouldn't want to do it forever. I think it's more important to get married.'

'I'd like to have someone madly in love with me,' Lizzie said. 'Like Rhett Butler.' They'd seen *Gone with the Wind* three times when it came to Woking. 'I'm not sure I'd want to marry them, though.'

Mary was surprised and rather shocked. 'Why ever not?' she asked. 'I mean if someone loves you and you love them, you get married. I mean, that's only natural.'

'In some jobs you have to leave work if you get married,' Lizzie explained, 'and that's not natural. I think it's ridiculous. Imagine getting a really good job, something you really enjoy, something that's valuable and worthwhile, and then falling in love and getting married and being told you've got to resign.'

'But they don't do that now, do they?' Mary asked. 'I mean look at all those advertisements in the paper asking for women to do war work. They're always on about it and they never say anything about not being married, do they?'

That was true but Lizzie didn't have time to consider it because someone was knocking at the door to their room.

'Come in!' she called. 'Don't be shy.'

It was Miss Henry. 'Aren't you coming down to breakfast you three?' she said. 'It's bacon and tomatoes.'

That was temptation. Bacon was a rarity.

'We're not dressed,' Lizzie pointed out.

'Come as you are,' Maggie Henry said. 'Cook won't mind. It's holiday time.' She'd been making a special fuss of Lizzie Meriton since Miss Smith told her about her mother. It was awful to look at her pretty face and to know that she was going to be told that her mother had been killed. Miss Smith *had* said it was just possible the person they'd found wasn't her mother but if they'd sent for Major Meriton to identify the body there didn't seem to be much doubt about it. 'I'll tell them you're on your way.'

Tommy Meriton drove to Woking as slowly as he could. It was miserable and cold and the roads were icy but his mind wasn't on his driving, as it would have been in any other circumstances. He was trying to find the right form of words to break his dreadful news to Lizzie. He was still in shock, although he wasn't prepared to admit it, still unable to absorb what had happened, although he knew with the reasoning part of his mind that it had and that he'd accepted it.

Woking was virtually empty and the few people in Chertsey Street were swathed in scarves and had their hats pulled well down over their foreheads and were skulking along as though they were actors in some awful American thriller. He looked at them with loathing, thinking, why are you alive and walking about when my Elizabeth is dead? Then he felt ashamed of himself because he was being unreasonable and cruel and his thoughts went spinning off into an uncomfortable mixture of anger and regret and grief. I can't do this, he thought, as he

190

reached the entrance to Downview and turned in at the drive. How can any man tell his daughter that her mother is dead?

There was nobody out in the grounds and it took far too long for someone to answer when he rang the bell. He stood under the porch shivering and miserable and when the door was finally opened by a rather small girl, he walked in and followed her up the stairs to the matron's room without saying a word. Now that he was here the sooner he got this over with the better.

Maggie Henry was standing just outside her room talking to a group of little girls. 'Come to see Lizzie,' he said gruffly. 'Is she in?'

One of the girls was sent to find her and he was ushered into Miss Henry's room and the door was discreetly closed.

Maggie gestured towards her easy chair and he sat in it feeling horribly ill at ease. 'Am I right in thinking you will need to be private when you talk to Lizzie?' she asked gently.

He admitted it, staring at her carpet. Her voice was so full of sympathy he was afraid it would unman him.

'You can use this room,' Maggie said. 'You'll be quite private here. I'll hang my *Do not disturb* sign on the door for you.'

Then there was nothing either of them could say and they waited in silence, as the noise of the school racketed beneath them and a lone bird chirruped in the branches of the tree outside the window and the clock on the mantelpiece ticked the seconds away.

A knock, a whispered voice, a rush of cold air, and Lizzie was in the room, looking at him anxiously. And Miss Henry was gone. He stood up, gathered his courage, held out his arms to her.

'Oh Lizzie, my little love,' he said, 'your mother's been killed.'

She put her arms round his neck and stood for a long time holding on to him, cheek against cheek, not speaking. Tears rolled out of his eyes and fell on her hair. He simply couldn't stop them.

She was murmuring to him, comforting him the way Elizabeth used to do, kissing his cheek, his tears salt on her lips. 'Poor Pa! Poor, poor old Pa!'

'I'm so sorry,' he said.

She drew away from him so that she could look up at him, her arms still round his neck and those grey eyes dry. 'It's not your fault,' she said. 'You didn't kill her.'

He was shaken by how calm she was. 'It's just...' he said. But there were no words to tell her how he felt.

'I know,' she soothed, wiping away his tears with her fingers. 'I know, Pa. It's terrible. The worst.' (Wasn't that what Miss Henry always said?) 'But you've still got me. I'll look after you.'

It wasn't until he was driving away that he realised that she'd been comforting him when it should have been the other way round.

Lizzie walked back up the stairs to her bedroom in the attic, sat in the window seat, took up her book and went on reading where she'd left off. It was Robert Browning's *Men and Women* and before her father had arrived she'd been reading *One Word More*, wondering whether she would ever find someone who would love her as much as Robert Browning had loved his Elizabeth. Talking about Rhett Butler that morning has set her thinking. Now it was as if her thoughts had congealed. She was surprised by how coolly she was accepting this death, almost as if it hadn't happened to her mother but to someone else, like poor little Iris's mother or Penny's, or Dorothy Brown's father who'd been torpedoed in the Atlantic. Not a real death at all. Just something you heard about and then said how sorry you were. For a few minutes she wondered whether she ought to tell her friends and decided against it. What was the point? It wouldn't bring her mother back to life. It was all very simple. She'd been in a house that had been hit by a bomb and she'd been killed. It happened all the time.

Then she put her head in her hands and howled with grief, overwhelmed by it, aching with it, out of her depths in it.

Tommy had been driving round Woking for more than an hour, hardly aware of where he was going or what he was doing. It was as if he'd lost all volition, as if the car was going its own way, with no more substance than thistledown. He'd driven down the same road twice before he realised where he was. Then he understood that it was Ridgeway and that he'd come to a halt outside Octavia's house. He turned in at the drive and switched off the ignition. Then he just sat there, staring through the windscreen. He had no idea what he ought to do next.

Janet was setting the table for dinner when she became aware of him and she went off at once to report to Emmeline.

'I think it's wor Major Meriton,' she said. 'Onny he's not movin', like. He's just sittin' there.' And Emmeline, who wasn't in the least surprised, put on her hat and coat and went out to speak to him.

She had to tap on the window for quite a long time before he became aware of her and rolled it down.

'Tommy, my dear,' she said. 'Aren't you coming in?'

'No, no,' he said. 'Thanks all the same. Can't stop. Things to do. Reports to write. That sort of thing. Regards to Tavy.' And before she could persuade him, he put the car in gear and drove away.

Emmeline stood in the moonlit garden flanked by the dead twigs of winter, with the gravel hard under her slippers – why hadn't she thought to change her shoes? – and the night air chilling her lungs. She was fraught with pity for him. What a terrible time this is, she thought. There are so many deaths and so much misery. And she wondered how Tavy would cope with that poor child.

At that moment she was sitting in the window seat with Lizzie in her arms, holding her while she cried. 'It's the worst,' Lizzie sobbed. 'The very, very worst. Life will never be the same again.'

'No,' Octavia agreed, 'it won't. It will be different from now on. You have to face that. We all do when we lose someone we love. But I can promise you that there will be good things as well as bad.'

'How can you possibly say that?' Lizzie said, raising her head. Her eyes were bloodshot with weeping and her face wild with grief. 'How can you possibly, possibly say that?'

'Because it's true,' Octavia told her. 'I know you can't believe it now, but it *is* true.'

# Chapter Fourteen

Spring was a long time coming that year. It was as if the trees were shrinking into themselves, as if their trunks had grown tough-skinned against so much brutality and their blossom had been blighted by the dust of so much destruction and the fury of so many fires. Even the songbirds were subdued, their calls delicate and hesitant. We have broken the natural exuberance of the season, Octavia thought. There is too much death. And she set herself to think what could be done about it. We will paint this spring, she decided, to remind ourselves that it's coming and we'll fill our classrooms with the colour of it, and celebrate it in poetry and song in every way we can. We mustn't let this war defeat us.

But it was a difficult time no matter what she tried to do about it. There was a battle going on in North Africa between the British and the Italians, which didn't make sense to her because they seemed to be fighting over a few hundred miles of desert. The newspapers were full of it, with stories of how the Italians were surrendering in droves to the 'Aussies' and there were newsreel pictures of long columns of Italian prisoners, with the occasional Australian soldier to guard them, trudging through the sand waving at the cameras. It was all a little unreal. Hitler's campaigns on the other hand were as swift and ruthless as ever. In April, when the lilac was just beginning to put out a few delicate buds in Octavia's rented garden, he launched a massive invasion of Yugoslavia, entering the country simultaneously from Hungary, Rumania and Bulgaria, and at the end of the month he invaded Greece, drove out the British army and marched in triumph through Athens. There didn't seem to be anything anyone could do to stop him, although the RAF, as Flight Lieutenant Mark Meriton reported to his father, 'did their darnedest'.

Tommy Meriton drove down to Woking every other weekend to see Lizzie, once with Mark, who caused much head turning when he stepped out of the car in the Downview drive. Tommy and his children were beginning to establish some sort of family pattern and although Lizzie was always much too quiet, he felt she was glad to see him. At home in Wimbledon he was lonely and taciturn, in Woking he did what he could to cheer his little girl, in the Foreign Office he worked. Sometimes he wished he could visit Tavy for an hour or two – she was the one person who would understand what he was feeling – but it didn't seem proper without Elizabeth and in any case she had quite enough to do without him imposing on her.

It wasn't until May, when there was another massive air raid on the City of London, that anything was to change and then it was because of Lizzie's anxiety.

The 10th of May was one of the coldest May nights on record and, once again, there was a low tide on the Thames and a bombers' moon of terrifying brightness. All the German bombers had to do that night was to follow the white ribbon of the Thames until they reached the familiar basins of the docks. Once they were above their first target, they dropped incendiary bombs in such numbers that the warehouses were rapidly set ablaze. Then, guided by moonlight and their own fires, they turned their attention to Central London and the mainline railway stations which they bombed with high explosives. The attack went on all night and the bombers came over in continuous waves, returning to their bases in Northern France simply to refuel and then setting out again.

It wasn't long before the fires stretched from Romford to Hammersmith, east to west, and from Hampstead to Norwood, north to south. The City had never withstood such a long, concentrated attack nor seen so much damage. Seven Wren churches were gutted, the Tower of London, Westminster Abbey and the Chamber of the House of Commons were on fire, and seven hundred gas mains were fractured and burning like torches to light the way for their tormentors. Hospitals were hit too, just when they were most needed. St Thomas's Hospital was very badly damaged and so was the Greycoat Hospital. And of course, hundreds of factories were destroyed and thousands of homes. Everything was on an apocalyptic scale. The LCC had over twelve hundred fire engines in use that night but they were overwhelmed by the number of fires and the lack of water and radioed for help to the outlying suburbs, who sent another seven hundred and fifty engines to assist as soon as they could. Even they weren't enough and the fires continued to spread. Cast-iron water mains cracked in the heat, six of the city's telephone exchanges were out of action, all the main railway stations were closed, every bridge across the Thames was blocked and so were over eight thousand streets. By the early hours of the morning seven hundred acres of London were on fire, and some of the fires went on burning for eleven days and nights. It was the worst raid anyone had ever seen.

News of the scale of it percolated slowly, for the papers played it down and so did the wireless. But the next day, people all over London could see the fires and smell the sugar that was still burning in the docks, and all day long small scraps of charred paper fell on them like an ominous black snowfall. And the sun was red.

'We've had the most dreadful raid,' Dora said, when she finally managed to phone her mother. 'They hit the docks. It's been raining bits of black paper all day.'

Emmeline wasn't interested in bits of black paper. 'Are you all right?' she said.

'Yes,' Dora told her, serious about it for once. 'I'm fine. It was all in the docks and the City. Our AFS boys went up to help. They said it was a nightmare. The City was on fire from one end to the other.'

Lizzie didn't hear about it until the following morning, when one of her old school friends sent her a letter with a graphic description of the height of the flames and the extent of the fire. She'd been working in the City ever since she left school and had seen it all when she tried to get into her office. *I walked over London Bridge because the Tubes were shut,* she wrote, *but then I couldn't get any further because all the roads were covered in debris and blocked off and lots of places were still on fire. I've never seen anything like it. The wardens told us to go home because we couldn't do any work in that mess, so we did.* Lizzie noticed that she didn't say anything about how many people had been killed and injured but there must have been hundreds in a raid like that. What if Pa...?

No, no, he simply mustn't. Suddenly, she needed to hear his voice, to know he was all right. Oh Pa, she thought, as she ran down the road towards the phone box, dear, dear Pa. Don't you be killed too. I couldn't bear it. By the time she reached the box her fingers were sticky with sweat and it took her a few fumbling minutes before she could get her pennies into the slot. And then the number rang and rang and nobody answered.

Oh come on! Come on! she thought. Somebody pick it up. There must be someone there. Mrs Dunnaway, if nobody else. But the ringing tone stopped and was replaced by that awful long burring noise that meant the phone had gone dead. She struggled to keep control of herself, pressed button B for the return of her coins and dialled again. And exactly the same thing happened. He's been killed, she thought. He's dead and they've sent for Mrs Dunnaway to identify his body. It's like my mother all over again. I can't bear it.

She stood in the nasty smelly coffin of a box, breathing in other people's stale cigarette smoke, trying to think what to do. She was still thinking frantically when a woman in a headscarf came and stood outside the box and looked at her in a nasty pointed way.

She struggled to open the door, stepped out of the fug, muttered 'Sorry' and ran back the way she'd come. What was she going to do? Oh, for heaven's sake, what was she going to do? He could be dead and she couldn't think of anything.

And there was Smithie, wheeling that old bike of hers round the side of the house with its basket heaped with books, just as it always was, dear old Smithie, with her fuzzy hair and her tatty old scarf and those scuffed shoes. She'd know. She ran towards her, calling, 'Miss Smith! Miss Smith!'

Octavia propped her bike against the wall. One glance at Lizzie's face told her this was serious. 'What is it?' she said.

Lizzie was incoherent. 'There's been...' she said, weeping. 'It's Pa. He could be... Amber sent me a letter. She said it was...awful. I can't get through and I've tried and tried. What am I going to do?'

Octavia understood that it was to do with the raid. 'Come with me,' she said. And as they walked into the building she went on, speaking calmly, 'It's about the raid on London, isn't it? I've been talking to Mr Chivers about it. A very bad one, so he says.'

'Yes. Yes,' Lizzie sobbed. 'I've tried to…phone. I couldn't get… There wasn't…'

'The telephone exchanges were hit,' Octavia told her. 'That's probably why you couldn't get through. Don't worry. We'll try again from my office.'

They'd reached the door and there was Miss Henry hard at work at the desk, looking up with her little foxy face all concerned. She stood up at once and put the kettle on when Octavia signalled to her. Then she waited with her arm round Lizzie's shoulder and cuddled her while Octavia dialled Tommy's home number.

Even from the other side of the little room, Lizzie could hear Mrs Dunnaway's gruff voice, confirming the number. Oh thank God, at least *she's* there. And if she's there she'll know if there's anything. Oh please don't let there be anything.

'It's Miss Smith, Mrs Dunnaway,' Octavia said, 'from Roehampton Secondary School. Is Major Meriton at home?'

'No, ma'am. He hasn't got back from work yet – if he ever got there. We had a bad raid the night before yesterday you see and everything's topsy turvy.'

'But he's well?'

'Oh yes, he's fine. We didn't have any bombs here, I'm glad to say. He went out this morning to see if he could get into the City – he couldn't get through yesterday – anyway he hasn't come back so I presume he did. He should be home by five o'clock. Or six maybe. Depending. Like I said, everything's topsy-turvy.'

'Perhaps you could ask him to ring me when he gets back,' Octavia said. 'He has my home number. It's not urgent but Lizzie's been worried about him.'

The assurance was given at once. 'Of course.'

'There you are,' Octavia said to Lizzie. 'He's quite all right and he'll ring you tonight as soon as he gets in. Have your supper and then come over. You've got your bike, haven't you?'

In fact Tommy did rather better than make a phone call. He turned up on Octavia's doorstep a mere five minutes after Lizzie had cycled into the drive.

It was an extraordinary evening. Lizzie was so relieved so see him that she wept and fell into his arms as soon as he entered the hall, and when they were all gathered in a circle round Emmeline's necessary fire, she sat by his side as if she'd been glued there. Nothing was said about the raid, of course, they were all too deliberately busy talking about other things, like what was happening at school and how late the spring was, and what it was like to live in the country, which was 'smashing' according to Maggie and Barbara, and how ridiculously small the rations were. 'Next time,' Tommy promised, 'I shall come bearing gifts.' They were so easy with one another and so happy to be together that when Octavia produced the last two bottles of her father's champagne, chill from the cellar, and Emmeline brought out the cake tin to reveal half a fruit cake, no less, the evening became a celebration. Even the three little'uns had a sip of champagne and got giggly, and the cake was devoured to the last crumb. Soon, they were all laughing and remembering old times, which was wonderfully comforting, even though Janet found some of it baffling. Eleven o'clock struck and they were still sitting round the fire and still talking.

'I must be off,' Tommy said looking at his watch, 'or I shall never wake up in the morning and Mrs D will have to come upstairs and whack me with the poker.'

'Oh Pa,' Lizzie said. 'You're so funny. And I thought you were dead.'

'Well, I'm not, as you see,' he said, hugging her. 'I live a charmed life, don't I, Tavy.'

'I think he was a cat in a previous existence,' Octavia said.

He kissed them all goodbye at the door, little'uns, Janet and all. 'It's been a lovely evening,' he said. 'We must do it again. My treat though next time, Emmeline.'

Then he drove Lizzie back to Downview, gave her one last cuddle and went home singing. It was the first time he'd done such a thing since Elizabeth died.

From then on he visited them every other week and, true to his promise, he always arrived with a hamper. 'It's like Christmas,' Emmeline said when she opened the first one, and he winked at Octavia and grinned at Lizzie and said he was very glad to hear it. But it wasn't Christmas. It was spring, at last, and the weather was as warm as their mood. Best of all, there had been no air raids since that last awful raid on the City and they were beginning to hope that the Blitz was over.

Dora said she didn't know what to do with herself now that everything had gone quiet. 'I mean,' she said when she phoned Emmeline, 'there's nothing going on in the office. Who wants to buy a house in London these days? Even if we had any to sell. I wonder he doesn't close down and have done with it.'

'How about coming down here for a few days?' Emmeline suggested. 'Would he let you? We haven't seen you for ages.'

'What would I do about the rations?'

'Get a temporary card,' Emmeline said. 'That's what the servicemen do. But you don't have to worry. We've got our own private source of supply.'

So the family grew even bigger and the 'Tommy parties' even more cheerful. Now it wasn't just food and drink but dancing to Octavia's famous gramophone. And when news came through that the Germans had invaded Russia, which meant that they wouldn't be invading England, they had a Saturday night party that went on into the small hours. So late in fact that Emmeline told Tommy he was to sleep on the sofa instead of driving back in the blackout, and made him up a bed there and then to settle the matter.

'Sweet dreams,' she said, as she and Octavia left him alone in the dishevelled drawing room. 'See you in the morning.'

Octavia walked up the stairs to her room feeling happily exhausted, glad that her family were together again, even if Johnnie hadn't been able to join them, and pleased that she'd played host to such a very big party and that they'd all had such a good time. Now that she'd stopped dancing she realised that her feet were aching and the first thing she did when she reached her room was to take off her shoes. Then she sat on the edge of the bed and reached for her nightdress under the pillow. I shall sleep like a top after all this, she thought. But she was wrong.

She lay on her back, watching the pin-point stars and the creamy crescent of the moon in the black square of her window, and gave herself up to her thoughts as she waited to drift off. It was such a joy to dance with Tommy again. She couldn't tell him so, naturally, that wouldn't be proper or kind when he'd just lost Elizabeth. But even if she had to keep it secret, it was a joy just the same, to be in his arms again, breathing in the warm familiar smell of him, smiling at him and talking to him, the way she used to do all those years ago when they were young and in love and nothing else mattered. It made her remember so many good things, as if the years hadn't happened, and it aroused her feelings too, although she certainly couldn't say anything about *that*, not to anyone. I did love him, she thought. I ought to have married him. We were good for one another. Memories danced into her mind, swirling and youthful and pleasurable and she surrendered to them, luxuriating in them, warmed and absorbed.

The moon was still hanging like a milk-white cradle in the square of her window. We change, she thought, but the moon stays the same, always the same and always watching us. The romantic notion rather pleased her. But then her wits returned and she realised that this particular moon had actually changed while she was watching it. When she'd first looked up at it, it had been in the far corner of the window, now it was in the middle. I must have been lying here for hours, she thought, and switched on the bedside light to look at the clock. It was half past four. Good God, she thought. I've been awake all night.

There was no point in lying in bed any longer. She was wide awake and not likely to sleep now. She got up, walked to the window and opened it so that she could lean out. Now she could see that the dawn had begun. The sky beyond the trees was misty pink and the garden shrubs were greening as they emerged from the darkness. It's going to be a fine day, she thought, and wondered how long it would be before the roses bloomed. The last time she'd looked at them they'd been in bud. Now, of course, they were just black shapes in the flower-beds. She could only just make out the odd leaf, silhouetted against... Then she froze with a sudden horror. There was

204

somebody walking about in the garden. She could see the dark shape quite clearly. A man, heading for the house.

A burglar, she thought. Well, I'm not having that, and she put on her dressing gown at once while she thought of something large and heavy to defend herself with. There was a cricket bat in the hallstand. Right. That would do. She went downstairs, as quietly as she could, found the bat, took a deep breath, opened the french windows and strode out onto the lawn. The figure was under the willow tree.

'Stop!' she called. 'Stop right there!' And marched towards him, bat raised.

'It's a fair cop, guv!' the figure said, walking towards her with his hands in the air. 'I give in! Don't hit me!'

For a second she wondered why he was talking such nonsense. It was like something out of some stupid murder mystery. Then she saw who it was.

'Tommy, you idiot,' she said. 'I thought you were a burglar. What are you doing in the garden?'

'Couldn't sleep, old thing,' he said. 'Too much to think about.'

'Me too,' she confessed. 'I've been awake all night.'

He took her hand, slipped it through the crook of his arm and walked them towards the fruit patch at the end of the garden. Almost at his first step a robin began to sing. 'Just in time for the dawn chorus,' he said. And sure enough, as they walked companionably together along the shadowed path, the chorus began, at first chirruping and carolling, and then weaving extraordinary complications as more and more birds joined in.

They'd reached the fruit patch and the hedge that shielded it from the rest of the garden. They were on their own, hidden and private, in the pearly half light. 'Do you remember the first time we heard this?' he asked.

Oh she did. She did. 'In your flat,' she said. 'That first summer.'

'What times they were,' he said. 'I've been thinking about them all night. Remembering.'

'Me too,' she said. They had moved from the cheerful language of farce to a sudden intimacy and tenderness that was making it difficult for her to breathe. 'We were very young,' she said, feeling she ought to make excuses for them.

'And very happy.'

'Yes.'

He smiled at her, his grey eyes dawn-dark. 'Are you happy now?'

She tried to be sensible. 'At this moment or generally?'

'Both.'

'I suppose I'm generally fairly happy,' she told him, avoiding the more personal question. 'Very happy sometimes. It's a good life. It depends on what's happening.'

He persisted, teasing her. 'And at this moment?'

It had to be admitted. 'Yes,' she said. 'I am. Very happy.' And she offered a deflecting explanation. 'It was such a good party. I've been thinking about it all night.'

'It won't wash, Tikki-Tavy,' he said. 'I'm talking about now. About us. About this moment.'

That old loving nickname gave her heart a palpable tug. How could she refuse him the answer he wanted, even if it wasn't sensible to give it? 'All right then,' she said, rather grudgingly. 'I'm happy now.'

He gave a crow of delight. 'You didn't have to tell me,' he said, beaming at her. 'It's written all over your face.'

She grimaced. He'd always said he could read her face. 'Then why did you push me?'

'I wanted to hear the words,' he said. And he put his arms round her, pulled her towards him, cricket bat and all, and kissed her full on the mouth.

In the reasonable part of her brain she knew she ought to resist, to pull away, to make him stop. But it was such a joy to be kissed by him again, here in the dawn in the quiet of the garden, that she stood where she was, dropped the bat and kissed him back.

'Darling, darling Tavy,' he said.

Now and a bit late she tried to put up some opposition. 'We mustn't…' she began.

He put a gentle finger on her lips, his eyes laughing. 'We have,' he said. 'My dear, dear Tikki-Tavy. We have.'

'My feet are soaking wet,' she said, trying to disarm him with practicalities. 'I think we ought to go back to the house.'

'We will go wherever you like,' he said, picking up the bat. 'All you have to do is lead the way.'

Emmeline had woken early that morning too and she and Janet were in the kitchen setting the table for breakfast when Octavia and Tommy came in through the kitchen door.

'Good heavens above,' she said. 'Where have you two sprung from? And why have you got that cricket bat? Don't tell me you've been playing cricket because I'll never believe it.'

'She thought I was a burglar,' Tommy explained. 'She was going to hit me with it.'

'Nothing ever surprises me with Tavy,' Emmeline said. Then she noticed how wet Octavia's slippers were. 'Oh Tavy, for heaven's sake! Look at the state of your slippers. You look as if you've been swimming in them. You'd better get upstairs and get dressed. I don't want you taking cold. I'm afraid I've only got corn flakes for breakfast, Tommy, but you're welcome to what there is.'

'Thanks all the same, Em, but no,' Tommy said. 'It's time I was getting back. I'm expecting a few colleagues this afternoon and I need a change of clothes. Thank you for putting me up – or putting up with me.'

'Next time bring your pyjamas,' Emmeline said. 'And your Wellington boots if you're going to wander about in the garden.'

That Sunday was the oddest day. The house was still full of people so there was constant talk and lots of games to play with the children and plenty to do, but Octavia couldn't keep her mind on any of it. Despite admonishing herself most sternly and telling herself that she really must be sensible, her idling mind kept sloping off to relive those few extraordinary moments in the garden. It was barely six months since Elizabeth had been killed and she knew perfectly well how much Tommy had loved her. That had been plain to her every time she'd seen them together. Too plain sometimes. They were a strong, loving couple. Elizabeth had understood him and handled him well. And now this. She knew she should have been shocked by the way they'd been behaving out in the garden. And yet she wasn't. She hadn't been at the time and she wasn't then. It was too good to be true, of course, and probably simply a matter of too much partying and too little sleep, coupled with the effect of dawn and birdsong. But it had happened. It couldn't be denied. It *had* happened. And if she was honest, which she always tried to be, she had to admit that she was glad of it. But what would happen now? Would he just go home and forget it? Or would something more come of it? And did she want it to? She thought and thought, all day long, returning to her questions like a tongue to an aching tooth, and she was no nearer knowing what she felt or wanted at the end of the day than she'd been at the beginning.

The next morning there was a letter lying beside her plate addressed in his unmistakable handwriting.

*Dear Tikki-Tavy,* he said.

*I have two tickets for a show on Saturday night. They say it's very good. How about taking time off work for once and coming to see it? I will ring you later and see what you think.*

*Give my love to Emmeline and please tell her the party was the highlight of my week.*

*Yours,*

*Tommy*

She passed it across the table for Emmeline to read. It was innocuous enough for general consumption and she didn't want to appear secretive about it.

Emmeline read it with her toast in one hand and the letter in the other. 'That's nice,' she said. 'You'll go, won't you. Bit of time off would do you good.'

So she went, in her prettiest dress and her least-worn coat, with her most respectable hat on her head and the most troubled misgivings in her heart.

Tommy took the Silver Cloud to meet her at Wimbledon station and he'd dressed for the occasion too, as Octavia was quick to notice.

'Spot on time,' he said, as he strode forward to take her hands and kiss her. A respectable kiss this time but a minor pleasure, brief though it was.

'This is a lovely car,' she said, relaxing into the passenger seat. 'I do like a bit of luxury.'

He grinned at her. 'Me too.'

'You're lucky to get the petrol for it. I've had to give up driving and take to a bicycle.'

'Perks of the job,' he said lightly. 'Ready for the off?'

It was a ridiculous play but sitting beside him in the stalls she enjoyed every silly word of it. Afterwards he took her to supper, which to her ration-restricted palate was almost too rich.

'How the other half live,' she said, as a rum baba was put before her.

'You can join the other half whenever you like,' he offered.

'I most certainly could not,' she told him. 'I have a socialist soul.'

He grinned at that. 'That's what I was afraid you'd say. So I suppose you'll refuse to eat your sweet.'

She took the first spoonful at once. 'That would be stupid,' she said. 'I can't let good food go to waste.'

'That's what I love about you, Tikki-Tavy,' he said. 'Socialist principles and aristocratic tastes.'

Oh, it was a good meal. But they took so long over it that she was afraid she'd miss the last train.

'You've missed it already,' he said, stirring his coffee. 'That's all catered for.'

She could hardly misunderstand him. But then she didn't want to misunderstand him. 'You've had this all planned from the beginning, haven't you?'

'Tools of my trade, old thing,' he said, grinning at her. 'Diplomacy is eighty per cent planning.'

'I would have said it was eighty per cent artfulness.'

'There's that too.'

'So where are we going now?'

'Home,' he said.

* * *

He drove her to Parkside Avenue and, while she was rummaging through her bag for the key and thinking what a long time it had been since she'd last used it, he took a hamper from the boot.

She laughed. 'Not more food, surely?'

'This is breakfast,' he said, carrying it into the kitchen. 'Mrs Dunnaway made it up for me.' And when she made a face at him, 'It's all right. She thinks I'm staying with friends.'

She put her hands flat on the kitchen table and took a preparatory breath. It was time to make their position clear. They had to be sensible. 'Now look,' she said. 'It's no good thinking we can just pick up where we left off. We've got to be sensible about this. We can't just... We have positions to think of...'

He put his hand under her chin, lifted her head and kissed her long and passionately. 'My dear, darling, ridiculous Tavy,' he said. 'Come to bed.'

# Chapter Fifteen

Octavia stayed in Wimbledon until five o'clock that Sunday afternoon and she only went back to Woking then because she didn't want to upset Emmeline by being late for dinner.

Tommy couldn't see that there was a problem. 'Phone her,' he said. 'Tell her you're staying here and I'm going to feed you. There's no need for you to rush off. I'm sure she wouldn't mind.'

'She would,' Octavia told him. 'She'd mind very much. I'd never hear the end of it. It's the most important meal of the week. Our one and only roast. And she's cooking it all herself tonight because Janet's gone to see her family. Don't make that face. It's all very well for you. You can eat roast meat whenever you like. You only have to book a table at one of your restaurants. We have to exist on our rations.'

'All right,' he said easily. 'Point taken. I think you're making more of it than she would but if that's the way you feel…'

The two of them were strolling in the garden arm in arm. It was peaceful there and, although it was woefully overgrown, there were still fish in the pond and flowers among the weeds and the rose arch was heavy with blossom. 'I don't want to leave you,' she said. 'You know that. But I must play fair.'

'You and your passion for justice,' he teased. 'So when am

I going to see you again?'

'Soon,' she said vaguely, stopping to weave a trailing shoot into the arch.

He took her hands away from the roses and held them, turning her so that they were face to face. 'This is important, Tavy.'

She felt chastened. 'I know it is,' she said. 'But it's complicated. You've got a high-powered job to do. I've got a school to run. We can't just take off whenever we feel like it.'

His face was stubborn. 'Yes we can.'

'Be reasonable, Tommy,' she said. 'We've got responsibilities.'

He gave her imprisoned hands an exasperated shake. 'Now look,' he said. 'We've been given a second chance, which is a damned sight more than we deserved, and I'm damned if I'm going to let it go. We're not young any more and there's a war on and nobody knows what will happen next. OK, we're not going to be invaded. We've escaped that. But everything else is uncertain. I want to spend the rest of my life with you and I don't want to waste a minute of it. When you're offered a second chance you grab it with both hands. Or you do if you've got any sense. I thought you felt the same way.'

Did she? She wasn't sure. Last night in the privacy of her bedroom in her empty house, she would have said yes without even stopping to think about it. But that was last night. It was wonderful to be back with him, wonderful to be loved by him, but here, in the garden, in the clear light of day, she had to face the fact that she wasn't a free agent. The school had to be run. There were people depending on her.

'Don't you?' he insisted. 'I seem to remember you saying you loved me.'

'I do love you,' she said honestly. 'I've always loved you. Right from the very beginning. You know that.'

'Very well then,' he said, lifting her hand and kissing her

fingers. 'Prove it. Tell me I can come down and see you on Wednesday.'

'Yes, of course you can.'

'And stay the night?'

She frowned and pulled her hand away from him. 'That's the problem,' she said, continuing her walk.

'Only if we allow it to be,' he said walking beside her.

She slipped her hand through his elbow and turned to look at him as they walked, her face an entreaty. 'We must be sensible, Tommy. If Em were to find out we were lovers she'd be mortified. She's a very conventional woman.'

'Then we must show her how stupid the conventions are.'

It was time to talk about the one thing neither of them had mentioned. 'It's only six months since Elizabeth was killed,' she said. 'I think most people would be shocked to know you'd started a love affair so soon. There are *some* proprieties.'

They'd reached the garden seat which looked decidedly grubby. He took his handkerchief out of his pocket and dusted it down, quickly and with irritable determination.

'For a start it's nearly seven months,' he said, as they sat down, 'but we'll let that pass. What's important for you to understand is that our marriage wasn't a love affair in the accepted sense.'

'Oh, come now,' Octavia said. 'I've seen you together too many times to let you get away with that. It was a very good marriage. You're surely not going to deny her that, poor woman. That's shabby.'

'No, I'm not,' he said. 'It was a very good marriage. You're right. She was a wonderful wife, superb at parties, ran the house like clockwork, looked after the children – and me too, sometimes – a good companion. There's no denying any of that. I was very fond of her and she of me, but it wasn't a love

214

affair. Not the way it was with you. The way it can be again if you want it to be.'

'That sounds like emotional blackmail to me,' she said in her direct way. 'Am I supposed to be pleased to hear you say such things?'

'No,' he said, 'that's not why I'm telling you.' It wasn't entirely true. He *had* hoped to please her. In fact he'd *expected* to please her. 'I just wanted you to know how things really were. You always said we had to be honest with one another.'

'True,' she said, 'but not to the detriment of someone else's character. It's no good, Tommy. You can say what you like but it won't make a ha'p'orth of difference. If we make our affair public the people who know us will be upset. They're bound to be. We must take our time over this and be discreet.'

'How long for?'

'Another eight months, at least. Possibly more.'

'That's the trouble with you,' he said. 'You're always so bloody direct.'

She laughed at that. 'And you want to spend the rest of your life with me?'

'Yes. I do. God help me!'

'And marry me?'

'That too. Naturally. I thought I'd made that clear years ago.'

Her smile was rueful, for all this was true and couldn't be denied. 'I wouldn't be the sort of wife you want.'

'I don't want a sort of wife,' he said. 'I want you. Always have.'

It was such a perfect answer it made her want to cry. She controlled herself by turning her sympathy to someone else. It was an old well-tried trick. 'But you married Elizabeth.'

'It seemed the right thing to do at the time,' he told her,

and he was rueful too. 'She was there, she was suitable, she loved me. I thought we could make a go of it. And we did in our own way. Everyone thought we were the perfect pair. And it was terrible when she was killed. Terrible.' He turned his head away from her, irritated by the turn their conversation had taken. 'Look, do we have to talk about all this?'

She felt so sorry for him and cross with herself for having pushed him into a memory that hurt him so much. 'Not if you don't want to,' she said.

'Well, I don't. I want to talk about us. About when we're going to see one another again.'

'Wednesday,' she said. 'You can sleep in the dressing room. I'll get Em to make you up a bed there. It'll only be a camp bed and it'll be very uncomfortable but you won't have to stay in it. Not for long anyway. It'll only be a token. Just to keep up the proprieties. You can come in and join me when the house is quiet.'

'Now that's more like it,' he said. 'I thought you were going to hold me at arm's length.'

'Perhaps you don't know me as well as you thought.'

'Obviously not,' he said, putting his arms round her. 'I'm glad to say.'

Lizzie was rather surprised to get a letter from her father to say that he was coming down to see her in the middle of the week.

'Unheard of,' she said to Poppy. 'I mean, when have you ever known him to come down on a Wednesday?'

Poppy was sitting in the window seat angling her compact mirror to catch the light as she applied a necessary coating of Max Factor to her face. They were off to the pictures in half an hour and she did so want to cover up her spots. They looked perfectly frightful that evening. 'Maybe he's lonely,' she said. 'I mean, after your mother and everything.'

That was a novel idea to Lizzie Meriton. It had never occurred to her that her father could suffer from anything as mundane as loneliness. 'I can't see why he should be,' she said. 'He's got heaps of friends. Our house was always full of them, drinking cocktails and going haw-haw-haw all the time and telling me how I'd grown.' Even the memory of it made her shudder.

'It was only a thought,' Poppy said and gave her friend an apologetic grin.

'No, no,' Lizzie said, accepting the apology and shamed into being a bit more gracious. 'You could be right. I just wish it wasn't Wednesday, that's all. I shall have to miss choir practice. Still if he's lonely, poor old thing...'

'Wednesday?' Emmeline said. 'This Wednesday do you mean?'

'That's what he says,' Octavia told her, as calmly as she could. 'He's coming to see Lizzie and he'd like to stay over and take us all to dinner.'

'But he was only here last Saturday,' Emmeline said. 'I thought he saw her then? What's up with the man?'

'I expect he's lonely, Ma,' Edith said. 'All on his own in that great house. Where's he going to take us, Aunt? Does he say?' The thought of having a meal in a restaurant was making her mouth water. If there was one thing Tommy Meriton really did know about, it was food. 'Don't make that face, Ma. Think of the fun we'll have and all the lovely things we'll eat.'

Thank God for Edie, Octavia thought, smiling at her.

'Well, I don't know,' Emmeline grumbled on. 'Where's he going to sleep? Have you thought of that? I can't keep putting him on the sofa.'

'We could bring one of the camp beds down and put it in the dressing room,' Octavia said, trying to sound as though she'd just thought of it. 'It wouldn't be wonderful, I'll grant you that, but at least it would be more private than the drawing room.'

'Well, I don't know,' Emmeline said again. 'I'll think about it.'

It was a successful evening, despite Octavia's misgivings. Tommy was an excellent host, and wined and dined them so well that Edie said she hadn't eaten so much for weeks and even Emmeline admitted that it was a very good meal. 'The steak pie was just right,' she said. 'Done to a turn. Just the way I like it.'

What a difference a bit of luxury makes, Octavia thought, and gave Tommy a grin when no one was looking.

When the house was quiet he tiptoed into her bedroom and stretched himself out in her bed with a sigh of relief. 'Bloody camp bed,' he said. 'It's like being on the rack.'

'Whisper,' she whispered to him, and quoted the latest slogan. 'Walls have ears.'

'I *must* love you to put up with this sort of caper,' he whispered. 'I hope you appreciate it.'

'You are nobility itself,' she teased him.

'Can you be noble and carnal at the same time?'

'Let's see,' she said. Oh, it was so good to be together again.

It wasn't quite so good the next morning when she woke up feeling distinctly jaded. Tommy was already in the bathroom, singing tunelessly. Where does he get his energy from? But she lay where she was for another fifteen minutes, wishing she could stay in bed all day, and when she finally bestirred herself and sat at the dressing table to brush the tangles from her hair, she was appalled by the weary face that stared back at her from the mirror. This is going to take a bit of getting used to, she thought. I hope it's a quiet day at school on Monday.

It wasn't. Naturally. But it began with a happy announcement. She'd only just walked into her study at Downview when Helen Staples arrived, breathless and rosy, to say she had some rather good news.

'Have you got time?' she asked hopefully. 'I'll come back later if it's difficult.'

'Come in,' Octavia said. 'I've always got time for good news.'

'Well, I say rather good news,' Helen said, blushing. 'Actually it's very good news, only I suppose that depends on the way you look at it. Very good for me I ought to say. Anyway I've come straight to tell you because I thought you ought to be the first to hear it. I'm engaged to be married.'

Octavia knew what it was without being told. One look at Helen's glowing face and the splendid sheen of her hair would have been enough, even if she hadn't caught the flash of a diamond on her finger. 'My dear,' she said. 'That's wonderful. I'm so happy for you. When will the wedding be?'

'Soon,' Helen said. 'Well, very soon actually. He's off back to sea in a week or two and he wants it to be on his next leave.'

'So I suppose this means you'll be handing in your notice.'

'I'm afraid so,' Helen said. 'That's the one sad thing about it.' But she was so happy she was beaming and didn't look sad at all.

'And where will you be living?'

'Portsmouth.'

'A sailor's wife,' Octavia said.

'A second lieutenant's wife,' Helen said, with obvious pride.

'You must look after him,' Octavia told her. 'Our sailors are valuable.'

'Oh, I shall.'

There was a knock at the door and Maggie Henry arrived. 'Sorry to trouble you, Miss Smith,' she said, 'but we've got a problem. I'll call back, shall I?'

'No,' Octavia said. 'I think we've finished for the moment, haven't we, Helen. We can talk again later.'

The problem was two cases of chicken pox and would necessitate the creation of an isolation ward so that the invalids could have some peace from the rush of the dormitories and the other girls could be protected from taking the infection. It took the best part of the morning to arrange it and by the time the doctor called and the change-over was prepared for, they had a third case and a girl whom Maggie said 'looked suspicious'.

'There's never a dull moment in this place,' Octavia said, when she and Maggie finally sat down in Maggie's room to eat their midday meal. The cook had kept it warm for them and warned them that they'd got to eat it to keep their strength up. 'We can't have you going down with something too.'

Octavia laughed at that. 'I've had every childhood disease you could mention,' she said. 'I don't think you need have any fears on my account.'

'Well, I hope you'll eat it all up just the same,' the cook said. 'We've got to look after you.'

By the time Octavia cycled home that afternoon, the isolation ward was organised, their fourth invalid had been diagnosed beyond doubt and she was feeling so tired her back was aching.

'Am I glad to be home!' she said, as she walked into the kitchen. 'Is there any tea in that pot?'

There was, but for the moment Emmeline had her hands firmly over the tea cosy and an extremely disapproving expression on her face and, seeing it, Octavia realised that there was an atmosphere and that she'd walked straight into it. She glanced round the room quickly trying to work out what it was. The girls were out in the garden playing some game in a tent made out of an old sheet, Edie was looking anxious, but then she often did, Janet was standing beside the sink, with her head bent over the washing-up bowl, not looking up. Then it's something to do with Janet. Speak to her first. 'Nice to see you again, Janet,' she said. 'Was it a good holiday?'

But Janet just mumbled 'Yes, mum' and went on looking at the washing-up bowl.

'Janet's got some news for you,' Emmeline said, sternly. 'Haven't you, Janet? She's just been telling us.'

'I hope it's good news,' Octavia said. 'We've all had enough bad news to last us a lifetime. Not that I can complain. I had a piece of very good news only this morning. One of my teachers came to tell me she was engaged to be married. Young Helen Staples, Em. The pretty blonde. Teaches English. I expect you've seen her too haven't you, Janet.'

'Yes, mum,' Janet said. 'But woan't that mean she'll be givin' you noatice, like? I mean to say, woan't you have to find another teacher?'

'Yes, I shall,' Octavia said, 'and I shall miss her, there's no denying that, but that's the way things are. It happens all the time. The great thing is she's found someone who loves her and she loves him and they're going to get married. That's what's important. I think it's splendid.'

Quick glance round the room to see what effect she was

having. Edie looking relieved, Em suspicious, Janet blushing a really pretty pink and stammering. 'The thing is, Miss Smith…'

'Let me guess,' Octavia said, sure of herself now. 'You're engaged too. Am I right?'

'Well, yes,' Janet admitted, 'onny, you see, it'll mean me leavin' me woark.'

'Pour me some tea,' Octavia said, 'because I'm gasping and then come and sit down and tell me all about it. What's his name?'

'Ted,' Janet said, as she poured the tea. 'And he's in the Merchant Navy an' he's real lovely an' he wants for us to wed before his next trip. It'll be a bit of a scramble but I canna say no, can I? Not when there are all those U-boats, if you see what I mean.'

'I do indeed. So when's the wedding?'

Her answer was rather a surprise. 'Sat'day week. Me mam's arrangin' everythin'. All I got to do is turn up on the day. Or the night before if you'd be agreeable to it.'

She's pregnant, poor girl, Octavia thought. 'Have you got your dress yet?' she asked.

'No, mum, not yet. It wor all a bit of a rush, like. An' a' course there's coupons now.'

'You could have mine if I'd still got it,' Edith offered. 'Only of course I lost it in the bomb. But I tell you what, Dora had one almost the same. I bet she'd let you have it. Or borrow it anyway. It's only hanging in her wardrobe. Would you like me to ask her?'

The kindness was obviously unexpected and it was no surprise to Octavia that Janet began to cry. Edith was across the room in a second and had her arms round her shoulders to comfort her. 'It's always the same,' she said. 'Don't worry.

222

Brides always cry. I know I cried buckets.'

'I don't remember you crying,' Emmeline protested.

'No, 'course you don't,' Edith said, easily. 'I did it in secret.' And she turned her attention back to Janet. 'Now, what about a veil?'

Emmeline made a grimace at her cousin but she didn't say anything more until the two of them were on their own in the drawing room after supper. Then she spoke her mind forcefully.

'That's a shot-gun wedding if ever I saw one,' she said, and her face was a study in disapproval.

'Quite probably,' Octavia said. 'Does it matter?'

'Does it matter?' Emmeline echoed in disbelief. 'Oh, Tavy, how can you say such things?'

'Times are changing, Em,' Octavia said, leaning back in her armchair. 'You can't expect young couples to stay chaste and wait, not these days, not when one or the other of them has got to go back to sea to face the U-boats or back to North Africa to face tanks, or off to a big city to face being bombed. There's too much risk around. I think it's a good thing that love can triumph even in the middle of the war. It encourages me.'

Emmeline shook her head. 'There are times when I despair of you,' she said.

Octavia smiled at her. 'Quite possibly. But we'll wish our Janet well, won't we, no matter what sort of wedding it is, and send her a wedding present.'

In fact, they did rather better than that. The next morning Janet put an invitation beside both their plates and said she knew it was a long way for them to travel but she'd be honoured, she really would, if they could come to her wedding. And as Emmeline's opinion had gentled somewhat

223

overnight and Octavia was delighted to be asked, they both agreed. It was a very pleasant moment but it provoked a lover's quarrel.

Tommy phoned that evening full of plans for another trip to the theatre. 'I've got the tickets,' he said happily. 'Table's booked. I thought we'd go to the same place as last time. It's all arranged. Two seats in the stalls, Saturday week. How's that for organisation?'

'Not good,' Octavia told him.

'Why not?'

'I shall be in Gateshead.'

He was surprised. 'Gateshead?' he said. 'Whatever for?'

'I'm going to a wedding.'

'Oh, for heaven's sake,' he said crossly. 'Whose wedding? Can't you put it off?' He was very annoyed when she told him she most certainly could not and explained why.

'What's the good of me getting everything organised,' he said, 'if you're going off to some stupid wedding?'

'It's no good you getting grumpy,' she said. 'It's not a stupid wedding, and in any case, even if it were I should be attending it.'

'Grumpy?' he said 'Well I like that. I'm a bit annoyed, that's all. Well, jolly annoyed actually. Who wouldn't be? Those tickets are like gold dust.'

'Then you should have checked with me before you booked them.'

'And I suppose you've got something planned for this Saturday too.'

'No. Why should I have?'

'Don't ask me. How do I know what you're doing? You never tell me.'

That was so petty it made *her* cross. 'You're being ridiculous,' she said and hung up on him.

It was two days before he rang again and then it was to tell her that he'd had the most extraordinary letter from Lizzie. 'I don't know how to answer it,' he said. 'I'll show you on Saturday before I take her to tea, if that's all right. I'd appreciate a bit of womanly advice.'

'I shan't be home till five,' Octavia told him. 'I've got a meeting with Mr Chivers. But you could ask Em. She's a great one for womanly advice.'

'I'd rather it were you,' he said, and he sounded almost chastened. 'Em's a darling and I'm sure she'd help if she could but it's your advice I want. Could we meet for lunch perhaps?'

So they met for lunch and he *was* chastened and not at all his ebullient self. He took the letter from the inside pocket of his jacket as soon as the first course was served and passed it across the table to her almost humbly. It was a touching letter.

*Dearest Pa,* it said.

*In a day or two I shall have finished my examinations and after that I shall break up, which means I shall have some time on my hands. I have been thinking about this a great deal and I've been wondering whether you would like me to come back to London and keep you company for a little while. It must be very lonely for you all on your own and I could look after you. I shan't be as good at it as Ma was but I would do my best.*

*Let me know what you think the next time you come down.*

*Your ever loving daughter,*

*Lizzie.*

'That's a very loving letter,' Octavia said, smiling at it. 'She thinks you're lonely.'

'Yes,' he agreed, 'I can see that. But what on earth am I going to say to her? I can't say I'm not, can I?'

'No, you can't.'

'Then what shall I say? She's put me on the spot.'

'I think you might have to let her come home and look after you. You'll hurt her feelings if you say no.'

'But that will mean…'

'Yes, I know, but I don't think we have any option. You could suggest she stays with her friends until the end of term and then comes home. That would give us a bit of leeway.'

It was a possible compromise but he didn't like it. 'I *had* hoped we could take a holiday in the summer.'

She was touched by how tentative he was. 'We still could,' she said, 'if we play our cards right. See what she says.'

'Yes,' he said, 'I will. And thanks for the advice.' He gave her his old confident grin, as if he was going to tease her. 'It wasn't a problem that could be taken to Em, you see, was it.'

Lizzie came straight back from tea with her father to tell Poppy that she'd been quite right. 'He is lonely,' she confided. 'He as good as said so. I'm going back to Wimbledon to look after him as soon as we break up. He said I was a dear girl. Wasn't that sweet.'

'What will you have to do?' Poppy wanted to know. 'I mean you can't cook, can you? Except beans on toast. How will you manage?'

'Oh, we've got a cook/housekeeper to do all that,' Lizzie said. 'It'll be my job to be there in the evenings to eat dinner and talk to him like Ma used to do. If he has a party I might have to play the hostess but I could do that. It's only a matter of standing around making the right noises and looking pretty. I've seen Ma do it plenty of times.'

'But would you know what to say?' Poppy worried.

'You don't have to say anything really,' Lizzie told her. 'You just have to agree with whatever they're saying. It's a sort of game.'

'Heavens!' Poppy said. 'I wouldn't like to have to play it.'

'So anyway,' Lizzie said. 'It's all settled.'

It was unsettled three weeks later by two events that neither she nor her father could have foreseen.

# Chapter Sixteen

Roehampton Secondary School was shrinking. There was no doubt about it. The number of first-formers had been slightly down last September but it hadn't been enough to concern them. Most of the girls who had opted to come to the school had been happy to be re-evacuated to Woking so they'd only lost about half a dozen, whose parents had decided they should stay where they were. But this year was a different matter. Now the new entrants had been living in their evacuated homes for nearly two years and many of them didn't want to be uprooted. They'd solved the problem by finding other London grammar schools that were nearer their billets and would take them until the war was over. In addition to that, many of Roehampton's present second- and third-formers had begun to drift back to London to be with their parents. There was no more bombing now, it was safe, and there was an emergency school not far from where they lived. It didn't operate the Dalton system but it was a grammar school and it would do until Roehampton Secondary School came back to London. Admittedly Octavia had picked up one or two London grammar school girls who lived locally and ought to have been going to other schools in other areas but it wasn't enough to run three first forms.

'They should have thought of this when they planned the

evacuation in the first place,' Maggie said crossly. 'If they'd sent our elementary schools into the same area as us there wouldn't have been such a muddle. They could have stayed in their billets and just changed schools.'

'I think it was a big enough undertaking without that sort of forward planning,' Octavia said. 'They got four million children out of London in three days don't forget.' But the drop in numbers was worrying because it would have an effect on staffing. She wasn't sure now, having seen next year's figures, whether she would be able to replace Helen Staples or whether they would be justified in keeping both their school houses. 'I will talk to Mr Chivers and see what he says about it,' she promised Maggie. 'Look on the bright side. At least there will be more room at our assemblies.' And when Maggie grimaced, she turned their conversation to other matters and asked how their invalids were.

Mr Chivers came down to Woking the next week. He arrived in a shower of rain and came dripping into the hall at Barricane House with a very wet umbrella.

'Such weather, dear lady!' he said to Octavia. 'But we mustn't grumble. These things are sent to try us.'

'I've got some coffee ready for us,' Octavia told him. 'You look as though you could do with it.'

'That sounds splendid,' he said. 'Then I will show you my plans.'

He was such an ally and, despite his rotund appearance, a man full of ideas. When the coffee had been drunk and enjoyed, he spread the plans of Barricane House across her desk and explained what he had in mind.

'If we were to extend this kitchen,' he said, 'with an archway here and more sinks and cookers, this could be a domestic science room, which would free the rooms you are currently using in Woking School and mean that your domestic science staff wouldn't be so isolated there.'

It was a very good idea and she told him so at once. 'That will please our Miss Fletcher,' she said. But she was thinking that Miss Fennimore and Mabel Ollerington would then be left all on their own in the Science labs at Woking school and although she knew they would never complain, something really would have to be done about it. Study rooms in Barricane perhaps. Could we run to that? It would save time for the girls and a lot of wandering about the town.

'Now, as to your new English teacher,' Mr Chivers said. 'The governors have asked me to tell you they are quite happy for you to advertise the post. You might be somewhat overstaffed for a year or two but we feel we must do all we can to keep the Dalton system running, and English is such an important subject.'

'That will be a great relief to all of us,' she told him and it was no more than the truth. 'Are you joining us for lunch?'

'No, no, dear lady,' he said. 'It would be a great pleasure but I have to be in County Hall this afternoon. Especially if we are to set this work in hand. The sooner it is started the better, as I'm sure you agree.'

So he took the train back to London and Octavia cycled to Downview to have lunch with her shower-damp pupils. They were all quite cheerful despite the rain but it made her yearn for a single school building where they could stay dry and warm all day. What a long time it had been since they left Roehampton. And yet here they all were, still cheerful and coping, still getting amazingly good examination results, still helping one another – and people were still falling in love and getting married, war or no war. And tomorrow is Wednesday.

\* \* \*

230

It was also a sunny day and Emmeline was in a very good mood because the local greengrocers were full of plums and she was going to make a plum pie for their dinner that night.

'It's about time we had a glut of *something*,' she said. 'We've been on short commons for such a long time I wonder we're healthy. There are days when I don't know how to make ends meet. And that dried egg is disgusting. It might be all right in cakes and puddings, but it's no good them trying to tell us you can scramble the stuff. It's like eating rubber.' She had what Johnnie would call 'a very dim view' of the Ministry of Food and took all their propaganda with heavy cynicism. But she'd certainly become a lot slimmer since the rationing began, which was no bad thing, and she was much quicker on her feet.

They'd had plums for school dinner that day, although Octavia certainly wasn't going to tell her that. I don't suppose a double dose of plums will do any of us any harm, she thought, and they're very tasty.

That was Lizzie Meriton's opinion too. As Octavia was cycling home to give Emmeline a hand with the evening meal, she was ambling along the canal path, eating yet more plums from a brown paper bag. She'd changed into her coolest clothes, sandals, an old thin skirt and her PE shirt, because it was too hot to wear anything else. Not that she'd had a great deal of choice since clothing went on the ration. Most of the time she simply wore whatever was clean and came to hand. But what did it matter what her clothes were like? Nobody was going to see her down there by the canal. The important thing was that school was over for the day and she was walking into town to meet her father *and* she had a pound of plums and could eat them all if she wanted to. They were very sweet and very juicy.

She had to pause from time to time to wipe the juice from her chin and she was getting more and more sticky. But sticky or not, she made a very pretty picture ambling along by the sky-tinted water with her long, fair hair dappled by sun and shade, and the short, thin, skirt clinging to her brown legs, but she was carelessly unaware of it, for she had other things on her mind.

It wouldn't be long now before she went back to Wimbledon and started looking after her father. In one way she was looking forward to it – it would be nice to have him all to herself for a few weeks and to be back in her own home – but in another way she was just a little bit worried. Despite the bravado she put on when she told Mary and Poppy what she was going to do, she wasn't actually as sure of herself as she sounded. At first, acting the hostess had sounded dashing and easy but, as the likelihood of being asked to do it drew closer, she was beginning to think that it might turn out to be difficult. Her father's guests might look down on her because she was only a schoolgirl, or they might think she was too poorly dressed. They all seemed to have such wonderful clothes and they wore them with style. Maybe I could find something of Ma's, she thought, and get Mrs Dunnaway to alter it for me. But then it might not be suitable or I might look odd in it, as if I was trying to be too grown up. Sighing, she reached into the paper bag for another mouthful of comfort.

Private Ben Hardy, of the 7th tank brigade, who was home on leave for ten days and at something of a loose end, rounded the bend just as she lifted the plum to her mouth and was dazzled by the sight of her. In the few love-struck moments while his brain was still functioning he knew she was the most beautiful girl he'd ever seen in his life. Then he realised that he was walking straight towards her and that if he didn't watch out he would bump into her. He side-stepped just as she looked up and tried to get out of his way and for several seconds they stepped and swerved to avoid one another, both moving in the same direction as though they were performing some complicated dance. Then he tried to lunge away from her just as she too was moving and they collided, flailing arm to far-too-solid shoulder. As she stumbled, the plums fell from the bag and rolled towards the canal.

The sight of good food going to waste was more than she could bear. 'You clumsy oaf!' she shouted at him. 'You great big silly stupid clumsy oaf! Look what you've done. Those are my plums!'

He was bewitched. Bereft of the power of speech but utterly bewitched. He fell to his khaki knees and began to scrabble about at the water's edge catching as many of the plums as he could and stashing them in his cap, wincing as yet another one plopped into the canal, while those lovely brown arms and those gorgeous legs flashed in and out of his line of vision. Finally, when the last plum had been caught, he sat back on his heels and offered her the capful. 'I'm so sorry,' he said.

Her face was furious. 'And so you should be,' she said, taking the cap and transferring her plums to the paper bag.

'I caught most of them,' he said, but she was already walking away, those long legs striding, that long hair golden in the green.

There were three little girls in school frocks walking towards her along the tow path and, as he watched, she stopped and spoke to them. They were gazing at her in admiration, as well they might, and after a few minutes she offered them some of her plums, wiping them on her skirt before she handed them over. What luck! She must be a teacher or something. If he could find out the name of their school he could see her again.

He sat on a fallen tree trunk by the side of the path, hooked his cigarettes from the breast pocket of his tunic and lit one to give himself a reason for loitering. Then when the girls drew up alongside him, eating their plums, he said good afternoon and remarked that it was a lovely day.

They agreed that it was.

He took a drag on the cigarette. 'Those plums look good,' he said.

They agreed about that too.

'Was that your teacher?' he asked. 'The young lady who gave them to you.'

That provoked giggles. 'Oh no,' the tallest girl said. 'Our teachers aren't like that. They're all old. Really old. Out of the ark, some of them. That's Lizzie Meriton. She's a prefect.' And she spoke the words with awe.

'She looks nice.'

'She is,' the girl said. 'Ever so nice. We're in her house.'

'Come on, Iris,' the smallest girl said, looking a bit anxious, 'or we shall be late for supper.'

'Can't have that,' he said, smiling, and he stood up and walked away from them. Well, you've got her name, he told himself happily, and you know she's a prefect at a school where they wear blue checked frocks, so that must be either a private school or a grammar. They're not Woking Girls. I do know that. I'll bet they're evacuees. Those kids sounded like Londoners to me. I'll ask Aunt Min. She'll know which one it is. There can't be many. Then I'll buy her some more plums and give them to her when I see her again. There was no doubt in his mind that he would see her again. It was just a matter of a little detective work. And hadn't he always wanted to be a detective? Lizzie Meriton, he thought, savouring her name. You're the girl of my dreams.

*   *   *

234

At that moment, the girl of his dreams was sitting opposite her father in the respectable dining room of the Albion Hotel, with her grubby bag of plums on the white tablecloth in front of her – to the barely concealed annoyance of the waitresses – and a terrible scowl on her face. After working everything out, even down to what sort of dresses she ought to wear at his parties, and thinking of all the things she could talk to him about in the evenings, he'd come straight in to this dining room, sat himself down and told her he wasn't going to be in London at all during the summer. She was appalled.

'I thought I was going to stay with you and look after you,' she said. 'I thought it was all arranged.'

Tommy recognised that he'd told her badly. It had sounded perfectly reasonable while he was speaking but it seemed to have gone wrong somehow. 'I'm sorry about that, little one,' he said in his most affectionate voice. 'But that's the war for you. Can't be helped. Marching orders and all that sort of thing.'

Lizzie wasn't impressed by marching orders. 'Well, I think it's ridiculous,' she said crossly. 'They can't expect you to work all through the summer. Nobody does. Don't they have any consideration for you? Couldn't you do it some other time?'

'No, I couldn't,' Tommy said. 'It's an Anglo–American conference and it has to be now because that's what Mr Churchill wants.' Then he realised that he was being indiscreet and hastened to warn her not to talk about it. 'It's hush-hush, so you mustn't say a word about it to anyone. Careless talk and all that sort of thing. I know it's not convenient but it could make a difference to the war.'

She shrugged her shoulders. 'Oh, well then I must put up with it.'

'That's my girl,' he said. 'Now, what would you like for tea? Do you fancy some scones?'

Disappointment – and a surfeit of plums – had taken away her appetite. 'I'm not hungry thanks,' she said. 'I ought to be getting back. Thank you for coming down to see me.'

Her stiff formality hurt him more than her anger had done. 'I'm really sorry about this, little one,' he said.

'Yes, well,' she said. 'That's the war for you.' And she stood up, picked up her bag of plums, walked round the table to kiss his cheek and left him.

One of the waitresses appeared at his elbow. 'Is the young lady not staying to tea?' she asked.

'The young lady has got to get back to school,' he told her, 'and I'm afraid I can't stay either.' He looked at his watch to convince her. 'I've got an appointment.'

She gave the proper answer, 'Very good, sir,' looked pointedly at the crumpled tablecloth and walked away from him.

He left her a tip – at least she'd been polite – and drove to Ridgeway as fast as he dared. He needed to see Tavy. Now. This minute. It was probably childish and she would probably take him to task for handling this badly but that's what he needed. Besides, he had a present for her. Two, if you counted the holiday. He might not be too good at handling his daughter. He had to face that. Daughters could be tricky. Everybody said so. But it was different with Tavy. Oh, come on you fool, he said, glaring at an old man doddering along on a bicycle, you're blocking the road and I've got things to do.

Lizzie was in a bad mood too. She walked back to Downview at a furious pace, making stray dogs bark and scattering a flock of scavenging pigeons into clattering alarm. So much

236

for feeling sorry for people, she thought. So much for trying to help them. They don't thank you for it. Well, I shall know better next time. She felt as if she'd been deserted. For Pa, of all people, to turn down her offer. It was hideous. I offered out of the kindness of my heart, she thought, kicking a stone out of her way, and this is what I get for it.

By the time she reached Downview she was hot and sweaty but she'd walked a lot of her bad temper away. Wait till I tell Poppy and Mary, she thought. They'll be horrified. She was quite looking forward to it. There was nobody about in the grounds, although Smithie's bicycle was propped against the wall and there was a soldier waiting by the porch. They're all indoors getting ready for supper, she thought, and strode towards the door to join them. And the soldier turned his head and began to walk towards her, smiling as if he knew her.

'Replacement plums,' he said, holding out a paper bag.

'What?'

'To make amends for the ones I knocked in the canal.'

Oh, good heavens. It was the oaf. 'You didn't have to do that,' she said.

'I did,' he insisted, holding the bag nearer. 'I knocked them in the canal, which I wouldn't have done for worlds. So this is to say sorry.'

'That's very kind of you,' Lizzie said. Now that she was looking at him she could see that he was really quite handsome, tall and slim, like her brothers, and with a certain pride about him that reminded her of her brothers too, especially when they were in uniform. He was wearing his cap on his shoulder so she could see that he had a lot of thick, dark hair – and very brown eyes – and a lovely mouth, wide and full-lipped, exactly the sort of mouth that she and Poppy had decided would be the best for kissing. And here it was, smiling at her. Good gracious heavens.

'I was wondering,' the handsome mouth was saying, 'if you'd like to come to the pictures with me. There's a James Cagney on at the Ritz. It's supposed to be good.'

'What time's it on?' she asked. 'Only I've got to go in and have supper.'

'Do you have to? Have supper I mean.'

'I shall starve if I don't.'

'I tell you what,' he said, 'why don't we have fish and chips? There's a very good fish and chip shop down my way. Then you wouldn't starve and we could go to the second house.'

She made up her mind at once. Pa could reject her all he wanted. She would go out with this young man. 'I'll have to just nip in and tell my friend I might be late,' she said, 'and get a coat or something.'

He was beaming at her. 'Take your plums,' he said.

Over cod and two penn'orth, which they ate out of the newspaper as they walked along the road and which was much better than the beans on toast she'd have got at Downview and much, much better than Pa's ridiculous scones, she asked him how he'd managed to find her.

'I'm a detective,' he said.

She was impressed. 'I didn't know they had detectives in the army.'

'They don't,' he said. 'In the army I drive a tank. But I like a bit of detective work when I can get it.'

'So how did you do it this time?'

'Actually, I asked my Aunt Min,' he said honestly. 'She's lived here for years so there's not much about the local schools she doesn't know and when I told her your summer uniform was blue check, she said Roehampton Secondary at once. Roehampton Secondary evacuated to Woking Girls. So I went to Woking Girls and a girl there said try Barricane House, which had to be in Barricane Road, which it was, and they said you'd be having supper here. Piece of cake.'

It was jolly flattering to be hunted down so assiduously. She picked up a chip and ate it slowly, savouring the flavour and thinking of some way she could answer him. 'But how did you know I was at school?' she asked. 'I'm not in uniform. Do I look that young?'

'I asked the little girls,' he told her.

'What little girls?'

'The ones you talked to on the towpath. They told me your name and what a lovely prefect you are and everything.'

'I shall have words to say to *them*,' she said, pretending to be stern. Oh, this was fun.

And so was the picture, although Jimmy Cagney was pretty silly, but it was nice to be sitting in the darkness with this handsome stranger beside her, feeling immensely grown-up and smoking cigarettes openly instead of dodging off behind the bike sheds. I wonder what Pa would say if he could see me now, she thought, and it occurred to her that he might well be cross. And that made the evening better than ever.

Her father was eating steak and onion pie that had been made with the two tins of steak he'd brought down with him as this week's contribution to the feast, and was regaling his listeners with tales of the various conferences he'd had to attend and telling them how complicated it had been to arrange them.

'Take the one I've got to work on in a week or two,' he said. 'All very hush-hush so you mustn't breathe a word. They want it to be on neutral ground, not in our country and not in theirs, and not in a country that could be compromised by hosting it. You've no idea how difficult that makes things. I'm beginning to think we shall have to hold it at sea.'

'Very good idea,' Octavia said. 'Why not?'

'Because it would be a gift for the U-boats.'

'Not if it was being held on a ship belonging to the biggest "neutral" power and sailing in their home waters. They would hardly want to provoke *them* into war, now would they?'

'You should be working in the Foreign Office,' he told her.

'Pass,' she said, laughing at him. 'I've got quite enough to do running a school.'

She'd made a perfect opening for him. 'You should take a holiday,' he said. 'Shouldn't she, Em?'

'That's what I keep telling her,' Em told him. 'But no. She must keep on and on. She never listens to what I say.'

'I'll bet you haven't had a holiday since before the war,' Tommy said, as if the idea had just occurred to him.

'Well, no,' Octavia admitted. 'But people don't take holidays in war time.'

'I do,' he said. 'In fact I'm going to take one when this conference is over. In the West Indies. Why don't you come with me?'

'I couldn't do that.' Could she?

'Why not? I'll bet half your pupils go back to London in August. Or more. They do, don't they?'

'Well, yes.'

'Very well, then. Take a holiday. You'd love the Caribbean.'

'Oh Aunt,' Edith said. 'The Caribbean! I mean, think of it. That's a once in a lifetime place. I'd go like a shot if it was me.'

'I tell you what, Edith,' Tommy said, grinning at her. 'I'll take your aunt out after dinner and put pressure on her and get her to say yes. How would that be?'

'Highly unlikely,' Octavia warned.

'Who's for more pie?' Emmeline said. 'We can't have it going to waste.'

Lizzie and Ben strolled out of the smoke-filled fug of the Ritz into a moonlit evening. The road was crowded with picture-goers, smoking and chattering and laughing, but above them the sky was an infinite dark blue sea, speckled with shining stars, where the full moon shone like a battered paper lantern. Lizzie gazed at it as she walked and thought how romantic it was. She could almost hear the violins playing.

'It's early yet,' Ben said, 'and it's a lovely night. You don't have to go straight back do you?'

'Well, yes,' she said, 'I do really. Matron'll be looking out for me.'

Oh,' he said, his face falling. 'Just for a few more minutes?'

She thought about it, knowing she ought to say no and go straight home. But she didn't want to do either and it *was* just about possible to stay. Miss Henry would think she was out with her father and he'd brought her back very late sometimes. 'Oh all right then, yes,' she said. 'But not for long, mind.'

So they walked to Horsell Common, which they had entirely to themselves.

It was wonderfully peaceful out there under the stars, strolling along the narrow pathways between the jagged shapes of the gorse bushes and the heather, listening to the swoosh of the pines and the occasional distant sounds from the town – a bicycle bell chirruping, two voices calling to one another, a car revving up. Neither of them said anything until they'd reached the top of a short rise and could see the dip where the sand pits were.

'That's where the Martians landed,' Ben said.

'I know,' she told him. 'I've read it.'

'We had to do it for General Schools,' he said. 'That and Hardy. Funny sort of mixture.'

'We did Hardy too,' she said. '*The Return of the Native.* Which one did you do?'

'*Mayor of Casterbridge.*'

So he's a grammar school boy, she thought. 'Was that Woking Boys?'

'For my sins.'

'We were evacuated to Woking Girls.'

'I know. I told you.'

'Pretty daft, really,' she said. 'We were much too big to fit into five little huts.'

'That's what my aunt said.'

The path had narrowed so much that they were walking side by side and almost close enough to touch. She decided to find out a bit more about him. 'Do you live in Woking or are you just visiting?'

'I live here.'

'Have you always?'

'No,' he said, looking at her. 'I came here when my Mum died. Dad buggered off and me and my brother came to live with Aunt Min.'

'I'm sorry,' she said. 'I didn't mean to pry.'

'It's all right,' he told her easily. 'These things happen. It was all a long time ago. Anyway, Aunt Min took us in and we've been here ever since.'

She was uncomfortable, feeling that she'd said the wrong thing and, now that it had been said, she couldn't think of a way to put it right. To make matters worse the path was now so narrow they were walking in single file and she couldn't see his face.

'What about you?' he asked, looking at her over his shoulder. 'Where do you live? When you're not being evacuated, I mean.'

'Wimbledon. Up by the Common.'

'Sounds nice.'

'Yes. It is rather,' she said and added, feeling she had to explain her affluence, 'my father works for the Foreign Office. Actually, I was going to go home for the holiday and look after him. We had it all arranged and now he's off to some stupid conference somewhere and I can't go.'

He was cheering – privately – thinking, what luck. But she was still speaking. 'I was going to be a real help to him,' she complained. 'I was going to look after him and get him breakfast and be there in the evenings so's he'd have someone to talk to and he wouldn't be lonely. I'd got it all worked out. Every last little detail. I was doing it out of the kindness of my heart and it wasn't going to be easy but I was prepared to do it, and then he comes bowling into that stupid hotel by the station and says it's all off because he's got to go to some stupid conference.'

There was a long pause and the path widened again so they could walk side by side. Her face was delectably fierce.

'I don't suppose he had much option though, did he?' he said. 'I mean, you do as you're told in war time. They don't ask you.'

It was true but she didn't want to hear it. 'I was going to look after him,' she said. 'I was going to make amends for Ma being killed.' Then she realised that she'd gone much too far, that he was a stranger and she shouldn't be talking about any of this, and to her horror she began to weep. 'I'm sorry,' she said. 'Just ignore me.' But then she was sobbing, in the terrible way she'd sobbed when her mother died and she couldn't stop.

She was aware that he'd put his arms round her and that he was holding her against his shoulder, rubbing her back, and that it was comfortable, as if he was holding her up. 'Cry all you want,' he was saying. 'Don't hold it in. Let it go. Just cry. I'll look after you.'

'She was killed,' she wept. 'Blown up. By a bloody bomb. I shall never see her again.'

Somehow or other, they were sitting underneath a pine tree and she had her back against the trunk and he was still holding her hands. She tried to apologise. 'I'm – so – sorry,' she said. 'I – shouldn't – be…'

'Shush! Shush,' he soothed. 'We all cry. It's all right. Cry it all out.'

She cried until there were no more tears left. Then she gave him a bleak smile, found her handkerchief and dried her eyes.

'Was it very recent?' he asked.

'Six months ago.'

'Ah! No wonder you're crying.'

'Did you…?'

'Over and over and over,' he said. 'I thought I'd never stop.'

'Did she…? Was she killed?'

'She had consumption,' he told her. 'She was the skinniest thing you ever saw. Quiet and gentle and terribly skinny. I was twelve when she died. But you never get over it. Not really. You just learn ways of coping.'

'Yes. That's what Matron says. "It doesn't get better, it gets different." My God. Matron! I'd better be getting back or she'll be sending out a search party.'

'I'll walk you to the gate,' he reassured her. 'I know a short cut over the common.'

'Will it take long?'

'No time at all,' he said. Unfortunately.

They followed the next footpath companionably, digesting what they'd just been saying to one another. It seemed amazing to him that he'd been holding her in his arms.

'Look,' he said eventually. 'I know this isn't the way to go on but I've only got ten days' leave and two of them are gone already and then I shall have to go back to Salisbury Plain. Can I see you tomorrow?'

'What are you doing on Salisbury Plain?' she asked, avoiding his question.

'Driving a tank,' he said, dismissing it as if it wasn't important. 'Exercises. That sort of thing. Can I see you tomorrow? Please.'

His urgency was so touching it had to be answered. And besides, he'd been so kind to her she could hardly turn him down. 'It would have to be after supper,' she said. 'I can't cut meals two days in a row or they'll smell a rat.'

'After supper would be fine.' Any time at all would be fine, just so long as he could see her again. 'We could go to the Gaumont. What time shall I call for you?'

Tommy and Octavia were finishing their evening in the Wheatsheaf Inn, drinking cognac, and enjoying a precious hour on their own before they had to go back to whispered caution in Ridgeway. It was one of the most comfortable pubs in the area and he'd chosen it with some care, finding a quiet corner where they wouldn't be noticed or interrupted and ordering her favourite drink as soon as they were settled.

She wasn't fooled by his attentions. 'You're so transparent when you want something, Tommy,' she teased. 'And it won't wash.'

'Now, that's where you're wrong for once,' he said. 'I'm not after anything.'

She grinned at him. 'No?'

'No,' he said firmly. 'Actually I've got something to give to you. A present.' And he took it from the inner pocket of his jacket, wrapped and flat in brown paper and laid it on the table in front of her.

'Heavens!' she said. 'It's not my birthday.'

'I can't wait for your birthday,' he told her. 'Open it.'

It was a thin book of poetry and to his delight she was surprised by it.

'Poems?' she said.

'Couldn't resist it,' he told her. 'Well actually, couldn't resist the one on page nine. It says everything I want to say to you.' Then he waited hopefully while she found page nine and read it.

*'Song and Dance' by RG Gregory.*

*Do you think an old heart can't sing*
*Do you think an old heart can't dance*
*With a love that belongs to spring –*
*Nor I – till I took this glance*

*In a mirror long put-by – denied*
*The least touch of light (there being*
*No cause but to let it hide)*
*Yet now there's this sudden seeing*

*This astonishing flow of longing*
*That gives the dulled glass a shine*
*And so many lost wants thronging*
*(must I fear the eyes aren't mine)*

*dream has shaken its sheets out*
*a freshness (discarded) restored*
*muted rhythms let loud beats out*
*(scared hopes being reassured)*

*unfathomable scores its chances*
*(love's fingers plucking the strings)*
*can't you see – this lame heart dances*
*can't you hear – this dried heart sings*

She was touched by it. 'Tommy, my dear man,' she said. 'That's perfectly lovely. I never knew you liked poetry.'

'I do when it's written for me,' he said. 'And it is, isn't it?'

'It's written for both of us.'

It was the perfect moment to ask her. 'You will come on holiday with me, Tavy, won't you?'

'I'll ask the staff what they think about it,' she temporised. 'I can't say more than that. It will all depend on what they say.'

'Can't you just tell them?'

'No, I can not,' she told him, returning to her cognac. 'We work as a team. I will tell them and, if they're agreeable to it, I will come with you. You'll have to be satisfied with that.'

'Fair enough,' he said and crossed his fingers. They were sensible women. They wouldn't let him down.

## Chapter Seventeen

Octavia fell in love with Grenada, even before she'd sailed into St George's Bay. It was the luscious scent of it, drifting across the sea towards her as their launch approached, and the sight of those lush green mountains silhouetted against the cobalt sky and those amazing white beaches. She'd never seen sand so white in the whole of her life, nor sea such a dazzling peacock blue.

'It's a paradise,' she said to Tommy.

He grinned at her, standing beside her at the ship's rail. 'It's not bad, is it.'

She laughed at his studied insouciance. Sometimes he was so English. 'Well, it beats Eastbourne.'

'You'll have to stay indoors in the middle of the day,' he warned. 'This is actually the wrong time of the year to make the most of the place because it's too hot in high summer. But it is lovely. I'll grant you that.'

It was also peaceful and a long way away from rations and bombs and all the appalling things that were going on in Europe and Africa.

'I can quite see why the Americans want to keep out of this war,' she said to Tommy as they finished their first dinner on the island. 'That was absolutely delicious. I haven't eaten a banana split for years. I'd forgotten such food existed.'

'Don't get too used to it,' he told her. 'We've only got a fortnight.'

'A fortnight!' she said happily. 'Two whole weeks of good food and warm weather and idleness. I shall go home a changed woman.'

'I can't imagine you changing,' Tommy said, 'or being idle come to that. You're not the sort of woman who lies around on a beach all day. You've got too much go.'

'What are we going to do tomorrow?' she said, proving his point.

He had an excursion planned for almost every day – 'somewhere where we can keep out of the sun' – and the first was to a sulphur pool at the top of the highest mountain on the island. 'It's supposed to have magical powers,' he told her. 'If you bathe there it will heal all your aches and pains and cure all your diseases and give you your heart's desire for good measure, or so they say.'

They set out early next morning when it was relatively cool, in a pony and trap which ambled them past fields of spices and bananas and coconuts, and through several shanty towns, which Octavia found decidedly shocking. One or two of the rough wooden houses looked fairly new but most were dirty and decaying, and the sight of such extreme poverty distressed her. They were all built on wooden stilts and all roofed with corrugated iron, some of it new and painted bright red, but most of it rusty and rotting. Snotty-nosed children played on the bare earth in front of the verandas or squatted on their haunches eating bananas or slices of melon or chunks of coconut, and a variety of mongrel dogs ran among the stilts, yapping and wagging their tatty tails.

'Yes,' Tommy said, catching her expression. 'That's poverty

for you. It's the same the world over. There were villages like this in the Balkans.'

'Something should be done about it,' Octavia said.

'But not by you,' he begged, 'and certainly not while we're on holiday. Save your strength for climbing the mountain.'

It was a very long haul and a very hot one, for now they were away from the plain and climbing through a tropical forest where perpetual rain dropped water down their perspiring backs and made the earth paths sodden and slippery. It was quite a challenge and, when the path diminished to a narrow track, it got worse. Then there were streams to negotiate as well as earth paths, and the way across was over extremely slippery stepping stones. Eventually they passed a long waterfall, tumbling snow-white against the tropical green, and found themselves beside a small, steaming, olive green pool that smelt strongly of sulphur. They had arrived.

Octavia was disappointed with it. 'Is this it?' she asked. 'It's a bit on the small side.'

Tommy was already stripping to his swimming shorts. 'You can't expect size and magic powers,' he said, looking around for the least damp spot where he could put his clothes.

She took off her frock and her shoes but she was still dubious. 'How are you supposed to get in?' she said.

'You jump,' he said. And jumped.

The water was warm and soft and obviously full of sulphur. Within minutes it had stained their fingernails and swimming costumes bright orange.

'What do you think?' he said, swimming beside her and putting an orange palm on her arm.

'Extraordinary.'

'Now,' he said, smiling into her eyes, 'we shall both be granted our heart's desire.'

'Which one?' she teased.

'How many have you got?' he teased back.

'Two,' she said, suddenly serious. 'But they've both been granted already.'

'I've only got one,' he said, 'and I've got to wait until Christmas to know whether that's going to be granted. Isn't that right?'

She leant towards him in the velvety water and kissed him lovingly. 'Right and proper,' she said.

That night they dined on turtle soup, grilled fish, melon and mangoes and went for a stroll round the harbour afterwards to walk off their excesses, and the next day they travelled into the interior to see a mangrove swamp and a grove full of humming birds, whirring among the blossoms like flying jewels. Every day brought another excursion and more pleasures. It wasn't until their holiday was more than half over that Octavia thought about her school and her colleagues and wondered how they were getting on. And that was because Tommy had a telephone call.

They'd been sitting over coffee in the bloom of the evening talking about the day's events when a waiter came quietly up to tell them that Major Meriton was wanted on the telephone. 'That'll be the conference,' Tommy said. 'Shan't be a tick.'

He returned to their table looking pleased with himself.

'I was right,' he said. 'That was Tubby. Just got ashore. Apparently, it's all gone rather well. They're issuing a joint statement tomorrow.'

'Now perhaps you can tell me who "they" were,' she said. 'And where they met. Or shall I guess?'

There was no harm in telling her about it now. The conference was over and they were on their own together under the stars, where no one could possibly hear them and they couldn't be accused of careless talk. 'Winston Churchill and President Roosevelt,' he said. 'But you worked that out a long time ago, didn't you?'

'And they met at sea, presumably.'

'In Placentia Bay,' he told her, 'just off Newfoundland, on a British battleship and an American cruiser. You were right about neutral waters.'

'So now what will happen?'

'I'll be able to tell you that when I've read the statement. It'll be in the papers tomorrow.'

Talk of news and newspapers made her think of the school and all the people in it still struggling on in the thick of things. 'I wonder how they are in Woking,' she said, frowning.

'They'll be fine,' he told her. 'Don't worry about them.'

But she was feeling guilty. 'I haven't even *thought* about them till now.'

'Good.'

'It's not good,' she said sternly. 'Anything could have happened.'

'Could you have done anything about it if it had?'

'Not if I wasn't there, no.'

'Well, there you are then,' he said and smiled at her. 'If there's one thing the first war taught me, it's that you can only be responsible for the men and the action where you are. Everything else is beyond your control and the sensible thing is to put it out of your mind and concentrate on the job in hand.'

It was probably true but it was a harsh doctrine nevertheless. She tried to argue against it. 'You're not going to tell me you don't worry about your family.'

'I think about them,' he admitted, 'naturally, and I wonder how they are, especially Mark and Matthew, but worrying is pointless.'

'What about Lizzie? Don't you worry about her?'

'Good heavens, no,' he said. 'Lizzie's no problem. She's a straightforward, sensible, little girl and she's in a safe place, getting on with her studies, heading for Oxford. No problem at all.'

He might not have spoken so cheerfully if he could have seen his straightforward, sensible, little girl at that moment, for she wasn't in a nice safe place getting on with her studies, she was on Horsell Common holding hands with a young man he'd never seen and never heard of.

It was a soft summer evening just as it had been every evening for the last eight wonderful days and Horsell Common was swathed in the soothing half-light of a languorous dusk. Lizzie was caught up in a dream of sensation and bewildered delight, enjoying every minute of the time they spent together but, in a peculiar and uncharacteristic way, not quite able to believe that it was actually happening, as if her ability to think was lagging behind the uproar of her senses. They'd talked about so many things – their families, her Pa, his Aunt Min, the war, their hopes and ambitions – it was hard to remember that they'd only met a mere eight days ago. She felt as if she'd known him all her life. And in all the time they'd been together the promise of kisses charged the air between them, he wondering, *could I?* she hoping that he would.

They had reached the sand pits and the grassy knoll where they usually sat and talked. But this time he stood where he was and went on holding her hand, looking down at her from his lovely height and so close she could feel the warmth of his body.

'I wish I didn't have to go back tomorrow,' he said.

The electricity between them was so strong it was making

it difficult for her to breathe. 'Me too,' she said huskily.

'I'll write to you every day,' he promised. 'You will write back, won't you?'

She felt as if they were exchanging vows. 'Yes.'

'Oh, Lizzie,' he said, 'my darling Lizzie.'

'Yes,' she said again. And this time the small, breathed word was a permission.

He kissed her, at first gently and then, when she responded – how could she not respond? – with more and more passion until they were both breathless.

Above their heads the stars shone steadfastly and somewhere across the common a nightingale began to sing, jug, jug, jug, teroo.

'Darling Lizzie,' he said. 'I think I love you.'

Tommy and Octavia were impressed by the Atlantic Charter, which was published in full in the papers the next morning and which they read at breakfast on the veranda, she because of the altruism of its sentiments, he because of the cunning of its diplomacy.

'You've got to hand it to Roosevelt,' he said, pouring himself more orange juice. 'He's a first-rate politician. A declaration of the – how does he put it? – "joint war and peace aims of the US and the UK" will make it harder for the isolationists to resist.'

'Will they join in the war though?' Octavia asked.

'No,' he had to admit, 'but it's a good first step. They can't fail to accept the peace aims, nobody could, and if they accept them publicly they will be assumed to be accepting the entire package. It's very clever.'

The peace aims *were* good. There was no denying it. The Allies would seek 'no aggrandisement, territorial or other', there were to be 'no territorial changes that do not accord with the freely expressed wishes of the people concerned', they would seek to ensure 'the enjoyment by all States, on equal terms, of access to the trade and raw materials of the world', they would establish 'a peace in which all men can live out their lives in freedom from fear and want', they believed that all the nations of the world 'for realistic as well as spiritual reasons, must come to the abandonment of the use of force'.

'You can't fault it,' Octavia said. 'They've even made provision for a new League of Nations. Just look at this.' And she read the words aloud. '*Since no future peace can be maintained if land, sea or air armaments continue to be employed by nations which threaten, or may threaten, aggression outside of their frontiers, they believe, pending the establishment of a wider and more permanent system of general security, that the disarmament of such nations is essential.* It's superb.'

'It is, but we must remember all the other audiences it's been written for and hope it doesn't fall on deaf ears,' Tommy said. 'Is there any more coffee?'

'You're such a cynic,' Octavia said, taking the lid off the coffee pot.

'And you're such an idealist,' he said, signalling to one of the waiters for attention. 'We make a good pair.'

It gave Octavia quite a jolt to fly back to Croydon and pick up her life again in wartime Britain. After a fortnight's colour and luxurious living in Grenada, London looked shabby and uncared for. Now, heading for Woking on a dirty train with its windows obscured by sticky tape, she noticed how uniformly grey and grubby everything was, how tired people looked, trudging about the streets, and how many bomb sites there were. She couldn't avoid seeing them, for they were covered in the bright pink flowers of the fire weed that people called London Pride. It seemed sad to her that a weed should be the only patch of living colour in the whole place. In a few weeks we shall be into the third year of this war, she thought, and we're no nearer to winning it than we were at the beginning. If only the Americans would come in and join us. That would make such a difference. But it wasn't likely and she had to face it. We must go on living on our inadequate rations, she thought, and enduring the blackout and skimping and saving and making ends meet until we're strong enough to invade France and start the long battle to push the Germans back to Germany. It felt like an impossible task.

The train gave a shudder, as if continuing was beyond its strength and creaked to a halt. They'd stopped right in front of a very large bomb crater and she looked out at it idly. Even here the fireweed was growing boldly, its pink flowers bright against the dark dead earth, the remains of the foundations, the splintered doors and the heaps of broken brick. Even here, she thought, and it occurred to her that this was new life she was looking at, new vibrant life taking root in the remains of death and destruction, and the thought cheered her. But it was jolly cold, even if it *was* August.

Lizzie was warm with love, sitting in her window seat in the afternoon sun, reading Ben's latest letter. It was a long one this time telling her how much he missed her and how much he wanted to see her again and, best of all, saying that he might be able to swing a weekend pass and get back to Woking in a fortnight's time.

'I do so hope you can,' she wrote back. 'I feel as if I haven't seen you for years.'

I shall tell Matron I'm going to see Pa, she planned, as she licked the envelope. It was an established excuse now. There wouldn't be any problem with it. *Then we can be together again and I can kiss you and tell you I love you.* Because she did love him. There was no doubt about it now. She loved him and when they were together again she would tell him so.

Maggie Henry was glad to see her Miss Smith back in Downview again. 'And looking so well,' she said. 'You've got quite a tan. It's done you good.'

'So, how are things?' Octavia said, settling into her familiar chair. 'How's the chicken pox?'

Maggie gave her report with some pride. The epidemic was over, she was very glad to say. 'No more cases for a week, so we've seen the worst of it.' The girls had organised a sports day on the lawn and Iris had won the prize for the long jump. They'd had wonderful weather. 'Nine whole days' sunshine. It did us all a power of good. Especially our Lizzie. It came just at the right time for her.'

'Why was that?' Octavia asked, intrigued.

'Well, her father came down, didn't he, Poppy told me, and he took her out every single day and it was sunny the whole time. I've never seen a girl so happy. Then we had a cookery contest and we all ate the exhibits, even the peculiar ones, and a paper chase and an excursion to Guildford to see the castle. It's been non-stop.'

Octavia listened to the list of events while she decided what to do. It would be best to keep her misgivings to herself for the moment but she would have to check what Lizzie had really been up to and who she'd been with. Using Poppy to provide an alibi was highly suspect. *I'll talk to Tommy about it,* she decided, *and see what he says.*

Tommy arrived that Wednesday with an armful of roses.

He was in one of his most cheerful moods, smiling broadly. 'Couldn't resist them,' he said, as he held them out to Octavia. 'What weather, Em! Isn't it grand?'

'I gather you had a good holiday,' Emmeline said, giving him her shrewd look.

He missed the look entirely. 'Top-hole,' he said.

'You must tell us about it over dinner,' she said.

Which he did and at considerable length. It was well past midnight before Emmeline finally decided they really ought to go to bed 'or we shall never get up in the morning', and by that time Octavia was fidgety with the need to talk to him in private. As she stood by the window waiting for him to join her she was plucking the curtains.

He strolled into the room, wearing his pyjama trousers, joined her at the window and put his arms round her. 'Well, that was a very nice evening, don't you think,' he whispered. 'Not quite Grenada, but nice.'

She turned in his arms to face him squarely. 'I need to talk to you,' she said and her voice was serious.

'You're going to say yes,' he said, delightedly. 'I haven't got to wait till Christmas after all.'

He was so happy she felt quite mean to have to press on with what she had to say, but it had to be done. 'It's about Lizzie,' she said.

'Oxford,' he said. 'It's the only place.'

'That's decided,' she said. 'It's not about her career.'

'Then what is it? She's well, isn't she? She looks as fit as a flea. Fairly gobbled up her tea. You'd think she hadn't eaten for weeks. Had to put in a second order.' It had been a really happy meal and he was still feeling the pleasure of it. 'Don't let's bother about her. She's fine. Come to bed.'

'I think she's got a boyfriend.'

His face changed in an instant, darkening and scowling. 'Nonsense,' he said, forgetting to whisper. 'She's much too young.'

She put a finger to her lips to warn him. 'She's not much younger than we were when we met, if you remember.'

'That's got nothing to do with it.'

'It's got everything to do with it. It's no good looking like that, Tommy. I wouldn't be saying this if I didn't have reasons.' And she told him what they were, remembering to keep her voice down.

Her explanation didn't change his opinion in the slightest. 'She was cutting off with her friends,' he said. 'Didn't want to make anything of it in case she was refused permission. Used me as an excuse. Obvious.'

'One of her friends provided her alibi.'

'Well, naturally. They were in it together.'

'I don't think so.'

'You're seeing more into it than there is, that's all,' he said.

'I'm seeing straight, Tommy, which is more than you are. Look at the facts.'

He turned away from her. 'Don't tell me what to do,' he said crossly. 'I won't have that. Just allow me to know my own daughter, that's all you need to do. She's much too young for boyfriends, you can take my word for it, and if she *did* have one, I should know because she'd tell me about it.'

Being put down made her angry. 'For a renowned diplomat you can be very obtuse,' she said.

'For a renowned headmistress you can be very rude.'

'Oh, come on, Tommy, I'm telling you the truth. Or aren't you man enough to face it?'

He looked at her with such fury on his face it was almost like loathing, then he strode away from her without another word, too angry to speak, dressed, slammed out of the dressing room door, stamped down the stairs, banged the front door after him and drove away. Oh, for heaven's sake, Octavia thought, how childish! Well, if that's the way he wants to behave, let him. But it kept her awake for a very long time, wondering how it could have gone so badly wrong. When she woke in the morning she had a throbbing headache and felt quite sick.

She was mixing an Alka Seltzer when Emmeline came yawning into the kitchen.

'What was all that about last night?' she said, scratching her head as she always did in the morning.

'Lizzie,' Octavia told her. 'I think she's got a boyfriend and he won't hear of it.'

'Ah! I thought it was something. He made enough row.'

'Row is about the right word for it, I'm afraid,' Octavia said, drinking her mixture.

'Headache?'

Octavia sat in her chair and rubbed her eyes. 'Um.'

'I'm not surprised,' Emmeline said, as she carried the kettle to the tap. 'It's always the same with a lovers' tiff.'

Even through the squeeze of the headache Octavia recognised what was being said. There was something about the tension in Emmeline's back, and the way she was hiding her face. She knows, she thought, and struggled to find the words to acknowledge it without upsetting either of them. 'Lovers I'll admit to,' she said carefully, 'but it's not a lovers' tiff, or at least not in the way most people would understand.'

Emmeline put the kettle on the stove and lit the gas and didn't say anything. But she was pursing her lips and obviously thinking.

'How long have you known?' Octavia asked.

'Since the beginning,' Emmeline said and smiled. 'It was

always on the cards, wasn't it?'

'Yes, I suppose it was. It feels as though it was.'

'Right, that's settled then,' Emmeline said, leaning her hands on the table. 'Now you can tell him to sleep in your bed and stop pretending. It'll save me washing all those sheets he never uses.'

So that's how she knew, Octavia thought, and smiled back at her cousin, feeling almost conspiratorial. What a long way we've both come, she thought. In the old days she'd have been shocked to the core. Now she's accepting *this*. It doesn't solve the problem of what's to be done about Lizzie though.

At that point, Barbara and Maggie came bouncing into the kitchen and scraped their chairs towards the table, chirruping their early morning greetings. 'Morning Gran. Morning Aunt Tavy. Did you hear the blackbird?' So she had to pause in her thoughts to answer them, wondering why the young always made so much noise. And then Edie and Joanie came down and there was the usual bustle of breakfast. The day was upon her, headache, problems and surprises notwithstanding and she would have to get on with it.

'There's the post,' Edie said, hearing the flump of the arriving letters. 'I'll get it. Should be a card from Dora.'

There was, among several bills and a letter from Arthur to say that he was well but very homesick and missed her terribly. 'Poor man.' Octavia had a long letter from Janet saying she and her husband were both safe and well, and Emmeline got a short one from Johnnie who said he was being posted to another airfield and had a spot of leave owing. And at the bottom of the heap there was an airmail letter from America addressed to Octavia in Mr Mannheim's elegant handwriting.

She opened it last, looking forward to hearing how he was. But in fact it was a very disturbing letter, and the news it contained

261

was so appalling it took her a while to comprehend it.

*Dear Miss Smith,* he said.

*I trust you are well and that the news I have to tell you will not distress you too much. I have been trying to contact Miss Henderson but without success. I fear she may have moved or been bombed. If you know where she is, could you perhaps forward this letter to her? It is for her information as well as yours and I am earnest that she should receive it.*

*I fear that the situation of the Jews in Germany and the occupied countries has become very grave. From what our correspondents are able to tell us, and they have to be extremely careful as you will understand, there is now an official German programme to exterminate as many Jews as they can. They call it 'The solution to the Jewish problem'. They have set up four* Einsatzgruppen *and given them the job of carrying out the killings. At first they took groups of Jews out into the streets or the fields and shot them where they stood, but now their methods have become crueller and more sophisticated. According to our correspondents they have built a special concentration camp that is designed for mass murder. They have gas chambers there where the Jews are killed and massive ovens where their bodies are burnt and large new railway sidings where the trains bringing their victims to the camp can be unloaded. It should be possible for the RAF to spot the sidings and pinpoint the location of this camp. It is not hidden.*

*Forgive me for burdening you with such information but I would feel I was doing less than my duty if I did not try to warn whomever I can.*

*I will write again when I have better news to impart. Please give my regards to the rest of your family and particularly to Mrs Thompson. We think of you all with great affection.*

*Ernst Mannheim.*

'Dear God!' Octavia said when she finally put the letter down. 'Just read that, Em.'

'What's up, Aunty?' Barbara said, anxiously. 'Is it Uncle Johnnie?'

'Your Uncle Johnnie's fine,' Emmeline told her quickly. 'He sent you his love and he's going to come to see us in a fortnight. You can read the letter if you like.'

'Then what's up?' Barbara persisted. 'You said, "Dear God."'

'It's a bit of bad news from someone we know in America,' Octavia reassured her. 'Nothing worrying, just a bit sad.'

'My word, just look at the clock,' Edith intervened. 'Come on you three, if you want to go swimming, we shall have to look sharp.'

'*Are* we going swimming?' Barbara said, half-delighted and half-surprised. It was news to her but very welcome because she loved swimming.

'That's what you said you wanted,' Edie said. 'But if we're going, you'll have to be quick.'

Barbara was out of her seat already.

'Right then,' Edie said. 'Upstairs and spend a quick penny.' And she bustled them out of the room.

'Is it true, do you think?' Emmeline asked when they were safely out of earshot. 'It can't be, can it? I mean, they wouldn't do anything so barbaric. Would they? They wouldn't, surely. I mean, killing people in gas chambers. He must have got it wrong.'

Octavia was lighting a cigarette. 'If it were anyone other than Mr Mannheim I would say it was just a dreadful rumour,' she said, 'because you're right, it's just too horrific for words. But as it's from him I think we must face the fact that it could very well be true. He's an honest man – we've

263

always known that – and I can't imagine him passing on a rumour. I tell you what I'll do. I'll phone Tommy tonight and see if he knows anything. And now I must copy the letter for Mrs Henderson. I'll keep the original. It could be important. And after that I think I'd better go to Downview and see how they're getting on.' She might be able to find out more about Lizzie's escapade and being there, with plenty to do, would put this horror out of her mind.

But it didn't work. The terrible words of the letter haunted her all through the day. Lizzie and her two friends had gone to town to buy Horlicks tablets according to Maggie, which seemed likely enough because they all bought the little tablets whenever they could as a substitute for sweets, but meant that she'd lost the chance to talk to them as she'd intended. She strolled through the garden, praising the girls for the good work they were doing among the soft fruits and in the vegetable patch, but instead of her own happy, healthy pupils she was seeing Jewish children being taken out into the streets to be shot; as she sat in Maggie's parlour, eating their rather frugal sandwiches, she saw gas chambers full of corpses and huge ovens waiting to burn them. No matter whom she saw or what she did, Mr Mannheim's terrible words crushed her heart. *Designed for mass murder... mass murder...mass murder.* How could such dreadful things be happening? she thought. What sort of a world have we created? And how are we ever going to set it right?

By the time she got home that afternoon, she was tired to her bones and an unnecessary phone was ringing. She was glad to see Emmeline walking out of the kitchen to greet her and thought yearningly of a cup of tea but thought, with a sigh, the phone would have to be attended to first.

'Yes,' she said wearily.

'Tavy,' Tommy's voice said. 'Sorry about last night, old thing. Look, I've been thinking. I think I ought to come down and see my Lizzie and sort this out. Find out what she's been up to, sort of thing. Bit of straight talking. Don't you think that's right? I can't come next Saturday, I'm afraid. We've got a big reception and I'm hosting. But the Saturday after. How would that be?'

It took her an effort to drag her mind back to what he was saying. Why do so many men think a problem can be solved by straight talking? she thought. It isn't straight you need with problems, it's devious. He's a diplomat. He ought to know that. But she didn't have the energy to argue with him. 'Yes,' she said and her voice was flat.

'Tavy?' he said. 'Are you all right?'

'No, Tommy,' she admitted. 'To tell you the truth, I'm not.'

Now, and rather late in the conversation, he was worried. 'It's not me storming off, is it?'

'No,' she reassured him. 'Nothing like that. I had a terrible letter this morning from Mr Manheim. He says the Germans are building gas chambers to kill the Jews.'

'Ah!' he said and there was a long pause. 'He's heard it too.'

'So it's true.'

'We're afraid it might be. Yes. There've been quite a few reports about it recently. Can I see the letter?'

'I'll show it to you on Saturday.'

'Chin up,' he said. 'I'll see you then.' And rang off.

Emmeline was still standing in the hall, waiting for her to finish. 'So it *is* true,' she said.

'Seems like it,' Octavia told her. 'He's heard it too.'

'Heaven help us all,' Emmeline said.

# Chapter Eighteen

It was such a beautiful summer morning, warm and languid even at nine o'clock and the sky was a perfect cloudless blue. The narrow High Street in front of Woking station, which Lizzie had never seen as a particularly exciting place, was transformed by a singing alchemy of love and sunlight. The long posters on the hoardings called with colour, the bus clonking to a halt outside the station entrance was as green as grass, the news vendor was actually smiling, the Albion Hotel, with its solid porch and its high wide windows, looked positively benign, the dust in the air swirled like specks of gold. As she walked into the station and stood on the platform waiting for Ben's train to come in, Lizzie felt she had never been so happy in all her life. Oh hurry up do, she urged the train. I want to see my darling Ben. My dear, darling Ben. There isn't a minute to spare.

He was standing on the step even before the train came to a halt, the door swinging open, his handsome face bright with greeting. She hurled herself into his arms and kissed him openly, the way she'd seen so many people do on the films, smelling his skin and thrillingly aware of him. 'Darling, darling Ben,' she said.

'You got time off, then,' he said.

''Course,' she told him. 'It was easy.'

'Two whole days,' he said rapturously. And kissed her again.

To Flight Lieutenant Johnnie Thompson, stepping more circumspectly from his own carriage further down the train, the sight of them was more heart-tugging than he cared to admit. Lovers always made him feel envious and aware of how shy he was. That chap's a tankie, he thought, noticing his insignia, so good luck to him. He knew what happened when a tank 'brewed up' and the occupants were burnt to death, and he had a profound respect for anyone who was prepared to run such a risk. They were on a par with flyers. The hazards were similar and so was the style. His girl's a peach, he thought. Just look at those pins! She'd rival Betty Grable. Well, good luck to her too. I wonder where he found her – and whether she's got a sister. Not for the first time he wondered if he would ever get a girl. It was all very well for the other chaps. They weren't tongue-tied like he was. They knew what to say. Life was very odd. Up in the sky, among the shredded clouds, with the intercom crackling and the engine purring, he could fight like a maniac and take impossible risks without even breaking into a sweat, but one look from a pretty girl could reduce him to uncontrollable blushing and stammering. He stopped in the station entrance and lit a cigarette to cheer himself up. Then he stepped out into the sunshine and went strolling off to visit his mother.

Tommy Meriton had risen early that morning too, woken by the twin demands of strong sunshine and his determination to drive down to Woking as soon as he could and sort out all this damned silly nonsense once and for all. He arrived at

267

Ridgeway minutes after Johnnie had come striding through the door. A good chap, Johnnie Thompson. Flyer of course, like Mark and Matthew.

'I'll put the coffee on,' Emmeline said happily. 'Then you can tell us all your news.'

'Not for me, thanks,' Tommy said. 'I've just come to see Tavy for a minute or two and then I must be off to the school to pick Lizzie up.'

Emmeline was remembering what Octavia had told her about young Lizzie. 'Did you tell her you were coming?' she asked.

'No,' he said, grinning impishly. 'It's a surprise. I'm going to take her out to lunch and devote the afternoon to her. Where's Tavy?'

'In the garden with Edie and the girls. Shall I call her?'

'No,' he said. 'It's OK. I'll find her.'

She was sitting on a bench under the rose arch where it was marginally cooler, dressed in a biscuit-coloured skirt and a rather pretty blue blouse, taking pretend tea with her nieces. 'You're early,' she said.

'I thought I'd go to the school first,' he said, 'then we can talk over this letter of yours later. I've been making enquiries.'

'And?'

'It *is* true, I'm afraid,' he said. 'There's been quite a lot of information coming through recently. I'll tell you this afternoon.'

'*Pas devant les enfants*,' she warned.

'No, of course not. Naturally.'

'Would you like a slice of cake, Aunt Tavy?' Maggie offered with solemn politeness, holding out a raspberry leaf.

'That would be delicious,' Octavia said, receiving the leaf. She smiled at Tommy. 'Good luck with your lunch.'

'It'll be a piece of cake,' he said, looking at the leaf.

Octavia watched him as he strode out of the garden, admiring his broad shoulders and those long legs and his easy way of walking. He's so confident, she thought, so much the master of his universe. And she offered up a silent prayer that it *would* be a piece of cake and that he wouldn't be disappointed.

To Tommy's surprise, Downview was completely empty, the front door wide open and no sight or sound of any pupils at all. It was rather off-putting to find himself in a deserted schoolhouse but he walked in nevertheless and strode along an echoing corridor to see if he could find anyone at home. Presently he heard the chink of spoons in china and followed the sound until he discovered the kitchen. There were two women in aprons sitting at the central table drinking tea and chatting. The older of the two looked round as he walked in and asked if she could help him.

'Where have all the girls gone?' he asked, smiling at her.

'They're having a picnic on Horsell Common, sir,' the cook told him. 'That's where you'll find most of them. Or at the swimming pool, a' course. There's a group gone swimming. Only a little group though. Who were you looking for? We've got the lists here.'

'Lizzie Meriton.'

'Ah now, you won't find her at either place,' the cook told him. 'She's one of the ones off on her own today, isn't she, Mavis.'

'Day out with her father,' Mavis said. 'Went off at the crack of dawn. Ever so excited she was. I'm afraid you won't find her here till tomorrow, 'cause she gets back ever so late when she's with her father, and you'll have to be quick to catch her then because he's down for the weekend and she's going to be with him all the time. She told me so.'

The shock of it made him feel as if he'd been punched in the stomach. So she *was* using him as a cover. Tavy was right. Naughty little thing, he thought. No, dammit, this is worse than naughty. This is devious. 'Well, thank you,' he said, remembering to be polite. 'Sorry to have troubled you.' And he left them to their tea.

God dammit, he thought as he walked back to his car, she's got no business treating me like this. If I hadn't handled that well I could have looked a complete fool. A complete and utter fool. He couldn't think what had got into her. No, that wasn't true. He could think but he didn't want to. How could she do this to me? When I've loved her so much, all these years, and looked after her and given her everything she could possibly want. It's downright treacherous. He drove back to Ridgeway in a mounting temper, roared down Kettlewell Hill in a scowl, turned in at Octavia's drive in a bad-tempered screech of brakes, hurt and furious.

Octavia was still in the garden, only this time she was picking lettuces for lunch. 'Ah!' she said when he frowned towards her. 'She's told you.'

'She wasn't bloody there,' he said. 'She'd told them she was going out with me and she wouldn't be home till late. Going out with me! The nerve of it! She didn't even know I was coming because I didn't tell her. It was going to be a surprise. So she was lying. My little Lizzie was lying! How could she do this to me, Tavy? It's cruel.'

'She's in love,' Octavia said, sitting back on her heels. 'We do cruel things when we're in love. It makes us careless.'

'*We* didn't.'

She ignored that. 'What will you do now?' she asked,

standing up and hooking the loaded trug over her arm.

'God knows,' he said. 'What can I do?'

Octavia was cleaning her trowel on a piece of mud-coloured rag. 'Talk to her?' she suggested.

'I'd like to give her a damned good hiding,' he said angrily. 'That's what she needs.'

She ignored that too. 'Would you like me to talk to her?' she offered.

He was relieved and his expression showed it. 'It might come better from you than it would from me,' he said. 'If you wouldn't mind.'

'It's part of the job,' she said, heading towards the house and thinking what a difficult job it would be. '*In loco parentis.*'

'How could she do this to me?' he mourned, following her. 'That's what I don't understand.'

'Come and help us with the lunch,' she said, holding his arm with her free hand. 'We've got a full house today.'

So he helped prepare the salad, under Tavy's instruction, while Edie and her brother set the table and Emmeline did what she could to cook omelettes with that 'ghastly scrambled egg', and by the time he sat at the table he was beginning to recover. He and Johnnie spent the first part of the meal talking about the RAF and what a top-hole plane the Spitfire was.

'I saw one of the prototypes,' he said. 'At Southampton in '36. We knew we were onto a winner then.'

'I can remember you telling us about it,' Johnnie said. 'Back in Parkside Avenue. I can remember sitting at the dining room table thinking "that's for me".'

'And you were right,' Tommy said. 'I don't know what we'd have done without the RAF.'

Johnnie made a self-deprecating face. 'Don't forget the Merchant Navy,' he said. 'You think of the great job they've been doing. We'd all be half starved if it wasn't for them. First rate chaps. They've taken some terrible casualties And the tankies, of course, battling on in Africa. It's not just us.'

'Very true,' Edie said, encouraging him. 'We're all in this together.'

'Which reminds me,' her brother said. 'I saw a tankie in Woking this morning, down at the station, kissing his girl. Very pretty girl she was, long blonde hair and legs like Betty Grable. I felt quite envious.' And he gave the studied chuckle he'd learnt to use to cover any possible embarrassment there might be when he'd dared to admit a weakness.

But it didn't work that time. They were sending eye messages all round the table, Edie to his mother, his mother to Aunt Tavy. He was rather alarmed. Were they warning one another? And if they were, what about? What on earth had he said? And what should he say *now*?

Fortunately he was rescued by Joanie, who picked a lettuce leaf from her plate, held it up in the air in front of them and declared it had got a fly on it.

'Eat it up then,' Tommy teased. 'Good source of protein, flies.'

The child wasn't impressed. 'Ugh! That's disgusting.'

And Barbara, ever curious, asked, 'What's protein?'

'Now look what you've started,' Aunt Tavy said to Tommy. 'We shall be questioned to within an inch of our lives.'

So the moment passed, as the fly was removed and Barbara was given her explanation, and Johnnie was able to relax.

'Tell us about this new base of yours,' Emmeline said to him when order had been restored. 'What's it like?'

'Within flying distance of France,' he told her.

She was instantly anxious, her forehead puckered. 'But you're not going there, surely to goodness.'

'We go where we're sent, Ma,' he said, piling food on his fork.

Emmeline shook her head. 'Heaven forbid,' she said.

'Oh Ma!' he said, laughing at her. 'You never change.'

Her face darkened. 'We've all changed, Johnnie,' she said 'Every single one of us. That's what war does to you.'

After the meal, Tommy told them he'd got to go back to London. 'Duty calls and all that,' he said, speaking to Emmeline but looking at Octavia out of the corner of his eye. 'I was hoping I might persuade your cousin to come with me. Tickets for the theatre and that sort of thing. What do you think?'

'And a chance to tell her what you know about Mr Mannheim's letter,' Emmeline said, looking at the children.

He smiled at her. 'Exactly so.'

'I'd go if I were you,' Emmeline said to Octavia. 'Have a night off. It would do you good.'

So they went, leaving Emmeline on her own with her family. But of course it wasn't Mr Mannheim's letter they talked about as he drove back to Wimbledon, it was Lizzie's incomprehensible behaviour.

It was a difficult conversation because Tommy had recovered himself sufficiently to start giving orders. 'You must make her see sense, Tavy,' he said. 'Send for her first thing on Monday morning and tell her she's making a big mistake.'

'By falling in love or not telling you about it?' she said, trying to tease him away from being dictatorial.

'Both,' he said decidedly. 'Sneaking off to see some stupid young man is quite bad enough, without using me as a cover for it. That's bloody devious, and it's got to stop. I mean any one can see that. And bloody dishonest. You must tell her she's not to do it. Keep her in detention or something. Give her lines. Lay down the law.'

The idea of giving a sixteen-year-old lines for falling in love struck Octavia as so ridiculous that she would have laughed out loud if it hadn't been for the determined expression on his face. 'Now look,' she said, turning in her seat so that she could face him. 'If I'm going to handle this for you, you must allow me to do it as I see fit. I'm not one of your subordinates to be told what to do and how to do it. I have my own way of handling things and you must allow me to use it.'

'OK. OK,' he said, lifting a placatory hand. 'I'm only giving you a few suggestions.'

'They sounded like orders to me.'

He recognised that he'd gone too far and hastened to backtrack. 'They weren't meant to be, honestly,' he said. 'They were only suggestions. She *must* be told. I mean, we both know that. But that's all. The way you tell her is up to you. Naturally. Just so long as you make things clear to her.'

Octavia looked at the set of his jaw and found herself wondering, not for the first time, how a man so sensitive and delicate in his private life could be so uncompromisingly heavy in public. 'No, Tommy,' she said, gathering her strength to oppose him. 'This won't do. You're asking me to sit in judgement on her. You want me to scold and bully. And you'd better know, here and now, that I won't do it. That's not the way I work.' She paused considering what she ought to say next. 'I'll tell you something,' she said at last. 'I've got a personal motto on my desk. I must show it to you sometime. It says *Don't judge, try to understand*. That's the way I work and the way the girls expect me to work. It's the way I shall work this time too. I won't do it at all, unless you accept that.'

'My stars, Tavy,' he said, with grudging admiration. 'You are a tough nut.'

'I have to be,' she told him. 'I'm a headmistress. And while we're at it, don't expect me to do anything for at least a day or two. I've only got a week till the start of term and there's a lot of preparation to do.'

He gave her his melting smile. 'You're the boss,' he said.

It was actually four days before Octavia had completed all her pre-term chores and by then the staff were beginning to return, new books were being delivered and both her school houses were in disarray. Nevertheless, the time had come. She'd thought out a possible approach. She was more or less ready. So Lizzie was sent for, made comfortable in the visitor's armchair, and welcomed with a smile and an easy question.

'Tell me Lizzie, what would you say if I were to tell you that you are quite likely to be chosen as head girl next year?'

Now it was Lizzie's turn to smile. The question wasn't exactly a surprise, even though she hadn't expected it at that moment. But to be honest she hadn't been thinking about school very much at all over the last few weeks. 'I'd be pleased,' she said, and then thought she should add, 'and honoured of course.'

'I'm not making any promises, you understand,' Octavia told her. 'It will depend on the way the staff vote, but I would say you were the front runner.'

As an answer seemed to be expected, Lizzie said, 'Thank you for telling me.'

'I usually forewarn my likely senior prefects,' Octavia said. 'I think you need to be prepared.' Then she paused and looked at Lizzie for several thoughtful seconds. 'And now,' she said, 'there is something else you can tell me.'

Lizzie settled into her chair and waited. Smithie's study was such a nice homely place to be, with its chintz curtains and the red chenille cloth on that little round table and the rows of books on the wall and Smithie's slippers waiting by the fireplace in case she got her feet wet in the garden. 'Yes, Miss Smith,' she said. 'Of course.'

'I gather your young man is in a tank regiment,' Octavia said. 'Is that right?'

The question was such a shock that Lizzie didn't know what to do or say. The homely room was splintering all around her, the books spinning from the walls, all order and comfort shattered. Oh my dear, good God! she thought. My dear, good God. Her first instinct was to deny it but there was something so calmly implacable about Smithie's gaze that she couldn't do it. In any case she'd see through a lie straight away. She always did. But how does she know? How could she possibly know? The room stopped spinning but now it had become a cage, holding her where she was to suffer and endure. She could hear birds chirruping out in the garden – lucky things – and the flop, flop, flop of someone's footsteps on the floorboards outside the door. The silence in the room was beginning to be oppressive. What could she possibly say? She had to say something. She couldn't just sit there. In the end, she said yes and was then painfully aware that she was blushing.

'I ask,' Octavia said gently, 'because your father came down last Saturday to take you out and he was very upset to find that you'd already gone and that you'd told Cook that you were spending the day with him. It gave him quite a shock.'

'I shouldn't have done that,' Lizzie admitted. It was always best to admit your faults when you were dealing with Smithie. 'It was wrong.'

'Yes. It was,' Octavia said. 'And you must put it right.'

'I will,' Lizzie said. 'I promise. Was he very cross?'

'Furious.'

Lizzie winced.

'I gather he's rather special, this young man of yours.' Octavia said, smiling at her.

'Yes. He is.'

Time to prompt. 'He's in a tank regiment.'

'Yes.'

'Does he drive it,' Octavia encouraged, 'or is he one of the crew?'

'He drives it,' Lizzie told her. 'He doesn't talk about it much. He's waiting to be sent out to Africa.'

'Then he's very special.'

'Yes,' Lizzie said, miserably. 'Oh, Miss Smith, I know I shouldn't have said what I did about being out with Pa. I mean, I know it was wrong, I knew it at the time, but I didn't know what else to say. I had to see him. We can only see one another when he gets leave or a weekend pass and I miss him dreadfully when he's not here. He's the nicest man I've ever met. Really kind. And we've got so much in common, and he's such fun, and gentle even though he *is* a tankie.'

'So if I were to say the sensible thing to do would be to obey your father and promise never to see him again…?'

An honest answer was necessary and possible. 'I couldn't do it. I really couldn't. I think I love him. And I know you'll say I'm too young, but I'm not. And anyway, even if I am, it's too late to say it now.'

'You'll be seventeen in a few weeks,' Octavia said reasonably. 'A lot of young women are married by the time they're seventeen, especially these days. Juliet wasn't fourteen when she met Romeo.'

Lizzie realised that she was staring and that her mouth had fallen open. She made an effort and managed to close her mouth but she went on staring. She was too amazed to do anything else. She's giving me permission, she thought. She's

277

actually sitting there giving me permission. She's as good as said it's all OK.

'You will have to put things right with your father, of course,' Octavia said, 'and the sooner the better, but I see no reason why you shouldn't continue to go out with your young man. You must be discreet about it, naturally, as I'm sure you will be, and you must let me know whenever you are going out, as a matter of course, and who you are going with, no matter who it is. It need go no further than these four walls but while you are a pupil of the school – and I hope you will continue to be a pupil until you've sat your Higher Schools Certificate – somebody has to be responsible for you, by law, as I'm sure you understand.'

'Thank you,' Lizzie said huskily. 'Thank you very much.'

'That's all settled then,' Octavia said. 'I shall see you on the platform on the first day of term.'

So Tommy got his apology which was so lovingly and humbly written it healed his damaged opinion of her in the short time it took him to read it. And Ben got a long and much more loving letter in which she told him how absolutely extraordinary Smithie had been and how she couldn't wait to see him again. And the new school year began in its familiar way, with 'Lord behold us with thy blessing', Smithie's welcome to the first-formers and the introduction of the new English teacher, who was a buxom sort of lady called Mrs Trench. When it was time for the junior prefects to be given their red sashes and the senior prefects to be helped into their black gowns, Lizzie found she had quite a lump in her throat and when her name was called to receive her special badge as head girl the cheers were so loud and so happily prolonged she was quite overwhelmed. This is such a good school, she thought, beaming at the girls below her in the hall, and I will do my very best for it.

However, despite Tommy's delight at the apparent conversion of his errant daughter and Lizzie's happiness in her new charmed life and Octavia's satisfaction at a delicate matter well handled, in the rest of the world matters were not going well. The war news was bad on every side. In Russia, Leningrad had been surrounded and was under siege and German troops were advancing along a front that stretched for over three hundred miles and were pushing inexorably towards Moscow. In North Africa, the Afrika Korps were besieging Tobruk and had pushed to within striking distance of Egypt and the Suez Canal so that Ben said he didn't think it would be long before his lot were sent out there to join the beleaguered Eighth Army. Newspaper commentators made much of the valiant defence that was being put up by the half-starved people of Leningrad and praised the extraordinary valour of the British troops that they were now calling the Desert Rats, but they couldn't disguise the fact that the Germans were winning.

'It needs a miracle to save those poor Russians now,' Emmeline said, setting the paper aside with a sigh. 'And I can't see that happening.'

She was wrong. The miracle began at the end of November when the German High Command discovered how punishingly cold the Russian winter could be and how poorly equipped they were to deal with it. With temperatures of 27 degrees below freezing, the German tanks ground to a frozen halt and it wasn't long before the storm troopers were freezing alongside them. The Russians were used to extreme winters and quickly adapted to this one, issuing thick winter greatcoats and fur-lined hats to keep their troops warm and using horses to deliver their supplies and sledges to transport their heavy guns. Within days the German impetus had stopped; within a week the Russians had begun to push them back. It was the first good news in a very long time.

But there was shocking and unexpected news to come. On a quiet Sunday evening at the beginning of December when the juniors at Roehampton Secondary School were busy making Christmas cards for their families and Lizzie was perched in her window seat wondering what she could get to give Ben for a special Christmas present, and Tommy and Octavia were sitting down to dinner with Em and Edie, the teleprinters in New York began to rattle out some alarming information. By the next morning the papers were full of it. Three hundred and sixty planes of the Japanese Air Force, flying from six aircraft carriers, had launched a violent and unprovoked attack on Pearl Harbour, the American naval base in Hawaii. The raid had lasted for two hours and in that time five battleships and fourteen smaller ships had been sunk, two hundred aircraft had been destroyed and over two and a half thousand men had been killed. The pictures in the papers showed huge black clouds billowing over the stricken ships and eye witnesses spoke of how sudden and terrifying the attack had been. It was, in every sense of the words, an outrage, especially as the Japanese ambassador in Washington had been meeting the American Secretary of State at the very moment the raid had been taking place.

That evening President Roosevelt called an emergency meeting of his cabinet, together with leading members of Congress. By the next afternoon the USA was officially at war.

'And about time too,' Emmeline said. 'Now we can get on with the Second Front and invade France and get our poor Arthur out of that prison camp. Oh, I know what you're going to say, Tavy. It's awful for all those poor young men being killed, absolutely dreadful, and I'm very, very sorry for them, but if it shortens the war...'

'I'm afraid we may find it will make the war drag on even longer,' Octavia warned. 'We shall have to fight the Japanese now as well as the other two.'

'Well, if that's your opinion of it, don't say anything to Edie, that's all,' Emmeline said. 'She's counting the days. What a Christmas we shall have with them on our side. It's going to make all the difference. Dora and John are coming and young David, which will be nice for him, poor little man, stuck out there in the country all on his own, and Johnnie says he'll try, but you never know with Johnnie. Tommy'll come, of course.'

'Yes,' Octavia said. 'He's determined to come. He says he wouldn't miss it for worlds.' But she was thinking of the real reason for his determination. On Christmas Day she would have to give him the answer he'd been waiting for. She couldn't put it off any longer. She'd promised and now she would have to do it. The trouble was she was no nearer to knowing what the answer ought to be than she'd been when their affair began. There was so little time for serious thought, her days were too full and her nights too exhausted. She'd struggled with the problem whenever she could, pausing as she brushed her teeth in the morning to consider her reflection in the mirror and wonder whether she really wanted to be a married woman with all the effort that that entailed, standing, coffee cup in hand, looking at the pile of marking on her desk and wondering whether she had room in her life for a husband. A lover, yes. That was almost pure pleasure. But a husband? Oh Tommy, she thought, what *am* I going to say to you?

Perhaps it was just as well that Winston Churchill had

other plans for Major Meriton that Christmas.

'He's off to Washington for talks with FDR,' Tommy said when he rang her that evening. 'We've been planning it all day. It's going to make rather a mess of Christmas. I *am* sorry. We shan't be back until the New Year.'

'We shall miss you,' Octavia said.

'Look after my Lizzie for me,' he said.

'Of course. Don't worry. She'll be fine.'

'Can't stop. I'm off to meet Tubby and the others. Never known a rush like this one. We've been at it since the news broke. Still that's war for you. See you soon.'

She stood in the hall with the receiver still in her hand, and was battered by so many emotions that it was all she could do to absorb them. Disappointment that she wouldn't see him until after Christmas, pride in him because he was at the centre of momentous events, annoyance because he'd told her so quickly and been in such a rush, almost as if he wasn't thinking about her at all, and irritation at herself because she was being petty. But underneath it all, purring away like a contented cat, an undeniable and really rather shaming sense of relief.

# Chapter Nineteen

The staff at Roehampton Secondary School welcomed the news about Pearl Harbour and America's entry into the war with unreserved approval. Like everyone else they deplored the loss of life but were glad that America was off the fence at last.

'We've certainly got something to celebrate this Christmas,' Morag Gordon said. 'We must make it a special occasion.'

That was the general opinion at the first staff meeting after the news broke. More than half the girls were going back to London to spend Christmas with their families. That was an established pattern. But there were nearly a hundred and twenty who would be spending the holiday either in their billets or at Downview and they needed something to lift their spirits. There was the sixth form pantomime of course but that was on the last day of term. What could be done on Christmas Eve and Christmas Day? A party certainly, which Sarah Fletcher would organise, carols round the Christmas tree on Christmas Eve, led by Jenny Jones, the best Christmas dinner they could contrive, given the restrictions of the rationing system, decorations for the tables and the hall by Phillida Bertram and her team and a gift for every girl.

'Let's have a bran tub,' Joan Marshall suggested. 'We can

have lots of games at the party and give a present to every winner. We've got three prefects with us this year and they're going to help with the games. I bet they'd make a bran tub too if we asked them.'

'Where would we get the sawdust?' Jenny asked.

'Oh, they'll find some somewhere,' Joan said. 'There's bound to be a wood-yard somewhere around. I'll ask Lizzie.'

'Bit of luck she's with us this year, if you ask me,' Morag said. 'I thought she'd go home to be with her father.'

'He's in Washington,' Joan said. 'She told me about it yesterday.'

''I'll bet that didn't please her,' Morag said. 'She's so fond of her father. It must be hard to be parted from him, especially at this time of year.'

Octavia listened to them and kept her counsel, wondering what they would say if they knew the true state of affairs – and thinking what an apposite word that was in the present situation. There were times when knowing so much about her staff and her pupils made her feel isolated.

'Actually,' Joan said, 'she's taking it quite well. She's a sensible girl. I think she's throwing herself into the life of the school instead.'

She would have been surprised to see their sensible girl at that moment, for it wasn't the life of the school she was throwing herself into, it was the arms of her lover.

The two of them were walking on Horsell Common as the afternoon darkened into night, well hidden among the bushes, stopping to kiss at every tenth step and clinging to one another with every kiss, lost to sensation. 'It's so good to be home,' Ben said, between kisses. 'Darling, darling Lizzie, you don't know how I've missed you.'

'I do,' Lizzie said. 'I've missed you the same way. It's been such a long time. They could have let you come home before this.'

'Kiss me again.'

And again. And again until their lips were sore.

'I love you so much,' he said, holding her close. The need to go further than kisses was making him tremble.

'You're cold,' she said, putting her hand against his cheek. It felt warm enough but he *was* shivering.

'No,' he told her, 'it's not that.' They were both bundled against the weather, he in his army greatcoat and a khaki muffler, she in her thickest winter coat, her fur hat, her fur-lined boots and two woollen scarves, so they were warm enough. 'It's just kissing you makes me tremble, that's all. It makes me want to… It makes me wish I could…'

They stood cheek to cheek as the night wind blew around them and the stars sent pinpoints of light towards them from the blue/black heights of the sky. They were lost to the delights of a powerful temptation. 'I wish we could go home to our own house,' he said, 'and go to bed in our own bed, without all these stupid clothes getting in the way, and be right away from everyone else, where no one can see us, and stay together all night.' Thinking such a thing made him tremble again. 'Oh my dear, darling Lizzie. I love you so much.'

'Kiss me,' she said. At least kisses were possible, even if everything else was a dream.

They kissed for a very long time, as they always did. But eventually they came to their senses and he remembered that he'd got to walk her back to the school and looked at his watch.

'What time is it?' she asked.

'Bit late,' he admitted. 'Not much though. We've got time to…'

She turned his hand so that she could see the clock face herself. 'It's very late,' she said. 'I shall have to go.'

He couldn't bear the thought of parting from her. 'Not yet.'

'I gave Smithie my word.'

'There are times,' he said, 'when I don't like your Smithie one little bit.'

'She's an ally,' Lizzie told him. 'I made a bargain with her and I'm going to keep it. Come on.' And she set off along the path, walking briskly to show him she meant it.

Now that they'd stopped kissing he remembered that he had something to ask her. 'Aunt Min said I was to ask you what you're doing at Christmas,' he said. 'I suppose you're going home to your father, aren't you.'

'No,' she said. 'I'm not. He's gone to Washington. He'll be there till the New Year.'

'Good,' Ben said, and when she gave him a quizzical look, added, 'Not good he's in Washington. I don't mean that. Although I suppose that's good in a way. Politically good anyway. I mean, good you'll be here. How would you like to come to Christmas dinner with my Aunt Min?'

It was asked casually, almost as if it wasn't important, but they both knew exactly how very important it was. She was going to be introduced to his family. 'Yes,' she said, 'if it's all right. I mean, I wouldn't want to impose on her, with the rations and everything.'

He put his arm round her and gave her a hug. She was the dearest girl to be concerned. ''Course it's all right,' he said. 'It was her idea. I'll call for you on Christmas morning and we can spend the whole day together in the warm. How would that be?'

Not quite as good as spending the whole day in bed would have been, but good enough. 'Blissful,' she said.

'The other thing is…' he began and then stopped. Maybe he was rushing her and he didn't want to do that.

'What other thing?' she said.

Her expression was encouraging, wasn't it? She was smiling. Looking happy. He took a necessary breath and plunged into the unknown. 'How would you like to get engaged?'

He knew as soon as the words were out of his mouth that he *was* rushing her because her face changed. Now it was clouded and anxious. 'I can't,' she said. 'I'm at school. I mean, you can't be engaged when you're at school, now can you? Anyway I've got to be discreet. I promised Smithie.'

He persisted because she wasn't exactly turning him down. 'But would you like to?'

'Yes,' she said, ''course I would. You know I would. Only I don't see how we can.'

'Then I can buy you a ring?'

That was possible. 'Yes.'

'And you'll wear it at Christmas?'

That was possible too. She could wear it on her finger when she was with him and hang it on a ribbon round her neck under her jersey when she was at school.

'We'll buy it on Christmas Eve,' he said. 'First thing when I get back.' And kissed her to seal the bargain.

It wasn't until she was inside the hall at Downview that Lizzie realised exactly what she'd promised. An engagement means we'll be getting married, she thought, and heaven only knows what Pa will say if I tell him that. And I shall have to tell him sooner or later. It's not something you can keep a secret. He'll go bananas. Fortunately, she didn't have much chance to dread it because Miss Marshall bumped into her on the stairs and Miss Marshall was full of some plan to make a bran tub for Christmas and was bubbling with excitement.

'I'll tell you all about it tomorrow morning,' she said. 'You'll help us with it, won't you.'

'Yes,' Lizzie said, vaguely, 'of course.' She didn't really care about bran tubs and Christmas but you couldn't say no to Miss Marshall when she'd got a bee in her bonnet and, anyway, she was suddenly very tired and needed to go to bed.

'Good show,' Miss Marshall said. 'See you at breakfast.'

She was even more excited at breakfast than she'd been the previous evening. 'You'll need a group to help you,' she said, 'to wrap up the presents and decorate the tub and that sort of thing. I should think about four or five but if more of them offer you can always use them. There's a wood-yard in Horsell. I've got the address. I suggest you go down on Monday morning and see what they say. You'll need a wheelbarrow to get it back here, of course, when the time comes, but we've got one in the garden that should do. What larks, eh?'

After a weekend of delicious but achingly unsatisfied lovemaking, Lizzie was tired on Monday morning and could have done without a trip to a wood-yard. But she'd given her word, so she and Polly gathered their team and all eight of them set off through the damp air to find the yard. It was at the bottom of Brewery Road, just past Horsell Moor, and they knew they'd come to the right place because they could smell the wood even before they walked through the gates.

There was a boy in overalls walking across the yard with a cigarette between his lips. He was a bit taken aback to see a gang of schoolgirls chattering towards him but when Lizzie told him why they'd come, he took his cigarette out of his mouth and told her she wanted Bert. 'He's the foreman,' he explained. 'I'll get him for you. Hold on a tick.'

Bert was a long time coming and after a while the juniors sat down on a pile of planks to wait for him. Iris had bought a tube of Horlicks tablets, which they passed round like sweets. Poppy stamped her feet and put her hands in her armpits and complained that she was getting cold. Lizzie thought of Ben and wondered what he was doing. She was so lost in her thoughts that she didn't notice the foreman's arrival and looked up to find that he was standing right in front of her, a tall, thick-set man, with a kind smile and eyes as brown as Ben's.

'How can I help you, ladies?' he said.

The juniors giggled at being called ladies and Lizzie explained their errand.

His answer was immediate and practical. 'You can have as much sawdust as you want,' he said. 'Have you got a tub? No. Try the hardware shop. They're the ones. Get your tub, bring it back here and we'll fill it for you. I'll tell Tom to look after you. OK?'

'What a nice man,' Poppy said as they left the yard. 'So what do we do now?'

'Go and see if we can buy a tub,' Lizzie said, 'and if we can, we'll go back to Downview and get the wheelbarrow to put it in. Come on.'

It took them all morning and Iris said it was the best fun ever, even though pushing the loaded wheelbarrow up the hill was jolly hard work. They had to take it in turns to do it, working in pairs because it was so heavy. But the excitement when the tub was set up in the hall made all the effort well worthwhile.

'We're the heroines of the hour,' Iris grinned.

'Never mind that,' Poppy said, taking off her gloves and examining her fingers. 'I've got chilblains coming.'

But Christmas is coming too, Lizzie thought, and I'm going to meet Aunt Min.

\* \* \*

Emmeline and Octavia had a full house that Christmas for, although Tommy wasn't with them, Dora and John and David were so they sat nine to the table and, without Tommy's contribution to the feast, Emmeline was hard put to it to provide sufficient food for them all. The rations had been increased over the Christmas period as they usually were and Dora provided biscuits and a bottle of port wine, but even so it was short commons and Emmeline felt guilty at her impoverished table.

'I'd kill for a turkey,' she said to Octavia. 'Chickens are all very well but they don't go anywhere near far enough.'

But it was a happy meal notwithstanding the shortages. Octavia had made crackers out of brown paper covered with painted stars and party hats out of brightly painted newspaper and every last scrap of food was eaten and pronounced first rate. In fact, when David had finished his slice of Christmas pudding he licked the plate, to his mother's consternation.

'David! David! Whatever are you thinking of?' she rebuked him. 'We don't lick our plates. It's bad manners.'

But to everybody's surprise, John encouraged him. 'You lick away all you like, son,' he said. 'Never let nothing go to waste. That's my advice. Food's too precious to waste.'

'That's all very well,' Dora said, 'but what about manners?'

'Manners don't come into it no more,' John told her. Was this really their quiet John standing up to Dora? 'There's many a good man been torpedoed to get that lot on your plate. If you'd seen some a' the things I've seen these last few years you'd never waste another mouthful in your life and you'd be licking your plate an' all.'

So David went on licking his plate until he'd polished it clean and, greatly daring, the three girls followed his example and licked theirs too. And Uncle John patted them on the head and said, 'That's the style!' Then the port wine was produced to finish off the meal and toasts were drunk to their new allies and absent friends, and when they'd sat by the fire for an hour or two, 'to let their food go down', Octavia got out the gramophone records and they danced and giggled for the rest of the afternoon.

It wasn't until it was midnight and she was finally in bed that Octavia had time to think of Tommy and Lizzie and to wonder what sort of Christmas they'd had, and by then she was so tired she fell asleep in the middle of her thoughts.

Ben Hardy came to collect his darling halfway though the afternoon on Christmas Eve and by teatime he'd bought the ring and they were engaged. Lizzie thought it was the prettiest ring she'd ever seen, made of tiny diamonds set round a central amethyst like the petals of a flower, but it cost the unheard of sum of £14 and seeing so much money being handed across the counter worried her.

When they were out of the jewellers and walking towards the fish and chip shop, he stopped to take the ring from its box and put it on her finger. 'You do like it, don't you?' he said. That anxious expression of hers was worrying him.

'It's gorgeous,' she said, gazing at it. 'I shall wear it all my life. It's just...'

'Just what?' he asked. 'Go on, Lizzie, spit it out. What's worrying you?'

'It was so much money,' she said. 'It makes me feel like a gold-digger.'

He gave such a roar of laughter that passing shoppers stopped to peer at him. 'Oh that's priceless!' he said. 'You, a gold-digger! The idea! No one could ever think that.'

'But it *was* a lot of money.'

'I've been saving up.' They'd reached the chippie. 'Cod and two penn'orth?' he asked and teased, 'It's OK. It won't break the bank.'

So cod and two penn'orth it was, and when they'd eaten it and licked every last trace of grease from their fingers, they went to the local dance hall, which was a pink confection known as the Ata, where they danced quicksteps and foxtrots on the famous sprung floor and admired the way their ring sparkled in the light from the glitter ball and held one another breathlessly close through every waltz. They had to leave early so that she would be back at Downview at her appointed time and there were too few moments for kissing but she didn't mind. She would have to keep her beautiful ring hidden away while she was in the school house but she didn't mind that either. They were engaged and tomorrow was Christmas day.

It was dank and cold and trying to rain, the sort of day for sitting indoors by the fire with your family opening presents or throwing a big school party with lots of games and presents in a bran tub, or if you were newly engaged, walking beside Horsell Moor with your fiancé and taking off your glove so that you could look at your ring. And suddenly realising that you knew where you were.

'I came down this way on Thursday,' Lizzie said. 'Me and the others. We were getting sawdust for the bran tub.'

'I know.'

That was a surprise. 'How do you know?' she said. 'Did I tell you?' She hadn't, had she? She'd have remembered if she had.

'I have my spies,' he said, laughing at her.

'No seriously. How do you know?'

They'd reached a line of small, terraced houses, backing

on to the canal, with grey slate roofs and prettily patterned brickwork and a warmth of smoke rising from the chimneys. 'Come and see,' he said, leading her to the house in the centre of the terrace. 'This is where I live.'

There were faces looking out of the downstairs window, all wide eyes and welcoming smiles and the door was opened before he could knock. Then they took two steps into a room crowded with more people than she could count, all talking at once saying 'come in' and 'make yourself at home' and 'pleased to meet you' and Lizzie smiled until her jaw ached as she tried to work out who they all were, looking from one to the other. But it was all a blur. She had an impression of a crowded table in the middle of the room set about with a collection of chairs, a fire blazing in the hearth, paper chains strung across the room from side to side, a black and white dog sitting on the hearth, watching the action as she was, turning its head from side to side. And she turned her own head to look for Ben and found herself staring at the broad shoulders and amiable face of the foreman from the wood-yard.

'Good heavens!' she said. 'Bert!' and then corrected herself. 'I'm sorry, I should have said Mr Hardy.'

'Bert'll do fine,' he said. 'I knew it was you last night. The minute he told us about you, I said to Min, "That's the girl that came to the yard. Couldn't be two as pretty as that." Didn't I, Min?'

She was blushing but nobody minded, and a tall, smiling woman came and stood beside her husband and took her hand and led her to the table. 'Never know'd him so sure about anything,' she said. 'The minute our Ben said long blonde hair. There now, if you'll sit here and make yourself comfy and then Ben can sit beside you and I can dish up. I'm so glad you could join us. We've been dying to meet you.'

293

There was a scramble as they all sat down and then the blur resolved itself into individuals. She was introduced to 'my brother Bob' who was tall and gangly and smiled at her shyly, and 'my cousin Heather' who was very like her mother with the same brown hair and grey eyes, and, as her heart steadied, she recognised that there were only five of them after all, not dozens, and a serving plate containing two plump chickens was carried proudly into the room and Bert said grace and the meal began.

After so many Christmases at home with just her and Ma and Pa on their own in their vast dining room, this crowded, happy meal was a revelation. Passing the vegetables was like some complicated dance, carving the chickens was a splendid ritual, offering a glass of Hock made it an occasion. As they ate and talked and questioned, she watched and answered and warmed to them. They were so loving with one another and so happy to be together. 'Happy Christmas,' she said, joining the toast. And it was. It was. Pa could be as cross as he liked, but she was engaged and there was nothing he could do about it and Ben's family had welcomed her.

Tommy came home from his trip to the States saying he was totally exhausted. 'We've been hard at it, dawn to midnight every blessed day,' he complained to Octavia, when he came down to visit her. 'I don't know where Winnie gets the energy from. I need to marry and settle down and get a bit of peace in my life.'

The two of them were sitting in the armchairs on either side of the fire and for the moment they were on their own together, as the children were in bed and Edie and Em were doing the washing-up. But the one thing Octavia didn't want to talk about was getting married. She still hadn't made up her mind what to say and her unusual indecision was making her nervous and rather irritable.

'You'd be bored stiff if you had to settle down,' she said, trying to make a joke of it.

He understood her motive just a little too well. 'Give me the try,' he said. 'You might be surprised.'

'I doubt it,' she said. 'You're too used to being in the middle of the action.'

He leant forwards towards her, his hands on his knees. 'Tavy,' he said, 'I'm asking you to marry me.'

It couldn't be avoided. 'Yes,' she said. 'I know.'

'And?'

She tried to temporise. 'We'll talk about it.'

'I don't need to talk about it,' he said. 'We've said all that has to be said. All I need is an answer. Will you or won't you?'

He was so straight and to the point. But what could she say? She thought for a little and then offered, 'Well then, the answer is yes, but not yet.'

'Oh, come on, Tavy, what sort of answer is that?'

'It's the best I can do at the present moment.'

'What's wrong with the present moment?'

'There's too much going on.'

'Like what?'

'Like getting as many of our girls into colleges and universities as I can, your Lizzie among them. I can't arrange a wedding in the middle of all that.'

It was a clever answer, if not entirely honest, and it was unanswerable. 'All right,' he said. 'Have it your own way, but I shall ask again.'

'I know,' she said. 'And I will tell you. As soon as I can. I promise.'

He grunted and turned away from her to take out his cigarette case, obviously annoyed.

'Tell me how you got on,' she said. 'Apart from being driven to exhaustion.'

He took a cigarette from the case, tapped it on the lid and lit it. Then he sat back and put his feet on the fender and inhaled deeply. 'Pretty well, all things considered,' he said. 'They should be in action by the end of the spring or early summer at the latest. Everything's being set in motion. And of course the Yanks are always very hospitable. Poor old Tubby got the short straw this time. He had a very rough ride by all accounts.'

She was relieved to see how deftly he had followed her suggestion. This is better, she thought. Talking about diplomacy is a lot easier than discussing a possible marriage. 'Where was *he*?'

'Moscow.'

'Ah.'

'Went with Anthony Eden,' he told her. 'It was a tricky delegation. He says Stalin is a very difficult customer. Wants his own way all the time. Won't sign any treaty with us or America unless we recognise his 1941 frontiers, which is quite out of the question. I mean, that would give him part of Finland, the Baltic States and Bessarabia, and we can't have that. Out of the question. And on top of all that, there's another chap there called Molotov who would keep banging on about when the Second Front was going to begin, and that didn't make matters easier either.'

'We'd all like to know that,' Octavia said. 'I'm on his side. I mean, we're never going to end this war until we invade France, now, are we? I'm not surprised he's pressuring you. They want to know when it's going to happen.'

'They don't want to know,' he told her. 'They want to give orders and have them obeyed. Dictators are bloody hard work.'

'Does that surprise you?' she asked. 'These are men who get their own way all the time. They're not open to compromise like you and me.'

He gave her his wry grin. 'I might have accepted a compromise this time,' he said, 'but that's because of Lizzie's career. I shan't be so amenable next time round. Be warned.'

At that moment, Emmeline and Edie came back from the kitchen and, to Octavia's relief, the subject had to be changed. But the question was still there, charged and unanswered, filling the space between them and sooner or later she would have to tackle it.

# Chapter Twenty

When Tommy drove off to London the following morning, Octavia was left feeling the most disquieting pangs of conscience. It wasn't her style to indulge in introspection, there being very little to be said for it and even less to be gained, but that morning she sat at the kitchen table not drinking her tea and feeling troubled and ashamed. She really had treated him extremely badly, poor Tommy. She should have given him his answer at Christmas the way she'd promised. It was ridiculous to be still making excuses. It wasn't as if she didn't want to live with him and she loved him almost as much as she'd ever done, given that they were both older and wiser, so she ought to have said yes and agreed to a date. Was it any wonder he was upset? But she'd been right to point out how busy she was going to be. That was true too and they had to accept it. They were both busy. It was the nature of their lives and it was bound to make problems for them.

'Have you finished with that tea?' Emmeline said.

Octavia sipped at it and grimaced.

'There you are, you see, you've let it go cold,' her cousin rebuked. 'Shall I make you a fresh pot?'

'No thanks, Em,' Octavia said. 'It's time to go. I'm seeing

Poppy Turner at half past nine and it's nearly that now. What did I do with my gloves?'

There were seven possible candidates for universities and training colleges that year and, as always, she wanted to be sure that the girls applied to the best possible places in the best possible way. She would interview them all, as she always did, one after the other, explaining and encouraging. Some, like Poppy, were unsure of their abilities and would need to be told how talented they were, others would need help with applications for grants to ensure that they had enough to live on, some were still undecided about the course they ought to follow and would need practical advice about their careers. In fact, they all required care of one kind or another. It was only Lizzie Meriton who was straightforward. Tommy would pay for her and see that she had everything she needed, she had a first-rate attitude to study and would pass all her examinations with distinctions, she was widely read, she'd been an excellent head girl, there was nothing to stop her upward path. Her interview would be the easiest of the lot and she would save it until last as a special treat when all the others had had their lives settled.

It took the entire week to see them all and to make all the necessary arrangements. It wasn't until late on Friday afternoon that she finally got around to fixing Lizzie's appointment and she only managed to do it then because they passed one another on the stairs.

'Ah, Lizzie,' she said, pausing with her hand on the banister. 'Could I see you on Monday morning, do you think? Period three?'

A smile, an agreement, then a request. 'I shall be going out with Ben tonight,' Lizzie said. 'Is that all right?'

'Of course,' Octavia said. 'As long as you're back by ten-thirty.' And she walked off towards her teaching room thinking how sensible her head girl was being and what a pleasure it would be to interview her.

It was a miserably cold evening and Lizzie was quite glad that she was going to have supper with Aunt Min and could sit by the fire for a little while afterwards. Fires were the one thing she really missed at Downview and Aunt Min always kept a good one going, as she had that evening. The warmth of it reached out to her like an embrace the minute she stepped into the house.

'You're like ice, child,' Min said, when she kissed Lizzie's cold cheek. 'That won't do. Come and sit by the fire and get yourself warm. It's no weather to be out walking. I've only got the tea to make and we can have our supper. We're a bit early tonight because we're going to the club. Gala evening tonight. Mustn't miss that.'

Lizzie looked a question at Ben.

'It's the highlight of the year,' Ben told her, grinning at his aunt. 'The one club meeting nobody misses.'

'You could come with us if you like,' Min offered.

'No thanks,' he said. 'We're going to the pictures, aren't we, Lizzie?'

But when they'd eaten Min's rissoles and he and Lizzie had washed the dishes and stacked them neatly away and the table had been cleared and folded and set against the wall and the rest of the family had bundled themselves into coats and scarves and woolly hats and gone giggling off to the gala, he didn't seem inclined to go anywhere. He pulled the settee up to the fire, switched off the light, settled them both among the cushions and began to kiss her, luxuriously as if they had all the time in the world, as if they were a married couple on their own in their own home, as the fire flicked shadows on the wall behind them and the coals shifted and shuffled and the dog slept on the hearth rug beside them.

'We don't really want to go out, do we?' he asked, when he finally paused to take breath.

It was an unnecessary question. She was so drowsed with pleasure she barely had the sense to answer it. 'Um,' she said, reaching up to kiss him again.

He turned as they kissed until he was lying on top of her. The shock of it was so delicious she could hardly breathe. She put her arms right round him and held him close, kissing and kissing. She could feel his heart beating against her chest, such a strong insistent beat, and his legs were heavy as if he was pinning her down, and his hands were warm and tender and coaxing, persuading her further and further. 'Darling, darling Lizzie,' he said. 'I love you so much.'

After a while she realised that she was actually rather uncomfortable and struggled to sit up.

He raised himself to give her room to move and looked down at her, his face gilded by firelight. 'What is it?' he said.

'You're squashing me,' she told him. 'There's a lump in this settee and it's sticking in my back.'

'I tell you what,' he said. 'If we were to go upstairs, we could have a bed to lie on.' His expression was at once hopeful and bashful and touching. 'Only if you want to though.'

She stayed quite still for a few seconds, half-sitting half-lying, and thought about it while he waited. 'They won't come back, will they?' she asked. 'I mean, I wouldn't want them to come home and find us upstairs. I mean, I wouldn't want to shock them or anything.'

'On gala night?' he laughed. 'No fear. They'll be there till midnight. So what do you think? Shall we...?'

She knew exactly what he was asking her and that she ought to say no but she couldn't do it. She was swimming in sensation, carried along by it, impelled by the urgency of it.

'I won't do anything you don't want me to do,' he urged. 'I mean, if you say no, I'll stop, no matter what.'

How could she possibly refuse an invitation like that? 'Yes,' she said. 'I know.'

'Then you will?'

'Yes,' she said, and kissed him to prove it.

They walked up the dark stairs with their arms round each other, stopping to kiss on every step, and he led her to a small cramped bedroom with two beds in it, both with the covers tightly tucked in. She was vaguely aware of a wardrobe, a chest of drawers, a bookcase full of books, but by then she was too breathless to care about any of it. He stood in the darkness of the room with one arm holding her close and switched on a little bedside lamp. It shed a circle of yellow light across the pillow of the nearest bed, pointing the way, and she took it, eager and uncertain, allowing him to take off her jersey and her blouse and her petticoat and her shoes and stockings, watching him all the time.

She felt cold and exposed and as if she was being judged and she tried to joke the feeling away. 'Will I do? Only I'm getting cold.'

He answered her seriously, cupping her breasts in his hands. 'You're the most beautiful girl I've ever seen in my life,' he said. 'Come under the covers and get warm again.'

It wasn't until much later, when she'd got her breath back and they were lying cuddled together under the eiderdown for warmth, he half asleep and grinning like the Cheshire cat, she wide awake and thoughts drifting, that she realised that her life was now totally changed. She was married now, or as good as married. They were one flesh and they belonged together and they would make love again whenever they could. She wasn't at all sure how they would manage it but she knew they would. And sooner or later, when she'd left school, they would marry properly in a church and belong together as man and wife, and live in their own home, all on their own together and make love whenever they wanted to and stay in bed as long as they wanted to afterwards, instead of having to get up and go back to Downview. The thought of her billet brought her to her senses with a start. She had to get back. She'd almost forgotten. What was the time? Did he have a clock in the room? She sat up, clutching the eiderdown about her, and peered at the clutter of books and boxes on the bedside table.

'Ten o'clock,' he said from the pillows. 'It's just struck. There's no rush.'

She was looking for her clothes, searching with her right hand while her left still clutched the eiderdown. 'There is,' she said. 'I mustn't be late. I've promised Smithie.'

'You and your Smithie,' he laughed. 'All right then. Don't worry. You won't be late. I'll take you back on my bike. You can ride on the crossbar. Only on one condition, mind.'

She'd found her petticoat and was pulling it over her head. 'What's that?' she said from among the folds of cloth.

'That you see me all day tomorrow and all day Sunday.'

'And tomorrow and tomorrow and tomorrow,' she promised.

'Well, no,' he said seriously. 'Only Saturday and Sunday. I've got to be back in camp by midnight.'

It was a difficult weekend. Saturday was cold and spitting with rain and there wasn't much they could do in the morning except walk on Horsell Common with nowhere to go to be warm and private. In the afternoon they went to the pictures where it was warm but not exactly private. It gave them a chance to sit in the back row and kiss one another but that was as far as they could go. By the time they emerged into the darkness of the winter night they were both aching with frustration.

'If we were married we could have a room of our own and stay in it all day and do whatever we liked,' Ben complained, as he cuddled her back to Downview.

It couldn't be denied. 'But we can't, can we?' Lizzie said. 'Not till I leave school.' And possibly not even then if her father had anything to do with it. She couldn't imagine him giving his consent. And what if she went to Oxford, the way she was planning? They didn't take married students at university did they? She'd never heard of such a thing. But she did so want them to be married. Oh, why was life so complicated?

'I tell you something,' he said, 'it's going to be a long time till my next leave.'

'I'd make it come quicker if I could,' she said.

Sunday was easier, although it took a bit of crafty persuasion. He met her at the school gate in the early afternoon glowing with the news that the folks were going to tea with their cousins and that they'd have the house to themselves for an hour or two.

'Are they all going?' she asked.

'No,' he said, 'just Aunt and Uncle and Heather. I've given young Robert the wherewithal to go to the flicks. I had to twist his arm a bit but he agreed in the end.'

'That's bribery,' she laughed. Oh, it was good to think they were going to have time on their own!

'That's necessary,' he said and kissed her. 'Come on.'

They stayed in the warm until his family came home,

bubbling with news of their cousins and then, after a decent interval when they listened to the gossip, they walked slowly back to the school house. They were languid with love and torn with the misery of being parted again and stood just out of sight of the school with their arms round each other in the darkness kissing goodbye again and again.

'Come back soon,' she begged. 'It's going to be awful not seeing you.'

'I'll do what I can,' he said, 'but I can't promise anything. We're going on manoeuvres.'

'Which means weeks, doesn't it,' she said dolefully. 'I hate this war.'

'We all hate it,' he said, suddenly feeling far older than she was and very protective. And he tried to cheer her. 'It could be worse. We could be sent to Africa. At least we're not going there yet.'

That didn't cheer her at all. 'Don't even say it,' she told him, fiercely. 'Manoeuvres are bad enough without you going to Africa.'

'We shall have to go eventually,' he warned. 'That's what we're training for.'

It was all too much. After such a weekend her emotions were raw. 'I can't bear it,' she said and burst into tears.

It took him a long time and a lot of gentling before he could comfort her calm again and consequently she was more than twenty minutes late. Mary was in the bathroom and Poppy was already in bed, sitting up against the pillows with her face creamed and a comb in her hand, putting in her curlers.

'You're late,' she said, mildly. And then she stopped because she'd caught the gleam of the ring on her friend's finger. 'Lizzie Meriton! Is that an engagement ring? Oh, do show.'

Lizzie looked at the ring and felt cross with herself. Fancy forgetting to hide it. That's what comes of getting upset. 'Well, yes,' she said, holding out her hand so that Poppy could see the ring. 'It is. But it's a secret.'

'It's gorgeous,' Poppy said, touching it reverently, and Mary came shivering back into the room. 'Look at this, Mary! What do you think? Lizzie's engaged.'

'That corridor's like ice this evening,' Mary said, getting into bed. 'You get nice and warm in the bath and then freeze to death on the way back. So come on then, tell us. Who's the lucky man?'

It was too late for Lizzie to be discreet so she told them – how they met, how handsome he was, how his uncle was the foreman at the wood-yard – 'the one who was so nice to us' – how he was in the tank corps and was going back to Salisbury Plain to start manoeuvres.

'You are a dark horse,' Poppy said admiringly. 'I never even knew you were going out with anyone. Did you, Mary?'

'Nobody knew,' Lizzie told them. 'I mean, nobody does, except you, so please don't go spreading it about. Smithie told me to be discreet.'

Poppy's eyes were a study in surprise. 'She knows about it?'

It was rather warming to be able to say yes.

'Heavens!' Poppy said. 'That woman never ceases to amaze me. Do you mean she actually knows and she didn't tell you not to or anything?'

'She said I was to be discreet, that's all. Oh, and that Juliet wasn't fourteen when she met Romeo.'

Poppy was still coping with surprise. 'Good Lord!' she said.

Mary was more practical. 'So when are you going to get married?' she said, getting into bed.

'When I leave school I expect.'

'I thought you were going to Oxford.'

'I might not be able to. Not if I get married. I mean, I don't think they take married students.'

'Oh Lizzie,' Poppy said, 'you can't not go to Oxford. I mean, it's the best university in the world. You can't not. You simply can't.'

'What did Smithie say about it?' Mary asked.

'She doesn't know,' Lizzie confessed. 'I haven't seen her yet. My appointment's not till tomorrow.'

'Well, rather you than me,' Mary said, ominously. 'If you turn down a place at St Hilda's, she'll be furious. You mark my words.'

'No she won't,' Poppy said, defending her heroine. 'She's not like that.'

Mary pulled the covers up under her chin. 'This is Oxford we're talking about,' she said. 'She will. You mark my words.'

Her words kept Lizzie awake for most of the night. What on earth was she going to say? She would have to tell her. It wasn't something she could keep to herself. Anyway, Smithie would know – she always did, God knows how, she always knew everything – and once it was out in the open, she was bound to be cross, because getting a Roehampton girl to Oxford was a matter of prestige. *Crème de la crème* and all that sort of thing. It was all hideously difficult and it got worse as the hours toiled past.

Octavia had had a trying weekend too. For a start it had been a weekend for visitors and Tommy wasn't one of them, which was rather a disappointment. He'd rung to say that Molotov was flying to London and that there was to be a reception in his honour on Saturday night. All the top brass in the Foreign Office had been told that their attendance was required,

307

'although what good that will do I can't possibly imagine. He's only coming here to bully us into opening the Second Front. It's all he ever talks about.'

'I shall miss you,' she said.

'I'm glad to hear it,' he told her and she could hear him grinning. 'Let me know how you get on with my Lizzie.'

So it was just family members who arrived that Saturday, first Dora, bearing a home-made meat pie, with David beside her, looking very tall and grown up, and then, to Emmeline's surprise, Johnnie, sagging with fatigue and in one of his disgruntled moods. The sight of him sent Emmeline into alarm at once.

'My dear boy,' she said. 'What is the matter? You look all in.'

'Nothing,' Johnnie said. 'Don't fuss.' He'd just been turned down flat by a rather pretty girl but he certainly wasn't going to tell her that. 'I'm tired, that's all.'

'Come and have a slice of my nice meat pie,' Dora said to him. 'That'll cheer you up.'

But of course it won't, Octavia thought, watching him as he sighed to the table, because whatever it is, it's well beyond the comfort of a pie. And food won't comfort Edith much today either because she's missing Arthur and wishing he were here with us. There's sadness all over her face. I wish we could get this dammed war over and done with. We're into the third year of it now and it's beginning to drag us all down. Em's getting thinner by the day, Edie's lonely, Johnnie's hiding his misery, I haven't given Tommy his answer. And as she took her first forkful of the pie, she was glad to think that on Monday morning she would have her nice easy interview with Lizzie.

* * *

It was a quiet, misty morning and the girls were sleepy. Lizzie was stifling a yawn as she walked into Smithie's study and didn't seem her usual cheerful self at all.

'I'm sorry it's so cold in here,' Octavia said, when they'd both settled into their chairs beside the limited warmth of the fire. 'That fire will take presently. It's just being a bit slow this morning.'

Lizzie looked at it and didn't say anything.

'Well now,' Octavia said. 'It's St Hilda's for you, isn't it?' She expected to be answered with a smile and an agreement and was alerted when Lizzie winced. 'What is it, my dear?' she asked. 'Is there a problem?'

There's nothing for it, Lizzie thought. I shall have to tell her. 'I don't think I shall be able to go,' she said.

Octavia was instantly on full alert. This has something to do with her love affair, she thought. I must handle it carefully. 'Why is that?' she asked. 'Are you having second thoughts about the course?'

'No, no,' Lizzie said. 'It's nothing like that.' Then she stopped and tried to gather her courage. 'I just don't think I shall be able to go to university after all.'

'Because?' Octavia prompted.

'Because Ben wants us to get married. Oh, I know I'm young and I know Pa won't approve because he's set his heart on me going to St Hilda's but that's how things are. It won't be long before he gets sent to Africa. I mean, there's no secret about it. They all know it. He reckons it'll be early summer, June or July probably, so his next long leave will be embarkation leave and he'd like us to get married before he goes. That's only right when you think what he's got ahead of him. I mean, he could be wounded or killed. There's no knowing what will happen once he's out there.' The thought brought tears to her eyes and she had to swallow hard before she could go on. 'I can't put my education before that, now, can I? It wouldn't be right.'

Octavia didn't argue with her. It wasn't the right moment. 'No, my dear, when you put it like that, it wouldn't be. Have you talked it over with him?'

Lizzie had to admit she hadn't. 'But there's nothing to say really, is there? If he's going out to join the Eighth Army and he wants us to get married, that's all there is to it.'

Not if I have my way, Octavia thought, and she rolled up imaginary sleeves and prepared to make as good a case as she could. 'Do I take it that you don't have any objection to St Hilda's *per se*?'

'Oh no,' Lizzie said at once. 'I mean it's a wonderful place. It would be a privilege to go there. I know that. No, I'm not against it at all. If I could marry Ben *and* go there, I'd go like a shot. But I couldn't, could I? I mean, they don't have married students at Oxford, do they?'

So far so good, Octavia thought. 'I have to admit I've never heard of any,' she said. 'But that is not to say it's impossible. I see no reason why they shouldn't. It's just that no one has asked the question before. You're a pioneer and St Hilda's is a pioneering college. I can remember how they welcomed speakers from the WSPU.'

Lizzie smiled at that, for the first time since she'd entered the room. She liked the idea of being a pioneer. It made solutions seem possible.

Octavia pressed home her advantage. 'If you will take my advice,' she said, 'you won't do anything precipitous. Things change all the time during a war, habits, opinions, lifestyles, even in the most entrenched sectors of the establishment. What was thought to be totally out of the question in peacetime becomes an imperative when we're at war. You've only got to look at the suffragette movement to see that. We campaigned for women's suffrage for years and years but it wasn't until we were needed for war work that we finally got the vote. I would say press on with your application, visit St Hilda's and see what it has to offer you, attend your interview, sit your Higher Schools and make up your mind to get the highest grades you can and then bide your time. Make your decision as late as you can. There's no rush.'

'Well...' Lizzie said, thinking about it. It sounded sensible, just so long as Smithie understood that there was no question about whether she would marry Ben or not. 'I shall marry him sooner or later,' she warned. 'That's a given.'

'Of course,' Octavia said, 'and good will come of it. We need young women like you to show that it is possible to marry and have a career. Change doesn't usually come of its own accord. We need someone or something to give it a push.'

So it was settled. Lizzie would go ahead with her application, sit her examinations, do everything according to her original plan, but not lose sight of the possibility that she might marry at any time. When she finally said, 'Thank you, Miss Smith' and left, Octavia was exhausted. She stayed where she was beside the fire and lit a cigarette to give herself a chance to recover before she had to take her next study period. As she drew in her first calming lungful of smoke she began to make plans. She wouldn't tell Tommy what had been said. It would only upset him and then there would be ructions and that wouldn't do at all. She wanted Lizzie's life to be as calm as possible in the weeks ahead. But thinking of Tommy and remembering what she'd been saying here in this room only a few minutes ago made her feel ashamed. *We need young women like you to show that it is possible to marry and have a career.'* What a hypocrite she was being. I must make my mind up and set a date and tell him, she thought. I can't put it off any longer. I will do it as soon as I get home.

But she got home to two letters that took her mind away from weddings and dates for the rest of the evening. The first one was a happy note from Janet announcing the birth of her baby.

'There you are,' Emmeline said. 'Didn't I say it would be January? What did she have?'

'A boy,' Octavia told her, handing her the letter. 'A canny lad, so she says. They're going to call him Norman. She's staying with her mother because her husband's at sea and she can't get the pram up and down the stairs on her own.'

Emmeline said that was very wise. 'She was always sensible even if she did get herself into trouble, if you know what I mean.'

That made Octavia smile because she knew so exactly what her cousin meant. But the smile was frozen as soon as she opened her second letter because this one was from Mr Mannheim and the news it contained was so grim as to be almost unbelievable.

*My dear friend,* he wrote,

*I hope you will forgive me for unburdening myself to you again but I feel I must pass on this news to everyone who might be able to help. It is necessary that these terrible things be revealed. To conceal them would be to condone them as I am sure you would agree and these are horrors that should never, never be condoned.*

*To put the matter briefly, there is news coming out of Germany that what they are now openly calling 'the Jewish solution' has become a full scale programme of mass extermination. It is terrible to write such words, hard to believe that there are human beings who would do such inhuman things, but there are such men. One is the man in charge of the programme. His name is Rienhard Heydrich. He is second in command to Himmler of the Gestapo. According to my informant, who I must tell you is usually reliable, he has plans to kill all the Jews now under German rule in Europe, which is to say over eleven million men, women and children for they do not spare the young. There are now several concentration camps built and in action with gas chambers equipped for the killing and crematoria to dispose of the bodies. It is hard for us to comprehend such ruthless enormity but I fear that news of what they plan is true. Do please send this letter on, I beg you dear friend, and forgive me for bringing such distressing things to your attention. There are days when I am half mad with the terror of the things I hear. We live in evil times.*

Octavia lit a cigarette and smoked as she tried to digest the horror on the page. Her senses were roaring at her that this simply couldn't be true, that no man could be so totally inhuman. But her reason was telling a different story. Mr Mannheim was a truthful man. He didn't exaggerate. He was careful to check his facts. If he said this was so, it was only too horribly likely that it was true. I'll show it to Tommy, she decided, and see what he says. If Mr Mannheim has heard it, he might have had wind of it, too.

'News from America?' Emmeline asked, sending a warning glance in the direction of her granddaughters.

Octavia handed the letter across. 'We'll talk about it after dinner,' she said, speaking lightly so as not to alert the children. Barbara was already looking up with a question on her face. 'Do you need a hand in the kitchen?'

'No, that's fine,' Edith said. 'We've done most of it. Can I see it after you, Mum?'

They talked about it until late into the night, anguishing that such a monstrous thing could be planned, let alone put into action. 'What makes them so cruel?' Emmeline said. 'They can't be born that way. I mean, to be planning to kill eleven million people, it's obscene.'

'What I can't understand,' Edith said, 'is why we don't invade France and push the Germans out and free the prisoners and have all this awful business over and done with. What are we waiting for? We should stop all this messing about in Africa and invade France, that's what we should do.'

They were hideous thoughts to take to bed and they kept Octavia awake for far too many hours, wondering how many Jews would be killed in the gas chambers before the Allies could save them and whether there was anything else she could do to help, apart from sending the letter on to Mrs Henderson. I'll talk to Tommy about it on Wednesday, she thought.

But the next morning he phoned just as she was leaving for work to tell her that he wouldn't be able to get down to see her for several days. 'Something's come up,' he said.

'Serious?' she said, reading the tone of his voice.

''Fraid so. We've had some alarming reports from our sources in Germany.'

'About the concentration camps?'

'Ah! You've heard too.'

'Mr Mannheim told me. I was going to show you his letter.'

He sighed. 'So you see how it is. There's a conference being planned. We're all going to be hard at it. I'll be down as soon as I can get away. Give my love to Lizzie.' And he was gone.

Octavia sighed too as she hung up the receiver. Mr Mannheim is right, she thought. We live in evil times.

# Chapter Twenty-One

Lizzie travelled to Oxford in her most recalcitrant mood, planning rebellion all the way, determined not to like the town or the college. I shan't fit in there, she brooded, as the winter fields drifted ethereally past her criss-crossed window. It'll be hateful. I know it will. I'm doing this as a favour to Smithie, that's all, and to please Pa, of course, and it's just plain stupid. I don't want to go one bit. I want to marry Ben and live in our own home, not be stuck in some academic backwater.

By the time she pulled in at the station, she was ready to turn straight round and go back again. But as the next train wasn't for an hour and there was a crowd streaming out of the station and heading off towards the town, she decided to follow where they led. She might as well take a look now she was here. It was a long way to come just to do nothing and it wouldn't make the slightest difference to the way she felt. So having sorted it all out in her head, she walked into the High Street – and was bewitched.

She ambled the length of the street, walking slowly because she had plenty of time, stopping to succumb to the tempting windows of a bookshop, or to admire the Gothic stonework of a church, or to peer through an opened doorway into a grassy courtyard where black-gowned figures were walking and talking. Despite herself she was calmed by the grace of the town, charmed by the honeyed colour of its ancient stones, jollied along by a jingle of cycle bells as young men and women swept past her, black gowns billowing. It was quite a different place from the sombre monochrome of the photographs she'd seen. They'd looked stuffy and antiquated. This town was full of young people enjoying themselves. By the time she'd crossed Magdalene Bridge and reached the gates of St Hilda's she felt thoroughly at home.

And St Hilda's had the welcome mat out for her. There was a uniformed porter standing in his lodge who addressed her as Miss Meriton, told her that her interview would be 'in Hall' and came out to show her the way; the grounds were like a well laid out park, bordering the river where she could see a line of brown punts waiting for custom; there was a magnificent pine tree to give shade to the house in summer and a low brick wall to mark the border between the lawn and the river bank; and the house was everything she could have wanted. It stood four-square to the river bank, secluded and secure in elegant grounds, an imposing Edwardian building with high gables and high arched windows. She liked it at once and knew she would be privileged to be living there, and when she was met at the door by a middle-aged woman in a suit that was so like the sort of thing Smithie wore, what was left of her preconceptions simply melted away. From that moment on she was pleased by everything she saw, the tiled hall, the two interconnecting common rooms with their imposing fireplaces and their expensive carpets — what style they have here! — the panelled dining room, the splendid oak staircase which reminded her of a lesser Downview, the quietly

316

understated elegance of the principal's study to which she was finally escorted for her interview with Miss Mann.

After Smithie's untidiness and open exuberance, she found Miss Mann neat and contained and distant and was perplexed by how little she said, although her questions seemed shrewd. It wasn't until she offered that it would be possible for some of next year's students to take their degrees in two years instead of the usual three that Lizzie gave her full attention to what was being said. Two years instead of three sounded like very good sense, if it could be done. It would mean that she and Ben could marry in two years' time, always providing Pa gave his consent once she'd graduated, and he'd have to do that, surely?

'How would you feel about such an eventuality?' Miss Mann was asking.

'I would consider it a challenge and hope to rise to it,' Lizzie said.

Octavia was pleased to hear how well the interview had gone and felt sure that Lizzie would be accepted, which, after a few busy days, she duly was.

'It's a feather in our Lizzie's cap,' she told the school at that morning's assembly, 'and an honour for our school.'

The cheers were so rapturous they made Lizzie blush. It was a lovely warming moment and, as she stood smiling at her admirers, she thought that if she could get Ben to understand what a good thing this was, she would never ask for anything else in her whole life ever again.

The letter of acceptance had arrived at just the right time for Tommy too, because he was coming down to visit at last. It had been an exhausting fortnight with far too much work for him to do so it was pleasant to sit round Octavia's table and enjoy the company and drink a toast to Lizzie's success. It had to be in beer because wine couldn't be had for love nor money, but it was a toast just the same and they all said 'cheers' and meant it. After the meal he talked about Oxford and what an ideal place it was if you were a student. Then he told them he had another bit of good news.

'Had a letter from Mark this morning,' he said. 'Apparently he's going to get married.'

'How lovely!' Edith said.

But Octavia asked, 'Who to?', thinking of Ben and Lizzie.

'Girl called Joan, apparently. Another Joan, Edith. She's a WAAF, which is how he met her.'

'What's she like?' Emmeline asked.

'No idea,' Tommy admitted. 'Haven't met her yet. She's bound to be all right though. I mean, Mark's got his head screwed on. He wouldn't pick anyone who wasn't. At any rate, it's all set.'

'And when's it going to be?' Octavia asked.

'The Saturday after Easter.'

Emmeline and Octavia exchanged glances, both thinking the same thing.

'Bit of a rush,' Tommy admitted, 'but there's a reason for it. All hush-hush, so you mustn't breathe a word. Bomber Command has got an offensive planned. Munitions factories, air bases, goods yards, that sort of thing. It's to cripple the German war effort and soften them up before the Second Front. Anyway, my two will be involved in it, providing fighter cover, so Mark wants to get married before it starts. Understandable given the circumstances.'

They agreed that it was and Edith said they were being very sensible, 'because you never know what's going to happen' and

Emmeline smiled and nodded and wondered whether they would invite Tavy to the wedding, thinking, I bet Tommy will arrange it if he can. Octavia was still anguishing about the concentration camps and she was wondering whether Bomber Command intended to bomb them too and what would happen to the inmates if they did. It was obvious that Tommy wasn't going to mention them at the moment so she would have to ask him later.

It was past midnight before she got the chance and then he was reluctant to tell her what he knew.

'It's an evil business,' he said. 'Do you really want to talk about it now?'

'Yes,' she said firmly. 'We owe it to those poor devils to check our facts and find out everything we can.'

He gave a resigned shrug. 'Well then,' he said, 'there are at least six camps up and running to our certain knowledge and we think there are more planned. They're killing people by the thousand. We estimate that there must be hundreds every day. And it's not just Jews, although they form the bulk of the killings. They're persecuting other groups too, gypsies, communists, homosexuals. It's all quite hideous.'

'Then they'll have to speed up the Second Front, won't they,' Octavia said.

'Can't be done,' he told her. 'A full scale invasion will be an enormous undertaking. The logistics are formidable. It's being planned now but the military don't reckon they can have it ready until late next year at the earliest. Winnie wants to get the Eyeties out of the war first. Clear the decks, sort of thing.'

'And in the meantime people are being slaughtered.'

''Fraid so.'

She got out of bed and went to stand at the window

so that she could look down at the garden, where it was peaceful and moon-washed and nobody was being gassed to death. She was very near tears. They couldn't just ignore this awful thing. They had to do something about it. After a while she remembered the bombing campaign.

'Are we going to bomb the camps?' she asked. 'Is that what this new offensive is about?'

'Good God, no,' he said. 'That would be doing their dirty work for them. We don't want that.'

She supposed not. 'But something should be done, Tommy. We can't just stand by and let them kill people in their thousands. It's inhuman.' She was crying now at the enormity of it. 'They must do something.'

He got up and came to stand behind her, wrapping his arms round her as if he was protecting her. 'Don't cry, Tikki-Tavy,' he said. 'It's not your fault.'

'Something should be done,' she wept. 'It's just too dreadful to think of all those people being killed and our useless leaders sitting on their hands doing nothing. Can't they see how abominable it is?'

He held her close and let her rant until she'd cried the worst of her anger away. 'I hate this war,' she said, blowing her nose.

He tried to soothe her. 'I know, my darling, I know.'

'It's an abomination, Tommy. A total and utter abomination. It diminishes us. It makes us less than human. We sit back and let these dreadful things happen and we should be doing everything and anything to make them stop. I can't bear it. It strips away our basic human instincts. We're capable of such good and we allow these obscene people to get their own way and rule our lives.'

'We'll defeat them in the end, Tavy,' he said. 'It's just a matter of time.'

It was probably true but it didn't comfort her. 'But how many victims will have to die before we do?' she said.

He turned her in his arms and smoothed her damp hair out of her eyes, very gently and tenderly. 'If I could change the world for you, I would,' he said.

'I know,' she relented. 'You're a dear man.'

'Then come back to bed,' he said. 'Your hands are like ice and I don't want you catching pneumonia on top of everything else. What would your pupils do without you?'

She was returning to her senses. 'They would cope,' she told him, shivering back to the bed. 'They're trained to be resilient.'

They had a lot of practice at being resilient that winter. It was extremely cold and the rations were smaller than they'd ever been. Cook did her best with what little there was, producing roly-poly puddings and spotted dick and stews, which were mostly vegetable but were at least filling, and she made sure that every girl had a pot of jam or marmalade once a month and her own individual ration of butter and sugar, doled out once a week, all carefully marked with their names, but she knew their diet was meagre and dull and often complained to Octavia about it. 'Not that there's much you can do to help us, Miss Smith,' she said. 'I do know that. But it helps to get it off my chest.'

Lizzie never complained. Food was the least of her worries that January. What was troubling her was the war in North Africa. The Germans had been pushing the Eighth Army further and further back towards Egypt. They'd reached a place called Benghazi already and Ben said the closer they got to Cairo the sooner his brigade would be sent out as reinforcements. He'd taken her news without much comment, beyond saying 'Lucky you!' and, although it was upsetting, his attitude was understandable. The thought of him being sent to Africa filled her with such foreboding that an education at St Hilda's seemed unimportant by comparison. She agonised until his daily letter arrived and followed the news every day, pouring over the papers for the least little detail. When the invitation to Mark's wedding turned up she barely noticed it and didn't answer it for more than four days, which was rude of her and rather silly, because putting it aside meant she missed how important it was. When she finally got around to writing a reply and read it for the second time she realised that it was a godsend. If Pa can agree to Mark getting married, she thought, and he obviously has, then he can't very well say no when I ask him if I can get married too. Sauce for the goose, sort of thing. I'll wear my pretty frock and that nice hat he likes and I'll catch him at the right moment and ask him sweetly, like Ma used to do. Easy-peasy.

*Thank you for your invitation*, she wrote to her brother. *I shall be there with bells on.*

Octavia wasn't at all sure whether she ought to be there at all. She was spending that weekend in Wimbledon, back in her own neglected home, with a pale sunlight making patterns on her dusty kitchen table and revealing how extremely dirty the windows were, and the sight of it was making her feel unsettled. Of course, there wasn't time to do any housework and very little point because it would all get dusty again as soon as she turned her back on it, and it certainly wasn't like her to be houseproud, but she felt guilty to be neglecting the place and aware that Tommy's house would all be in apple-pie order.

'About this wedding,' she said, pouring a second cup of tea and thinking that at least the tea cups were clean.

'Buy a new hat,' he said, stirring his tea.

'Never mind a hat,' she said sternly. 'I don't think I ought to be there.'

'Can't see why not.'

'Because a wedding is a family affair and I'm not family.'

'But you will be,' he said, giving her his most devilish grin. 'Time to give 'em a foretaste, don't you think.'

'You might give them a shock,' she said. 'Have you thought of that?'

'You worry too much,' he said. 'They'll love you. And anyway, it's a wedding. There'll be far too much going on for anyone to be shocked. Trust me. Just buy a pretty hat. That's all you need to do.'

She bought the hat – although with serious misgivings. It was all very well for Tommy to tell her not to worry. He took things so easily – or at least he did when it came to family matters. It was different when he was at the Foreign Office. He obviously planned everything down to the last little detail when he was there but when it came to his children, at the very time when he should have been thinking everything through most carefully, he didn't think at all. There were times when she found him really quite hard to understand.

But there was no time to brood on it. She sent a letter of acceptance, put the hat away on top of the wardrobe and got on with the term. In a few weeks the applications for next year's first form would be coming in and she wanted to be ready for them, especially as one of them could be young Barbara. She and David had both sat the scholarship examination that year and Edith had been watching the post with fidgeting anxiety.

'I do so want her to pass,' she said to Octavia. 'I know there's nothing we can do about it if she doesn't but I do so

323

want her to. It could be the making of her.'

It was the first time Octavia had really appreciated what a once-in-a-lifetime chance the examination was. Until then she'd simply interviewed all the applicants on the list the LCC had sent her, chosen the best and most suitable ones and thought no more about it. Now Edith was making her consider the ones who failed. There can't be very much difference between the children who pass and the ones who have to accept failure. They've all been considered bright enough to enter. When this horrible war is over I must put my mind to it.

Meantime there was work to be done and girls to be interviewed, among them Barbara Ames, to her mother's damp-eyed relief. Octavia was pleasantly surprised to see how overawed she was when she came to the school. She sat by her mother's side, round-eyed and shy, and answered every question politely, calling her 'Miss Smith' instead of 'Aunt', like the sensible, well-coached child she was. When Edith led her out of the room she was still solemn.

'She'll do,' Octavia said to Maggie and she put a firm tick by Barbara's name.

Emmeline wasn't anywhere near so discreet. 'Well?' she asked, when Octavia finally came home that afternoon. 'What's the verdict?'

Octavia gave her the thumbs-up. 'But don't say anything until it's official,' she warned.

'You know me,' Emmeline said. 'Soul of discretion, me. The tea's made.'

The next day's news brought a disappointment. Dora phoned in the evening to say that David hadn't passed. She sounded cross and irritable and when her mother tried to comfort her by saying he could always try again when he was thirteen, she snorted.

'He can see out the year,' she said, 'and then he can come home. It's quite safe now and he might as well be taught in the emergency school as stay down there not learning anything. I always said that school was no use.'

As Tommy and Mark had predicted, the war was taking a new turn. At the end of March when the first tentative daffodils were trembling in the flower-beds at Ridgeway, Bomber Command launched its new bombing offensive with raids on Lubeck and the mighty Krupps works at Essen. Two days later, the port of Le Havre was bombed too and Matthew Meriton phoned his father to say that his squadron had put up a jolly good show there and had shot down eight German fighters – and was called a stout feller, which was very high praise.

But as always in war, one attack led to another and another. In April the Germans decided to retaliate by bombing some of England's most beautiful cathedral cities; first Exeter, then Bath, then Norwich and York. The papers called them the Baedeker raids and printed shocking pictures of the damage they'd done. And Emmeline got the letter she'd been dreading ever since Johnnie joined up.

She knew it was bad news as soon as she saw the envelope because although it was addressed in Johnnie's familiar handwriting it was so scruffily written that her heart contracted at the sight of it. Her hands were shaking so much it took her several fumbling seconds to open the envelope and when she'd read the letter she lifted her head and howled in anguish.

'I knew this would happen,' she wept. 'Didn't I say so? I never wanted him to fly those horrible Spitfires in the first place. I said so at the start. I did, didn't I, Tavy. First Squirrel and then Podge and now my Johnnie.' The tears were torrenting down her cheeks, making her look haggard and distraught. 'Oh my poor Johnnie. My poor, dear Johnnie. I can't bear it.'

Edith had picked up the letter and was reading it, while her daughters watched her and didn't say a word. 'It's all right,' she said to them. 'He's not dead. Just wounded, that's all.'

'That's all!' Emmeline cried. 'All! What are you talking about? He's been wounded. Don't you understand? Wounded. They get terribly wounded in a war. They die of wounds. You don't know the half of it.'

Edith gave her a warning look but she was too far gone in her distress to see it and went on weeping, rocking backwards and forwards in her chair.

'He's in hospital, Ma,' Edith said, passing the letter to Octavia. 'Which is the best place. And we can go and visit him. I'll phone them up and find out when the visiting hours are and we'll go the minute we can. Today if it's possible. Don't cry. It'll be all right. Really. Now I've got to get these girls to school or they'll be late and that would never do, would it, girls? Not when it's the last day of term.' And she gave Octavia a look which *was* responded to and shepherded her children upstairs to the bathroom.

While she was out of the room and Emmeline was still weeping and rocking, Octavia phoned the hospital. By the time Edie came downstairs again, she had the address and the visiting hours written on the notepad and ready for her.

'There it is,' she said. 'He's in the burns unit and you can visit him this afternoon. I've written it all down. Don't worry about Joanie. She can come to Downview with me for the day. That'll be nice won't it, Joanie. You can see our garden. And I'll pick the girls up this afternoon. Don't worry. They'll be all right.'

'Thanks,' Edie said, and the word was heartfelt. 'There you are, Joanie. You're going to the big school. Aren't you the lucky one. I'll be back directly, Ma. Don't worry. Aunt's got it all under control.'

'I don't know what the world's coming to,' Emmeline wept. 'I really don't.'

It was a difficult journey to Tonbridge Wells, because they had to take a train into London and then travel out again but they arrived at the hospital in plenty of time and found the burns unit without any trouble at all because the wards were so clearly marked. Emmeline was appalled by it. All those young men burnt until their flesh was like raw meat or bandaged up, which was even worse because she had no idea what horrors were underneath the bandages. Edith did her best to smile at them as they passed their beds and one or two smiled back but her mother passed them frozen-faced.

Johnnie was in the end bed, lying on his back with his eyes tightly shut, his face pale as putty, a cradle over his legs and both hands heavily bandaged. He opened his eyes as he heard their approach and instantly became bright and cheerful, saying, 'Hello you two. Nice to see you.' But he didn't fool either of them.

'Oh, Johnnie,' Emmeline mourned, 'my poor dear boy. Look at the state of you.'

Her sympathy annoyed him. 'I'm fine, Ma,' he said and his voice was tetchy. 'Don't fuss. I'm doing OK.'

But Emmeline ploughed on. 'What's up with your leg?' she said.

'Got a bit burnt. That's all. You know how it is when you prang the old kite. How are the kids?'

Emmeline didn't want to talk about the children. They were unimportant compared to seeing him injured and not knowing exactly what was wrong with him but his face was shut, the way it used to be when he got into trouble with his father as a boy, and he obviously wasn't going to tell her anything. So she told him about the scholarship and how Barbara had passed and he said he was glad to hear it and closed his eyes again.

'Let him rest,' Edie whispered. 'Stay here with him and I'll go and find Sister or a doctor or someone. Won't be long.'

She was nearly half an hour and when she came back, her face was shut too and her brother was fast asleep.

'Well?' Emmeline asked.

'They're very pleased with him,' Edie temporised. 'They say he's a fighter. I'll tell you all the details when we get home.'

'How long can we stay?'

'Another twenty minutes,' Edie said, looking at the wall clock.

'We'll just sit here then shall we?'

They sat until the tea trolley arrived and a nurse with a nice kind face came along to wake him up and feed him bread and butter and tea in a cup with a spout. Emmeline winced to see that he couldn't use his hands at all but to Edie's relief she didn't remark on it, and after a while the bell was sounded and they had to say goodbye and leave.

'We'll come again soon,' Emmeline promised as she kissed him.

He was being bright again. 'Look forward to it,' he said.

They waved all the way to the door and Emmeline didn't say anything until they were halfway along the corridor. Then she took Edie's arm and gave it an urgent shake. 'Now tell me what they really said,' she ordered.

'Well,' Edith said slowly. 'His hands are burnt, as you saw. They're giving him salt baths to help them to heal and they said they were quite hopeful. He might need surgery to repair them where they're sort of pulled into claws but they're hopeful.'

'And his legs?'

'They're not so good,' Edie said. 'They were badly burnt. He was trapped in the plane you see and they burnt while they were trying to get him out.'

Emmeline was anguished beyond caution. 'How badly burnt?'

'They had to amputate one of them, I'm afraid. He's lost his right leg below the knee.'

'Oh, my dear, good God!' Emmeline said. 'My poor, poor boy. What *will* he do now?'

At that moment he'd turned his face into his pillows and was weeping like a child and the nurse with the kind face was rubbing his arm which was the only part of him she could reach to offer any comfort.

'I'm finished,' he wept. 'It's all over with me.'

'No it's not,' the nurse said. 'You're healing nicely.'

'It is. It is. I shall never fly again.'

She countered that too, speaking gently. 'You will if you want to.'

He lifted his head to glare at her. 'With a tin leg?'

'Douglas Bader flew again. And he's got two.'

That was true but he was too down to respond to it. 'I might as well be dead. They should have left me where I was.'

'Don't talk rubbish,' the nurse said. 'They were good brave men and they got burnt too, I'll have you know. Two of them were treated here.'

Until that moment he hadn't thought of his rescuers. 'Badly burnt?'

'Hands mostly. We looked after them.' And as he seemed to be recovering, 'Now then, what do you want for supper?'

'Sorry to belly-ache,' he said.

She smiled at that. 'It's all right.'

'No,' he told her seriously. 'It's not. I shouldn't burden other people with my troubles. You've probably got enough of your own.'

'Burden all you like,' she said. 'That's what we're here for.'

He was looking at her, still with that serious expression on his face. 'I know you're Nurse Jones,' he said, 'but what's your Christian name? If you don't mind telling me, that is.'

'Gwyneth,' she said. 'And before you ask how I came by it, I'm from Glamorgan.'

'Gwyneth,' he said and smiled at her. 'That's a beautiful name.'

'So what are you having for supper? Rissoles, or fish pie?'

For the next six days Edith and Dora and Emmeline took it in turns to visit. It was the Easter holiday and Octavia was around to look after the children, although as she pointed out, she would be away herself on Saturday, attending Mark Meriton's wedding. Whatever else, Johnnie's injuries had put that event into perspective. She knew now that it really didn't matter whether his family approved of her presence there or not. It was a wedding and a chance to celebrate and be happy and she was glad to take it.

# Chapter Twenty-Two

Mark Meriton's wedding was a study in Air Force blue. It was a delicate April day, the sun shone tentatively, there was lilac blooming in the neighbouring gardens and yet the little church in St Albans was sober with uniforms. For a bemused second Octavia wondered whether they'd come to the right place. Then she saw Mark and Matthew standing together at the altar rail and realised that the church was full of their RAF friends and, while she was looking round to see if there was anyone there she recognised, a young boy in a very white shirt came up to ask Tommy if they were 'bride or groom'.

'Father of the groom,' he said, beaming.

'Yes, sir,' the boy said. 'Major Meriton, isn't it? If you'll come this way, sir.' And he escorted them to the front pew where they found Lizzie in a very pretty dress and a blue straw hat, and beside her a familiar face who turned out to be Tommy's younger brother James, there with his wife Laura and their two dumpy daughters. There was a difficult moment when Tommy introduced Octavia to Laura as 'an old family friend' and she was given a look of such sneering animosity that she felt quite upset, but then the organist began to play the wedding march and she was rescued by the arrival of the bride and the congregation settled down to follow the service.

When it was over, she and Lizzie left the church together.

'They're just horrible inverted snobs,' Lizzie said, glaring at her cousins who were following their mother in the opposite direction. 'They were picking on me all the way here. Why didn't I have my hair permed? And didn't I find high heels uncomfortable? I mean, I wouldn't wear them if I did. And was a straw hat suitable for my brother's wedding? On and on. And do you know what they said when I told them I was going to St Hilda's? You'll never believe this. They said it was a waste of time because I'd only get married. *Only!* That's all they know.'

Octavia took her by the arm and steered her out of earshot. 'No Ben?' she asked.

'He's on manoeuvres,' Lizzie said. 'Mark said it would be all right to bring him but the army had other ideas.' She was still glaring at the departing backs of her aunt and cousins. 'I don't know which of them I like least,' she said. 'Aunt Laura's always sneering at someone or other. Nobody's ever right. Except her. I mean fancy saying it's a waste of time to go to Oxford? I bet they wouldn't say it if it was them.'

'Exactly so,' Octavia said.

'Uncle Jim's all right,' Lizzie said, smiling at him as he passed. 'He went out of his way to pick me up at Downview. When Pa said he was driving up from Wimbledon, *he* said I couldn't travel by train and he didn't mind coming to get me in the least. I thought that was really nice of him. But the others! Words fail me.'

'Your father can drive you to the reception,' Octavia said, as Tommy strolled up to join them. 'Can't you, Tommy?'

'Can't I what, old thing?' Tommy said.

'Drive Lizzie to the reception.'

'Naturally. Pretty wedding, I thought. Like the hat, Lizzie.

Nice to see old James again.'

The photographer was calling for the 'immediate family'.

'That's us,' Tommy said. 'Come on, you two.'

Lizzie went off happily holding his arm but Octavia contrived to slip away and hide herself among a group of very tall and very friendly airmen. After what she'd just heard about James's wife and daughters, she felt her presence in such a public family photograph would be a provocation and she had no intention of provoking anybody if she could help it. But she rejoined them at the reception because it wasn't a sit-down meal so she could eat sausage rolls and cheese straws and pretend to sip a rather revolting cordial and wander about the room, talking to as many people as she liked and keeping out of Laura's way, which was far more satisfactory. Now and then she and Lizzie passed one another in the crowd, and once Tommy came to find her because he wanted to introduce her to a man he called the Wing Co, and once brother James appeared at her elbow to tell her he did so admire what she was doing 'at that school of yours'. So the afternoon passed pleasantly. Mark made a charming speech, the bride blushed, toasts were drunk, everything went according to the old established pattern.

But when the guests were gathered outside the hall to wave their newly-weds goodbye, Tommy made a serious mistake. The bride had thrown her bouquet at the crowd in the traditional way and had clapped with the rest when it was caught by one of the WAAFS and James had turned to his brother and said, 'One thing leads to another, eh, Tommy?' with quite a roguish gleam in his eye.

'Could well be,' Tommy said. 'How would you fancy another wedding in the family?'

James nodded his head. 'Young Matt, is it?'

'Well actually…' Tommy began. But he was pre-empted by his daughter, who held out her hand to her uncle so that he could see her ring.

'No, Uncle James,' she said. 'It's not Matthew, it's me.'

'Well, congratulations, my dear,' James said. 'Is your young man here?'

'I'm afraid not,' Lizzie told him. 'He's on Salisbury Plain on manoeuvres, otherwise he would be. He's in the tank corps.'

'Ah,' James said. 'That accounts. So when is this wedding to be?'

This time it was Lizzie who was forestalled. 'Not for years yet,' Tommy said. 'She's got to get her degree first, haven't you, Lizzie. It's not something to rush. Only fools rush in, eh, Lizzie?'

'Well actually…' Lizzie said, but her father was turning his brother aside.

'Have you met the Wing Co, James? No! Oh, you must.' He moved them both into the crowd, talking as he went. 'Stout feller. Thinks the world of young Mark.'

It was more than Lizzie could bear. To be cut by your own father, at your brother's wedding, where she couldn't contradict him or even answer him was so painful it was as if he'd punched her. 'How can he do this to me?' she said to Octavia. 'I thought he was supposed to love me.' And then she caught the sneering expression on her aunt's face and the tears began to flow. She put her hands to her mouth, turned and ran away from them.

'Excuse me,' Octavia said, and followed after her, walking as quickly as she could without actually running. She found her behind the hall, leaning against the wooden wall and sobbing like a child.

'How could he do this to me?' she wept. 'How could he?'

It was time to take action. Talk could come later. 'Stay there,' Octavia commanded. 'Don't move. I'll just go and make my farewells and then we'll go home.'

'Home?'

'To Downview.'

'How can we do that?' Lizzie wept. 'I'm not going in his car. Or Uncle James's. I couldn't bear it. Not after this.'

'Of course not,' Octavia said. 'We'll go by train. Stay there. I'll be as quick as I can.'

As she was. Lizzie had only just dried her eyes when she brisked round the corner, with her handbag over her arm and the most determined expression on her face. 'Come along,' she said.

It was a long journey and a very tiring one, for they missed their connection at Waterloo and both the London termini were suffocatingly crowded. It wasn't until they were alone in an empty carriage on the Woking train and heading out of the city that Lizzie had a chance to talk and then what she had to say was urgent and alarming.

'The thing is, Miss Smith,' she said, 'Ben's going to be sent to Africa. They're waiting for their embarkation leave. That's why he couldn't get away for the wedding. He says they'll hear any day. Only the thing is, he wants us to get married before he goes. I was going to soften Pa up at this wedding and ask him to arrange it but he won't, will he? Even if he hadn't lost his temper. The fact is, he doesn't want me to get married and he won't give his consent and if he won't give his consent I can't get married. My poor Ben's been planning our honeymoon and everything and now what am I going to tell him? I don't know why Pa has to be so hateful. Anyway, I can't ask him. Not now. Not after cutting me like that. I'd only get my head bitten off. So I'm stuck, aren't I?'

'Not necessarily,' Octavia said, thinking hard. 'Let's see if we can get this into some sort of perspective. Presumably you'd marry Ben if you could. That goes without saying.'

'Yes. I would.'

'But you *do* want to go to Oxford? Or you would if everything else was equal?'

'Yes. I suppose so. I haven't really thought.'

'Then think now.'

'Well then, yes, I would. It's a wonderful place. But it isn't possible to have everything you want, is it?'

'Well…' Octavia said, smiling at her. 'It all depends on how you go about it.' The solution was obvious and entirely improper. It would infuriate Tommy if he heard about it, which of course he shouldn't and wouldn't. She would have to make sure of that. But it *was* the solution. Mischief rose in her as strong as a life force. 'Let me tell you what I have in mind,' she said. 'I think you should go ahead with that honeymoon he's planning and take it and enjoy it. You'll have to wear a wedding ring of course, otherwise you'll get questions, but I'm sure he'll provide that, won't he? And you'll have to take care you don't get pregnant. But if I'm any judge of your young man he'll manage that too. You'll have to be exceptionally discreet and not discuss it with anyone at all – and particularly not your father. And when Ben has been sent to Africa, you can go to St Hilda's and study there while you wait for him to come home again. It would be a waste of your talents not to do it and there's no need for anyone there to know what you are doing in your private life, providing there's no baby to give the game away. If he gets leave during term time you'll have to make some excuse to absent yourself from college for however long you've got. But I'm sure you'll be able to think of something. It won't be easy but it *is* all possible.'

Lizzie listened with growing admiration and amazement. That the famous Miss Smith should be sitting there, calmly advocating an affair was so extraordinary she could barely believe it. But she was right. It was the answer.

'So what do you think?' Octavia said.

'I'll write to him tonight,' Lizzie said. 'As soon as I get in.'

It was late by the time Octavia got home because, when Lizzie had trailed upstairs to her room, she went to find Maggie Henry to check on how her girls had been during the day. When she finally walked into the drive at Ridgeway she saw Emmeline standing by the dining room window and knew by the set of her shoulders that she'd been watching out for her. Not a good sign for it usually meant trouble. And sure enough, when she put her key in the lock her cousin was already in the hall, waiting for her and looking ruffled.

'Where's Tommy?' she said. 'I thought he was bringing you home.'

'It's a long story,' Octavia told her. 'Is there any tea? I'm gasping for a drink.'

Emmeline sniffed. 'Didn't they have drinks at this wedding of yours?'

Octavia registered the sniff. There *was* something up. 'They had cordial,' she said, 'and it was undrinkable. I poured mine in the flower-bed.'

Tea was produced. There was always tea. It was the one thing that wasn't rationed. She and Emmeline and Edith and the girls sat round the kitchen table and had tea and a slice of apple cake.

'So what have you all been doing today?' she asked as she poured herself a second cup.

'Mummy's got a job,' Barbara told her.

'If you ever heard of anything so ridiculous,' Emmeline said.

So that's what's the matter, Octavia thought. 'It doesn't sound ridiculous to me,' she said.

'There's no need for it,' Emmeline said.

'I have tried to explain,' Edith said to her aunt. 'Once Joanie's at school I shall have to go to work. I shall be drafted. You know that, Ma. So I thought if I've got to go anyway, I'll find something for myself and I have.'

'Very sensible,' Octavia approved. 'What sort of work is it?'

'Making parachutes,' Edith told her. 'They were advertising last week for machinists so I wrote in. GQ Parachutes. It's in Maybury down by the infants' school. They're a jolly lot. They took me round and showed me what I'd have to do and they were ever so friendly. They make new parachutes and repair damaged ones. The place was stacked with them. It didn't look too difficult, really, Ma, and it's all treadle machines. They told me all sorts of things. There are two bosses apparently, Mr Gregory's the brains and Mr Quilter's the money, so they say. Anyway it'll be nice to be earning my living. I know you don't like the idea, Ma, but it will. I've been pinching and scraping long enough and if I've got to buy furniture, and God knows what when this lot's over, I shall need some cash put by.'

'Very sensible,' Octavia said again but she was wondering why family life had to be so prickly and difficult. First Tommy trampling all over poor Lizzie and now Em laying down the law to Edie when she was being perfectly reasonable.

That night, when she finally got to her bedroom and was writing up her journal, she returned to her wondering. *I sometimes think it was just as well Tommy and I didn't marry when we were young,* she wrote. *We would have had children because his heart was set on it and we would never have agreed about how to bring them up. I wonder when he will phone me. I must give him a day or two to recover.*

Lizzie was writing at that moment too, sitting in her window seat with her bedside lamp to light the page, while her two companions slept. It was the letter to Ben that she'd promised Smithie she would write and it was a long one. She'd already given him a description of the wedding and her father's perfidious behaviour, and now she was telling him all about Smithie's solution. *Write soon and let me know what you think,'* she wrote. *'I shall be worrying until I get a letter.*

He answered by return of post. *Your Smithie is a giddy marvel. We'll do it. I will book us a room at Weston-super-Mare. That is the place, isn't it? See you ASAP.*

So the new school term began. Joanie went to school and returned home with her shoes scuffed and an ink stain on her jersey saying it was OK and she was Joan now "cos they don't call you Joanie at school', and two days later Edith started work at the factory. She found it a great deal more tiring than she was prepared to admit although she did her share of the cooking when she got home and was careful to clear the table and sweep the kitchen floor just as she'd always done. Emmeline grumbled to Octavia that she looked like a little ghost, but after a week she got used to her new lifestyle and began to pace herself better and didn't look quite so drawn.

Emmeline went on complaining nevertheless. 'It's never-ending change,' she said. 'You just about get used to one thing and another turns up. I don't know how we're supposed to manage.'

'By taking it in our stride,' Octavia said. 'Isn't that right,

Edie?' She was privately congratulating herself at how well she was striding over difficulties that summer. Only that afternoon she'd given Lizzie permission to be absent for the next ten days and now she was wondering how Tommy would take it when he found out about it – and rather looking forward to his anger.

It exploded upon her in a telephone call the following morning.

'I've just had a card from Lizzie,' he said. 'What's all this nonsense about her going on holiday?'

Octavia's heart constricted. Surely she hasn't told him? she thought. She wouldn't be so silly. Not after all I've said to her. Fortunately he was still complaining, which gave her a chance to catch her breath and think.

'I left a message with that matron of yours. Said I'd be coming down on Wednesday, and what do I get? A postcard! A postcard! I ask you. Says she's going on holiday with some silly friend. Do you know about it?'

'Yes,' Octavia said, calmly. 'I gave her permission.'

'You did what?'

'I gave her permission.'

'For God's sake, Tavy. It's not up to you to give her permission. She should have asked me. I *am* her father, in case you've forgotten.'

'And I'm her headmistress,' Octavia said, thinking *checkmate*, 'in case *you've* forgotten. *In loco parentis.*'

'And what about her Entrance Exam? Or have you all forgotten that?'

'She's well prepared,' Octavia told him, 'and she'll be back in plenty of time to take it. There's no need for you to worry.'

There was a pause and then he changed direction. 'And where the hell did you get to after the reception? I searched

340

all over the place for you.'

'I was looking after your daughter,' Octavia said. 'I took her home. Do you have any idea how much you upset her?'

'Don't tell me how to treat my own daughter,' he said furiously. 'She had to be told. You can't let your children do whatever they like. You ought to know that.'

'She's not a child, Tommy. She's a woman.'

'She's a child.'

'She's the same age as we were when we met.'

'You're so bloody aggravating,' he said and hung up.

And you only know the half of it, Octavia thought, as she put the receiver back on its hook. There are times, Tommy Meriton, when you are really quite insufferable. It's just as well I have to go to school or I'd have lost my temper too. And she wondered how Lizzie was, out there in Weston-super-Mare on her 'honeymoon'.

She was in bed, of course, and she wasn't going to get up for hours. She and Ben had promised one another right at the start that they would do whatever they wanted to, whenever they wanted to, and, as their landlady rather liked the idea of having a tankie and his wife honeymooning under her roof, they'd been given plenty of latitude. For, as the permissive lady explained to her neighbour, 'He's off to that dreadful desert in a week or two and he could be killed, poor boy. We owe it to them really, don't we?'

The weather was kind to them that first week, with plenty of sun to warm them as they strolled beside the sea or walked on the Grand Pier, and balmy evenings to enjoy on their way to the pictures or the local dancehall.

'I wish this could go on forever,' Ben said as they strolled back to the boarding house through the salty darkness on their last precious evening. 'Ten days is too little. They should have given us a month.' Now that the moment of parting was so close he was torn by the anguish of it.

'Next time,' she said, trying to comfort him.

He was sinking under the weight of an impossible sadness. 'If there is a next time.'

She put her hand over his mouth. 'Don't say such a thing,' she said fiercely. 'Don't even think it. There *will* be a next time. And we *will* get married. I promise you.'

He put his arms round her and held her so tightly she could barely breathe. 'Darling, darling Lizzie,' he said. 'I love you so much. I'd go AWOL if you asked me to.'

'I don't ask you to.'

'I would.'

'I know,' she said, and offered the best comfort she knew. 'Don't let's stand out here. Let's get back and go to bed.'

It was three weeks before Tommy rang Octavia again and then it was to apologise 'for losing his rag' and to offer to take her to the West End. 'Might be the last chance we get for a while,' he said. 'I'm off to Washington again.'

Octavia was quite glad to hear it. Lizzie had come back from her 'holiday' looking drawn beyond her years and had spent the next week either doggedly sitting examinations or hidden away in her room, supposedly revising. It was Octavia's custom to be there as the candidates went in, to wish them luck and see that they were all right, and the sight of Lizzie's pale face made her ache with pity. It must be peculiarly difficult to have to say goodbye to your lover and watch him go off to war and then come back to school and sit examinations. In one way at least, Tommy's trip to Washington was opportune. It would give his daughter a chance to recover her spirits a little before she had to face him again.

But the trip to the West End was a temptation, besides being a chance to kiss and make up, so she took it and used it. She was beginning to understand that there was a pattern to his outbursts – first fury in which he said all sorts of silly things, then a long silence, then repentance and apology and finally a treat of some kind – and although it seemed pretty childish, at least she understood it. And his repentant tenderness almost made up for it.

They went to see the latest Hollywood musical which was showing in Leicester Square. It was called *Me and my Girl* and was an anodyne confection starring Judy Garland. It was pleasant enough although not exactly thought-provoking. Afterwards he took her to dinner and made a great fuss of her.

'Sorry about all that earlier on,' he said, when the meal had been served. 'You know, with Lizzie and the holiday.'

She was stern with him. 'So you should be.'

'I've always been a bit obsessive when it comes to Lizzie,' he confessed. 'Silly I know, but I can't help it. I want the best for her, that's the trouble. Always have. Elizabeth was forever on at me about it.'

There was so much that ought to have been said but Octavia forbore. It wasn't the right moment. Not yet. She felt sure a better one would present itself, sooner or later, and there was no point in quarrelling with him needlessly. So they enjoyed their meal and spent a loving night together and the next day he took flight to Washington, quite his old cheerful self, promising to bring her back 'some goodies from the land of plenty'. Which, she thought, will at least please Em.

\* \* \*

343

Emmeline had had a difficult few weeks. She'd travelled to Tonbridge Wells every other day and grieved because Johnnie never seemed to be getting any better.

'He's as bad now as when we first saw him,' she confided to Octavia. 'He's marginally better when that nice nurse is with him – the one he calls Gwyneth – but his hands are in a terrible state and now they say they're going to operate on him, which seems dreadful to me. I mean what can they do, when his fingers are all curled up like claws?'

Octavia didn't know what to say to cheer her, especially as she tossed every scrap of offered comfort aside as if it made her angry. Eventually all she could find to say was 'Well, we shall see, won't we?' and that seemed pretty fatuous.

'This damned awful war!' Emmeline growled. 'How's Lizzie's young man? Is he there yet?'

He was there, and he'd written home, once to his aunt and uncle and three times to Lizzie, telling her what a foul place the desert was, *like an oven and when the wind blows the sand gets everywhere, in your food and your hair and up your nose, everywhere.* In the second letter he told her how depressing it was to hear the old hands saying they hadn't got a cat in hell's chance of beating the Germans. In the third he reported that everything had come to a halt at a place called El Alamein. *It's a difficult terrain to fight in. You can't go north because you'd be in the Mediterranean and you can't go south because there's a line of cliffs there and a huge depression called Qattara, which is actually a salt marsh and not the right place for tanks, and there are minefields everywhere. Although I don't know why I'm writing all this because I bet it'll be blue-pencilled.*

She wrote back to him after every letter, telling him how much she loved him and how much she missed him and urging him to look after himself. She didn't say anything about the examination or about her life in school. It didn't seem appropriate somehow, not when they were as good as married.

The summer term ambled away. Her father came back from the States and took her out to tea, but seemed a bit put out because she didn't have much of an appetite. Ben wrote a letter every week although, as he reported, *There's not much to say. Jerry's keeping quiet for the moment. The sand is sand.* Smithie took her final assembly and most of her senior pupils either went out to work or back to London for the summer. By the middle of August, Lizzie and Polly were the only two prefects left in the building. They entertained themselves with organising picnics and going to the pictures and telling stories to the juniors. And then there was a sudden flurry of news. Churchill had decided to replace General Auchinleck with another general called Alexander, and another one called Montgomery had been given command of the 'forces in the field'. Within a week Ben was writing to tell her what an extraordinary man he was.

*He's not much to look at,* he said, *bit on the short side, funny-looking face, big hooter, not exactly what you'd call prepossessing, and he's got the most peculiar voice, sort of high-pitched and nasal, but I tell you, he came down here and stood on a tank and talked to us and you could have heard a pin drop. I've never heard anybody in the army talk to us like that. He says we're the best army the world has ever seen and the most highly trained and we're going to hit the Germans for six. He says there's no doubt about it. Rommel's had a good run for his money, he says, but all that's going to stop. Our campaign is going to be planned to the last detail, we've got powerful new tanks coming, we're going to train and prepare until we're in tip-top condition, and there'll be no stopping us. What do you think of that?*

It sounded extraordinary to Lizzie and not particularly likely. After all, the Germans had been having everything their own way ever since the war began so one speech was hardly going to turn it all round. Was it?

Poppy was of the same opinion. 'I mean, anyone can say things,' she said. 'It doesn't necessarily mean they can do them.' Nevertheless, she sat in the window seat holding the letter reverently, like something special and from another world. It thrilled her to be on the edge of Lizzie's love affair and to think that Ben was a fighter. 'I wonder what will happen next.'

What happened next was that Rommel's army attacked, and for the first time in the campaign they couldn't press their attack home. After five days of heavy fighting they were forced to retreat and, eventually and ignominiously, ended up back in exactly the same position they'd come from. The British newspapers were cock-a-hoop and called it a splendid victory, and even Ben, who knew the territory better than the news editors, said it was a good show, although he admitted that they'd taken a lot of casualties, *but don't worry. I've come through without a scratch. Monty's right. Next time we'll push them out of Africa altogether.*

Lizzie couldn't show this letter to Poppy because as well as reporting the battle it spoke too movingly of remembered and private delights. But she read out the bits about the battle and Poppy said he was very brave, which was perfectly true. Then, since the new term was about to begin and they couldn't stay in Downview, they put their minds to what they were going to do until they went up in October.

Poppy was all for taking a temporary job as a land girl. 'It'll be jolly hard work,' she said, 'but it's a healthy sort of life and the pay's not bad and it's only for six weeks.'

'I'll phone Pa,' Lizzie said. 'See what he thinks.' She'd barely seen him since the wedding, except for when he took her out to tea, but this sort of request was possible and might be a sort of olive branch. Not that he deserved one but she couldn't stay angry with him for ever.

She was right about it being an olive branch and pleased by how happily her father accepted it. 'Jolly good idea,' he said and asked if she needed funds, 'for travel and so forth.'

'She's coming to her senses, you see,' he said to Octavia when he saw her that Saturday. 'She's got over all that silly nonsense with the soldier. I knew she would, only you wouldn't have it. Bit of firm handling. That's all she needed. It'll do her the world of good to be working in the open air. Put some colour in her cheeks. Just what she needs before she gets on with her studies.'

So Lizzie and Poppy said goodbye to Smithie and their nice Miss Henry, promised to write to them and let them know how they were getting on, and went to work on a farm in Cambridgeshire where they picked potatoes and fed chickens and learnt to plough and milk cows, and Octavia welcomed her new first-formers and gave sashes and gowns to her new prefects, and Edie sewed more parachutes than ever, and Tommy took it easy, for the first time in years, and Ben and his fellow tankies prepared themselves for the decisive battle that Monty had promised.

It began on the night of the 23$^{rd}$ of October, while Lizzie was asleep in her elegant room at St Hilda's and Tommy was at his club and Octavia was writing up her journal in her quiet bedroom, and it opened with a massive bombardment. It was put up by a thousand heavy guns and the noise of it was so deafening that Ben wrote afterwards that it was a wonder it

347

didn't split their eardrums. But it had the desired effect. By the early hours the New Zealand Division were in action clearing a gap through the minefields in front of the German forward position and they were followed by the armoured divisions. For the next two days what Montgomery called 'a crumbling process' went on slowly and inexorably as pockets of resistance were tackled and 'mopped up'. Then on November 2nd the New Zealanders broke through the enemy lines followed by the 7th Armoured Division and the Germans began to retreat. From that moment on the battle became a rout. It was, as Monty had promised, a decisive victory.

Back home, the headlines yelled 'Success' and 'Victory' and parliament gave permission for church bells to be rung in celebration. It was the first time they'd been heard since war was declared and the sound of them was heart lifting. 'Now,' people said, listening to them as they sang across winter fields and peaceful villages and bomb-battered towns, 'we're on the way to winning, at last.'

But it was Churchill who put the situation into words in a speech to the House of Commons. True to character, he was careful to sound a note of caution but the triumph of his tone was unmistakable. 'It is not the end,' he said in his fruity voice. 'It is not even the beginning of the end. But it is perhaps the end of the beginning.'

On the day that the speech was reported in the papers, Tommy rang Octavia in one of his happiest moods.

'End of the beginning, you see,' he said. 'Monty's done a great job. Now we're on our way. We've just been having a party.'

She laughed at that. 'It sounds like it.'

'I'd rather have a wedding though,' he said. 'Just the time

348

for it, don't you think? Great victory, celebrations, end of the beginning, that sort of thing.'

She'd been buoyed up by the good news ever since it broke, feeling relieved and excited, and now his bubbling happiness was so infectious, it tipped her into a decision. He was right. It *was* the time for it. 'We shall have to consult our diaries,' she said.

He cheered. 'Dearest girl,' he said. 'I'll bring mine with me on Saturday.'

# Chapter Twenty-Three

Like everyone else in the burns unit, Johnnie Thompson was pleased by the news from El Alamein too, although privately he was even more pleased by the fact that after two painful operations his hands were so much improved. They were still scarred, of course, and more clawed than they should have been. That was something he would have to live with. But they were serviceable. They would hold a knife and fork or a cup. They would even do up the buttons on his tunic and that was a real achievement.

He was practising his new trick at that moment, sitting in a chair alongside his bed and feeling rather pleased with himself.

'Look at you!' Nurse Jones said, as she walked up the ward.

Not for the first time, Johnnie thought what a very nice voice she had. It was so warm and encouraging and it had that nice lilt to it. 'Good or what?' he said beaming at her.

'First rate,' she said. 'I've come to change your dressings but don't stop. Finish what you're doing.'

'Will I get marks out of ten?' he asked.

She smiled at that because it was a long-standing joke between them that she gave him marks for what he endured.

'I've brought your paper for you,' she said, 'and you've got a letter. Which do you want first?'

'Both.'

'That's the trouble with you lot,' she said, putting the newspaper and the letter on his locker. 'You're such greedy-guts. I never knew such a bunch. Right then. Are you ready for the torture?'

And that was another thing, he thought, as he eased back onto the bed. She was always gentle. She never hurt him if she could possibly avoid it. He picked up the paper and began to read it as she started work on his remaining foot, lowering it into its bath of salt water. 'Ten out of ten,' she said. 'That's coming along lovely. Mr Ferguson's visiting presently. He *will* be pleased.'

Her praise was pleasant but he was too caught up in the news to notice it. 'Look at this, Gwyneth,' he said. 'The Yanks are in the war at last.' And he read the headlines to her. *'Anglo-American force lands in North Africa.'*

'About time too,' she said, turning his foot to one side.

Johnnie went on reading aloud. *'The greatest armada of ships and aircraft ever assembled for a single operation today landed American troops in Vichy-French North Africa. As Rangers, Marines and infantry landed from the sea, paratroopers dropped on key airports in Morocco and Algeria. They had taken all their objectives by nightfall.* They're going to encircle the buggers. Pardon my French, Gwyneth.'

'Never mind pardon your French,' Gwyneth told him. 'Hold your foot still or you won't get ten out of ten. It's more like seven at the moment.'

Johnnie picked up his letter and opened it. 'Sorry about that,' he said and settled down to read quietly. It lasted all of five seconds and then he was chortling again. 'Will you look at this,' he said, waving the letter. 'This is my Wing Co. He's found me a job.'

'Well good for him,' Gwyneth said. 'What is it?'

'Tutor pilot, teaching the trainees. He says I'm just the sort of chap they're looking for. Plenty of flying hours, Spitfire pilot, that sort of thing.' Outside the window the sky was crumpled and colourless, like old sheets, but in this little corner of the ward the air was suddenly rosy with hope.

'Will you go for it?' she asked.

He tried to be sensible although his heart was racing with excitement. 'Yes,' he said. 'I think I might. I'll have to get my tin leg fitted first but when I'm up and running...'

'Good things happen in threes,' she said, gentling his foot back into the bath. 'I wonder what the third will be.'

It came later that morning when Mr Ferguson did his rounds and examined Johnnie's stump. 'Yes,' he said, 'I think you're ready to have your prosthesis fitted. I will make the arrangements. I hear you've had the offer of a job.'

'Not exactly an offer, sir. I can apply for it.'

'Then I trust you will. We shall have you up and walking in no time at all now. If I were you I would put in the application today. Strike while the iron's hot.' There was nothing like the thought of being back in harness to keep up his patients' morale. 'Well done.'

Johnnie saluted him. Nothing less than a salute would do.

Emmeline was none too pleased to be told that he was going to be moved. 'It's miles out of the way,' she complained to Edith, 'as if Tonbridge wasn't bad enough, and he's not allowed visitors. I told you, didn't I? What sort of a hospital is that?'

'It's where they fit artificial limbs, Ma,' Edith said. 'One of the girls had a brother there. He swore by it. Do you want the sprouts doing?'

Emmeline looked at the clock. 'They said they'd be ten minutes,' she said, 'and they've been half an hour already. Yes, you'd better do them. They should have finished by the time we're ready, but if they haven't, they'll have to take a break and get on with it afterwards. Although why they should be making all this to-do about choosing a wedding day I can't imagine. They've had long enough to think about it, in all conscience, and they've got enough days to choose from.'

But as Tommy and Octavia were discovering, the number of days that were actually available to them was strictly limited and choosing a date for their wedding, followed by the ten days that Tommy said was the very minimum they needed for a honeymoon, was proving irritatingly difficult. At that moment, they were sitting on either side of the fire in the dining room, scowling at one another.

Tommy had started the discussion by suggesting the Christmas holiday, and had been told at once that *that* was out of the question.

'Much too soon,' Octavia said firmly. 'Anyway, Maggie Henry's going to have a holiday with her cousin. Long overdue I might say. She hasn't taken a break since the war began.'

'Will that matter?'

'Well, of course it will. We always share the care of our Downview girls over the holidays and one of us has got to be there. So that's out. Sorry.'

'Can't some of the other teachers do it?'

'No they can't. And I'm not going to ask them. Anyway, what about Lizzie?'

'*What* about Lizzie?'

'Won't she be home for Christmas?'

'Apparently not,' he said. 'She's going back to that farm with her friend Poppy, so she says. So we don't have to worry about her.'

His casual manner annoyed her. She thought of Lizzie waiting and worrying about Ben and felt cross on her behalf. 'You might at least have given her a thought.'

'Well, we've given her a thought and she won't be there. If we want to marry at Christmas, it's fine by me.'

'You're not listening to me, Tommy,' she said, trying to be patient and not making a very good job of it. 'Haven't I just told you it's out of the question?'

He held up his hands to placate her. 'All right. All right. Have it your own way. Easter then. That should give us plenty of time.'

But, as he found out when he consulted his own diary, Easter was ruined by a conference he had to attend. 'God damn it all. Will you look at that.'

'Fifteen all,' Octavia said, trying not to sound too smug and failing at that too. 'So that brings us to the summer half term. What about that?'

'You only get a week though, don't you?'

'Yes, we do,' she admitted. 'But do we really need ten days for our honeymoon? I mean, we could compromise, couldn't we?'

Apparently not. 'Out of the question,' he said. 'If we can't have a decent honeymoon what's the point of getting married?'

'I'm beginning to wonder,' she said. The euphoria that had carried her along when he first suggested choosing a date was being pecked away by all these ridiculous difficulties. It should have been so easy, and yet here they were on the verge of a row and they hadn't got anywhere.

'I'm beginning to think your heart's not in it,' he complained and his face was dark. 'I mean, God damn it, Tavy. There are three hundred and sixty five days in a year. Don't tell me we can't find one.'

'It's not my heart,' she told him. 'It's my diary. Come on Tommy, be fair. I did warn you it would be tricky. We've got busy lives.'

'I'm dishing up,' Emmeline said from the doorway. 'How are you getting on?'

Tommy recovered himself and grimaced. 'We've gone through five or six years when nothing can be done,' he said, 'but apart from that...'

Emmeline laughed at him. 'Oh well then,' she said, 'you won't mind putting it aside and having your dinner.'

In the end, when the meal had fed them back to good humour, and he'd spent the rest of the evening talking about Johnnie and Mark and Matthew, and when he and Octavia were satisfied and companionable in bed together, he decided the best thing they could do was to pencil in the first two weeks of the summer holiday and think about it again at the end of the summer term.

'We could go on for ever, driving ourselves crazy and being disappointed,' he said. 'It'll sort itself out.'

She was half asleep but stirred herself to answer him. 'Very sensible,' she said. 'You never know what's going to turn up.'

'That's the problem,' he said.

What turned up on the 1st of December was revolutionary and encouraging. It was a report written by a man called Sir William Beveridge, who was the chairman of a committee set up to consider 'Social Insurance and Allied Services' and it could have been written specially to please Octavia, for it contained most of the ideas she and her father and the Fabians had been discussing and refining before the war. What Sir William was aiming at was 'a system to abolish want'. He proposed that everybody would be entitled to free medical and hospital treatment so that nobody would have to forego the treatment they needed because they couldn't afford it; that there would be retirement pensions for everybody and family allowances of eight shillings a week for every child after the first one. To pay for it all there would be a single weekly contribution – a sort of national insurance – of four shillings and threepence from every worker and two and sixpence from their employers. The much hated dole would be abolished. All working people and their families would be cared for 'from the cradle to the grave'.

When she'd read it, Octavia sat at the kitchen table and cheered. It was so exactly what was needed, so well thought out, so British, so timely. And she wasn't the only one who was approving. All through the day the BBC broadcast bulletins to the people in Nazi-occupied Europe to tell them what was being planned. *'In the midst of war,'* they said, *'Britain is grappling with her social problems and finding peaceful and positive answers to them.'* The implication was obvious. There is no need to conquer other nations and kill their people and exploit them to solve your social problems. You simply have to devise a fair system and finance it properly.

Emmeline had reservations about it. 'Do you think they'll do it?' she said when she'd read the newspaper.

'That will depend on what sort of government is elected when the war is over,' Octavia told her. 'We must work to see that we get the right one. I will write to Mr Dimond.'

Emmeline made a face. 'Haven't you got enough to do?'

'This is important,' Octavia said, stubbing out her cigarette.

'Well, I hope Tommy agrees with you, that's all. You'd better not let it get in the way of that wedding of yours or he'll have something to say.'

'There's the post,' Octavia said, glad of an excuse to change the subject, and she went to get it.

It was quite a bundle. A short letter from Tommy to say he'd booked seats for a show on Saturday; a long one from Lizzie to say how much she was enjoying life at St Hilda's and to report that she was going to spend Christmas with Poppy and her family. She said she'd had three more letters from Ben and that he was impressed with the new Churchill tank and was keeping out of harm's way, and that she herself was well, although anxious, *as you can imagine*; a letter from Janet to say that the baby was coming along lovely and was quite recovered from the mumps, *dear little man;* and to her surprise and delight, a short friendly note from Mr Dimond, pat on cue.

He said he was wondering whether she would be agreeable to addressing a parliamentary committee on the future of education. *The Beveridge Report is turning our thoughts towards the peace,* he wrote, *but there are other major issues besides health and social security which also have to be considered, although of course those two are of prime importance. I think you might be interested to know that Parliament is in the process of setting up a working party to consider the sort of direction school education should take once this war is over. I feel that your contribution to the debate would be invaluable and hope I can persuade you to give evidence.*

'Read that,' she said to Emmeline holding the letter out to her, 'and tell me you don't think it's funny. He must have been reading my mind.'

But Emmeline was concentrating on her own mail. 'He's

going to that other damned hospital tomorrow to be fitted with his new leg,' she said, not looking up from the page.

'Good,' Octavia said. 'I'm glad to hear it.'

'It's not all *that* good,' Emmeline complained. 'If they don't allow visitors and if he's going tomorrow, I've only got today to see him. I wish they'd given us more notice. It's going to be a dreadful rush to get there.'

But she rushed notwithstanding and came home to report that he was in good spirits and looked better than she'd seen him in weeks. 'That nice nurse was there,' she said. 'She's such a nice girl. She can cheer him up in seconds. I watched her do it. I wish she could go with him to this new place.'

Johnnie was saying exactly the same thing at that very moment, only in rather different words and half-joking. 'I shan't half miss you, Gwyneth. I wish I could stow you away in my pocket and take you with me.'

She looked at his pockets. 'Be a bit of a squeeze,' she said. 'Don't you think someone would notice?'

'I could say you were my iron rations.'

'Do I look like iron rations?'

He was suddenly and breathlessly serious. 'You look like the nicest girl I've ever met in my life,' he said. 'If it wasn't for the fact that I shall be some rotten old peg-leg I'd...' Then he was afraid that he'd gone too far and stopped.

She prompted him. 'You'd what?'

'It doesn't matter. It's silly really. You'd laugh.'

'Try me,' she said.

Oh God! Could he? She was looking at him so steadfastly with those lovely brown eyes it was making his heart jump about. 'The thing is, I mean, well the thing is, I suppose I'm...'

'Go on, Flight Lieutenant,' she said, 'spit it out.'

'What it is,' he said, 'is...well, if you want to know, I'm asking you to marry me. I know I'm no catch and if I'm speaking out of turn, I'll shut up.'

She leant forward, put her hands on his shoulders and kissed him full on the mouth.

'Is that yes?'

'Soppy happorth,' she said. 'What do you think it is?'

He put out his hand and stroked her cheek, very gently because his skin was still rough with scars and he didn't want to scratch her face. 'I love you so much,' he said.

That night, while he was lying wakeful in his narrow bed, too excited and too apprehensive to sleep, and Emmeline was sitting by the window in her bedroom, looking out at the cold garden and worrying about him, Octavia was answering her letters and gathering information to send to Mr Dimond.

His letter had come at a most opportune moment. Ever since she'd read the Beveridge Report she'd been thinking about other changes that ought to be brought in. The present education system was wasting far too many intelligent children. David's rejection and Dora's bitter reaction to it had shown her that, if nothing else, and when she began to gather her ideas she realised that there were other flaws in the system and that she'd been blindly accepting them for far too long. She'd always known that far more boys than girls were offered grammar school places in London, not because they were cleverer than the girls but because there were more grammar school places available for them. It had been an irritation but not one she'd felt moved to do anything about. She knew, too, that the pass rate for the scholarship examination varied from county to county. I must find out exactly how wide the variation is, she thought, and then I'll see if Mr Chivers can get hold of the LCC education figures for me. The thought of being part of a campaign was wonderfully uplifting. Now, she thought, as she took up her pen, what else?

Tommy was disgruntled. He sat at his capacious desk in the Foreign Office scowling and drumming his fingers with annoyance. He and Tubby had just been told they were to organise yet another conference for their globe-trotting Prime Minister, this time at Casablanca in Morocco.

'We've only just got back from the last one,' he complained.

'Join the Foreign Office and see the world,' Tubby joked. 'We might see Humphrey Bogart there. Or Ingrid Bergman even. Now that would be something.'

Tommy wasn't in the mood for jokes. 'I tell you Tubby,' he said, 'this war is getting in the way of my private life.'

'Private life, old boy?' Tubby scoffed. 'Since when have we had a private life? Chance would be a fine thing.'

Wouldn't it just, Tommy thought. Tavy's right. We're too busy for our own good.

But despite his gloom, the fourth January of the war began with good news. While Churchill and Roosevelt were putting the finishing touches to their plans for the invasion of Italy and the next stage of the war, Monty's army was entering Tripoli and in Russia the German army was finally surrendering to the Russians at Stalingrad.

*Will they let you come home now?* Lizzie wrote hopefully to Ben.

*No chance*, he wrote back. *Monty's got other plans. Watch the newspapers.*

# Chapter Twenty-Four

The Parliamentary Committee on the Future of Compulsory State Education was set up at the end of March that year and Miss Octavia Smith, headmistress of Roehampton Secondary School, was the third person called upon to give evidence. She was pleased to be consulted so early in the proceedings because it showed they were going to take her seriously and, naturally, she came well prepared.

'I have some statistics here that might interest the committee,' she said, when the introductory formalities were over. 'They concern the variation in the provision of grammar school education throughout the country.'

The chairman looked at the folder she was carrying and noted how thick it was. 'Could you perhaps summarise your findings for us?' he asked.

She could and did. 'Perhaps the first thing I should tell you is that there is a very wide variation from county to county,' she said. 'South Wales is the top of the list. They are very well provided with grammar schools, as you will see. Consequently 25 per cent of all eleven-years-olds in South Wales can expect to be offered a place at one. In London, under the LCC it is 21 per cent, although I should point out that there are more places for boys in London than there are for girls so the figure is the average for both sexes, considerably more for boys and considerably less for girls. In the shires, where grammar schools are in short supply, the figure is around 11 per cent. The variation is wide. I will leave the figures with you so that you can consider them at your leisure.'

'That would be helpful,' the chairman said. 'Of course your statistics do beg one or two questions.'

She nodded to show that she would be prepared to answer them if she could. 'Of course.'

'Is it possible perhaps that children in South Wales and London are of a – shall we say – higher intellectual calibre than children in the more rural parts of the country?'

'They might lag behind by one or two percentage pints,' Octavia said. 'That's possible. But certainly not by fourteen. In any case a child's intelligence is not static. It will grow and develop as the child develops. It is affected by a great many factors.'

'You could perhaps give us an example of some of them.'

Indeed she could. 'The quality of the teaching it receives for one,' she said. 'A skilled teacher who knows how to spark off a child's interest will lead her pupils into all sorts of directions and all sorts of extremely intellectual pursuits. Some of the things our pupils study would surprise you. And all of their own accord, of course.'

One of the committee members who introduced herself as Kathy Ellis asked the next question. 'I'm intrigued to hear you say that your pupils study "of their own accord",' she said. 'That's not at all how I remember my school days. Could you tell us a little more about how they go about it? Presumably they all follow the same syllabus.'

'Yes,' Octavia said, 'but they have a choice about how far their studies will take them. They are all given two suggestions

362

for each piece of work they have to undertake, a minimum task, which everybody has to tackle, and maximum tasks, which they can follow as far as they wish. We set no restrictions. That is up to each individual girl.'

'It must take a lot of preparation, on the part of the teachers, I mean,' Miss Ellis observed.

'Yes,' Octavia said, 'it does. But we consider it well worthwhile.'

'And in your opinion would such a system work for every eleven-year-old?'

Octavia gave her an honest answer. 'No,' she said. 'I'm afraid it wouldn't. There are some children who are so backward in their development, either physically or mentally or emotionally, that being asked to be responsible for their own studies would be more than they could manage. But the majority would rise to the challenge.'

'You will correct me if I am wrong,' Miss Ellis said, 'but you sound as if you would like to offer a grammar school education to the majority.'

Octavia was into her stride. 'I see no reason why the majority shouldn't benefit from it,' she said. 'At the moment we are wasting the talents of most of our children. I think that's a most unsatisfactory state of affairs and I would certainly like to put an end to it. I don't think we can afford to waste our children. We need their talents and we shall need them more than ever when the war is over.'

'So, Miss Smith,' the chairman said, 'I take it you would be in favour of raising the school leaving age to sixteen for all pupils in the state system.'

'That,' Octavia said, 'would be a consummation devoutly to be wished.'

'Then it will please you to know that it is something we

are presently considering,' the chairman said. 'There are concomitant problems, of course. Such an expansion would need a comparable expansion of the teaching force.' He smiled at her, almost conspiratorially. 'I don't suppose you have any ideas about how that might be brought about?'

Octavia hadn't expected to be asked her opinion on how to increase the number of teachers but she was on such good form that afternoon that the question didn't throw her in the least. 'We have just been talking about the waste of talent in our present system,' she said. 'There must be thousands of young men and women in the forces who have had to learn to do all sorts of things they never dreamt were possible when they were restricted to what they were taught at elementary school. If they could be trained as teachers after the war, we would have plenty of skills at our disposal and, being ex-servicemen and women, they would bring considerable experience into the workforce too. I take it requiring women teachers to resign when they get married is now well and truly over?'

'Oh, I think we've moved on from there,' Miss Ellis said. 'We're not in the dark ages now.'

'Married women teachers, ex-servicemen,' the chairman teased. 'What is the world coming to?'

Sitting there in that warmly panelled room, watching the intelligent faces ranged around her, Octavia felt so confident and optimistic that she could answer any question he threw at her, even a teasing one. 'Its senses,' she said.

'Well?' Emmeline asked, when Octavia finally arrived home. 'How did it go?' She was simmering with excitement, her hair tousled and her eyes bright.

'I think I told them what they wanted to know,' Octavia said. 'And I gave them a surprise or two to keep them on their toes.' She was still feeling inordinately pleased with herself. It *had* been a good afternoon.

'Glad to hear it,' Emmeline said. 'Now *I've* got some news for *you*. Johnnie's getting married.'

So that was what the excitement was about. 'To his nice nurse, of course.'

'Isn't it splendid,' Emmeline said. 'He's got to go to Canada though, that's the only trouble.'

Octavia sank into her easy chair feeling confused. 'To get married?' she asked. 'I thought you said she was Welsh.'

'No, no, not to get married,' Emmeline said happily. 'She *is* Welsh. The wedding's in Glamorgan at some place I can't pronounce. No, no, he's got to go to Canada to work. They've taken him back in the RAF – and so I should think after all he's been through, poor boy – and now he's going to be a tutor and teach the conscripts how to fly. Only he's got to do it in Canada, if you ever heard of anything so silly. Why they couldn't send him somewhere near in England I can't imagine. They've got enough bases. Anyway there it is, they're going to Canada and they want to get married before they go.'

'The trouble with you, Em,' Octavia said, laughing, 'is that you want the whole war to be organised to suit you.'

'Not the whole war,' Emmeline said. 'You do exaggerate. Just my little bit of it. Anyway, Johnnie's getting married. That's the main thing. Actually getting married. I never thought I'd live to see the day, he's been so slow. Well you know how slow he's been. I'd almost given up on him. Thirty-eight and not married! I mean to say! And that's another thing. What on earth am I going to wear?'

It was a very pretty wedding in a very pretty church in a village called Eglwys Brewis. The choir sang lustily, Gwyneth's family seemed absolutely enormous but they were all very welcoming and plainly very fond of their girl. And Johnnie gave a touching speech.

'I know I should be thanking you all for coming,' he said, 'and I do thank you, all of you, naturally, but what I really want to do is to thank my new mother and father-in-law for this dearest girl, your Gwyneth and my wife. I don't think she'll mind if I tell you something rather personal. She was the first person I saw when I came round after I was shot down and I truly believe that seeing her saved my life. I'd damn nearly given up the ghost, you see, and there she was, saying, "Come on, Flight Lieutenant, open your eyes. I'm not going to let you die on me." So I had to do as I was told and get on with it. Didn't have much option did I, Gwyneth?' He paused while they smiled at one another and his audience waited. 'But seriously,' he said, looking back at them all, 'I might pull her leg about it but I shall remember it to my dying day. So what I want to say to you is this. I promise you I will look after her and treasure her and love her for the rest of my life. Thank you.'

Every woman at the reception said 'Aah!' and most of them cried, Emmeline and Edith copiously. Even level-headed Dora was swimmy-eyed.

'That was a really lovely wedding,' she said as they headed off to catch the bus that would take them to the station and the long journey home. 'They're so happy together. It was a joy to see them.'

It upset her when her mother burst into tears all over again. 'Damned Canada,' she wept. 'They didn't have to send him there. I shall never see him again Dotty. I can feel it in my bones. I shall be pushing up the daisies before they let him home. Pushing up the daisies. It's all too dreadful. I can't bear it.'

366

'He'll be back before you know he's gone,' Dora tried to comfort. 'You'll see. Once we get on with the Second Front.'

'Once,' Emmeline wept. 'It's never once though is it? It's over and over again, killing all the young men, over and over again. Telling us it's the war to end all wars. And what's this war supposed to be? Tell me that. I can't bear it.' And she put her head in her hands and sobbed quite terribly.

By that time the people on the bus were looking at her, some awkwardly, some with sympathy, all three children were anxious, and Joan was clinging to her mother's arm. Dora and Edith felt most uncomfortable.

'Em dear,' Octavia said quietly, putting a clean handkerchief into her cousin's damp hand. 'Try not to cry. You'll make yourself ill.'

Dora was firmer. 'Don't keep on, Ma,' she whispered. 'People are looking at you.' But she got no response at all.

Edith tried to be positive. 'Cheer up, Ma,' she said. 'He's only got married. That's all. It's not the end of the world. You're upsetting the girls, look. You don't want that, do you?'

But Emmeline went on crying. There didn't seem to be anything any of them could say to stop her and in the end they simply left her to it and talked to the children, partly to reassure them, poor little things, and partly to cover the noise she was making. She cried all the way to the station and was still sniffing as they walked onto the platform.

'I hope she's not going to do this all the way to London,' Dora whispered to Octavia. 'I'm beginning to think there's something the matter with her. I mean it's not like her to go on and on like this, now is it.'

They eased her onto the train as if she was an invalid and sat her in the corner by the window, where she stared out at the gathering darkness and didn't say anything. None of

367

them could understand why she'd cried so much and for so little. They were used to her tears but there had always been a good reason for them up to now and she usually recovered much quicker than she was doing that evening. It was very upsetting, especially after such a lovely wedding.

She was silent all the way into London and all the way out again to Woking and, when Octavia had finally driven them home from the station, she went straight upstairs to bed without saying a word. And that *was* peculiar.

'Do you think she's ill?' Edith said, when she'd put the girls to bed and come down to join her aunt in the drawing room.

'I've never heard of an illness that started with a crying fit,' Octavia told her, 'but I suppose it's possible. Let's hope not. Perhaps she's just overwrought. She's had a lot to cope with, what with one thing and another. We'll see how she is in the morning and if she's no better we'll call the doctor.'

The next morning they all overslept, which didn't matter because it was a Sunday, and Emmeline stayed in bed later than any of them. It was midday before she came downstairs, looking very pale but not weeping, which was a great relief to Edith. 'I'll just get on with the potatoes,' she said, opening the larder.

'We'll do it for you if you like,' Edith said. 'Won't we, Aunt. Give you a bit of a rest.'

But Emmeline filled the colander with potatoes and settled at the kitchen table to peel them, her face set. 'I'll get the joint on presently,' she said.

So they left her to it. Edith made a rice pudding and washed up the breakfast things and Octavia cycled over to Downview to see how her pupils were. When she got back Emmeline was setting the table, working doggedly and not saying anything.

'She's been as quiet as a mouse since you left,' Edith

reported, when Octavia joined her in the kitchen. 'Not saying much and not smiling. It's very odd. I mean she hasn't said sorry or anything. Not that I think she ought to, I mean. But it's not like her not to say anything and she always says sorry after she's been crying. D'you think we ought to get the doctor?'

'Has she been crying again?' Octavia asked.

'No,' Edith said. 'Just quiet and not saying anything.'

'We'll leave it a day or two and see,' Octavia decided. 'There's no point in dragging him out if she's just tired.' Doctors worked long enough hours without being called out unnecessarily.

So they waited and although Emmeline didn't seem to be getting any better and was still far too quiet and unsmiling, at least she was listening to the children when they came home from school and cooking the meals in her usual way.

'Nerves,' Dora said, when she rang for the second time to see how she was. 'I thought that at the time. Women do get nerves, especially at her time of life.'

'She's fifty-nine, Dotty,' Edith protested. 'She's long past that.'

'Nerves,' Dora said firmly. 'You mark my words.'

'I think it's the change of life,' Poppy Turner said. 'Women go ever so peculiar at the change. You should see my mum.'

She and Lizzie were in the British Restaurant in Oxford, eating meat pie, dehydrated mashed potatoes and overcooked cabbage, and setting the world to rights. The person whose behaviour they were analysing at that moment was the cook at Poppy's hall of residence, who had taken to muttering to herself and throwing saucepan lids about.

'I don't think my mother ever reached the change of life,'

Lizzie said. 'She was only forty-two when she died.'

Poppy changed the subject at once, alerted by the sadness that was dragging her friend's pretty face. 'How's Ben?'

'Cheesed off, so he says,' Lizzie told her. 'They're waiting to invade Sicily and he says it's non-stop bull.'

'What's bull?'

'Unnecessary spit and polish, drill, that sort of thing. They all had to have a bath last week because Monty was coming to inspect them and apparently when he says "Have you had a bath, soldier?" they have to be able to answer "Yes, sir". He said it was absolutely ridiculous. I mean it must have been if you think about it, having a bath in the desert. He said it was ten men to a small tin bath, so the last one got out dirtier than he went in.'

'Heavens!' Poppy said. 'When's he coming on leave?'

Lizzie sighed. 'When they've conquered Italy, as far as I can make out.'

'Heavens!' Poppy said again. 'But that could be ages.'

'Yes,' Lizzie said. 'It could.' And every single day he was fighting she would worry about him and feel afraid. It was an anguish to wait for news when he was in the middle of some attack somewhere. It gave her a nasty scrabbling knot of fear in her belly nearly all the time and at night when she was on her own she wanted to howl. Even when a letter did finally come, it was still dreadful because although she knew he'd been all right when he'd posted it, anything could have happened to him while it was being sent to England. In one way this long wait for news of the invasion was better. She was lonely and missed him achingly but at least she wasn't frightened all the time.

She looked at her empty plate and sighed again. If only the war could be over and done with and they could be together.

But it went on and on and the news was dreadful, even if there were more victories now. The only respite from it was to disappear into her reading and live in the easier delights of romantic poetry, Elizabethan drama and the nineteenth-century novel, or to give herself over to the provocative stimulus of being taught by Helen Gardner and Dorothy Whitelock. She was well aware that, had it not been for the war, her life at Oxford would have been extremely pleasant, a bit like life at Downview really, each of them with their own carefully doled out rations of butter and jam and their own scuttleful of coal. The conversations in their rooms at night, when they drank cocoa and huddled over their inadequate fires, were a trifle more learned – they talked about sex and Shakespeare, politics and Priestley, deplored the deliberate elitism of Ezra Pound and T S Eliot, discussed the news. Of course they kept their most private thoughts to themselves. It was only when Poppy or Mary came to Oxford to visit her that she was able to talk about Ben, and even then there were a great many things she couldn't tell them, all of them censored in one way or another.

'What's for afters?' Poppy was asking the waitress.

'Apple pie and custard.'

Poppy made a grimace. 'Why is it always apple pie?'

'Search me,' the woman said. 'I suppose we en't run out of apples.'

'Two,' Lizzie told her. 'We've got to have something to keep out the cold.' It was a wintry sort of day and she'd left her gloves in her room. 'Now then, Poppy, tell me how you're getting on with your course. Last time you were here you said you weren't learning anything that Smithie hadn't taught you already.'

'Actually,' Poppy said, 'we had a very good lecture only last week from a woman called Miss Ellis. All about what schools are going to be like when the war's over.'

'And what *are* schools going to be like?'

'Well...' Poppy said. 'According to this Miss Ellis...'

Emmeline's 'nerves' kept her quiet and unresponsive until the third week of April, and by then Edith and the girls had grown used to the change in her and didn't pay much attention to it. Octavia had been watching her more closely and she was still worried. It was so unlike her competent, outspoken cousin to be subdued and quiet. She wasn't crying any more, which was one good thing, but there was something about her that was, well, disquieting to say the least. If Octavia had been asked to describe what it was, she'd have said she wasn't herself. Not that anybody did ask her opinion. They were all too busy getting on with their lives. So she watched and worried and was careful to hide the newspapers when the news was bad, just in case it provoked another outburst. And the news was bad, particularly that week.

The first sign that something terrible was happening was a report that somehow or other the Jews in the Warsaw ghetto had managed to get hold of some guns and were actually fighting the Germans. An SS officer called General Juergen Stroop had been sent to the ghetto with two thousand troops to 'subdue' them with machine guns, mortars and flame-throwers. As more details began to emerge it was obvious that the Jews were being massacred. Some of them had tried to escape by taking to the sewers, so the sewers had been flooded to flush them out. There was talk of thousands of deaths and of dead bodies lying in the streets covered in newspaper.

But it wasn't until Tommy came down for a long weekend that she found out exactly what had happened and by then she'd had an anguished letter from Mr Mannheim telling her what little he knew about it. *What a wicked world we live in,* he said, *that such things can be done.*

'All quite true, I'm afraid,' Tommy said. 'We've had some truly appalling reports coming out. There were over three hundred thousand Jews in the Warsaw ghetto when the Nazis set it up and now it's down to fifty thousand. A lot have been sent to concentration camps, of course, but a lot more have died of starvation. This uprising was sheer desperation.'

'It's too dreadful to think about,' Octavia said passionately, 'so what it must be like to be living there and enduring it and seeing it happening every day...'

'The *Mirror* says the Germans are going to kill them all,' Edith said.

Tommy sighed. 'That seems to be their intention, yes.'

Emmeline had been sitting at the table listening without saying a word. Now she stood up, her face wild. 'Those wicked, wicked Germans,' she said. 'Haven't we had enough of them? Killing and killing and killing. There's never any end to it. My poor dear Cyril gone and Podge gassed and Dickie and my poor Eddie and my Johnnie with his leg amputated and now all these Jews being burnt and gassed and all for what? That's what I want to know. All for what? It's evil. Don't you see? It should be stopped before we all go mad. That's what'll happen. We'll all go mad. I can't bear it. Why doesn't someone make it stop? I can't bear it.' She was crying so much her words were slurred. 'Bear it...' she wept. 'I can't...It's not fair...I can't.'

Edith and Octavia put out their hands to her, begging her to stop. 'Mum! Please don't.' 'Em dear, please...' But she shook them away and turned from them wildly. Then she ran headlong out into the garden, banging the kitchen door after her.

They looked round at Tommy, neither of them quite sure what to do. 'Leave her be,' he advised. 'She won't come to any harm in the garden.'

Edith was embarrassed that he should have seen such an outburst. 'I'm so sorry,' she said. 'What must you think of us?'

'I've seen men go off like that in the trenches,' he said. 'They used to babble and cry too. They called it shell-shock in those days.'

'Shell-shock?' Edith said in disbelief. 'But she's not been shelled. I mean, it's peaceful here. She hasn't even been bombed. She should try that if she wants to be shell-shocked.'

'Quite possibly,' Tommy said mildly. 'It looks the same to me, that's all.'

Octavia was remembering some of the things her cousin had been saying. 'Perhaps it's a not a matter of what happens to your body,' she said, 'but what happens to your mind. She lost your uncle Cyril in the first war, Edie – that was what she was talking about – and your two little brothers in the flu epidemic and both your grandparents in that road accident. Maybe she's just had more than she can take. Maybe that's what shell-shock was too. The thing is, what are we going to do about her?'

'If we move into the kitchen,' Tommy said, 'we can see what she's doing. Keep an eye on her sort of thing.'

So they moved to the kitchen and Edith made a pot of tea and Octavia watched her cousin pacing up and down in the vegetable garden. She seemed to be talking, because she was waving her arms in the air and stamping her feet and, after a long time, she sat down on the garden seat and put her head in her hands.

'You stay here,' Octavia said to Edith. 'I'll go and see how she is now.'

She was moaning as though she was in pain, and she didn't stop or look up when Octavia sat down beside her and put her arm round her shoulders. The physicality of the comfort she was offering reminded her of all the weeping girls she'd held in the same way and without even stopping to think about it, she started to say the same comforting things. 'You cry, my darling. Cry all you want to. It's all right.'

And Emmeline cried in the same way and with the same abandon. 'Oh, oh,' she wept. 'I want it all to be over, Tavy. I don't want to be in this awful house, scrubbing that awful floor and standing in queues all day. I want to go home.'

Now that's better, Octavia thought. That's practical. That's something I can arrange. 'Dry your eyes and come in and have a cup of tea,' she said, 'and I'll see what I can do about it.' After all, London was very rarely bombed these days. It might be possible for them all to go back. I'll write to Mr Chivers and see what he thinks.

She wrote her letter before she went to bed that night, even though Tommy complained that he couldn't see why it couldn't wait till morning. And the answer came back almost by return of post. Mr Chivers quite understood her point of view and, as she had pointed out, there *were* very few bombing raids nowadays, but he was sorry to have to tell her that the LCC didn't consider it safe enough for schools to return yet and he would strongly advise against it, at least until after the Second Front was underway and the airfields in France had been cleared. It should be safe enough then. As soon as it *was* possible for the school to return he would let her know.

It was a disappointment, there was no denying it, but not an unexpected one. When she'd thought about it calmly, which wasn't until after she'd posted the letter, she'd known what the answer was going to be.

By that time, Emmeline had dropped into apathy again but she read the letter when Octavia offered it to her. 'Well, thank you for trying,' she said and sighed. 'That's that, I suppose.'

'I'll try again, Em,' Octavia said. 'I'll keep on trying. I'll get you home just as soon as I can. I promise.'

But it was obvious that that would depend on the Second Front, and they hadn't even invaded Italy yet.

The news of the invasion came in a BBC bulletin four days later. Speaking in his usual calm and measured tones, the newsreader said that troops of the British 8th Army under General Montgomery had landed in Sicily in conjunction with the United States 7th Army under General Patton. They were attacking on a front one hundred miles long. The advance was swift. The next day the bulletins were reporting that the 8th Army had captured the port of Syracuse. Twenty-four hours later, Augusta surrendered to them and three days after that the Americans took Agrigento and Porto Empedocle.

Lizzie and Poppy followed the news in the farmhouse, standing by the kitchen table and holding hands for comfort. The familiar terrible fear was scrabbling in Lizzie's belly every time she thought of where he was and what he might be facing and the bulletins made it worse, although she had to hear them.

'He'll be all right,' Poppy said, squeezing her hand. 'You'll see. And it's ever such good news.'

That was true, Lizzie thought. But she did so wish he wasn't part of it. Please don't get hurt, she willed him. Please come through it.

\* \* \*

Octavia heard the bulletins sitting in the kitchen in Ridgeway with a cup of tea at her elbow. And at the end of the seventh bulletin there was a piece of 'news from home' that pleased her almost as much as the 'news from abroad'.

'A government white paper, published this morning,' the newsreader said, 'advocates free schooling for all pupils up to the age of sixteen. This will be a major change in the education system.'

'There you are, Em,' Octavia said. 'I might not have been able to get us all back home yet, but I've done *some* good.'

# Chapter Twenty-Five

'Now then,' Tommy said. 'Time to fix this wedding of ours. Your school breaks up in a fortnight – that's right, isn't it? – so that gives us three weeks to call the banns, fix the wedding, book the honeymoon and go ahead and enjoy it. All you've got to do is name the day.'

The two of them were on their own for once in the house at Ridgeway. The children had been fed, washed and put to bed, Emmeline and Edith had gone off to the pictures, and they were out in the garden strolling about between the bean poles and the herbaceous borders enjoying the colours of the evening and with the privacy to talk to one another more freely than they usually did. Not that Octavia really wanted to talk about a wedding.

'Don't rush me, Tommy,' she said.

'Rush you!' he said. 'Oh, that's rich, Tavy! That's bloody rich! It really is. I've been asking you for months and months. I've been the soul of patience. Or haven't you noticed? No, I don't think you have. I can't wait about for ever.'

'No,' she agreed. 'I know that. It's just a bit awkward at the moment.'

'That's what you always say.'

'It *is*, though. I can't just rush off and leave everything.'

He was heavily patient. 'That's what people do when they get married.'

'I know they do but I can't. It would mean leaving Em and I can't do that. Not at the moment. She's really not well at all.'

'She'll cope,' Tommy said. 'She's a tough old thing.'

'That's the trouble, Tommy. She isn't.'

He caught hold of her shoulders with both hands and looked at her for such a long time that she began to feel uncomfortable. 'You don't want to marry me,' he said at last. 'That's the real trouble. It's got nothing to do with Em or anything else. The plain fact of it is, you don't want to marry me.'

'No,' she said, trying to be patient, 'that's not true. I do. It's just that there are things in the way all the time. We're not free agents, either of us.'

'That's what you always say.'

'Because it's true, Tommy.'

He threw his hands in the air. 'I give up,' he said. Then he turned and walked away from her, heading towards the house.

She strode after him, persisting and feeling foolish. His anger always made her feel foolish and really this was so childish. 'It *is* true,' she called. But he ignored her and strode into the house. She found him in the drawing room, standing by the window, scowling at the gathering dusk.

'It may have escaped your notice,' he said, 'but we're in the middle of a war and, if the reports we've been hearing are accurate, things are going to get complicated. According to our spies, Mussolini's been summoned to attend the Fascist Grand Council and it looks as though they're going to get rid of him.'

It was a relief to hear him talking shop. That was safer ground altogether. 'Would that shorten the war?' she asked.

'It might,' he allowed. 'The point is, if it happens there will be diplomatic repercussions and we shall have to cope with them. It wouldn't surprise me if the new leaders didn't sue for peace. It's on the cards. The Italians don't have much of an appetite for war, especially when they're being beaten. They prefer an easy conquest like the one they had in Ethiopia. Anyway, what I'm saying is I might not get another chance to arrange this wedding for a long time. I think we should go ahead now, while we can. But you don't. OK. You don't have to say so. It's written all over your face. Very well then, I give you warning. I shall ask you once more when we get our next opportunity and if you don't say yes then I shall give up on the whole idea. I can't go on for ever waiting for you to make up your mind. Now I'm going home.'

And he went.

Octavia stood by the window and listened until the sound of his car had faded away. She felt demoralised and irritable. It was all so ridiculous. She couldn't just walk off and leave Em, not while she was still in this peculiar state. Since her last outburst she'd sunk deeper and deeper into apathy, doing the housework in a leaden, miserable way and barely saying anything to anybody. She'd only gone to the pictures with Edith because Edith had told her to, not because she particularly wanted to. She wasn't herself and she certainly wasn't well enough to be left. *After knowing us all these years, he really ought to understand how I feel about her.* But that was the trouble with Tommy, this now familiar dichotomy in his nature, meticulous planning and extreme care at work and rushing at things in his personal life, like a bull at a gate. *'Time to fix this wedding of ours'* without thought. It wasn't as if there was any real urgency about getting married. They *were* married to all intents and purposes. He could see her whenever he wanted to. They weren't exactly living together because he had to be in London and she was here in Woking but it was a marriage as near as, dammit. And now we're in the middle of another row and there's all that palaver to be got through before we can be normal with one another again.

Sighing, she left the window and walked across to her armchair and the coffee table where a pile of books lay waiting to be marked. It's just as well I've got work to do, she thought, as she opened the first one. But she still felt miserable and inadequate and there was still far too much to worry about.

It was an anxious summer. There were so many people waiting and worrying, as the Eighth Army battled its way across Sicily towards Messina, and Lizzie Meriton was among them.

'Ben says they've got to cut Messina off before the Germans get there,' she explained to Poppy, as they called the cows in for milking, 'otherwise they'll escape across the straits to Italy and live to fight another day, and we don't want that.'

Poppy agreed that they didn't. But that was what happened despite the most valiant efforts of the Eighth Army.

Ben was most upset about it. *Now they've got away to Italy,* he wrote, *and we shall have to fight them all over again, and they've taken all their equipment with them, which is almost as bad.*

But at least he wasn't fighting them at that moment which was a relief to Lizzie. She and Poppy were kept hard at work from dawn to dusk, milking cows and mucking out horses and ploughing the fields, and it was even more difficult when she wasn't sleeping properly. Her respite lasted for seventeen days. Then two pieces of news broke within a week of each other.

After a massive bombardment of the coastal defences, what the newspapers were now calling 'Allied forces' invaded Calabria on the toe of Italy and opened up the attack on the Italian mainland. Five days later, just as Tommy had predicted, the new Italian government surrendered. Within a fortnight, the Eighth Army had conquered southern Italy.

Ben's next letter was happily optimistic. *Not long now*, he said. *We're bowling 'em over like ninepins.*

It was good to open a new school year with such positive news filling the papers, particularly as it was now the fifth year of the war and girls like Iris Forbes and Sarah Turnbridge, who'd been evacuated as first-formers, were now house officers and preparing for their general schools examinations. Standing before her assembled school in the hall at Downview, Octavia looked across to where her sensible fifth-formers were gathered and smiled at the memory of how they'd been then, traipsing out of the old school hall in their hot new uniforms, with their luggage and their gas masks. It's been such a very long war, she thought, but it really *is* beginning to end now. Even old Churchill would have to admit that.

In fact, old Churchill was making plans for a meeting with President Roosevelt and Joseph Stalin to discuss the next phase of the war. Tommy wasn't looking forward to it.

'It's in Tehran for a start,' he complained, when he came down to visit, 'and Tubby says that's a hell of a place, even in November. But there you are, needs must when duty drives and all that sort of thing.' He'd quite recovered from their latest row and had arrived that weekend with a hamper of food, which even made Emmeline smile.

Listening to him, as he charmed her family in his familiar

easy way, Octavia found herself wondering what he would say if she suggested that he should excuse himself from this conference so that they could get married. It was catty and petty even to think such a thing but there were times when she couldn't help it. Still, he was charming, there was no denying that, and extremely generous.

'How on earth did you manage to get all this food?' she said, as she and Em unpacked the hamper.

'Guile and globetrotting,' he told her happily. 'I'll bring you back some Turkish delight next time.'

He came home in a foul mood, complaining that Joe Stalin was absolutely impossible. 'Bully, bully, bully,' he said. 'He never listens to a word anyone says. Marches in with a gang of armed thugs as bodyguards, all boots and machine guns, and then just ploughs on and on, saying the same thing over and over again. We had instructions that we were to host 'relaxed dinner parties'. The idea was to improve relations between us and the Ruskies. Wine and dine 'em. That sort of thing. Total waste of time. He wrecked every single one. We shall have trouble with him when the war's over, you mark my words.'

'But the war's going well,' Octavia said. 'I mean his army's been pushing the Germans back for months and the campaign in Italy might be a bit slower now but it's going in the right direction. He must be pleased about that surely.'

'He wants us to open the Second Front,' Tommy told her. 'It's all he ever talks about.'

'Well, so do we,' Octavia said. 'I'm with him on that one.'

'But we know it's got to be properly planned or it'll go off at half-cock. He just wants to bully us into obedience.'

It was a cold, slow winter. The troops in Italy were bogged down by rain and mud, their aircraft were grounded by fog and in Russia the arctic winter brought tanks to a frozen halt. There were days when it seemed as though the very forces of nature were conspiring against them. To Lizzie, crouched over her inadequate fire after a day at work in a chilly library, the world was black and cold and hopeless.

'I don't think this war is ever going to end,' she said sadly to Poppy, who'd come down to visit her for the weekend. 'I think it's going to go on and on and on getting worse and worse and I shall never see Ben again.'

'He's all right though, isn't he?' Poppy said, ever practical. 'And that's the main thing.'

Lizzie stretched her neck which was aching after all the reading she'd been doing. 'He was last time he wrote,' she said, 'but that's days ago and there's been some terrible fighting at Monte Cassino.' It was worrying her sick even to mention the place, leave alone think about it.

'Look on the bright side,' Poppy advised. 'I mean it'll be Christmas soon. What say we go Christmas shopping? I want to buy something nice for my mum.'

But Lizzie was looking at the dull grey of the sky and the bare black trees that edged the damp grounds of the college like spectres and couldn't see any brightness to cheer her. 'It just goes on and on,' she said.

'I tell you what,' Poppy said. 'Let's go to the pictures.'

'We must pull out all the stops this Christmas,' Octavia said to her staff. 'We need something really lively to keep us all going. Any ideas?'

'Stars,' Phillida Bertram said, tucking the ends of her shawl into her belt. 'Symbols of hope. We can use sheets of newspaper painted midnight blue and pin them up along the picture rails like a sky-scape and then the girls can design the stars and cover the sky with them. Bright colours, of course, and as many as we can paint. Should look good.'

'Do we have a sixth-form play?'

As sixth form mistress, Miss Gordon knew the answer to that. 'In rehearsal,' she said. 'Octavia Whittington and her Cat.'

'And a bran tub?'

'We shall need more bran,' Joan Marshall said. 'I'll get the prefects on to it.'

Not for the first time, Octavia thought what an extraordinary group of women they were and how fortunate she was to be able to count them as friends. There can't be many women who cope as well as they do, living in digs all this time and that can't have been easy, coping with the loss of friends and in some cases members of their family – Morag had lost a nephew in the Atlantic and one of Joan's cousins had been killed at Dieppe – living on their monotonous rations, scrimping and saving. Yet they took everything in their stride, they never complained, they were always willing and cheerful. I wish I could give them something really special this Christmas, she thought, as a reward for all their good work and she thought longingly of champagne and chocolates. But of course there was nothing she could give them. Luxuries just weren't available.

'How's the choir?' she asked Jenny Jones. And got the expected answer.

'Coming along lovely, Miss Smith. We've got a barbershop quartet.'

'That'll be a novelty,' Phillida laughed.

'Wait till you see them,' Jenny told her. 'They're all going to wear moustaches.' She looked round at the others and grinned. 'It's for the sixth-form play.'

'I can't wait,' Elizabeth Fennimore said, adjusting her pince-nez. 'Octavia Whittington and a cat *and* four sixth-formers with moustaches. The mind boggles.'

It was a hilarious play and the barbershop quartet performed to shrieks of delight and prolonged applause. And that Christmas Eve, like a timely Christmas present for all of them, there was an official announcement broadcast on the wireless. General Eisenhower was to be the supreme commander of the invasion of Europe with General Montgomery as his field commander. The Second Front was on its way at last.

The news lifted spirits all over the country. Even Lizzie took heart from it, especially as Ben wrote to say that there was a rumour that part of the Eighth Army was going to be sent back to England to join the new Army of Liberation.

*I do so hope you're right*, she wrote back. *Let me know the minute they tell you. I can't wait to see you again. Do you think this really is the beginning of the end?*

It was certainly the gathering of a huge army. By the middle of January, when Margaret was sitting her scholarship examination and David was re-sitting his, to Dora's considerable relief, the south of England seemed to be full of troops on the move, travelling in trucks and lorries all marked in a new way with a white, five-pointed star.

'It gives you such hope to see them all like this,' Phillida Bertram said, as she and Octavia watched a convoy pass. They'd been in Chertsey Road buying paper from Mr Elton's stationery shop, as the supplies from London had been delayed and the art classes had run out of nearly everything they needed, and the convoy had come through just as they were setting off to Downview again.

Octavia agreed that they did. 'And just when we needed it most,' she said.

'I wonder how long it will be before they're ready to invade,' Phillida said. 'It's about time we took this war to France.'

'I'll ask Tommy Meriton,' Octavia told her. 'He's usually a good source of information. Although he'll probably say it's hush-hush.'

But before she got a chance to speak to him the war came to Horsell Common in a way that none of them had expected.

It was a bright, cold Sunday and the Downview girls were happily occupied in their usual ways, reading, writing home, knitting or out in the garden digging over the vegetable patch. One or two had gone out for a walk on the common, among them Iris and Sarah, bundled and be-scarved and both wearing two pairs of gloves to keep their hands warm. They'd reached the Six Cross Roads and were discussing the relative merits of their various screen heroes, when they heard a plane coming their way. Iris looked up idly to see what it was. They were used to light planes flying over Horsell Common because there was an aerodrome not far away at Fairoaks, and sure enough this was one of their planes. The two girls watched as it circled and lost height.

'I think there's something the matter with it,' Iris said. 'It's dropping ever so quick.'

'It's on fire!' Sarah said. 'Oh my God, Iris, it's on fire.'

She was right. There was black smoke billowing out of its tail.

'We must do something,' Iris said, her eyes round with horror. But it was too late to do anything. Even as they watched, the little plane burst into flames and plummeted to the ground, its engines screaming.

The two girls clung together, too shocked to move. Then they saw that there were two men in Army uniform running through the bushes towards the flames.

'Come on,' Iris said. 'We've got to do something.' And ran after them.

What they found was so terrible that for a few seconds they couldn't accept what they were seeing.

The plane was burning like a bonfire, roaring flames and throwing up thick black clouds of smoke in a stink of burning fuel and rubber and hot steel. The superstructure was all that was left of it and that was burnt black and twisted in the heat and all around it the trees and bushes were burning too, crackling and spitting sparks. The two men were standing to one side of it, shielding their eyes from the intense heat, and lying on the charred grass at their feet there was a man writhing and moaning and so badly burnt he was black all over. His clothes were just black rags and his hair was shrivelled to his head like shreds of black cotton. As they watched one of the men took off his tunic and lowered it across him.

'Oh my dear, good God,' Iris said.

The second man was running over to them and now they could see that he was in the Army Cadet Force and not much older than they were. 'Don't come any closer,' he said. 'There's another one in the plane and we can't get him out.'

'Where's the nearest telephone?' Iris asked. 'One of us ought to phone.'

The cadet wasn't sure and while he was telling her so, they heard an ambulance ringing its bell and, turning towards the sound, they glimpsed the white sides of the vehicle as it bumped through the bushes. So somebody had phoned. Thank God for that.

Then they were all calling and waving their arms. 'Over

here! Over here! Oh please be quick!' And long seconds later the ambulance driver had taken command of the situation while his companion was down on his knees by the injured man. 'You two girls go home,' he said. 'There's nothing more you can do here. Leave it to us.'

As they walked away, Sarah began to shake. She was still shaking when they crossed the road and walked through Downview's front door.

'Go and get Matron,' Iris shouted to the nearest girl she saw, 'and be quick about it.'

Octavia had been cleaning her bedroom when she heard the roar of the plane's engines. Since Janet left them she'd got into the habit of cleaning it herself, because it wouldn't have been fair to expect Emmeline to do it, not on top of everything else she had to do. It wasn't done regularly, she had to admit, but she tackled it whenever she had the time and noticed how dishevelled it was getting. Now, she put down the carpet sweeper and opened the window to lean out and see what was wrong with the plane. She was just in time to watch it catch fire and to realise that it was falling towards the common. Then she heard the impact and the explosion and knew that she had to go to Downview straight away. Some of the girls would have been out on the common and they would need her. She left the sweeper where it was and ran down the stairs.

She was halfway down when Emmeline began to scream and by the time she reached the hall Edith and the girls were running out of the dining room and heading for the kitchen. They found Emmeline rolling about on the floor.

'We shall all be – killed,' she howled. 'All of us. Every single one. They won't – be satisfied – 'til they've – killed us all. Oh, oh, oh! I can't bear it. I can't. I can't. All killed.' Her sobs were as searing as they'd been on the last two occasions but now there was an hysterical edge to them, as if she didn't know where she was or what she was doing. She rolled from side to side, screaming and babbling, her face so wild she was almost unrecognisable. 'Oh! Oh! Blown – to bits. I can't bear it.'

'Get up!' Octavia said sternly. 'Nobody's been blown to bits. It was a plane crash. That's all.'

But that only made her worse. 'All?' she screamed. 'All? All of us dead. Is that all? Don't you see…?'

Octavia decided to try reasoning with her. 'You're upset and you're making yourself worse by rolling about,' she said. 'Get up and stop screaming.'

But she was wasting her breath. Emmeline went on rolling about and weeping that she couldn't bear it.

Edith was watching her with disbelief. 'What are we going to do?' she said to Octavia. 'We can't let her go on like this. She'll hurt herself.'

Octavia moved into second gear. Reasoning had failed. Now it was time to organise. 'Nip upstairs and get her a couple of pillows and her eiderdown,' she said to Barbara and Margaret. 'If she won't get up we can at least make her comfortable where she is. Joan, you can help your mother to make some tea, can't you. I'm going to phone the doctor. I know it's Sunday, but we can't let this go on. And then I must go to Downview. Some of my girls could have been out on the common and I want to be sure they're all right.'

The doctor was quiet and helpful. He was just on his way out to see another patient but he said he would come on to Ridgeway as soon as he could. 'Keep her warm,' he advised, 'and try to calm her if you can. There will be a Sunday fee, of course.'

So they eased the pillows under Emmeline's rolling head and wrapped the eiderdown around her as well as they could and offered her tea, which she refused, and although she didn't stop crying at least the screaming part of the fit seemed to be over.

'I won't be long,' Octavia promised. And cycled to Downview.

It was a relief to find that Miss Fennimore and Miss Gordon were there before her and that they'd run a check and knew that all their pupils were present and accounted for.

'Some of them were a bit upset,' Elizabeth reported, 'but they're calmer now. Two of them saw it, I'm afraid, and they came back in rather a state. Maggie's looking after them.'

Iris and Sarah were still sitting in her room, wrapped in blankets and drinking tea, having told her all about the crash, detail by horrific detail.

'We're over it now,' Maggie reported as Octavia came in. 'They've both been very good.'

'Of course they have,' Octavia said. 'They're Roehampton girls.'

But Roehampton girls or not, the crash had burnt itself into their brains and they needed to tell the story of it all over again. So she stayed with them and listened and told them she was sure the doctors would do everything they could to help the man they'd seen – 'they do some wonderful things with burns these days' – and let them talk for as long as they needed to. It was well over an hour before they were in a fit state to leave and she could cycle back to Ridgeway.

The doctor was still there and turned out to be an avuncular man with a gold watch chain draped across his belly and a white beard trimmed about his chin. To her relief, Emmeline was sitting at the kitchen table. Her face was still blotchy and she was still swathed in her eiderdown but she was talking to him more or less sensibly.

'Miss Smith?' the doctor said, when Octavia walked into the kitchen. And when she acknowledged her name, he stood up and prepared to take his leave. 'I have given your cousin a prescription for some nerve tablets,' he said, 'which I am sure will help her. We must hope so, mustn't we, Mrs Thompson. Let me know should you need another call.'

But once he and Octavia were out in the hall, his tone was decidedly more brisk and less avuncular. 'Hysteria is a difficult condition to diagnose,' he said, 'and even more difficult to treat, I'm sorry to say. The pills I have prescribed may alleviate her condition but on the other hand they may have little effect. It is necessary to get to the root of the problem, which in this case seems to be an anxiety of some sort. As far as I can see, what seems to be troubling your cousin is being an evacuee. She tells me the work is very hard here and she feels left out of things. Powerless, was the word she used. Did you know about this?'

'I had some idea,' Octavia told him, remembering. 'She said something similar in one of her other attacks.'

'Quite,' the doctor said. 'Well, the upshot of it is that she wants to go home to Wimbledon.'

It wasn't a surprise but it wasn't exactly timely. 'Do you think she would be better there?' Octavia asked. 'Happier?'

'I think it is possible,' the doctor said. 'I wouldn't go further than that. Is the house habitable?'

'It isn't damaged, if that's what you mean,' Octavia said. 'It's very dirty because nobody's lived in it since we were evacuated but, yes, it's habitable.'

'Then if you will take my advice,' the doctor said, 'you will arrange for her to return. I will send you my bill in due course. Good afternoon.'

'Well?' Edith asked, when he'd driven away.

Octavia led her into the drawing room, where the girls had returned to their jigsaw puzzle, and told her what had been said.

'Well, she can't go back on her own, that's for sure,' Edith said, sitting in one of the easy chairs by the fire. 'She'd never manage. We shall have to go with her.'

'I can't,' Octavia said sitting in the other chair. 'I can't leave the school and we've been advised not to go back until after the Second Front.'

'Could you stay here on your own?' Edith asked, poking the fire.

'I don't think I'd want to,' Octavia told her. 'It's a big house for one person. I might go to Downview. The school's shrunk so much we've got empty rooms there now. Anyway that's not the point at the moment. The first thing is to get your mother back to Wimbledon.'

She moved a fortnight later, with Edith and the girls to keep her company and help her run the house and with their few belongings crammed into the boot of Octavia's car. And the next morning, Octavia packed her own personal possessions into the empty car and moved into an empty room at Downview. It felt very strange and very sudden.

# Chapter Twenty-Six

That first morning back in Wimbledon was bitterly cold. The sky was colourless and threatening snow and there were frost ferns on the bedroom windows when they woke. Edith lay on her back with the covers pulled up to her chin and watched her breath steaming before her, loathe to leave the warmth of her bed, but Emmeline was up as soon as she was awake, dressed and active, down in the cellar filling the coal-scuttle as if she'd never been away.

'I'll soon have this stove lit,' she said, when Edith joined her in the kitchen, shivering in her pyjamas. 'Go and find a dressing gown for heaven's sake, child, or you'll catch pneumonia. There's one in my wardrobe. And put some socks on. The geyser's working so we've got warm water. You have to let it run through for a little while, that's the only thing. It's a bit rusty. I'll get the breakfast presently. You go and see to the girls. Make sure they put on plenty of clothes. This house is going to strike chill for a day or two.'

'It's absolutely extraordinary,' Edith said to Dora when she and David came over that afternoon to see how they were getting on. 'It's as if she's stepped back in time. She's been on the go all day, down to the shops to register the ration books, scrubbing the kitchen floor and the larder. She's even made a pie for supper. I can't keep up with her.'

'Maybe the doctor was right,' Dora said. 'Maybe she just needed to get home. Where is she now?'

'Checking the blackout,' Edith said.

'Very sensible,' Dora said, 'or she'll have the warden after her.'

'But you don't have raids nowadays, do you?' Edith said.

'We get the odd hit and run,' Dora told her. 'Nothing dreadful. Shall I put the kettle on? You could do with a cuppa, couldn't you, kids.'

But she was wrong. That night they had a real raid and a very alarming one.

When the sirens went they were all in bed and asleep, worn out by the exertions of the day. Edith woke at once, her heart pounding, feeling frightened and confused. Then she realised it was a raid and moved straight into her old Blitz-time routine. She got up and put on every item of clothing she could find, working as quickly as she could although her hands were too cold for speed. Then she went in to see to the girls. It pleased her to find that they were reacting in the same calm way as she was and were already dressing.

'Good girls,' she said. 'Put on all the clothes you can find.' And she picked up Joan's jersey and pulled it over her head. 'That's the ticket.'

'We're going in the cellar,' Margaret told her. 'Gran said. She says it'll be safe as houses there. Just like the underground. She's taking down the chairs and we're to bring our eiderdowns.'

So they brought their eiderdowns and Edith carried a blanket too, just in case. She found her mother shovelling the coal aside to make room for them. The cold air was full of coal dust and her hands were black with it. But she wasn't crying or even looking anxious. She was just her familiar practical self.

'What a to-do,' she said, 'waking us like that. Damned Hitler. Just when we were having a good sleep, too. I brought the deck chairs down, Edie. I thought we could sleep in them better. There's two more in the conservatory.'

They were settled in twenty minutes. Edith timed it. Then they waited. The girls dozed. The time passed. They could hear gunfire in the distance and the drone of the German bombers. The wait lulled them. When the first bomb fell it made them all jump.

'That was close,' Emmeline said. 'Wrap yourselves up warm, girls. We don't want you getting cold. Put your little hands under the eiderdown, Joanie.'

The next two explosions were so close they made the light bulb jump about on its dangling wire and they were followed by the alarming noises of falling glass and crashing walls.

'High explosives,' Edith said remembering. 'Big ones.'

'Yes, but we don't need to talk about it,' Emmeline told her. 'I brought some cards down. Who'd like to play Snap?'

The girls were too frightened for card games but, because their mother and grandmother were calm, they made the effort. No more bombs fell near them although they could hear the raid going on further away, and presently they heard an ambulance bell.

'There you are,' Emmeline said, listening to it. 'Now we shall be all right. They've come to look after us.'

The all clear sounded at a little after three o'clock.

'Thank God for that,' Emmeline said. 'Now you can get back to bed and have a bit more sleep.'

'What about you?' Edith said. 'I hope you're going back to bed, too.'

'No, not just yet,' Emmeline said. 'I'm just going to pop

down the road and see if I can lend them a hand.' And when Edith looked astonished, 'It's all right. I shall wrap up warm.'

'Is that wise?' Edith asked.

'Probably not,' her mother admitted, 'but it's necessary. This is a wicked war and we've all got to help one another.'

She didn't get back until four hours later and then she came shivering into the kitchen with her boots covered in mud and brick dust and a tin hat on her head

'It's snowing quite hard,' she said. 'Terrible to be bombed in the snow. Makes it all so much worse. Poor things. I've been helping them out of the wreckage and finding their things for them.'

Her granddaughters were impressed. 'You mean actually pulling people out?' Barbara asked. 'We saw them doing that last time, didn't we, Mum. When we came out the underground.'

'Me and the rescue teams and the nuns from St Teresa's,' Emmeline told her. 'You never saw such comedy turns as those nuns. They were all wearing tin hats and rubber boots and they'd tucked their habits right down into the boots. Splendid women. They gave me this.' And she took off her hat and put it on the kitchen table. 'The old people's homes were hit,' she explained to Edith. 'You know, the Catholic ones on The Downs. Nothing left of one of them. They're still lifting off the rubble. It's going to take hours, so Mr Cadwallader was telling me. I shall go back again when I've had some breakfast. Is there any tea?'

'I don't know when I've ever been so surprised,' Edith said to Octavia when she rang that evening to find out how they were. 'When the sirens went I thought we'd have screaming and crying and I don't know what all, but no, off she went as

397

cool as a cucumber. Can you credit it?'

'What's she doing now?' Octavia asked.

'In bed asleep,' Edith told her. 'I'm the only one awake.'

'Well, look after yourself,' Octavia said. 'It's worrying to think of you being in the middle of an air-raid.'

'We'll be fine, Aunt,' Edith said. 'We've got Queen Boadicea to look after us.'

Queen Boadicea took them down to the cellar the following night when the sirens went again. This time she made a pot of tea and brought that down with her too. 'Cup that cheers,' she said, pouring it out for them. 'Drink it up while it's hot.' She did the same thing two nights later when they had their third raid and by the following night it had become part of their routine. And then, as abruptly as they'd begun, the raids stopped.

'Well, thank God for that,' the royal lady said when a week had gone by and nothing had happened. 'Now perhaps we can get down to cleaning the house and then we'll have a special tea to celebrate because you've been such good children. I must see if I can make a fruit cake. How would that be?'

They told her it would be smashing and Joan wanted to know if Aunty Dora and David were coming.

'We'll all be coming,' Edith said. 'Now eat up your breakfast, like good girls, or you'll be late for school and we don't want that.'

'There's the post,' Barbara said. 'I'll get it.'

It was a most exciting post and kept them all happily occupied for the next ten bubbling minutes. Margaret had passed her scholarship and was hugged and patted and praised until she was breathless. And then just as the girls were finally putting on their coats and getting ready to leave the house, the phone rang and it was Dora with the news that David had passed too.

'Well, aren't you all the clever ones,' Emmeline said. 'Now we have got something to celebrate. I've got to make a fruit cake now, haven't I? It only needs your Aunt Tavy to come home and everything will be right back to normal. Won't she be pleased when she hears!'

In fact, their Aunt Tavy was lonely, and hearing their good news made the loneliness worse. Of course, she told herself it was silly to be feeling like that when she was in a house full of friends and colleagues and pupils but it was true no matter how sternly she took herself to task about it. During the day it wasn't so bad because she was too fully occupied with the needs and emotions of her pupils to pay attention to what she was feeling herself but at night, when she'd retreated into her small cramped room and lay in her unfamiliar bed looking round at the boxes full of books and papers that she hadn't had time to unpack, loneliness washed her to weeping. It felt unnatural to be staying in the school building at the end of the day and not going home to Em and her 'nice cup of tea' and she missed the chatter and closeness of her family, especially now when they had something to celebrate. And then of course there was Tommy, who'd been quite cross when she'd rung to tell him what she'd done and had seen at once that it would make difficulties.

'I mean, it's not exactly convenient, is it,' he'd said. 'I can hardly come down and stay with you in a school house.'

She supposed not. 'But I can come back to Wimbledon now and then.'

'Now and then?' he'd said crossly. 'We need more than now and then.'

'I'm sorry about it, Tommy,' she'd said, 'but I had to do it. I couldn't let Em go on the way she was.'

'Well, I don't think much of it,' he said.

He'd changed his tone by the time he rang again. 'Don't even think of coming up to Wimbledon,' he warned. 'The Blitz has started up again.'

'I know,' she said. 'Edith told me.'

'We caught a packet round here,' he said. 'Are they all right?' She told him how well Emmeline was coping.

'Doesn't surprise me,' he said. 'I told you she was tough. But you stay where you are. You mustn't come up. Not under any circumstances. I don't want *you* getting bombed.'

'I shan't get bombed,' she said.

'No, you won't,' he said sternly, 'because you'll stay in Woking. You will won't you, Tavy?'

He's remembering poor Elizabeth, she thought, and promised to stay where she was, 'for the time being anyway.'

'Good,' he said. 'I'm glad to hear it. Now, I've got a bit of news for you. I'm going to be a grandfather. Joan and Mark are expecting.'

That made her smile, as much with relief at his change of tone as amusement at his change of status. 'I can't imagine you as a grandfather.'

He laughed. 'Nor can I but that's what I'm going to be.'

'When's it due?'

'Beginning of March, so he says. He reckons it'll just about be born before the Second Front begins and they send him off to France.'

'Is it so close?'

'Yes, it is, according to the most reliable estimates. They're bringing the Desert Rats home to spearhead the attack.'

Octavia thought of Ben and Lizzie. 'All of them?' she asked.

'Quite a contingent, I believe. Crack troops, you see. Experienced.'

I wonder if Lizzie knows, Octavia thought.

Lizzie had known even before the news filtered through to the Foreign Office.

*It's still only a rumour*, Ben had written, *and we've had these sorts of rumours before but this time I really think we're being sent home. Fingers crossed.*

She'd lived in a state of exquisite tension ever since, watching for the post and quite unable to concentrate, waking early every morning to sit by her window and look out over the dark trees and the dew-grey lawns and think and hope. Let it be true, she prayed. Please God let it be true. Let me hear today.

She heard a fortnight later. He was coming home and, even better, he was being posted to Abingdon, a few short miles away.

*I'll see you at the station as soon as I can get a pass*, he wrote. *And then I shall put in for some leave. God knows I've earned it. Love you, love you, love you.*

She was waiting at the station for half an hour before his train came in. She'd cut a lecture and excused herself from a tutorial and washed her hair and put on her lipstick and when his train finally chuffed in, she was hopping from foot to foot with impatience. And then suddenly, there he was, jumping out of the train, still in uniform and looking darker and older, holding out his arms to her.

'Oh Ben!' she cried as she ran. 'Darling, darling Ben. I thought I'd never see you again.'

He kissed her fiercely and hungrily. 'Nor did I,' he said. 'Do you have a room somewhere?'

The question put her into a panic. We can't go there, she thought. It's not possible. Men aren't allowed. It was one of the strictest rules. But he was looking at her with such urgency and she loved him so much and she hadn't seen him for such a long time. And anyway rules were made to be broken, weren't they? It would be running a terrible risk but what was that compared to the risks he'd been running all this time? 'You'll have to say you're my cousin or something,' she warned. 'And we'll have to be really quiet.'

'I don't care what I have to say as long as I'm with you,' he said and kissed her again. 'Come on.'

She knew it was a bad idea when they reached the lodge and she had to tell her first lie to the porter and felt absolutely dreadful about it. And when they were in Hall and passing her friends and acquaintances in the corridors and on the stairs and she was telling the same lie over and over again, it got worse. This wasn't the sort of place to bring your lover. It wasn't the sort of place to *have* a lover. Once they were inside her room she put the chair against the door so that they'd have a bit of warning if anyone tried to walk in, but by then her anxiety had reached trembling point. He didn't seem to notice the state she was in and started to unbutton her blouse as soon as she'd shut the door, kissing her neck and fondling her breasts. But it wasn't any good. She was far too worried to respond to him and although she kissed him back and put her arms round his neck the way she'd always done, she didn't feel a thing. It was miserably disappointing. She lay on her back on her uncomfortable bed and wanted to cry.

When he'd got his breath back, he propped himself on one elbow and looked down at her, his face questioning. 'Are you all right?' he said.

It was too much. 'No,' she said, turning her own face away

from him. And burst into tears. 'We're not supposed to do this,' she wept. 'I shouldn't have brought you here. If they find out I shall get sent down. It's one of the cardinal rules. No men.'

He got up, buttoned his trousers, took command. 'We'll go out,' he said. 'Don't worry. I'll say I've come to take you out to tea. They can't not allow *that*. Make yourself respectable. Wash your face or something.' He was straightening the bed as he spoke, tucking in the corners and plumping up the pillows. 'Wear a thick coat,' he instructed as he moved the chair and opened the door. 'That other one's too thin. All set?'

Once they were in a tea shop and sipping a cup of very hot tea she felt a lot better. 'Sorry about that,' she said. 'Crying and everything.'

'That's all right,' he said cheerfully. 'No bones broken.'

'Do you always take command like that?'

'I'm a corporal,' he said. 'These scones aren't half bad.'

'What made them send you to Abingdon?' she asked, when she'd eaten a scone. 'I'm not complaining. I think it's wonderful. But why Abingdon?'

'They're sending us all over the place,' he said, biting into his second scone. 'We've got to knock the new recruits into shape so's they know what to do when the time comes. Show 'em the ropes.'

'But you're home,' she said, much cheered by the tea. 'You're out of it now.'

'Out of it?' he said bitterly. 'That's a joke.'

'You won't have to go back to Italy? Not now, surely.'

'Not Italy no,' he said. 'We're being fattened up for France. We're here to spearhead the invasion.'

She could feel her heart shrinking and falling. 'They can't do that to you,' she said.

''Fraid they can,' he said. 'They don't ask our permission. Anyway, don't let's talk about it. I've got ten days leave coming. What say we go to Weston-super-Mare? I'll write to Mrs Collingwood and fix it up.'

'I shall have to think of a good excuse to get time off,' she said.

'Lie through your teeth,' he advised. 'There's a war on.'

It was bitingly cold beside the sea. Neither of them had realised how bleak and empty their seaside town would be in winter. The pier was closed, the kiosks along the front were shut and shuttered, the sea grey and forbidding, the beaches deserted except for the occasional sea-scuffed mongrel. A walk on the prom left them shivering and pink-nosed and, when they emerged from the pictures on their first evening, there was such a fierce wind blowing that they ran all the way back to their lodgings. But what did it matter? They were together, they had sufficient to eat, a double bed to love in and there was no one to disturb them. What more could they want?

It wasn't until their last morning together that the outside world impinged on their consciousness in any way at all, and then it was because Lizzie was curled up on the bed, twisting her wedding ring round and round on her finger. Ben was shaving and he stopped in mid-scrape to watch her and admire her.

'Is your Pa still opposed?' he asked.

'No idea,' Lizzie said. 'I haven't seen him to ask him. Not since Mark's wedding when he was so... Well, I told you didn't I? Anyway, not since then. And that was months ago. Mark and Joan have got a baby on the way now.'

He put down his razor and came to sit beside her. 'I'd marry you tomorrow if I could,' he told her. 'You know that, don't you. Maybe being a grandfather'll mellow him. What d'you think?'

'Highly unlikely,' Lizzie said and joked, 'he's not the mellowing sort.'

'I'm serious, Lizzie,' he said. 'I'd like us to get married before the Second Front.'

She shivered. 'Don't let's talk about the Second Front,' she begged. 'It's too horrible. I know it's coming but I don't want to think about it until I have to. Wait till after my finals and I'll ask him then. He should be in a better mood by that time. He'll have a graduate daughter.'

'When *are* they?'

'May,' she said. 'Ages yet.'

'May's too late,' he said, catching her hand and kissing her fingers. 'I shall be in France by then.'

Her face was full of disbelief and shock. 'You won't.'

'That's what they say. Ask him now, Lizzie, and we'll marry at Easter.'

'He'll say no,' she said miserably. 'You know what he's like.'

'You could be wrong.'

'He'll say no,' she repeated.

'I tell you what,' he said. 'Write to Smithie and see what she says.'

'Smithie's good,' she told him, 'but even she couldn't persuade him to do something if he didn't want to. I'll write to her, just to satisfy you, but don't hold your breath.'

'Give us a kiss,' he said, pulling her towards him, 'you lovely girl.'

'I can't kiss you,' she protested. 'You're all over soap.'

'It'll be a new experience,' he told her, happily.

* * *

Tommy Meriton was in Parkside Avenue that Saturday having dinner with Emmeline, Edith and Octavia in their newly cleaned dining room, admiring the newly washed curtains, the newly polished furniture and the sparkling glass and telling Emmeline she was 'a giddy marvel'. The 'Little Blitz' was now obviously over and Octavia had driven home the previous evening, bringing some of her precious books with her. She'd spent the afternoon dusting them and restoring them to their places in the book cabinets, while Em and Edith cooked the meal and fed the girls and took them off to bed. Now they were all sitting round the table and Tommy was opening the bottle of claret he'd brought with him to complement the beef.

'There's a second bottle on the sideboard,' he said, 'so drink up.'

'Where did you get it from?' Emmeline said. 'I thought you couldn't get wine for love nor money.'

He tapped the side of his nose. 'Black market,' he told her.

'You're a wicked man,' she laughed. 'You'll have us all drunk.'

'And quite right too, after all the work you've done,' he said, beaming at her. 'Besides I've got something to celebrate.' He paused and smiled at them all before he made his announcement. 'I am now a grandfather. I can't say I've ordered my pipe and slippers yet, but that's what I am. Little girl, born yesterday, seven and a half pounds and they're going to call her Heather Elizabeth.'

There was a chorus of congratulation.

'Mother and baby doing well?' Octavia asked.

'Naturally. And now you must look out your prettiest hat ready for the christening.'

Octavia laughed. 'Is it planned already?'

'Got to be,' Tommy said. 'It's a tight schedule. Bombing campaign's already under way.'

'So how long will it be before the invasion?' Emmeline asked. 'If you're allowed to tell us.'

'Well it's very hush-hush,' he said, 'but as it's you Em, and I know you won't gossip, we're looking at the end of May.'

'Three months,' Emmeline said.

'If everything goes according to plan.'

There was certainly a lot of activity that spring. American troops arrived by the ship load and were soon building new camps and airfields, ready for their bombers to follow them. There were rows of field guns bristling in the fields like some huge alien crop, the roads were clogged with convoys and in country lanes army lorries and troop carriers were parked nose to tail, their roofs and bonnets marked with the familiar five-pointed white star. According to rumour a fleet of minesweepers had gathered in the Channel to clear away the German mines and the skies were loud with bombers on their way to attack marshalling yards and airfields and sometimes, to Edith's approval, to bomb Berlin. 'Serve 'em right,' she said. Give 'em a taste of their own medicine. See how they like it.' There was no doubt that the invasion was coming and that it was going to be massive. And in the middle of it all, Octavia received her expected invitation to the christening of Heather Elizabeth and a long letter from Lizzie telling her that Ben was home and that they were both very happy but that she had a problem and she would appreciate some advice.

*The thing is, Miss Smith*, she wrote, *he wants to get married before the invasion and so do I but I can't see Pa giving his consent. He wouldn't do it before and he's not a man to change his mind. What do you think I should do?*

Octavia put the letter down on her desk beside the invitation and began to consider. Lizzie was right. He could be terribly stubborn and he didn't like losing face. So what could be done? She stared down at her desk, idly admiring the elegance of the invitation and noticing the passion of Lizzie's bold handwriting. And the juxtaposition gave her an idea. She took up her pen, found a postcard and sent a quick message to her pupil. *Phone me.* Then she went off to her first lesson, treasuring her plan like the sweetie it was.

Lizzie phoned the following afternoon at the end of the school day, when she knew Smithie would be back in her room.

'I'll be quick,' Octavia said. 'I don't want you getting cut off in the middle. Now then. You've been invited to the christening, of course.'

'I'm a godmother.'

'Splendid. Now what I advise you to do is this. Write to your brother and ask him to send an invitation to Ben.'

'Yes but…'

'Make sure Ben knows how important it is for him to be there. It's a Sunday so it shouldn't be too difficult. But – and this is important, Lizzie – don't arrive together and don't pay any attention to one another when you're in the church. And tell him to wear his beret. Then leave it to me.'

'I will obey you "point-device",' Lizzie said.

And did.


The new Heather Elizabeth had a fine day for her welcome to the Anglican Church and behaved herself impeccably, only protesting slightly when her head was doused with unexpected water. Afterwards, cradled in her mother's arms, in her grandmother's crowded front room, she gazed solemnly at her admirers as they told her what a dear little thing she was and didn't remind her mother that feeding was an absolute necessity until a full twenty minutes had passed.

'She's a good baby,' Tommy said to her doting father when she'd been carried away to be fed.

'She's not bad, is she?' Mark said. Then he remembered what Octavia had instructed him to do. 'You haven't met my friend Ben Hardy, have you?' he asked and signalled to Ben that he should join them. 'Corporal Hardy. Major Meriton.'

They shook hands and sized one another up.

'Eighth Army,' Tommy said, noting the beret.

'Joined at El Alamein,' Ben said, with some pride. 'Just before the battle.'

'First-rate show.'

'Yes. It was. Monty knows what he's doing.'

'Tell me, what do you think of the new Churchill tank?'

Mark drifted away from them and left them to it. Now he had to find Octavia and tell her the deed was done.

'Excellent,' she approved. 'I'll give them a few more minutes to get going. Just one more thing. Could you find Lizzie for me and tell her to watch for my signal?'

'This is better than a thriller,' Mark said. 'I keep expecting a spy to leap out and confront us with a Luger.'

'Keep watching,' Octavia told him, 'and you'll see a headmistress confront a Major with a Ben.'

She left the two men talking until Tommy moved on to make conversation with someone else, then she inched after him.

'Nice chap?' she asked, as the christening party talked and laughed and made approving noises around them.

He bent his head towards her. 'Who?'

'The soldier you were talking to.'

'First rate,' he said. 'Eighth Army. One of Monty's mob. Seen a lot of action. They had a hell of a time at Monte Cassino.'

'So I believe,' Octavia said. 'You approve of him then?'

He was smiling at his brother, who was smiling and walking towards him and not paying overmuch attention. 'Stout feller,' he said. 'Salt of the earth. We could do with a few more like him.'

'So he'll make a good son-in-law,' she said.

He turned away from his brother's approach and looked at her quizzically. 'What are you talking about, Tavy? What son-in-law?'

'Yours,' she told him levelly. 'He's engaged to Lizzie. Isn't that right, you two?'

Ben and Lizzie were edging through the crush towards him, hand in hand. 'And you call me devious!' he said to Octavia. Then he looked at his brother. 'Hello, James,' he said. 'You've walked in on a family crisis.'

Octavia felt distinctly anxious. He hadn't refused the idea outright, he'd even made a joke of it but calling it a crisis wasn't a good sign. If only James wasn't there she might be able to tease him a bit, make it easier for him.

The brothers were shaking hands. 'Have I?' James said, smiling at Lizzie and Octavia. 'Well bless my soul. I thought it was a christening.'

Now Tommy was turning to Ben, squaring up to him, stretching up to his full height, looking stern. Oh God, the signs *were* bad.

'You never said you were engaged to my daughter,' he said.

'No, sir,' Ben said visibly standing his ground. 'You never asked me.'

Tommy shook his head, paused and began to grin. 'So I

suppose you want to get married before the balloon goes up,' he said. 'Is that it?'

Ben grinned too. 'Got it in one, sir.'

Octavia was so relieved she had to lean on the back of a chair. But she didn't get a chance to say anything because James and Lizzie were both talking at once, James saying, 'Well, they *are* engaged, Tom,' and Lizzie throwing her arms round her father's neck, saying 'Darling, darling Pa!'

Tommy was beaming but practical. 'What sort of date did you have in mind?' he said to Ben.

Ben and Lizzie answered in unison. 'Easter Saturday.'

Tommy grimaced. 'Bit short notice, isn't it?'

'That's the war for you,' Ben said, daring a joke.

'And what's Miss Mann going to say?' Tommy said, looking at Lizzie. 'I'll bet you haven't thought about that.'

'I have actually,' Lizzie said coolly, stepping away from him and going back to Ben. 'She's not going to say anything because I shan't tell her.'

'You mean you're going to get married and go back to college as if nothing's happened? Good God, girl, I've never heard the like.'

'Well, good for you,' James said to his niece. 'Never trouble trouble till trouble troubles you, eh.' And he laughed at his brother. 'You've bred a revolutionary, Tom. I never thought you had it in you.'

'Easter Saturday it is then,' Tommy said. 'You're not to cut finals mind Lizzie. And I shall expect a brilliant result.'

'Of course,' Lizzie said. 'You shall have one.'

He smiled at that. Then he looked at Octavia. 'I shall expect a bit of reciprocation too.'

'You shall have it,' Octavia promised. 'Just as soon as I'm back in London.'

Lizzie was looking over her shoulder into the crowd. 'Must tell Mark,' she said. 'Be back in a tick.' And she ran off to find her brothers, pulling Ben with her.

'What it is to be young!' James said and he moved into the crowd too.

Tommy and Octavia were left on their own together, hidden in the blur and buzz of the party.

'That felt like an Octavian put-up job to me,' he said.

She wasn't sure whether he was praising her or blaming her but she admitted her involvement. 'Yes,' she said. 'I suppose it was in a way. I thought you might need a bit of persuasion.'

'A more accurate word would be coercion.'

Yes. It did feel like blame. She would have to stand up to him. 'They're young, Tommy,' she said, 'and they're in love and they don't know how long they'll have together or whether he'll come through or be injured or killed or what will happen to them. I think they deserve their wedding and as much happiness as we can give them and if I have to use a bit of coercion to get it for them then so be it.'

He held out his hands, in the old familiar gesture, as if he were fending her off. 'All right. All right,' he said. 'You've got what you wanted. You don't have to bite my head off. But I shall hold you to your promise, mind.'

'I know,' Octavia said, smiling at him because she had been a bit fierce. 'But let's get this wedding organised first, shall we?'

He took out his cigarette case, offered it to her and lit up for both of them. 'And what's all this about you coming back to London?' he said.

'We can move as soon as the Second Front begins,' she said. 'That's official.'

# Chapter Twenty-Seven

Lizzie got married in her mother's classical wedding dress, skilfully cut down to size and tailored to fit, with Mary and Poppy as her bridesmaids in dresses made of parachute silk and run up by Mary's mother. It was the first time Lizzie had ever worn a full length gown and she looked vulnerable in it, very slender, very young and surprisingly shy, her long hair shining underneath her veil. As she walked up the aisle on her father's arm she was so nervous she tripped and would have fallen had it not been for his steadying hand, and she made her responses in such a soft voice that the congregation had to strain their ears to hear her. When she and Ben stepped out of the church as man and wife and ducked under the guard of honour his uniformed mates had provided, and their friends and family showered them with confetti and the clouds showered them with soft April rain, she was giggling with relief.

'Married!' she said to Ben.

'Married,' he agreed and kissed her.

'Hold it just like that,' the photographer called. 'That's perfect.'

The reception was in Tommy's fine house, food and wine provided courtesy of the black market. Ben's aunt and uncle were very impressed by it, and Jimmy, who'd acted as best man and had been almost as nervous as the bride, was totally subdued. 'You never said you were rich,' he said to Lizzie, when the meal was over.

'I am *now*,' she said, hanging on to Ben's arm.

Rich and stupid with happiness but with that horrible scrabbling anxiety lurking in her belly. Oh Ben, my darling, darling Ben, she thought, why do we have to have a war? Why can't we just go away and live happily ever after, the way people did before all this horrible mess began?

'A lovely wedding,' James said, wandering over to join his brother with his wife trailing behind him. 'Hello, Octavia. You've done them proud, Tom.'

'We did our best,' Tommy agreed, 'didn't we, Tavy?'

'Wherever did she get that dress?' Laura said, preparing to criticise.

'From Chanel,' Tommy told her. 'I wanted her to have something special.'

The name made her catch her breath. 'How did you manage that?' she said, much put out. 'I mean she's French. She's in Paris. You're not going to tell me you went there.'

'Wheels within wheels,' Tommy said. 'It cost a small fortune.'

'That's the trouble with you, Tom,' she complained. 'I never know when you're serious.' And she drifted away from them.

'That was naughty,' Octavia said, as James grimaced and walked after her.

'Couldn't resist it, old thing,' Tommy said. 'She asks for it sometimes. Anyway it put a spoke in her wheels. I can't have her being acid at my Lizzie's wedding.'

There was a stir on the far side of the room. Lizzie had changed out of her finery and she and Ben were ready to leave. She was still carrying her posy and stopped at the door to toss it to her guests. 'Catch!' she called. And as the flowers fluttered through the air, losing some of their petals as they fell, she was gone.

'I do so hope they'll be all right,' Octavia said

'They'll be fine,' Tommy told her. 'Come and have some more champagne.'

'But how long have they got?' Octavia said. 'That's the question.'

Lizzie was asking exactly the same question, sitting beside her new husband as they were driven to the station.

'How long have we got, Ben?'

He put his arm round her and answered her seriously. 'Don't let's waste time thinking about it,' he said. 'We've got now.'


But however hard they tried not to think about it, their parting was scheduled and there was nothing they could do to delay it. Preparations for the invasion were visibly speeding up. On the day Lizzie went back to Oxford to sit her finals it was announced that all coastal areas had been banned to visitors. There were constant army convoys on the roads and constant air reconnaissance over France, railway timetables were reorganised to accommodate troop movements, bombers flew by day and night until the sound of their engines was so familiar that people barely noticed them. It was as if the entire country was fidgety with impatience. And four weeks after their wedding, when Lizzie's finals were over and she was looking forward to the moment when they could be together again, Ben was recalled to base and all camps were sealed.

*I can't tell you anything except that I love you,* he wrote to her. *There are guards on the gates so as no one can go in or out and they've sealed up the phones and they're censoring every letter. It's all bull and pep-talks. Another one tonight. Aren't we the lucky ones?*

*Love you, love you, love you,*
*Ben*

The pep-talk that night was a message from General Montgomery, Commander in Chief 21$^{st}$ Army, which was read to them by their Brigadier, and despite his cynicism Ben was moved by it.

'The time has come,' Monty had written, 'to deal the enemy a terrific blow in Western Europe. The blow will be struck by the combined sea, land and air forces of the Allies – together constituting one great Allied team, under the supreme command of General Eisenhower.

On the eve of this great adventure I send my best wishes to every soldier in the Allied team. To us is given the honour of striking a blow for freedom which will live in history; and in the better days that lie ahead men will speak with pride of our doings. We have a great and a righteous cause. Let us pray that 'The Lord Mighty in Battles' will go forth with our armies, and that His special providence will aid us in the struggle.

I want every soldier to know that I have every confidence in the successful outcome of the operations that we are about to begin. With stout hearts and with enthusiasm for the contest, let us go forward to victory. Good luck to each one of you. And good hunting on the mainland of Europe.'

Four days later they were crossing the Channel, struggling against a strong north-easterly wind, a sharp rain, fear and seasickness. The Second Front had begun.

\* \* \*

The BBC gave the news in its usual well controlled way but the newspapers threw it at their readers in headlines six inches high: 'Second Front – Allies invade Normandy' and the next day they had the pictures to prove it.

'Poor devils,' Emmeline said, studying the taut, grimed faces and the heavily laden packs of the young men struggling onto the beaches. 'God help them. Thousands of them it says.'

Edith changed the subject. She had no intention of letting her mother sink back into hysteria, not when she was doing so well, and those pictures were just the thing to set her off.

'I'm going down the shops,' she said, 'to get some more soap. Do we need any soda? I mean if we're going to start on Aunt's room. What d'you think?'

'We can't wash the curtains,' Emmeline told her. 'Not in this weather. They'd never dry.'

'But we can start on the picture rails and the skirting boards and give the carpet a good hoover and clean out the wardrobes,' Edith urged. 'I mean, she'll be coming home now, won't she. You know what she said. And once she makes her mind up, she's so quick. It wouldn't surprise me if she didn't come walking through that door tomorrow. Let's strike while the iron's hot, eh.'

Emmeline put the paper aside. Edith was right. They ought to get on. 'Wait a tick,' she said, 'and I'll get my hat and come with you.'

As Edith had predicted, Octavia drove back to Roehampton Secondary School on Saturday morning bringing Morag Gordon with her. The invasion was four days old by then and all the reports were saying that the Allied armies had established a bridgehead and that everything was going according to plan so it was time to start organising their return. It wouldn't be nearly as difficult as it had been when they were preparing for the evacuation all those years ago, because nearly half their pupils were already back in London. She'd already worked out which rooms should be cleaned first, ordered a van to transport their class libraries and ensured that the fifth- and sixth-formers could take their state examinations in the comfort of their own gym. Next term's syllabuses were written and printed. The LCC had been informed of their intentions. Now she was going to meet the school keeper and inspect the building and set the whole thing in motion.

It gave her the most peculiar sensation to be walking into the school hall. It was so quiet that their footsteps echoed – so quiet and so large and so empty. She climbed up onto the platform, trailed her hand along the table, where the dust was so thick she could have written her name in it, looked out at the school clock and noticed that it had stopped at 3.46, and memories of that last day tugged at her mind. All those girls sitting on the floor with their luggage and their gas masks and their sandwiches, hot and sticky in their winter uniforms, waiting and being so good and sensible and patient.

'The wireless is still here,' Morag Gordon said, stooping over it.

'Does it work?' Octavia asked.

It pleased them both to find that it did although it took a little while to get it tuned properly and, while Morag was turning the knobs, listening intently, the school keeper arrived in his shirt sleeves, apologising for being late.

'Not to worry,' Octavia told him. 'You're here now. I've got a list for you.' And she took it out of her file, shaking the ghosts away. The return had begun and they were all going to get on with it.

They came home two weeks later, on a pleasant summer day, when the Americans had just captured Cherbourg, the British were encircling Caen and General de Gaulle was walking along the streets of a newly liberated Bayeux. Now, Octavia thought, watching as her pupils tumbled out of their train into the waiting arms of their mothers and aunts, we can get back to normal. There isn't going to be any more bombing, the Allies are beating the Germans and driving them back, it's all over bar the shouting.

'What will you do now?' Mary O'Connor asked, looking at Lizzie and Poppy.

The three girls were sitting in a tea shop in Oxford enjoying what would probably be their last meeting in the city. They too had finished their exams and now they had to decide what they were going to do next. Mary, as a newly qualified SRN, had been offered a job in King's College Hospital and was due to start work in two weeks but Poppy and Lizzie had to wait till August for their results.

'We could go back to the farm, I suppose,' Poppy said. 'There's always work for us there.'

'But after that?' Mary said. 'When you get your results.'

'I expect I shall get a job somewhere, teaching,' Poppy told her.

'What about you Lizzie?' Mary asked. 'I mean will you go to work or will you just be a housewife?'

'I haven't got a house,' Lizzie said, 'so I can hardly be a housewife.'

'I thought you and Ben had a flat,' Mary said.

'That was just for a few weeks,' Lizzie told her. 'We let it go when he was sent to camp. There didn't seem to be any point in it.'

'Is he all right?' Poppy asked.

'He was the last time he wrote.'

'It must be awful, not knowing,' Poppy said.

'It is. Don't let's talk about it.'

It was peaceful in the tea shop and virtually empty. The elderly waitress smoothed her white apron, adjusted her white cap and sat down on a chair, there being nobody in the shop to tell her she shouldn't. Now that all the servicemen were gone and the students were going, it was so quiet she hardly had anything to do. Nice-looking girl, the one with the wedding ring, she thought. Not a student of course, being married. I wonder where her husband is.

The nice-looking girl was wondering that herself, and aching with the pain of not knowing. The terrible thing about being left behind was that there was nothing to keep your mind off what was happening. Since the end of finals she'd been drifting and worrying, listening to the news bulletins and trying to work out where his brigade would be and whether he was in a battle or, worse, whether he was hurt. Mary was right. What she needed was a job of work.

'I shall go to the farm,' she decided, 'and keep myself occupied.'

In Parkside Avenue, Edith and Emmeline were washing the bedroom curtains. They'd had the copper on the go since early morning and the green walls of the scullery were running with water. But the first two sets had been put through the mangle and were hanging on the line and a third set was washing and they were feeling very pleased with themselves. The roar of a distant explosion made them both jump.

'What on earth was that?' Emmeline said.

'It sounded like a bomb,' Edith said. 'Can't be though or they'd have sounded the sirens.'

420

'It was a jolly big one, whatever it was,' Emmeline said and went out in the garden to have a look.

There was a column of black smoke rising into the blue sky somewhere to the east. 'There you are,' Emmeline said. 'That's a bomb if ever I saw one.'

'Hit and run, I'll bet,' Edith said, remembering what her sister had told them. 'Do you think we should go down the cellar?'

'No point if it's a hit and run,' Emmeline said. 'They'll be gone long since.'

But the next morning, their neighbour told them he'd heard it was a gas main exploding. 'It was in the *Evening Standard*,' he said.

It was in the *Evening Standard* again the next day, when there was another even louder explosion and the same thick pall of smoke.

'Two gas mains in two days,' Emmeline said when she and Edith and Octavia were eating their dinner that evening. 'What's up with them? Are they all developing faults?'

'It's not very likely,' Octavia said, helping herself to another spoonful of mashed potato. 'Not one after another like this. If it weren't for the fact that the sirens didn't sound, I'd have said they were raids but it seems odd for a plane to come all this way and only drop one bomb. You'd have thought it would have been a stick at the very least.'

The mystery was solved two days later at half past three in the morning.

The family were all sound asleep but the sound of the explosion was so loud that it had them out of their beds and into their clothes in seconds. Octavia switched off all the lights, opened her bedroom window and leant out to have a look. This time there were flames in the sky as well as smoke and this time it was very close to them. There was no gunfire and no sound of a plane, just an eerie silence. 'I should say it's in South Wimbledon,' she said. 'Or Merton Park maybe. If it's a gas main we shall know about it in the morning.'

She was right. By breakfast time the news was spreading. The milkman told Emmeline when she went out to the step to fetch in the milk and his version was confirmed by the postman half an hour later. It *was* a bomb and a very big one and it had fallen in Cliveden Road. They were still digging people out of the rubble.

'Right, that's it,' Emmeline said, taking her hat off the hat stand and jamming it on her head. 'Damned Hitler.' And she called into the house, 'I'm going to see Mr Cadwallader.' Then she was off, stomping through the front garden in a temper.

Edith and Octavia ran out of the kitchen just in time to see the edge of her skirt disappearing out of the drive.

'Well, at least she's not screaming,' Edith said. 'That's one thing.'

'And at least we shall know what this is,' Octavia said. 'I knew it wasn't a gas main. Maybe I'll phone Tommy and see what he says. He ought to be awake by now.'

He was awake and informative. 'They're pilotless planes,' he told her. 'Rocket propelled and packed with high explosive. Sort of flying robots. They're launching them from the *Pas de Calais*. I can't tell you much more than that for the moment. Information's still coming in.'

'Dear God,' she said. 'It's like something out of *War of the Worlds*. Is there any way of stopping them?'

'The RAF Johnnies are on to it,' he said. 'Don't worry. There are contingency plans for another evacuation.'

'I'm not worried,' she told him. 'I'm furious. I brought my school back to London because I thought it was safe. We all did. And now look where we are. It's diabolical. We've had quite enough to put up with without robots being fired at us when we weren't expecting it. Bloody Hitler. The man's a scorpion.'

'I'll call in and see you on Saturday,' he promised. 'Chin up!'

When Octavia cycled into school that morning the school keeper was setting up the benches ready for assembly and there were already several teachers waiting for her in the hall.

'They're saying it was a bomb,' Elizabeth said. 'Have you heard anything?'

She led them into her study and told them what she knew. 'We'll have an after-school staff meeting tomorrow,' she said to Maggie Henry. 'I'll phone Mr Chivers presently. He might have more information. We don't have any girls from South Wimbledon, do we?'

They didn't, but that didn't stop them worrying about the girls who might get caught in other attacks.

'We didn't bring them home to have them killed by a flying bomb,' Barbara Trench said.

'Exactly so,' Octavia said grimly. 'So we will have a decision to make.'

It was upsetting to be sitting comfortably in her old staff room, with a cup of tea at her elbow and the familiar school grounds green and wind-tossed beyond the window, and have to face the fact that they might have to be evacuated all over again.

'I've told you all I know,' she said to the staff at the end of her report, 'and now we must put our minds to it and decide what is the best and proper thing for us to do.'

'It seems to me,' Elizabeth Fennimore said, 'that we have

two options. We can't disrupt the examinations. Not now they've begun. That would be unthinkable. So we either wait until the examinations are over and we all join the evacuation then, or we evacuate the rest of the school now but leave the fifth and sixth form here to finish their exams with sufficient staff to supervise them. Either way will be difficult.'

'Or,' Morag said, 'we can stay where we are and not join the evacuation scheme at all.'

That suggestion caused a palpable stir.

'Is that wise?' Barbara Trench said. 'I mean, wouldn't we be putting our girls at risk?'

'Yes,' Morag agreed, 'we would. But not for long. If these flying bombs are being launched from the *Pas de Calais*, we shan't have to endure them for more than a few weeks, a month at the most, just until our armies reach Calais and put paid to them. Besides that, they're going to sound the sirens now to give us warning that they're coming. So we ought to have time to take cover. I vote we stay where we are. I've had enough of being evacuated.'

'It's not a matter of taking cover,' Barbara Trench said hotly. 'They're terrible things. They destroy whole streets. We wouldn't stand an earthly. I think we should get out as soon as we can and not come back until they've been dealt with.'

'But what about our exam girls?' Alice Genevra said. 'I think we should stay here and give them a chance to sit their exams without being driven from pillar to post. I mean, it's not long. It'll all be over in a week or two and now they've started... I mean, I don't think we should uproot them in the middle of it all.'

'Better uprooted than dead though, Alice,' Elizabeth said.

'I'm with Alice,' Mabel Ollerinshaw said. 'I think we should stay where we are and carry on as normal, at least until the exams are over. After all, this isn't like the Blitz. It isn't one bomb after another all night long. These things are dreadful but they're few and far between.'

'We mustn't forget the others,' Sarah Fletcher suddenly put in.

'What others?' Mabel asked her. 'Do you mean ordinary bombs?'

'No,' Sarah explained. 'The other girls. I mean the ones who came back. Some of them have been home for months – years even – and they're over half of our numbers now. Are we going to take them?'

'Now that's a good point,' Elizabeth said. 'I hadn't thought of them.'

'And will they want to go?' Sarah said. 'I mean they've been here a long time and put up with the Little Blitz and everything. They might want to stay where they are. I know I do. I think it's lovely being home again, using my own cooker and everything, even if they do drop flying bombs on us.'

'Me too,' Phillida said. And sighed. 'But what are we to do?'

The three choices were debated until all of them had expressed an opinion. It was past five o'clock before they took a vote and by then they'd come to a compromise. They would stay where they were until after the examinations and then review the situation.

'Thank you ladies,' Octavia said. 'I will inform the parents and the LCC and the governors of our decision.'

She also had to tell Tommy, who arrived at Parkside Avenue at half past seven on Saturday evening with the details of the re-evacuation in his pocket.

'July 11th,' he said. 'It's all laid on.'

She made a grimace. 'We're not going,' she said.

'What do you mean not going?'

'What I said. We're not going.'

He was furious. 'Don't be so bloody ridiculous. Of course you're going.'

'No, Tommy. We're not. We're staying until our girls have finished their exams. We don't want to uproot them.'

'Get your hat,' he ordered. 'We're going out. The supper can wait, can't it, Em?'

'Well,' Emmeline said doubtfully. 'It's a pie.'

He took that as a yes. 'That's settled then,' he said. 'Come on.'

'Where are we going?' Octavia asked, following him out to his car.

'You'll see,' he said and his voice was grim.

He took her on a tour of all the worst bomb sites in Wimbledon, all round Wimbledon Park to Church Road, down Wimbledon Hill and into the Broadway, to Hartfield Road where there were four bomb sites and where an air raid shelter had been hit, to Palmerston Road and Gladstone Road, and back across the Broadway to Stanley Road where two shops had been destroyed, to Effra and Evelyn and Faraday Roads, and on to Haydon's Road, where there were more bomb sites than she could count, and finally south to Cliveden Road, where the first flying bomb had fallen. The road was still cordoned off, so they left the car and explored the site on foot, crunching through the brick dust and the splinters of wood and glass, with the strong powerful smell of the raid cloying their nostrils and wreckage all around them.

'My God!' Octavia said. 'It looks like an earthquake.' The devastation was so much worse than she'd expected that it took her a while simply to accept it. At least seventeen houses had been completely destroyed. There was nothing left of them but piles of broken brick and slate, wrecked doors and mangled furniture and jagged planks of wood. Four more were so badly damaged they were beyond repair. They still stood but they were like decaying teeth, jagged and blackened and broken. 'My God!' Octavia said again as they walked on. It was a sobering walk for there wasn't a single house in the entire street that hadn't been damaged.

'Twelve deaths and fifty-three serious injuries,' Tommy said, standing beside her in the rubble. 'That's what these bloody things do to you. *Now* do you want to stay here?'

She knew she ought to say no. She knew how much he wanted her to say it. But she couldn't do it. She had to tell him the truth even if it upset him. 'We've made our decision,' she said and was upset to realise how stubborn she sounded.

'Then change it.'

'I can't.'

'Of course you can. You're the Head.'

'That's not the way we work,' she told him. 'It was a democratic decision and we're going to stick to it.'

'God damn it, Tavy,' he said. 'You're not listening to me. Look at all this. Just look. We're not playing games. People are getting killed.'

'I know.'

He grabbed her by the shoulders and shook her. 'You don't,' he cried. 'You're not listening. Oh, for crying out loud! Have I got to lose you both?'

His anguish was almost more than she could bear but she still couldn't go back on her decision. And in the most peculiar way, seeing this terrible destruction had made her more determined to stay. Not that she could tell him that. 'You won't,' she said, trying to reassure him. 'Really. It'll be all right. You'll see. I've got a feeling about it.'

It was the worst thing she could have said and she knew it as soon as the words were out of her mouth.

He let go of her shoulders and turned away from her. 'This isn't about feelings,' he said bitterly. 'It's about high explosives.'

She tried to apologise. 'I'm sorry. I shouldn't have said that.'

'I'm wasting my breath,' he said, wearily. 'Come on. I'll take you home.'

They drove back in silence and he left her at the gate, not offering to kiss her goodbye and merely saying, 'I'll phone you.' She got out of the car feeling miserable and defeated. She hadn't meant to hurt him, poor Tommy, but how could she have done anything else?

Emmeline was in the kitchen sitting at the table reading the *Evening Star*. 'No Tommy,' she said and it was more a statement than a question.

'No,' Octavia said. 'He's gone home.'

Emmeline folded up the paper and put it on the dresser. 'Can't say I'm surprised,' she said. 'I suppose it's because we're staying on and not being evacuated.'

'Something like that,' Octavia admitted.

'Oh well,' Emmeline said. 'Come and have your pie. It's more kidney than steak but it's turned out lovely.' And she called towards the dining room. 'Tavy's home, Edie. We can dish up now.'


On Monday morning, as if to prove Tommy right, three flying bombs fell on Wimbledon in fairly rapid succession. The first one was at twenty to four in the morning and was preceded by an air raid siren which woke the house and gave them time to get down into the cellar; the second was at half past six and sounded very close; the third arrived at half past eight as Octavia was cycling to school. It was making a noise like a clapped-out motorbike and she looked up towards the sound and saw it quite clearly, a squat, black, evil-looking thing, belching fire and chugging towards South Wimbledon. As there didn't seem to be anything else she could do, she stopped cycling and watched it, feeling oddly calm as if she'd been anaesthetised. Even when the engine cut out and it began its dive, she was still calm because it wasn't anywhere near her. She watched until she heard the explosion and saw smoke and debris rising into the air. Then she cycled on to school.

It pleased her to see that her pupils were being as sensible as she was.

The fifth form sent a deputation to her before assembly to ask what they were to do if the sirens sounded while they were taking their examination.

'It's all in hand,' she told them. 'You will go down to the east cloakroom, and finish them there. I will tell you all about it at assembly. But I shouldn't think we'd have any more today. Three's enough.'

'Did you hear the doodlebugs this morning, Miss Smith?' one of the first-formers said cheerfully, as she walked along the corridor on her way to her first lesson.

'Yes, Connie,' Octavia said. 'I most certainly did. We could hardly be off hearing them, could we? Nasty, noisy things.' And she noted that the pilotless planes had acquired a nickname and thought it was rather a good one.

The morning continued without any more alarms, which was quite a relief, and at break, the girls went out into the grounds as if it was an ordinary day. Octavia was watching them from the window of her study, when Barbara Trench arrived to say that she'd got something to tell her.

'I'm taking my children back to Woking,' she said. 'I can't put *them* at risk, even if I were prepared to stay here myself. I've written to our landlady and she's quite happy to have us back. I'm sorry to do this to you, Miss Smith, but I'm sure you understand my position.'

Octavia understood it perfectly but it was an annoyance just the same.

'We shall have to put an advertisement in *The Times* as quickly as we can,' she said to Maggie, 'or we shall be a teacher short come September and I can't have that.'

'Leave it to me,' Maggie said. 'I'll do it straight away.'

All in all, it was an eventful day.


But there was a worse one just over a week before the end of term. The examinations were over and the fifth- and sixth-formers were rehearsing a play to lighten the last assembly. When the sirens went they were all in the gym and half of them were in costume.

'Never mind changing,' Joan Marshall told them, appearing in the doorway in her sports kit with a rounders bat in her hand. 'Just get into the cloakrooms as soon as you can. Leave everything where it is. We'll clear up afterwards.'

'It'll spoil the surprise,' they grumbled. But they did as they were told. Which was just as well, for the doodlebug fell seconds after they were all underground and it was so close they could feel the floor rippling under their feet from the shock wave it caused. Then the lights went out and there was a stunned pause while they heard the patter of shattering glass. Then there was a dull roar from somewhere in the building.

'Stay where you are,' Octavia called, striding through the dark. 'You're quite safe here. The lights will come on again presently.'

There was the flicker of a very small light and Joan Marshall was walking towards them with a candle in a saucer. 'Best I can do for the moment,' she said cheerfully. 'Has anyone got a torch?' A surprising number of torches were produced and Jenny Jones organised a sing-song to entertain them while they were waiting and after what seemed like a very long time the all clear sounded.

'Stay where you are,' Octavia said for the second time, 'and don't worry. Miss Gordon and I will just go up and take a look round and see where the damage is and then we'll come down and tell you when it's safe for you to go. We'll be as quick as we can.'

They toured the entire building, walking quickly from room to room and Octavia took notes in her pocket notebook as she went. There was dust everywhere. The floors were thick with it and it was still swirling visibly in the air. All the windows at the east end of the school were shattered and quite a lot of glass had fallen into the classrooms despite the sticky tape; the east door had been blown off its hinges and leant against the jamb at a crazy angle like a drunk about to fall over; and when they reached the music room, they found that the ceiling had fallen and now lay in pieces all over the floor and the piano. There was an air-raid warden standing in the mess, making notes.

'Any casualties?' he asked. 'I gather you were in the shelters.'

'We were,' Octavia told him, 'and nobody's hurt but I shall have to send them home, don't you think?'

The warden agreed with her. 'It's not safe enough to keep them here at the moment,' he said. 'You don't want another ceiling falling on them.'

'Quite right,' Octavia said, glad that the decision was made. And she turned to Morag. 'I shall write to their parents and keep them informed,' she said. 'I wonder whether the phones are still on.'

It took over an hour for the staff to shepherd all their pupils out of the building and for Octavia and Maggie to write and print the letter. By the time it was finished, Octavia was tired to her bones. When Maggie left her to see if she could make a cup of tea, she sat at her dusty desk and put her head in her hands, aching to lie down and have the day over and done with. I put them through this, she thought. It was my decision to stay and if that damned bomb had fallen just a little bit closer, they could all have been killed. She was torn with shame and fear and dragged down by the weight of her responsibility.

'Are you all right?' Maggie said, returning with the tray.

The question was so concerned and affectionate it nearly brought Octavia to tears. But she managed to control herself with what was left of her energy. 'Just tired,' she said. 'I shall be glad to see the back of this term.'

'It's been a day and a half,' Maggie sympathised. 'Nice cup of tea, eh?' But as she was pouring she suddenly stopped and put down the teapot and grinned. 'What an idiot I am!' she said. 'I had a treat for you. Came just before the alarm went. Fancy me forgetting.'

'A treat?' Octavia asked.

'Another application for the English job,' Maggie said, grinning more widely than ever. 'It's on top of the pile.'

It was from Lizzie. Octavia could feel her spirits rising at the sight of it.

'I recognised her writing,' Maggie said. 'I knew you'd be pleased. Our Lizzie Meriton. She'd fit us like a glove.'

'We shall have to interview all the suitable candidates,' Octavia said. 'It mustn't be a foregone conclusion. That wouldn't be proper.'

But it was and they both knew it.

# Chapter Twenty-Eight

'There you are, Edie,' Dora said, spreading a newspaper out on her kitchen table. 'This is for you.'

It was a warm afternoon at the start of September and the sisters were making the most of it. In four days' time the new term would begin and then there would be no more get-togethers until half term.

'What is it?' Edith said, easing Joan out of her coat.

'Prefabricated house,' Dora said, taking the coat and hanging it on a hook on the door. 'Read it. I'll just make the tea, you four, and then we can have some cake.'

The table was set for six with a home-made apple cake on its stand as a centrepiece and Joan had been eyeing it ever since she came in.

'They're building them on the commons,' Dora said, wetting the pot, 'and they're going to give priority to people who've been bombed out or are married to servicemen. That's you on both counts. Read it.'

Edith sat at the table and read the article. 'They look smashing,' she said, examining the picture.

'They're putting them up on Clapham Common already,' Dora said. 'I saw them this morning with a great queue of people standing outside and I wondered what they were and then I bought the paper and lo and behold there they were. What say we go and have a look?'

'Will they let us?' Edith said. 'I mean, are they ready for people to look at?'

'I'll bet that's what the queue was,' Dora said. 'People looking. Anyway it's worth a try. What d'you think, kids?'

'I thought we were going to the pictures,' David said, scowling.

'We shan't if you pull that face,' his mother warned. 'It'll all depend how you behave.'

'We're having our cake first though, aren't we?' Joan asked.

Half an hour later, thirsts slaked and cake replete, they walked down the High Street to the common to take a look at the new houses. After the shabby appearance of their battered High Street with its bomb sites and its grime and its worn-out paintwork, they looked fresh and band-box new, standing in neat rows beside the trees. Edith said it took her breath away just to look at them. Everything about them was appealing, from the smart green paint on their front doors and their two front windows, to the neat grey panels of their walls. They had flat roofs and tin chimneys and there were little white picket fences round the patches of grass that had been allocated to them as their front gardens.

'They're like country cottages,' Edith said.

They had to stand in line for a long time before they were allowed inside but, even though the girls were fidgety and David scowled and grumbled, it was well worth the wait, because if the outside was good, the inside was spectacular. There were three big bedrooms, with wardrobes and cupboards all built in, and a lovely bathroom and a living room with a lot more cupboards and a little table you could fold down and set against the wall to make more space when you weren't using it – and, wonder of wonders, a gas fire. 'Think of that,' Edith said. 'No more raking out the ashes and dragging coal up from the cellar and having to wait for it to warm through. The luxury of it.' But the kitchen was the best of all. It had everything that anyone could possibly want – a little white geyser so that you could have hot water whenever you needed it instead of having to wait for the kettle to boil, a copper for the washing and a lovely new gas cooker all grey and white and ready to use, and shelves and cupboards all built in like the ones in the bedrooms and, standing alongside them and looking like another white cupboard until you opened it, one of those new refrigerators with shelves for butter and milk and meat and little round spaces where you could put your eggs. It was like being at the pictures.

'If this is what the future's going to be like,' Edith said, 'I'm all for it.'

The lady who'd been showing them round gave her a smile. 'Then perhaps you'd better step next door and put your name down,' she said. 'There's a lady there who will take your particulars.'

'There you are,' Dora said, when the forms had been filled in and they were walking back along Balham High Street towards the cinema, 'won't that be something to tell your Arthur. Cheer him up no end this will.'

'He needs cheering,' Edith said. 'They've moved them to another camp.'

'Again?' Dora said. 'How many times's that?'

'Four.'

'They're getting edgy, that's what it is,' Dora said sagely. 'They know their number's up. That's why they keep on bombing us. They're doing it while they can.'

435

Talk of bombing reminded Edith of her brother-in-law. 'How's your John?' she said.

'He was all right last time I heard,' Dora said. 'Still cracking jokes. You know John. He'd make a joke of anything. He says he's doing the same job he was doing in Portsmouth and getting bombed for it in the same way. It sounds as if they're being plastered. Damned doodlebugs.'

'Sometimes I think the whole world's gone raving mad,' Edith said sadly. 'Here's our Johnnie in Canada with one leg, and Ma having hysterics, and your John being bombed by doodlebugs and us being bombed by doodlebugs, and my Arthur pining away in a prisoner a' war camp and I've been looking at new houses.'

'And why not?' Dora said fiercely. 'You take what's on offer, gel, that's my advice. Live while you can. You never know what's round the corner. And keep your old chin up. It can't go on forever.' Then she turned her attention to the children because they'd reached the cinema. And not before time. She couldn't have her Edie getting down. 'Here we are kids,' she said. 'Now it's *your* treat because you've been good. And afterwards we'll have fish and chips for supper. How about that?'

Despite the doodlebugs and the paucity of the rations there was quite a lot of optimism that autumn, for the European campaigns were going well. The Russians had captured Bucharest and reached the borders of East Prussia, the Americans were in Paris, the Allied armies in Italy had taken Florence and Montgomery's men were storming across Belgium, going at such a speed that Ben reported to Lizzie, *We ran right into the back of their retreat, fought them wheel to wheel. Bit bloody but we gave them a good trouncing. I took a slight flesh wound. Nothing to worry about.*

She *did* worry about it, naturally. A tank battle fought wheel to wheel sounded absolutely terrifying but it was over by the time she was reading the letter and there was no point in thinking about it. So she wrote back to tell him she'd got a job at Roehampton with Smithie, that she was living with her father *for the time being* and that she was starting work in two days' time. *I shall be a school teacher by the time you get this*, she wrote. Then she put down her pen and pondered.

There was so much she wanted to tell him, so much she needed to tell him if she was absolutely honest. She'd sent off her application for this job almost on impulse, thinking how wonderful it would be to be teaching at her old school, and when she'd been interviewed and appointed she'd been so happy and excited she hadn't thought about anything else, but now, as the beginning of the new term drew near and inescapable, she was having troubling second thoughts. What if she couldn't teach after all? What if she got things wrong? If only he were here beside her and they could talk about it. But they couldn't and it wasn't fair to burden him with her problems when he'd got more than enough of his own. Sighing, she picked up her pen again and wrote *PLEASE TAKE CARE OF YOURSELF*. Because that was the important thing, not whether she could teach or not.

Tommy was rather pleased to have his little girl back home with him although he warned her on their first evening together that they wouldn't see much of one another.

'It's mayhem at the Foreign Office with all this going on,' he said. 'We work all the hours God sends. There's a plan afoot to start up a new League of Nations and Tubby and I are in the thick of it. I shall have to go to Washington in a week or two.'

'Don't worry,' she told him. 'It's only for a little while. Just till I find my feet.'

'Mrs Dunnaway will look after you when I'm not here,' he told her. 'And at least we shan't have so many buzz bombs to worry about.'

'Really?' she asked.

'Should be, now we're in the *Pas de Calais*,' he told her.

'How much longer is this war going on, Pa?' she asked.

'Six months, nine, a year at the most,' he said. 'We're planning the peace already. That's what all these meetings are about. Cheer up, little one. He'll soon be home. Good times are coming.'

That was Octavia's theme at her first assembly of the year.

'We are starting a new school year in our own school building for the first time in six years,' she said. 'We have more pupils than we have ever had in our history and I think it is safe to say that this will be the last year of the war. Work hard, work well and, above all, enjoy what you do. The peace is coming and when it does there will be a great deal to do and we shall need all our skills if we are to do it well. We none of us know what lies ahead of us nor what challenges we shall have to face. But whatever happens I know you will rise to the challenge as Roehampton girls have done all through this long terrible war. I am very proud of you.

'Now we will start our new year in our usual way with our usual hymn, "Lord behold us with Thy blessing". If you please, Miss Jones.'

Iris Forbes and Sarah Turnbridge had just received their black gowns as senior prefects and were sitting on the platform behind Miss Smith with a good view of the assembled staff,

438

who were ranged on either side of the hall in their usual places.

'It *is* her,' Iris said, as they walked back to their form rooms. 'I knew it was.'

'I wonder whether she'll teach us,' Sarah said. Both of them were taking English at Higher Schools so it was possible.

'We shall have our timetables presently,' Iris said, 'and then we'll know.'

'Just so long as it isn't old mother Trench,' Sarah said.

'She's gone,' Iris told her. 'Didn't you know?'

'Good riddance,' Sarah said. 'She was the most boring teacher I've ever had.'

They turned up for their first lesson with Mrs Hardy at the end of the afternoon, seven young women in red sashes and black gowns, grinning like Cheshire cats. They were so excited to see her they didn't notice how nervous she was. She'd spent the morning with her form giving out timetables and plans of the school and telling them how the Dalton System worked and now she was feeling unaccountably tired and not at all sure how she was going to tackle this first lesson. It was all very well thinking you could do a thing but quite different when you actually had to do it.

'Fancy it being you,' Iris said, as they found their seats. 'We knew it was you the minute we saw you, didn't we, Sarah.'

'Yes,' Lizzie said. 'Now we're going to…'

'The last time we were all in that hall together was the day we were evacuated,' Sarah said. 'We never thought the next time we'd be in the sixth form and you'd be our teacher.'

'What a day that was,' their friend Margaret said. 'Do you remember how hot it was? Stifling. And we all had our winter uniforms on.'

'Yes,' Lizzie tried again. 'We're going to…'

But now they'd begun to reminisce, there was no way she could stop them. They were remembering the day detail by detail.

'We wanted to buy a drink at the sweet shop by the station and you wouldn't let us. Do you remember?'

'Iris cried.'

'I did not!'

'You did and Mary O'Connor's mum gave you a humbug.'

'I remember the humbug.'

'We all had to wait on the platform for the train to come and it took ages and ages.'

I've lost them, Lizzie thought. It was just the very thing she'd been afraid of. She'd lost them and she didn't have the faintest idea how she could get their attention back unless she shouted. And she couldn't shout at them. That was unthinkable. And particularly not to Iris and Sarah. They'd been in her house group.

'Do you remember that awful hut where they took us? Right out in the middle of nowhere.'

'And those terrible old coaches with the prickly seats.'

'And the Nitty Nora with her comb.'

'And here we are and you're teaching us,' Sarah said. 'Who'd have thought it?'

It was a chink of light. An opportunity. 'But I'm not, am I?' Lizzie said.

'Not what?' Iris said.

'Teaching you,' Lizzie said, grinning at them. 'I mean, I've got the text books, but I'm not teaching you.' Give them out quickly while they're listening. Keep them listening. 'Let me tell you what we're going to do. We're going to study Geoffrey

Chaucer. And you're going to love him.'

'Are we?' Margaret said dubiously. 'The others said he was difficult, didn't they, Iris?'

Is that what all the gossip was about? Lizzie wondered. Were they using delaying tactics? 'Then they were wrong,' she said firmly. 'He isn't difficult. He's great fun. He tells a good tale and he tells it well. And he's very rude.'

Now they were interested. 'Rude?' Margaret said.

'Very. Downright naughty sometimes.'

Iris had opened her book. 'It's in a foreign language,' she said.

Tackle it head on. 'No,' Lizzie said. 'It just looks like a foreign language, that's all, because the spelling is different. Don't try to read it for yourselves yet. Just listen while I read it to you.' And she began to read the opening lines of the Prologue, getting as near to modern English as she could without disturbing the word order or the rhythm.

'When April with its showers sweet, the drought of March has pierced to the root, and bathed every stem with that juice whose virtuous power engenders the flowers, when Zephyr too with his sweet breath has inspired in every holt and heath the tender crops and the young sun has run its half course in the sign of the Ram, and small birds make melody...' Then she paused. 'Spring you see,' she explained. 'April showers, spring flowers, young crops, birds singing. We're off to a sunny start.'

And so to her great relief they were. But it had been more by accident than design.

At the end of the afternoon she walked slowly through the hall on her way back to the staff room, deep in thought. She didn't notice Smithie's approach until they were almost toe to toe. Then she glanced up to find herself looking straight into her headmistress's eyes.

Octavia knew at once that her star pupil was troubled and that whatever it was would have to be tackled delicately. The droop of her shoulders was a disquieting sign. 'How did everything go?' she asked.

'I like my first form very much,' Lizzie told her. 'They're dears.' Then she paused, not quite sure whether she ought to confess her doubts or not. She didn't want to look a fool. Not on her first day.

'But?' Octavia prompted. And waited patiently.

Her patience and concern provoked an admission. 'I'm afraid I made a mess of my first lesson.'

'Come in and tell me about it,' Octavia said and led the way to her study.

It was a searching interview but not an unpleasant one. Octavia took her through the lesson step by step, listening and prompting, and when they'd finished she sat back in her easy chair and smiled at her new recruit. 'It seems to me,' she said, 'that you handled a potentially difficult situation extremely well.'

'It didn't feel like that to me,' Lizzie told her.

'That's because you were in the middle of it. I'm telling you how it looks to me. You made your first mistake and you learnt from it and that's fine because that's what mistakes are for. Your pupils will have come out of your lesson aware that Chaucer is worth studying, which is no mean feat. They also know you're fond of them, which is the secret of all good teaching. And you've learnt that you've got to have your opening move ready and organised before you enter the classroom. If I can offer you a bit of advice, I'd start the next lesson with a look at 'The Wife of Bath'. I've never met a class yet who didn't warm to

442

*her.* There's an excellent picture of her in the collected works in my teaching room.'

'I remember it,' Lizzie said. 'You showed us all of them one after the other as soon as we'd read Chaucer's description and we had to compare and contrast.'

'Exactly so.'

It's all right, Lizzie thought. I am going to be able to do this. But she was noticing how much older her Smithie looked and how tired.

'She's an extraordinary woman,' she told her father at dinner that evening. 'There she is in the middle of a war with a school to run and God knows what to attend to and yet she takes the time to put me on my feet again. Extraordinary.'

'She always was,' Tommy said. 'Even when she was a mere slip of a girl.'

He sounded wistful, which seemed rather peculiar. Why should he be wistful about Smithie? 'I didn't know you knew her when she was a girl.'

'Eighteen,' he confirmed. 'I was at school with her cousin. But that was in the dark ages. How did you get on with your form? Are they nice?'

The term continued and, once she'd got into the habit of planning exactly how her lessons would begin and gathering all the material she needed to make them run the way she wanted, Lizzie began to enjoy it. The sixth form were highly taken with 'The Wife of Bath', admiring her red stockings and her hat as big as a shield. 'Can't you just see her?'

'Five husbands,' they said and quoted, 'withouten other company in youth.'

They were happily comparing the portrait with the description when there was a distant explosion.

443

'Doodlebug?' Iris wondered.

'They haven't sounded the sirens,' Margaret pointed out

Seconds later there was another explosion, marginally louder.

'Should we go down to the cloakrooms?' Sarah asked. And while Lizzie was wondering what to say, the question was answered by the arrival of a fifth-former with a 'message from Miss Smith' to say they were to stay where they were unless the alarm went.

'Very odd,' the staff said to one another in the staff room. 'Why didn't they sound the alarm?'

'Maybe they forgot,' Joan Marshall said.

They forgot all through the next day and the day after that, when there were really rather a lot of explosions, some at a distance, others uncomfortably close.

'If these *are* doodlebugs,' Phillida said, 'it's funny they don't sound the sirens. I think they're something else and they're not telling us.'

'I'll ask my father,' Lizzie told them. 'See if he knows.'

It was the first time in her life she saw him being diplomatic and the sight struck ice-cold into her brain.

'Yes,' he said, 'they were bombs. We're not entirely sure what kind so I can't say very much about them at the moment. I'll let you know if and when we get any more information.'

Lizzie watched his guarded face and felt suddenly and terribly afraid. If he can't tell me, she thought, and he obviously can't, they're keeping it hushed up, and if they're keeping it hushed up, that means it's something too horrible for us to be told, in case they alarm us. Don't they know how our imaginations work?

'In other words,' she said, 'you know but you've been given orders not to tell anyone.'

444

He looked shamefaced. 'Well, I wouldn't go so far as to say that.'

'I would,' she said. 'It's obvious. Oh, come on, Pa, I'm not a child. I've got a husband in Belgium and God alone knows what could be happening to him out there and I have to face that every day of my life. I think I've got a right to know what might be going to happen to me. I don't believe in secrecy. I think it's much better to know the worst than to imagine it. It's all right. I understand about careless talk. I shan't pass any of it on if you tell me not to, but I need to know and you need to tell me.'

'I can't, little one,' he said. 'Official secrets and all that.'

'Official secrets, my aunt Fanny,' she said angrily. 'I'm your daughter. You can tell me. Nobody has official secrets from their daughter.'

Her insistence made him laugh and laughter loosened his tongue. She was right. It was unkind to keep her in the dark. 'It's another flying bomb,' he said, 'only worse than the doodlebugs. It carries the same amount of high explosive so it's just as destructive as they are, but it's not a pilotless plane, it's a rocket. It flies at speeds greater than the speed of sound, so we can't see it coming – or hear it coming for that matter – and the gunners can't shoot it down. The Germans can launch it from small transportable rocket pads almost anywhere, it's got a much longer range than the doodlebug and they've got thousands of the things in stock. Now can you see why the authorities want to keep quiet about it?'

'My God,' she said. 'It *is* bad.'

'Yes,' he said. 'It is. But keep it under your hat until it's official.'

* * *

It was official nine days later, when so many rumours were going the rounds that it was deemed less harmful for people to know what was actually going on than to keep them guessing and speculating. It surprised the authorities that Londoners took it phlegmatically.

'It's just one damned thing after another,' Emmeline said to Octavia, when the news broke. 'But what did I always say? If it's got your number on it it'll get you. No good worrying about it. We must just try and look on the bright side. At least we haven't got to keep jumping in and out of the cellar. I'll tell you one thing though. When this lot's over and we've caught the monsters who've been doing this, we should put a bullet through their rotten heads and string them up from the nearest tree.'

'She's so fierce,' Octavia said to Tommy when they were in bed that Saturday night. 'She doesn't have hysterics any more, she just gets angry.'

'That's a healthier reaction,' he said. 'She's got every right to get angry. We all have. It's an evil war. Which is why we've got to make damned certain the new League of Nations, or whatever we're going to call it, has a military arm this time and can insist on its decisions being carried out.'

'When do you go?' Octavia asked.

'Wednesday, for my sins.'

'I shall miss you,' she said. 'Just make sure they make the right decisions.'

'Yes, Miss Smith,' he said, giving her a mock salute. 'And if I do all the right things and they make all the right decisions, will you marry me?'

'When the war's over,' she said and sighed. 'I can't look after the school and cope with the rockets *and* arrange a wedding.

I should buckle under the strain.'

She'd tried to speak lightly, as if it was a joke, but he was so keenly attuned to her that night that he sensed the anxiety behind what she was saying. He propped himself up on his elbow and looked down at her, lying beside him, her face silver-edged and serious in the moonlight. Oh, how he loved that serious face. 'What's up, Tikki-Tavy?' he said. 'What are you worrying about?'

The tenderness of his voice provoked an honest reply. 'It's those bloody rockets,' she said. 'I keep thinking, what if I've made the wrong decision? What if one of them falls on the school and my girls are killed or injured, or on their houses, which they easily could, couldn't they, because there's no knowing where they're going to fall. Bloody awful things. It's my responsibility to care for my girls and my teachers. That's what I was appointed to do. And I do care for them. They're like my family. I love them dearly. And what have I done? It was my decision to keep them here. I'm the one who's supposed to protect them and look after them and what I've actually done is expose them to danger. Oh, I know the staff had a part in it. You don't have to tell me that. I mean I know it was a democratic decision. But I could have overruled them. I had the power to do it. And I didn't because I wanted to stay here too. I was being selfish and not thinking straight. And now we're entrenched. They keep saying "We've got to see it through" and it makes me feel absolutely dreadful every time they say it. Anything could happen, Tommy, and if it does it will be my fault.'

'That, if you don't mind me saying so, is illogical,' he told her. 'You didn't start the war and you didn't design the rockets.'

'No but...'

'What you're suffering from, my darling, is the weight of command. There isn't a leader alive who hasn't felt like that at some time or other. Except Hitler and you can't count him. And it's worse if your decisions mean that someone is going to get killed. Monty and Eisenhower face it every day and on a large scale. You think of all the men who were involved in the invasion and how many of them were killed. We have a decision to make, we weigh up the consequences, we make the decision. Then we have to watch the men under our command get shot and die in agony. Weight of command.'

Hearing the bitterness in his voice and watching the anguish on his face, she knew he was talking about the first war and his part in it. It was something she'd never heard him do before. 'You too,' she said.

'I've never forgotten it,' he said. 'It stays with you for the rest of your life. Watching men die. I remember the first one as if it were yesterday. Only a kid. Couldn't have been more than seventeen. If that. He did as he was told and he had both his legs shot away. His guts were spilling out of his body and he was trying to push them back in with his hands and there was blood everywhere. He kept crying for his mother. I shall remember it to my dying day.'

'Oh, Tommy,' she said, putting a hand on his arm, 'my dear, dear man.'

'Never told a soul till now,' he said gruffly. There were two moon-silver tears running down his cheeks. 'Couldn't face it.' He brushed the tears away. 'Anyway, I know what you're feeling, Tavy. We all feel it. That's the thing.'

'Were you afraid?' she asked. They were talking so freely now and with such honesty it was possible to ask him.

'Terrified,' he told her. 'We all were. Shit scared. Only you couldn't show it, of course, not if you were an officer. You had to keep a stiff upper lip. All that sort of thing. Keep up morale. Bloody stupid because we're all afraid under fire. Me, you, all of us.'

'Yes,' she said. 'You're right. We are. I certainly am. Only I'm like you. I can't show it. I have to keep up a bold front, especially to the girls. It does help, you know. It's necessary but it's bloody hard to do.'

'The weight of command,' he said.

'Yes,' she said. 'I suppose so. Have you got a cigarette?'

He found his cigarette case, and lit up for both of them and for a few minutes they smoked and recovered.

'I haven't talked like that since Pa died,' she told him.

He drew in a lungful of smoke. 'I've never talked like that *before*,' he said. 'Not to anyone.'

'Then I'm honoured,' she said.

'Don't keep things from me, Tavy,' he said. 'Tell me when things are bad. I might not be able to help much but I don't like to think of you battling on and feeling alone.'

She took the last drag on her cigarette. 'I love you very much,' she said. And kissed him.

# Chapter Twenty-Nine

Being under fire from a weapon as implacable and powerful as the German V2 bred a weary fatalism in the beleaguered citizens of London. There was no way they could defend themselves against an invisible attacker and nothing to be gained by worrying about their lack of defence. All they could do was get on with their lives and enjoy whatever pleasures came their way. The pubs did a rollicking trade and the cinemas were crowded with people watching the latest Hollywood musical and luxuriating in a technicoloured world where heroines were always beautiful and never smudged their lipstick, heroes were always square-jawed and impossibly handsome, good always triumphed and there was no such thing as war. 'Load a' cobblers,' they said to one another, as they emerged into the grime and dust of their down-trodden world, 'but it cheers you up a treat.'

Tommy confided to his old friend Tubby Ponsonby that he'd be quite glad to be out of it for a few days. 'I shall worry about my Lizzie, naturally,' he said, 'but I couldn't do anything to protect her even if I *was* here.'

'Make the most of the great US of A, old fruit,' Tubby said. 'That's my advice.'

Her father's departure left Lizzie in a quandary. It had been very good of him to offer her a home when she came back to London and she *was* grateful to him, of course she was, but the house was too full of ghosts to be a comfortable place for her to live in. The garden and the old nursery were particularly difficult places, for although they triggered cheerful memories of all the stupid games she and her brothers used to play when they were young, they were a daily reminder that they were in France now and in danger, just like Ben, and that brought that awful scrabbling anxiety back into her belly again. The stairs and the parlour were even worse. Every time she looked up at the stairs she could see her mother drifting down them in that flowing, fluid way of hers, wearing one of her lovely evening dresses and looking young and alive, and the memory was so painful it made her ache with grief all over again. The parlour had been shut up, according to Mrs Dunnaway. 'I polish it now and then,' she said, 'but he never goes in.' Lizzie could understand why. On one poignant occasion she'd gone into the room herself to look for one of her father's books and it had been painful in the extreme. The minute she opened the door, she could see her mother in the sharpest and cruellest focus, sitting in her easy chair beside the fire with Pa facing her, just the way they used to do when she came in to kiss them goodnight as a child, when the world was peaceful and sunny and there was no such thing as a Blitz. She was overwhelmed with a grief as tearing and terrible as it had been when her mother was killed. She fell into the chair as if she'd been thrown there and cried for a very long time. No, she thought, as she passed the safely closed door on her way to the kitchen each morning, I can't stay here. Not without Pa anyway. I must find somewhere else. It wouldn't be easy, she knew that, because so many houses had been bombed and weren't fit to live in, but she would try. The next morning she put cards in the shop windows of all the tobacconists within walking distance of the school and on the spur of the moment wrote a shorter appeal and pinned it to the staff notice board at school. Then she waited.

She got an answer at break the next morning and it came from the new art teacher, Fiona Fitzgerald, who wandered over to find her while she was pouring herself a cup of tea.

'About this flat you're looking for,' she said, putting out a paint-smeared hand to pick up a cup. 'I suppose you wouldn't be interested in sharing with me, would you? I live over the newsagent's. Mr Pearson's. You put a card in there yesterday.'

Lizzie was a bit surprised. She hadn't thought of sharing with another teacher. But it was a possibility. 'Well, I might,' she said. 'Could I see it?'

'You could come back with me this afternoon, if you like. It's a bit of a mess but it would give you an idea.'

So they cycled to the newsagent's together. It was a small flat and it *was* in a bit of a mess with the breakfast things left on the kitchen table and milk bottles and letters on the floor at the top of the stairs but it had two bedrooms on the second floor and a sizeable kitchen.

'I use the front room for painting,' Fiona explained, 'so I live in the kitchen. I used to share with another student before the war but I live on my own now and – well – to tell you the truth, I don't like it on my own. Not with the rockets. I'd rather have some company. What do you think?'

'Could we give it a try perhaps?' Lizzie asked. 'For a week or something. See how we get on.'

'I don't see why not,' Fiona said. 'A week sounds fine to me. We could go halves on the rent, couldn't we?'

'I ought to warn you, though,' Lizzie said, 'I've got rather a lot of books.'

'I ought to warn *you* I make a pig's ear of the place at Christmas,' Fiona confessed. 'That's my muckiest time because of the decorations and making cards. But you know the sort of chaos there is when there's a lot of artwork going on. You must have seen it when you were a pupil. You'd better take a look at my workroom though before we decide. You ought to know what you're in for.'

It looked like an extension of the art room at Roehampton. There was an old kitchen table in one corner, covered in paint pots and piles of paper and brushes standing in old jam jars, an easel set to catch the light with a large unfinished work on it and canvases stacked against the walls.

Lizzie laughed. 'Yes,' she said. 'I see what you mean.' And she walked over to look at the work on the easel. It was a study of a row of weary-looking women standing in line outside a butcher's shop. There was something about it that reminded her of Henry Moore's picture of people sheltering in the underground during the Blitz. 'It's good,' she said. 'You've caught their weariness.'

The compliment pleased Fiona but she didn't comment on it. 'So what do you think?' she asked.

Lizzie and her books moved in at the end of the week, courtesy of her father's wheelbarrow, and by Sunday evening she and Fiona had kept one another company through several explosions, all of them fairly distant, had exchanged life histories and had told one another about their love affairs, which in Fiona's case were plentiful and entertaining. On Monday morning Lizzie put their dirty dishes in the sink and left them to soak and they went cycling off to school together like old friends. By the time Tommy finally came home, the move was complete.

He was rather put out. 'I know she's not been home for very

long,' he said to Octavia, 'but it seems most peculiar to be in the house without her.'

'She's got to live her own life,' Octavia told him. 'You knew she wouldn't stay with you forever.' And she changed the subject. 'How was the conference?'

'Sensible,' he said. 'They're going to call the new organisation the United Nations and it's going to have an army, you'll be pleased to know. There are forty-six nations involved in it already and if they sign up to it they will have to pledge to supply armed forces in the event of any crisis.'

'I'm glad to hear it,' she said. 'We should have thought of *that* when we set up the League and then we wouldn't have had all this terrible trouble.'

'How have the rockets been?'

'Bloody awful,' she told him. 'Croydon's been really hammered, so Dora says. But at least we haven't had any in Wimbledon yet.'

Dora had been a full time warden ever since the doodlebugs began. There'd been no work for her at the estate agent's for a very long time apart from arranging the occasional let and she was useful and in demand as a warden. For the last six weeks she'd been on duty six days out of seven.

'My David's having to look after himself,' she told her mother. 'Just as well he's sensible.'

'He could come here and stay with me, if you like,' Emmeline offered. 'I'd look after him for you. I don't like to think of him being on his own.'

But Dora said it wasn't necessary. 'I leave him things to heat up,' she said, 'and he has his friends in to keep him company. He's a big lad now.'

'That's all very well,' Emmeline complained to Octavia

later that evening. 'He *is* a big lad, there's no denying that, but he's still young. He still needs looking after, especially with these damned rockets. Dora can be very hard sometimes. Maybe I ought to go over in the afternoons now and then, and give him his tea when he comes in. Only she'll probably say I shouldn't. I don't know what to do for the best.'

Octavia said she didn't know what to advise, which was more or less true, because Em would go her own way no matter what anyone said. But in the event the LCC solved her problem for her. At the end of October, Edith had a letter offering her one of the prefabs on Clapham Common. She was scatty with excitement, making lists of all the things she would need, and all the things she would like but probably couldn't afford, examining her post office book to see how much money she'd got, collecting tea chests and cardboard boxes so that she could start to pack.

'Not that we need all that much,' she said. 'That's the beauty of a prefab. It's all built in. It'll only be beds and bedding and a few pots and pans and things.'

'And china and cutlery and a door mat and chairs and curtains,' Emmeline said. 'You'll need nets being on the common or you'll have everybody looking in at you. You can take the bedding you've been using here, if you like. That'll be something to get you started and I shan't need it. We could go to Arding and Hobbs for the china. I'd suggest Ely's but they're a bit pricey. What do you think?'

They were so happy shopping and packing that it was several days before Emmeline realised that Edith would be living just along the road from Dora and David. 'What a bit of luck,' she said. 'He can come home to you when our Dora's out. That'll be much better.'

'He'll eat all the cake,' Joan warned.

'You and your cake,' Edith said. 'Put that tablecloth in the tea chest for me, there's a good girl.'

They moved a month later and the house was very quiet and very empty when they'd gone. Emmeline spent the rest of the day drifting from room to room like a ghost, picking things up and putting them down again, tweaking the curtains and brushing up imaginary dust.

'Now it's just us,' she sighed, as she and Octavia sat down to dinner on their first changed evening. 'I shall miss them.'

'And Tommy,' Octavia said. 'When he's not gadding about the planet. What's in the evening paper?'

'They're going to lift the blackout,' Emmeline told her. *'Lights are going on again in all our railway stations*, it says here. And about time too. I'm sick to death of being in the dark. Those damned rockets will get here no matter what we do, so why not have a bit of light?'

It was certainly cheering to think that they wouldn't have to stumble about in the dark any more and, like her cousin, Octavia felt in need of a bit of cheer. The Normandy invasion had been four months ago and yet the Allied armies were still battling their way towards Germany and had suffered a costly defeat at a place called Arnhem: the rockets were still causing far too many deaths and far too much destruction: the rations were as small and the food as dull as ever, the city as run down and dusty. If change was coming, it was coming very slowly.

'Concentrate on the future,' Tommy advised. 'That's what Tubby and I are doing.'

But the future seemed too distant for concentration and the present crowded it out. It wasn't until she had an unexpected phone call that there was any indication that her life would change in any way.

Emmeline was out visiting Edith and the girls and Octavia

was alone in her study, marking books and drinking yet another cup of tea, when the phone shrilled into her thoughts.

A cultured voice asked if she could speak to Miss Octavia Smith.

'Speaking,' Octavia said, putting down her red pencil.

'Kathy Ellis,' the voice said. 'We met when you gave evidence to the Parliamentary Committee on the future of education.'

'I remember it well,' Octavia said. And waited.

'We were wondering whether we could tempt you into meeting us again,' Miss Ellis said. 'There's an old friend of yours on the committee now and he's very keen to meet up with you again and we have one or two proposals we would like to put to you.'

Octavia opened her diary. 'It would depend on what day you had in mind,' she said. But although she was being cautious, excitement was bubbling in her chest, making her feel warm and hopeful and useful, and she knew she would meet up with Miss Ellis and this mysterious 'old friend' and listen to their proposals no matter what date they suggested.

They met at County Hall in a panelled room overlooking the grey and choppy waters of the Thames, on a cold, inauspicious day in the middle of December. The papers that morning were full of bad news. The Germans had started a sudden counter attack through the Ardennes forest and had advanced thirty miles into Belgium. Octavia had read the paper on her way up to Waterloo and she was still frowning as she walked into the room. There were only two people there: Miss Ellis, looking exactly the same as she remembered; and a middle-aged man in a battered brown suit and horn-rimmed spectacles with a lot of thick fair hair, worn in a cowlick over his forehead.

There was something vaguely familiar about the cowlick but she couldn't really say she recognised him.

'Brian Urquhart,' he said, holding out his hand towards her. 'We met at the College of St Gregory and All Souls. Rather a long time ago, I'm afraid. You came to give us a talk about how children learn. Best thing I ever heard. I've never forgotten it. I don't suppose you remember me.'

She was remembering as he spoke. There was something about the earnestness of his voice. That and the cowlick. 'You were one of the ones who came up to talk to me afterwards,' she said. 'You said you wanted to teach in a Dalton School. Did you ever manage it?'

'No,' he said. 'I went to an elementary school where they were very repressive.'

'I'm sorry to hear it.'

'Come and sit by the fire,' Miss Ellis said, leading the way, 'and let me tell you what we have in mind.'

They sat in a semi-circle round the limited warmth of a reluctant fire. 'I suppose you've heard that free secondary education is going to be given to all our children as soon as the war is over,' Miss Ellis said. And when Octavia nodded, 'Yes. I thought you would have done. What you will not have heard, as the news hasn't been released yet, is that the government plan to set up emergency teacher training colleges for returning servicemen to provide all the extra teachers we shall need for the expansion. We were wondering whether you would consider a post as a principal of one of these colleges. We are only talking about colleges in the London area you understand, although there will be others in other parts of the country.'

'I'm honoured that you should think of me,' Octavia said, 'but I must tell you straight away that my answer has to be no.

I couldn't leave my school and all the good work we're doing there, no matter how tempting these colleges might be.'

'We rather feared that was what you might say,' Miss Ellis told her. 'Then perhaps we could tempt you into a post as a visiting lecturer to spread the word about how children learn.'

'That would be possible.'

'With visits to your school?'

'That too,' Octavia said. 'We had a lot of visitors before the war. It was quite a regular thing. I would have to ask the staff of course, but I think they would be happy about it.'

'So far so good,' Miss Ellis said. 'Your turn now Brian.'

'You will probably think I'm being presumptuous,' Brian Urquhart said, brushing the cowlick away from the top of his glasses, 'but I was wondering if you'd write us a sort of booklet as a teaching aid. How children learn and what gets in the way of the natural learning process and how you see the future of education in this country. That sort of thing. I know it's a lot to ask but it would be invaluable to us. I've never met anyone who explained it as clearly as you did. No. Correction. I've never met anyone else who explained it at all. There are still far too many teachers who think teaching is a matter of shouting at children and bullying them and telling them what to do and mocking them if they can't do it.'

'Put like that,' Octavia laughed, 'how can I refuse?'

The coals shifted in the grate and one of them began to hiss. 'I think we should go down to the canteen and have a spot of lunch,' Kathy Ellis said. 'It's warmer down there and we've got something to celebrate.'

'What do you think of that?' Octavia said to Emmeline over supper that night.

'Just so long as you don't go working all the hours God

459

sends,' Emmeline warned. 'I know what you're like when you get a bee in your bonnet. And don't forget it's Christmas.'

'I haven't forgotten,' Octavia said. 'I'm going to buy a gramophone.'

But Emmeline was right about bees and bonnets. Her new-old friend's request had been perfectly timed and cunningly expressed. It upset her to think that there were still teachers who knew nothing about the art of teaching and believed that all they had to do was stand up in front of a class and tell the children what to do. That idea should have been shown up for the stupidity it was long, long ago. After school next day she got out her files and started to reread the notes she'd made for the talks she'd given before the war. It took her three evenings to sort them all through but on the fourth she was ready to write. She made up the fire in the drawing room, settled herself in her armchair with a note book on her knees and a pencil in her hand and began.

'I shall begin at the beginning,' she wrote. 'The first and most important thing for any intending teacher to understand is that learning is a natural process. We are all capable of learning and, if we are not impeded or made fearful or despondent, we learn throughout our lives. So let us start by looking at the process.

'It begins with something that is inborn and natural to all living creatures, namely curiosity. The child (or adult) wants to find out, to know how something is done, to discover a new skill, to follow an idea, as you are doing as you read this. Like all appetites it needs feeding. A good teacher will provide the 'food' as and when it is needed but he won't offer it before the child is ready for it and his initial appetite for it has been roused. Rousing the appetite is the first and most skilled part of our job as teachers and it can be done in a variety of ways, which I will deal with later.

'The second stage I shall call discovery. The child takes whatever food he needs and uses it. It is a time of trial and error and thought and effort and children vary in their approach to it. Some plunge into it happily, others need to be sustained and encouraged. A good teacher will praise whenever praise is truly earned. He will never scold a mistake, however silly it might appear to him. The golden rule is to remember that a mistake is not a sin or stupidity or deliberate naughtiness. It is one of the ways in which we all learn. In other words, it is a natural part of the process.

'The third stage comes when the child has acquired his new skill or found the answer to his questions. If the first two stages have gone well it is marked by serenity and satisfaction. Then there is a fourth and resting stage when the child moves on to a new topic and the completed investigation seems to be forgotten. It may surprise you to know that there is a fifth stage when the child returns to the skill he has learnt and he is still a complete master of it, remembering everything that is important about it with ease. Teachers who subscribe to the chalk and talk method of education are always surprised when they see this happen. Their surprise is an indication that they do not understand the natural process.'

'Are you still at it?' Emmeline said, appearing in the door. 'It's half past eleven. I'm off to bed.'

Octavia looked up, pushed up her glasses and stretched her back, surprised at how stiff she'd become and how much her neck was aching. 'I'm writing my credo, Em,' she said.

'Well don't write it all night,' Emmeline said.

But now that she'd begun, Octavia couldn't stop. There was so much she wanted to say and she was hot with energy and couldn't wait to get it down on paper. She knew from

461

her years in the classroom that it is better to have too much information than not enough. When the whole thing was written she would get Maggie Henry to type it for her and send a copy to Kathy Ellis and Brian and they could sort out what they needed. Meantime she would make a list of all the topics she felt she ought to tackle. Things that get in the way of learning. The value of praise and the destructive power of blame. Ways to spark a pupil's interest. What do we mean by discipline? It was nearly one o'clock before she decided that she really was too tired to go on writing any longer.

From then on she wrote whenever she had an opportunity, which wasn't as frequently as she would have liked with Christmas rushing upon them and the school abuzz with preparations. She bought her gramophone and a collection of records, wrapped presents and wrote cards and tried to enter into the spirit of the season but her mind was never far from the book.

On Christmas Eve, Tommy arrived bearing a hamper to say that he was throwing himself on their mercy because he was all on his own. 'Lizzie's gone to her friend Poppy's for Christmas,' he said, 'and Mrs Dunnaway's deserted me and gone back to Gloucester in my hour of need. I'm an orphan of the storm.'

'We can't have that,' Emmeline said, helping him out of his coat, 'and in all this cold too. Come in and have a drink, you poor, lorn critter.'

The poor lorn critter entertained them royally that Christmas, pulling crackers and carving their precious turkey at the Christmas table, leading the dance during the afternoon, telling impossible ghost stories round the fire in the evening. When the children had been sent to bed, despite very loud protests, and Emmeline had restored a little order to the drawing room, they sat round the fire and roasted chestnuts and discussed the war.

'It can't be very much longer now, surely,' Edith said.

'We're being held up by the weather,' Tommy told her. 'It's pretty impossible in the Low Countries by all accounts. Drifts four feet deep in some places. Once the spring comes and the tanks can get moving again, we shall cross the Rhine and then it won't be long before it's over.'

That was Ben's opinion of it too. *This is the worst winter I've ever known,* he wrote to Lizzie. *If it isn't bloody snowing, it's freezing fog and we can't see more than a foot in front of our faces. The Jerries lay fresh mines on top of the snow and wait for the next fall to cover them up. Crafty buggers. We've lost two men that way. I hate this war. I feel as if I've been stuck in it for ever. Love you, love you, love you. Can't wait to get home.*

Lizzie and Fiona followed the news every day, sitting in their kitchen with the wireless on the table between them, listening to every word. The German break-out, which was being called the Battle of the Bulge, was finally being contained and Fiona said she thought they'd be pushing the Germans back 'any time now' but Lizzie was thinking of Ben fighting in the snow with the Germans laying mines he couldn't see and aching with that terrible, crawling anxiety.

'In one way, I shall be quite glad to get back to school,' she said. 'At least when I'm working I don't have time to worry so much.'

Fiona leant across the table and patted her hand. 'Soon be over once the spring comes,' she said. 'You'll see.'

On New Year's Day, while Em and her daughters were clearing the table and doing the washing-up and the children were playing Pit, Octavia sat by the fire and started to write the section on 'Things that get in the way of learning'. She didn't finish it until term had started and by then the Battle of the Bulge was over and the Germans were retreating again.

'I'm so slow,' she said to Emmeline. 'At the rate I'm going, the war will be over before I've finished.'

'It's not a race,' Emmeline said.

But there were times when it felt like one, especially when there was so much going on at school that she was too tired to write or when she was woken in the night by the sound of yet another rocket and couldn't sleep again afterwards and was exhausted in the morning. Trivial news items triggered her into irritability. The BBC had been in the habit of preceding their news bulletins by playing the national anthems of all the Allied powers and suddenly all sorts of obscure nations, like Ecuador, Paraguay, Egypt and Saudi Arabia, decided to jump on the bandwagon and declare war on Germany and they wanted their national anthems played too. A new one was added to the list at every bulletin and playing them all took longer and longer.

'It's downright ridiculous,' Octavia said. 'Where were they when we were fighting the Germans all on our own? I didn't notice them rushing to join us then.'

But at least it was a sign that the end was coming and it was one of many. The German prisoner of war camps were being liberated one after the other and much too slowly to suit Edith. But in fact it wasn't very long before she had her hoped-for letter from Arthur to say that he was free.

*I can't come home just yet, though,* he wrote. *We've got to stay in hospital for a little while because they kept us a bit short of rations and we need building up. Not to worry. I'm not ill or wounded or anything, just a bit on the thin side.*

Edith was very upset and complained bitterly about it. 'We fed their damned prisoners,' she said. 'Years and years. We should have tried starving *them*, if that's the way they were going on.'

'Look on the bright side, Edie,' Dora said. 'At least he's free and he hasn't been hurt and he'll come home when they say he can. See if I'm not right.'

In February, while Octavia was busy writing the section on discipline, Tommy was sent to Yalta in the Crimean for a Big Three conference between Roosevelt, Churchill and Stalin. He left in a bad mood saying that they were going to carve Europe up between them and that Uncle Joe would get the lion's share. 'The victors dividing the spoils,' he growled, 'and we're not even over the Rhine yet.'

The Rhine was crossed five weeks later. From then on everything was sped up. Ben wrote to tell Lizzie that they were fairly charging through Germany and had covered a hundred miles in one day. The rockets stopped coming. The Russians and the Americans were racing to be the first to enter Berlin. The German army in Italy finally surrendered and without his German protectors Mussolini was hung by the partisans and his dead body strung up by the heels outside a garage for everyone to see, like a dirt-smeared side of pork. And there were rumours that Hitler had committed suicide.

'Look sharp,' Emmeline said to Octavia when she read the news, 'or it'll be over before you've written the last word.'

'It's written,' Octavia told her with great satisfaction. 'I wrote it yesterday evening.'

But she was wrong. There was still one more thing that had to be said.

At the end of the week, when the daffodils were brightening the garden and there were birds nesting in the hedges and

Octavia was feeling pleased with herself and her efforts, Tommy arrived to tell her that she must come to the pictures with him to see the newsreel.

'It's a terrible, terrible film,' he told her, 'but I think we should see it. Particularly in view of all the things that the Mannheims have told us.'

It was even more terrible than she feared and expected, for it was filmed at a place called Belsen and Belsen was one of Hitler's death camps. She sat in the dark cinema smoking for comfort and watched as skeletal men in filthy striped shirts and tattered trousers were fumigated to get rid of their lice, and shuddered as desperately thin children squatted on the ground too weak to stand, or lay on their sides as if they were dead, their shaven heads and huge eyes made grotesque by starvation, and groaned with horror as piles of the most pitiful dead bodies she had ever seen were shovelled into the dark earth of huge communal graves. At the end of the film she wept with pity and anger because this was a cruelty obscene beyond belief. And that night she added a postscript to her book.

*We have just lived through a war*, she wrote, *in which many ordinary human beings have shown amazing courage and fortitude under appalling conditions. But we must not forget that there have been others who have committed almost unbelievable atrocities, especially in death camps like Belsen and Buchenwald and Auschwitz. We need to look at these people and understand them if we are to prevent such terrible things from happening again. As teachers we know how much our pupils need to be appreciated, to feel that they are wanted and valued and to know that they are loved but, also as teachers, we should never forget that Belsen is what happens when people are taught to hate. The Germans were told in a steady drip, drip, drip of poisonous propaganda that the Jews were a lower race, that they were responsible for everything that was wrong in the German state and that they deserved to be killed, and Germans who were already full of hatred for a variety of reasons and who needed someone they were allowed to hate found a hideous cause. After what was discovered at Belsen, we cannot avoid the knowledge that a deep-seated long-lasting hatred is powerful, self-justifying and utterly cruel. Now, more than ever, we need to ensure that we teach our children in such a way that they know they are themselves loved, that they are loving to others and that they are allowed and encouraged to think things out for themselves. We cannot afford to do anything less.*

Four days later, in a school house in Rheims, the German General Alfred Jodl surrendered unconditionally to General Montgomery and Eisenhower's Chief of Staff, General Walter Bedell Smith. The war in Europe was over.

# Chapter Thirty

It was such a glorious summer day, that day of the victory parade, a day of smiles and sunshine, with paper flags all along the route, fluttering like flowers, and roaring cheers rolling and echoing along the Mall, a day to be really happy, despite all the dreadful things that had happened in the last six awful years, because the war was over at last and although they knew the peace was going to be difficult, they would never, never, never have to fight another one.

Octavia stood on the pavement with her family around her and cheered with the rest as the long columns of servicemen and women marched past, Americans, black and white, chewing gum and wearing their tin helmets, Australians in bush hats, Sikhs in turbans and splendid beards, British sailors with their blue collars flapping in the breeze, British airmen in their distinctive air force blue, British soldiers marching in well-drilled precision, men and women from the ARP and the fire service, nurses in full uniform, capes and all, the parade was endless and every marcher in it was proudly applauded.

Dora was intrigued by the logistics of it. 'It must have taken some planning to get all this lot into London just for this one day,' she said. 'I wonder where they've put them all.'

'In tents, duck,' the woman standing next to her said. 'All

over all the parks they are. You should see 'em.'

'Fancy,' Dora said and she looked round at the others. 'Shall we go and have a look, when the parade's over? What do you think?'

Edith and the children were all for it and so was Emmeline but Octavia said she'd have to be getting on to the Albert Hall. 'I mustn't miss the concert,' she told them. 'The choir would never forgive me. And nor would my dancers.'

'I thought you were going to some reception with Tommy,' Emmeline said. 'You mustn't miss that.'

'It's all taken care of, Em,' Octavia said. 'He's going to pick me up at the Albert Hall when the concert's over and you know what a stickler he is for being on time.'

'I'm glad to hear it,' Emmeline said. 'You wouldn't want to miss the reception.'

Octavia wasn't particularly keen on this reception, and wouldn't have minded missing it, if she was honest, but she'd agreed to it because he'd seemed so keen for her to be there and she couldn't very well go back on her promise now. Besides it was a special day.

'Here's some more Yanks coming,' Edith said, peering down the Mall. 'I do like their helmets.'

When the last of the marching men and women had passed them by and the long parade was over, Octavia said goodbye to her family and took the Tube to South Kensington. Exhibition Road was swarming with happy people all going in the same direction and all in a state of chirruping excitement. It's going to be a very good concert, if this is the audience, she thought, and she quickened her pace.

The great circular bulk of the Royal Albert Hall looked grubby and a bit battered, like every other building in London, but it was very definitely welcoming, as the crowds streamed into the various doors and attendants took their tickets and showed them the way. And once inside the hall, the atmosphere was sizzling. The members of the London Symphony Orchestra were already drifting onto the stage as she entered, carrying their instruments and greeting one another as they moved to their places, and the massed choirs of London schoolchildren were taking their seats too, in long multicoloured ranks below the organ, chattering and excited and peering out into the vast auditorium to see if they could catch sight of their families. There was such a happy buzz about the place that it lifted Octavia's heart simply to hear it.

And the concert was everything that anyone in the audience could have hoped for, happy, inventive, musical and full of life. There were children performing country dances in the arena, bouncing and skipping with cheerful abandon – her own girls danced the sailors' hornpipe – and the choirs sang 'Jerusalem' and 'Land of Hope and Glory' and 'Say not the Struggle Nought Availeth' and several of the songs that had kept people going through the war. At the end of it she clapped until her hands were sore. We've come through, she thought, as she applauded. Whatever happens to us now and whatever difficulties we have to face, we've defeated an appalling enemy and come through with our spirits high and that's something to be proud of.

She didn't notice that Tommy was at her elbow until the cheers died down.

'Good?' he asked.

'Wonderful.'

'Car's waiting,' he said. 'What a day it's been. Did you see the parade?'

She told him what she'd seen and how good it had been as they negotiated the curving corridors and found the exit he wanted. There was a taxi waiting outside, which surprised her a bit because she thought he would be driving her to this reception in his own car, but she got in obediently and was rattled away as they talked. They drove along Kensington Gore and Knightsbridge, round Hyde Park Corner, along Grosvenor Place, past the high walls of the palace gardens, edging through the crowds that were spilling off the pavements and wandering in the road, and finally came to the end of Buckingham Gate.

'We'll get off here,' Tommy said. 'We can walk the rest of the way.'

'Where are we going?' Octavia asked, when he'd paid the driver.

He took her hand, slipped it into the crook of his elbow and patted it. 'Not far,' he said. 'I know a short cut. Come on.'

'Caxton Street?' she said, noticing where they were going. 'Is that named after the famous printer or the famous Hall?'

'Both I expect,' he said. 'That's the famous Hall over there. See?'

It was a tall, rather forbidding building, and looked Gothic, with an imposing front entrance and very high windows. 'That one?' she said. 'Good heavens! Now that's not a bit how I would have imagined it.'

'We could go in and have a look if you like,' he offered, casually. 'It's rather nice inside.'

'It won't be open,' she said. 'Not today.'

'Oh, I think it will,' he said and he looked decidedly mischievous. 'Let's see, shall we?'

He's up to something, Octavia thought, noticing the look. I'll bet this is where the reception is. So they crossed the road.

The impressive door was open so they went in, he still

471

holding her hand in his elbow. A man in morning dress came forward to greet him.

'Major Meriton,' he said, holding out his hand.

Yes, he is up to something, Octavia thought, watching as the two men shook hands. The mischief on Tommy's face was now too marked to be missed.

'Allow me to introduce Miss Octavia Smith,' Tommy said.

The man said he was pleased to make her acquaintance and shook her hand too. Now what?

'If you'll follow me, sir,' the man suggested and he gave the merest of bows and led them across the hall to a tall door and through into a room that was full of the scent of flowers. Too small for a reception, Octavia thought, looking at the table and the two high-backed chairs that faced it. Then she realised where she was.

'This is the Register Office, isn't it?' she said.

His face wasn't simply mischievous now, it was devilish. 'Yes, I believe it is.'

'Where people get married.'

'I believe it is,' he said and added, casually. 'We could get married here if you'd like to.'

'Yes,' she said. 'We could but it would take a bit of planning.'

'Actually,' he said, 'it wouldn't. We could get married now, if you'd like to.'

'You're not serious, are you?'

'I've never been more serious in all my life,' he said, while the morning-suited man edged discreetly away from them and seemed to be signalling to someone.

Are they going to throw us out? Octavia thought, noticing the movement. I wouldn't blame them. 'You can't just get married on the spur of the moment,' she said. 'Don't you have to call the banns or have a licence or something?'

'We've got a licence,' he told her. 'A special one. It's all arranged. All you've got to do is say yes. And you will say yes, won't you, Tavy? I've waited a very long time. And it's a perfect day for it.'

She found herself laughing. It was all so unexpected, so typically Tommy, so right. 'Oh Tommy!' she said. 'What am I to do with you?'

'Say yes,' he told her. 'That's all you've got to do. Just say yes.'

So she did. And a very happy ceremony it was.

Afterwards, when they walked out of the Hall arm in arm, there was a wedding car waiting for them by the kerb, hung about with white ribbons.

'How long have you had this planned?' she asked as she climbed in.

'Years,' he said, sitting beside her and putting his arm round her. 'Planning's my forte, remember.'

'You're the most artful man I've ever met.'

'And if that's not the nicest thing a wife can say to her husband I'd like to know what is.'

'Where are we going?'

'To the reception.'

She'd forgotten the reception and it seemed a little out of place now. Not quite the sort of thing to be attending when you've just got married. 'We won't have to stay there long, will we?' she asked.

'Not if you don't want to,' he said.

She realised that she was being ungracious. 'Just for a little while then,' she said. 'To show willing.'

They seemed to arrive very quickly after that and from then on everything was sped up. They were out of the car and into the building in two steps, they were walking towards a door, he was opening it and ushering her through and then there was an uproar of cheers and squeals and the air was full of rose petals and she realised that this wasn't the official reception she'd expected but a wedding reception and that they were cheering the bride and groom, they were cheering her and Tommy. Oh my dear good, God, he *has* planned this well.

Emmeline's face swam into focus from the crowd of people smiling in front of them. 'Is the deed done?' she called.

He lifted her hand so that they could see the ring on her finger. 'Signed, sealed, ship-shape and orderly,' he said and walked her into the crowd.

There were so many people there and all of them old friends. She walked from one to the next, gasping in surprise and pleasure. Emmeline rushed to hug her, followed by Edith and Arthur.

'Good God!' Octavia said to him. 'When did you get back?'

'I've been here for ten days,' he said. 'Edie couldn't tell you because of the surprise.'

She leant forward to kiss him. 'How are you?'

'Glad to be home.'

'I'll bet.' And there was John, beaming at her, with Dora and David beside him. 'Oh John, how good to see you.'

He was shy, of course, stammering, 'C-congratulations, Aunt.' And now Emmeline was pulling another guest forward and it was Johnnie with Gwyneth beside him, prettily pregnant. 'Johnnie, my dear boy! How did you get here?'

'We flew.'

'And so did we,' another voice said from behind her, and she turned and there were Mr Mannheim and his wife. 'From Hamburg,' he said. 'Courtesy of your husband.'

'He must have been working on this for months,' Octavia

said, looking round for him. He was over by the table talking to Lizzie and Ben. And there were Frank Dimond and Mrs Henderson. And Janet, with two little boys. She never told us she'd had another baby. 'Oh, it is good to see you all,' she said as she walked towards them.

'A happy, happy day,' Mrs Henderson said, 'and well deserved.'

'And so say all of us,' Miss Gordon said, joining them.

'Morag, my dear,' Octavia said. 'This is so extraordinary I don't know what to say.' Then she noticed Phillida and Alice, and behind them Elizabeth Fennimore and Jenny Jones and Maggie Henry and Sarah Fletcher. 'Oh, oh, my dears, are you all here?'

'Naturally we are,' Joan Marshall said, striding into the group. 'We wouldn't have missed this for worlds.'

Time passed in a blur of greetings and congratulations as she moved from one old friend to another. Mr Mannheim told her that he and his wife were working in a camp for displaced persons, helping them to find their way home and doing what they could to ease them away from the horrors they'd endured.

'It is very hard work,' Mrs Mannheim said, 'but we are glad to do it. It is the least we can do.'

Then Ben and Lizzie were rushing towards her and they both kissed her and Ben told her he'd been in the parade.

'I didn't see you,' Octavia said.

'I saw *you*,' he told. 'Just after I'd spotted my Lizzie. You were only a few yards apart.'

'I didn't see you either, Lizzie,' Octavia confessed. Now that they were standing in front of one another she was feeling unsure of herself, wondering what this dear girl must be thinking to see her headmistress married to her father.

'Is it any wonder in that crowd?' Lizzie said. 'I've never seen so many people.'

'I expect this is a bit of a surprise,' Octavia said.

Lizzie grinned at her. Really she was so like her father sometimes. 'No,' she said. 'Not to us. We knew he wanted to marry you, didn't we, Ben?'

'Really?' Octavia said, feeling very surprised. 'Did he tell you?'

'Good God no,' Lizzie said. 'We just knew, didn't we, Ben? When we saw you together at our wedding.'

The question had to be asked. 'And you don't mind?'

'No. 'Course not. Why shouldn't you be happy together? Mind you, I'm not sure what I ought to call you now, but I expect we can sort something out.'

'Why not "Smithie"?' Octavia said, laughing. 'That's what you girls usually called me.'

Now it was Lizzie's turn to be surprised. 'We thought you didn't know.'

Tommy was suddenly standing between them, with his arms round them both. 'Aren't you starving?' he said. 'I know I am.'

Octavia was too excited to be hungry but she realised that she and Tommy had to lead their guests into the wedding breakfast and that they were all standing around waiting for them to do it.

'Oh Tommy,' she said, 'my dear, dear man. This is absolutely wonderful. All these people. I don't know how you managed it. You must have been working on it for months.'

He pretended to groan. 'Are we eating or not?' he said. 'Tubby says he's fading away. Isn't that right, Tubby? I don't want to have to catch him if he faints.'

'Then I must take pity on him and lead him to the food,' she said.

It was an extraordinarily good meal – how did he manage that? – and they had extraordinarily good champagne for the toasts. And when the first toast had been drunk he made an extraordinarily good speech.

'In a wedding like this,' he said, 'you mustn't expect anything to be done by the book. The invitations certainly weren't. And while I remember it, thank you all for keeping it under wraps the way you have. That wasn't done by the book either and it's much appreciated. Fact is, Tavy threw the book away years ago – and that doesn't surprise you does it? – so we all have to improvise. There was a time when that would have terrified me but, over the last few weeks, I've come to see that there are one or two advantages in having to improvise, especially when you're making a speech. For a start it usually results in something pretty honest. Or more honest than the general run of diplomatic speeches which I don't need to tell my friends here are usually sycophantic tosh.' He paused to give his friends a chance to laugh, which they did. 'So,' he went on, 'when I thank you all for coming here this afternoon, you will know that I mean it, and when I say I understand what your presence here means to Tavy, you will know that I mean that too.'

He paused again and gave Octavia a rapturous smile. 'Strictly speaking of course,' he said, 'we've got no right to be sitting here at the centre of the high table.' And when some of his guests looked surprised he explained. 'We should be sitting at the end of the high table, not at the centre. That was where we first met, at the end of the high table at Emmeline's wedding when we were both eighteen, and years later we met again at the end of the high table at the double wedding of Dora and Edith. Now and just for once, I think I've persuaded our Tavy to take centre stage although how long I shall be able to keep her there is open to question. But then I think I'm safe in saying that it is Tavy's method to question everything. And the one good thing to say about that is that it does keep you on your toes. It might present you with a few problems but it does keep you on your toes. Take for example the problem of what my new wife is to be called. When I first asked her to take my name she told me she'd already got a name. And a jolly good one too. So naturally I'm not going to ask her to change it now. She might be Mrs Meriton to me and to the Passport Office but in her school and in the wider educational world where she does so much good, she will always be Octavia Smith.'

He picked up his champagne glass and raised it to her. 'So when I give you the toast, ladies and gentlemen, you will understand that it has to be in these words. No others will do. To the incomparable Octavia Smith.'

'That,' she told him as the toast was drunk, 'was perfect.'